The
Secrets of
Dragonfly
Lodge

RACHEL HORE

The Secrets of Dragonfly Lodge

**SIMON &
SCHUSTER**

London · New York · Amsterdam/Antwerp · Sydney/Melbourne · Toronto · New Delhi

First published in Great Britain by Simon & Schuster UK Ltd, 2025

Copyright © Rachel Hore, 2025

The right of Rachel Hore to be identified as author of this work has been asserted in accordance with the Copyright, Designs and Patents Act, 1988.

1 3 5 7 9 10 8 6 4 2

Simon & Schuster UK Ltd, 1st Floor
222 Gray's Inn Road, London WC1X 8HB

Simon & Schuster Australia, Sydney
Simon & Schuster India, New Delhi

www.simonandschuster.co.uk
www.simonandschuster.com.au
www.simonandschuster.co.in

The authorised representative in the EEA is Simon & Schuster Netherlands BV, Herculesplein 96, 3584 AA Utrecht, Netherlands. info@simonandschuster.nl

Simon & Schuster strongly believes in freedom of expression and stands against censorship in all its forms. For more information, visit BooksBelong.com

A CIP catalogue record for this book is available from the British Library

Hardback ISBN: 978-1-3985-1800-1
eBook ISBN: 978-1-3985-1802-5
Audio ISBN: 978-1-3985-1803-2

This book is a work of fiction. Names, characters, places and incidents are either a product of the author's imagination or are used fictitiously. Any resemblance to actual people living or dead, events or locales is entirely coincidental.

Typeset in the UK by M Rules
Printed and Bound in the UK using 100% Renewable Electricity
at CPI Group (UK) Ltd

For Dr Phyllis Hore
and Dr Anne Roby

'Those who contemplate the beauty of the earth find reserves of strength that will endure as long as life lasts. There is symbolic as well as actual beauty in the migration of the birds, the ebb and flow of the tides, the folded bud ready for the spring.'

RACHEL CARSON

'The sedge is withered from the lake
And no birds sing.'

JOHN KEATS

For a third night Nancy lay sleepless for hours, anxious thoughts chasing around in her head. Heavy rain battered the window and rattled through the downpipes, while the wind tossed the branches of the trees, made the landing light flicker and the curtains shiver. The storm was like a stage set for the nightmare her life had become.

She must have dozed, for a noise downstairs snatched her to sudden wakefulness. The rain had dwindled to a gentle patter, but this had been a different sound, something strange and wrong. She lay quiet, listening, her skin clammy, the room alive with shadows. There it was again, a clink of metal, outside but close, very close. Then a scraping noise, as of a spade along stone, followed by silence. Someone was in the garden, she was certain. They'd come for her.

She dared not move, but move she must. To reach the telephone. She'd prowled her home the evening before, tightening every window, turning the keys in the doors, shooting the bolts, but if someone wanted to break in they'd do it somehow. By twisting a crowbar or thrusting a brick with a gloved hand through glass.

She sat up, then stilled. Should she call the police? They'd come out on the first night. She remembered the weariness in the sergeant's voice as he'd tried to reassure her: 'There's nobody here, Miss.'

'But there was, I know there was.' Her voice trembled.

His rookie constable had entered from the garden, wiping his boots on the doormat. 'No sign of a break-in.' She'd read contempt on his pale, spotty face.

'I did hear something,' she insisted, her nails digging into her palms.

'Don't mind me saying, Miss, but things can seem frightening at night, a young lady alone.' The older man was kind but firm.

She'd stared at him, disbelieving. 'I know what I heard. What I saw.'

Not the police, she thought now, she wouldn't trouble them again.

She flinched at a tapping sound downstairs. 'A twig,' she muttered aloud, 'it's only a twig against the window. Get up. Go and see.' She swung her bare feet down to the rough warmth of the rug, but fear sapped the strength in her legs and she covered her face with her hands.

Go! As she stood up, something pattered against her window, heavier than raindrops, and she froze. Then she took a step towards the window, and another. Grasped the curtain, breathed in and snatched it aside. She stared out at the wild night. The storm was passing now. Clouds like black cobwebs veiled the moon. She blinked at its brightness, then looked down, saw a figure and her eyes widened . . . 'Oh,' she breathed, 'it's you.'

One

London
June 2010

What a difference a year can make.

Late one Thursday afternoon, Stef Lansdown was taking a shower and didn't see a sparrow alight on the sill of the open window of her studio flat and peck at some breadcrumbs she'd scattered there. It glanced about, its beady eyes alert. After a moment, it spread its wings and darted inside.

The empty room lay bathed in sunshine, the roar of traffic from the street almost drowned out by a loping hiphop beat shaking the floor. The bird didn't seem frightened. It circled, perched briefly on a bedside lamp, then flitted back to the sill where it continued its meal.

Stef's flat was situated on the first floor of a modern block in Balham, South London. Its single room, with galley kitchen and bathroom cubicle, was light and airy but marred by clutter. An unmade double bed dominated the space. Washing was drying on a rack. Newspapers and spiral-bound notebooks lay tumbled across a tiny sofa pushed up against a wall of bookshelves. On a coffee table under the window, a modest clutch of birthday cards shivered in the breeze.

Among the books were piled a dozen copies of *Secrets of an Author's Wife* by Stephanie Lansdown. An anglepoise lamp stood sentry on a narrow pine desk over an open laptop next to a mobile phone and a mug of cooling tea. A light blue jacket hung on the back of the chair.

Suddenly, the room leapt into life. The rush of water cut out, loudening the throb of the music downstairs.

The startled sparrow flew away.

The shower room door swung open and Stef stepped out through a billowing cloud of vapour like a modern Venus, wrapped in a white towel. A birthday card caught in the draught and sailed to the floor. She picked it up and frowned at its message: 'Life is short. Smile while you still have teeth. Happy Birthday!' *Ha ha.* As she returned it to the table, her phone began to ring. She sighed, then answered it.

Stef had embraced turning thirty. On her birthday, her lawyer boyfriend Sam had thrown a party for her at a trendy wine bar near their luxurious flat in Clapham. She had a promising career as a journalist on a national broadsheet newspaper and was about to publish her first book. Personal happiness and success seemed secure and a bright future beckoned.

By the time she was thirty-one, that future had darkened. She and Sam had split up acrimoniously and since it was his flat she'd had to find somewhere else to live. Soon afterwards, her job went in a round of redundancies, and despite a small severance payment and the slightly larger advance she'd been given for her book it was becoming a struggle to pay the bills. She'd picked herself up and was making a new life for herself but she still felt battered and bruised.

'Mum. Hi.' Stef tucked the phone between shoulder and ear, gathered the towel more tightly in one hand and continued drying herself with the other while her mother rambled on about Stef's failure to call and the lack of rain for the garden. She listened with increasing impatience. Her mum had a habit of ringing on a whim and launching into a monologue without asking if it was convenient.

She took advantage of a pause for breath to ask, 'Was there anything urgent, Mum? Only I'm about to go out.'

'You should have said. With anyone nice?' Her mum's falsely casual tone could not disguise her real meaning: *Is there a young man involved?* Stef plucked a pair of socks from the airer and decided they were dry. She hated this constant interest in her love life. Her mother seemed more concerned by it than by Stef's professional difficulties, and last year's break-up with Sam, engendered by his stubborn refusal to discuss the possibility of ever having children, seemed to have upset her as much as it had Stef.

'I'm meeting Sarah for a drink. You know, agent Sarah. At six,' she emphasized, noticing with alarm that her bedside clock said five-thirty.

'Well, you'd better go.' Her mother sounded hurt. 'You know, I was hoping you'd come and stay sometime. It's months since I've seen you.'

'Oh, Mum, not months. I helped you move in. How many weeks ago was that?'

'Six weeks. That's an *awfully* long time. I'd come up to see you, but the hotels are so expensive.'

Stef looked round the cramped room and felt guilty. It wasn't easy to ask her mum to stay here. She was considering what to suggest, when her mother rushed on. 'There *was* a reason I rang, actually. I've found a woman who might interest you.'

'A *woman*?' Stef smiled. 'I thought it was *men* you wanted me to meet.'

'No, silly, a woman for that book you're going to write. I met her at an art exhibition in the village. Her name's – oh, Nancy something. Foster, that's it. Dr Nancy Foster. She's a naturist.'

Stef giggled. 'A nudist? Really? In respectable Hickston?'

'Don't be ridiculous, darling. She lives in a cottage on the wildlife reserve, she told me. Very remote, but she doesn't mind that because of the wonderful birds.'

'You mean she's a *naturalist*.' Stef's eyes twinkled as she tapped the speaker icon, then laid down her phone while she fastened her bra.

'Yes, I told you!' Her mother's voice sounded squawky in the room. 'We were both puzzling over a drawing of a badger. Nancy said something about its spine being wrong. Anyway, we got talking. A very interesting person, Stef. She studied Zoology back in the late 1940s, then worked in a lab doing research.'

'Really?' Stef stilled briefly before opening a drawer. 'That must make her, what, in her eighties?' She straightened, a pair of knickers in her hand, trying to think. Nancy Foster might indeed be worth meeting. The next book Stef was planning to write was about women scientists. A zoologist from that period could be useful.

'Eighty-something, yes, but you wouldn't think so to look at her. Very active and such an original dress sense. But listen, this is the important bit. She's giving a talk about swallowtail butterflies on Saturday evening at the reserve. I wish you'd come, darling. We could go to it together and you could talk to her afterwards.'

'Mum, I'd love to, honestly, but Saturday's the day after tomorrow!' Stef tried to remember what she was doing at the weekend. Nothing exciting. Working on an article for an ecology magazine. She had a deadline early next week.

'You need a rest, love.' Her mother's tone was wheedling. 'Given all you've gone through. You shouldn't work all the time.'

'I have to, Mum. That's the freelance life.' She paused. 'Look, I'll think about it, I promise, but I really have to go now. Love you.'

After they'd said goodbye, Stef pulled on some cleanish jeans, grabbed her jacket from the chair, then rummaged in the cupboard for shoes. All the time she was thinking about her mother with the usual mixture of fondness, guilt and irritation. It was true that she'd not been to visit her since helping her move into her country cottage, but it was typical of her mum to imagine that Stef could drop everything and race over at a moment's notice. Or was it Stef who was being selfish? Mum was living on her own in an unfamiliar village, and although Stef's sister Pippa lived nearby she ought to go and see for herself how Mum was getting on. Back and forth her mind darted.

She went to the bathroom mirror to put on the silver pendant and matching earrings that Pippa had given her for her thirtieth, and her attention moved to the evening ahead. Her literary agent wanted an update on Stef's next book.

Sarah was always so glamorous, Stef thought, as she frowned at the reflection of her round face in the mirror, still pink from the shower. She wished she'd washed her thick, shoulder-length blonde hair after her run, for it had developed a life of its own. Too late now. A few strokes of the hairbrush, a touch of concealer, a slick of lip gloss and she'd have to do.

She searched for her bag, eventually locating it under the duvet, then scooped up her phone from the desk and her door keys from beneath a scrumpled tax demand. There were few advantages to a studio flat, but one was that things in it couldn't get lost for long. The flat was rented from Jasmin, an ex-colleague who'd moved in with her new partner at the same time that Stef had moved out of Sam's place. Jasmin sensibly hadn't wanted to sell the flat in case her relationship didn't work out. Stef hadn't had that luxury. Now that she was single again and freelance, buying her own place looked impossible. She kept a car, despite the expense, as it gave her a sense of freedom, however illusory.

As she waited on the busy platform for a train to take her into Central London, her mother's suggestion preyed on her mind. She could, she supposed, do the four-hour drive to North Norfolk on Saturday and stay for a couple of nights. As long as her mother understood she had to work. On Stef's last visit, everything had been a mess. Stef's parents were long divorced and her father had finally forced the sale of the family home. Despite a huge clear-out, Stef's mum still had too much stuff. Since then, however, she had told Stef at least twice that she'd got rid of a lot more and the spare bedrooms were now ready for guests.

She hardly registered the train arriving and the carriage doors opening, for she was remembering the chaos of her mother's move. A particular memory, unbidden, made her shudder with embarrassment. She sank onto a free seat, replaying it in her mind.

It had been a stressful morning. The vendors had been late dropping off the keys at the estate agents, and Pippa rang to say she was unable to help after all because her kids had temperatures. Stef and their mother had reached Springfield Cottage to find to their dismay that several cars were parked outside and there would be no space for the furniture van to unload. Her mother knocked on the door of the house opposite and learned that the vehicles belonged to a visiting film unit who were using a characterful Georgian house nearby as a set. Stef was dispatched to seek them out and found only a grumpy girl sitting on the wall outside the house. She was the unit's runner, she said, and had been left to guard the equipment. Aaron, who was in charge, had taken everyone else to the Ilex Tree for a sandwich.

Seeing the furniture van roar past on its way to Springfield

Cottage, Stef shouted her thanks and rushed off to the village's only pub. She arrived out of breath and thoroughly out of temper.

Still, the ensuing confrontation needn't have happened in the way that it did, she reflected as the tube train stopped briefly between stations, and she wasn't proud of herself. She squeezed her eyes shut in embarrassment.

She'd found four young men seated at a wooden table in the pub's window, with glasses of beer and plates of sandwiches before them.

'Are you lot blocking my mum's cottage?' Self-conscious under their gaze, Stef's voice came out more sharply than she'd intended.

'Possibly.' The dark-haired man, presumably Aaron, for he appeared to be in charge, regarded her with a wary expression. 'We're sorry if it is us. Where is your mum's cottage?'

'Down there.' She waved in the general direction. 'Past the village shop, then it's one of the red-brick ones on the right with the "Sold" sign outside. There's a bloody great furniture lorry waiting to park, so can you move your cars, like, now?'

She and Aaron locked eyes and his flashed with annoyance. 'If you ask nicely,' he said, 'then I'm sure we will.'

'Just get on and move them,' she said; then, her courage running out, 'Please.'

'All right.' He pulled a key from his pocket. 'George? Sajit? We'd better do as the *lady* says right away.'

Stef followed their striding figures up the street and stood wanly aside as they manoeuvred their cars past the waiting furniture van. George and Sajit smiled at her as they left, but

Aaron's expression was furious and he drove so close she had to jump back. She swore and raised a finger as his car passed.

She recalled his angry face now as the tube train roared through the tunnels. The clean lines of his profile, his narrow face with its cropped beard, the springiness of his dark hair. And felt her face grow hot with shame at her behaviour.

When the signs for Embankment came into view, she was glad to disembark and shake off the memory.

Two

Delizioso, where Stef was meeting her agent, turned out to be a stylish Italian bistro with a scarlet, green and white striped canopy. Sarah, striking in an emerald shirt-dress that set off her cropped auburn hair, green eyes and pale skin, was already seated at a table outside. She was frowning as she tapped at her phone with quick fingers, but when she spotted Stef she laid it aside and rose with a welcoming smile. Of a similar age to Stef, agenting was a recent change for Sarah after years as an editor in a publishing house. They were both establishing new careers and, although Stef was in awe of Sarah, who could be fierce when roused, it felt like a close partnership.

A waiter brought them misted flutes of fizzing prosecco. Sipping the chilled bubbles gave Stef a thrill of pleasure and she felt herself finally relax.

Stef's first book was a biography of the wife of a mid-twentieth-century English novelist, whom she had studied at university. From a newly discovered collection of letters, she revealed that the woman had been more than a helpmeet to her famous husband; indeed she was more a collaborator on some of his best-known work. Rumours of this had been circulating for years since their deaths, but Stef had been surprised by the storm of controversy that her book stirred up, relatives and friends of the couple lining up on one side or the other. That had mostly quietened down now, the paperback was shortly to be published and Stef's editor Catherine was pressing for something new.

It hadn't taken Stef long to find a subject that interested her. A London university conference in January, shortly before she was made redundant from the *Globe*, had given her the idea. Stef had been sent to report on the conference instead of the newspaper's science correspondent. A middle-aged male, set in his ways, he had joked that he would surely be 'eaten alive' if he went.

Stef had been surprised by what she'd heard in the sessions and chatting to delegates in between. She hadn't appreciated the myriad small ways in which the lives of female scientists continued, even now, to be harder than men's. Overt discrimination wasn't always the greatest problem – progress had been made. It was the sheer number of persistent micro-aggressions that wore down female geneticists, engineers, zoologists and astrophysicists across the world. Stef's article impressed the *Globe*'s editor so much that he published it as news in the paper's opening pages and commissioned a noted female scientist to write an editorial piece about it, underlining its importance. *'The days might be over when Lise Meitner was passed over for a Nobel Prize in favour of her male co-physicist,'* this woman thundered, *'and biochemist Rosalind Franklin's discoveries about the structure of DNA were sidelined by caballing male colleagues, but humanity is losing out on cutting-edge discoveries because scientific research is still a man's world.'* Women who originated groundbreaking projects were still being hampered by matters such as smaller research budgets, less laboratory space and the continuing power of male networks.

Stef's report and the related editorial attracted a great deal of interest. Letters on the subject appeared in the paper for several days. She was interviewed on a BBC news programme and a shadow higher education spokeswoman asked a question about it in Parliament. And then it all died down. The issue continued to haunt Stef. She'd been interested in science herself at school in the 1990s, but remembered picking up on a subconscious message that 'hard' sciences like physics or chemistry 'weren't for girls'. Where this had come from she wasn't sure, but it was certainly linked to another circulating assumption, that 'girls weren't good at maths'. Both of these, Stef knew, were myths, yet they persisted. And when disaster struck several months ago and she became one of the casualties in the round of editorial redundancies, Sarah encouraged her to research a serious book about the topic.

'I'm still proposing to structure the book as a series of linked biographies,' Stef said as they sipped their prosecco. 'There'll be plenty of reflective commentary, but the idea is that the powerful individual experiences will create a strong overall pattern.'

'I agree. Especially if you have a good range of specialisms.

Your editor is expecting to see one or two big names – it'll help sales.'

'Yeah. It's difficult not to include Rosalind Franklin, she's such a towering example, but I'm also interested in those who didn't make it to the big league. It's important, Sarah. Those are the ones who will prove my point. I've found a really sparky American chemist from the 1970s. She complained about her papers not being accepted by journals. Then, after she married a colleague, hey presto, adding his name to her work got her published! There's an obvious trend here – I've come across it a lot.'

'She sounds a great example.' Sarah was writing in a little notebook. 'Anyone else?'

Stef listed a couple more names, then paused. 'Something interesting happened today.' She told Sarah about her mother's phone call. 'She's met a zoologist from the 1950s called Nancy Foster. I haven't heard of her, but I'll investigate.'

'Nancy Foster. Let's see what Uncle Google says.' Sarah typed the name into her phone. 'I've added "zoologist" and "1950s",' she said. She scrolled through the results. There was a vet practising in Australia with the name, who'd recently won a bravery award for saving the life of an ageing film star's sick dog and been feted in the media there. 'Clearly not she,' Sarah said with an ironic smile. She clicked onto the next page and swiped past numerous social media profiles of irrelevant Nancy Fosters. 'No good,' Sarah said, frowning. 'You'll have to do some digging.'

'Of course, she might have worked under a different surname,' Stef mused. 'If she married, I'm thinking.'

'Maybe. Let's look into it. What about a title for the book?'

'I was thinking of *Curious Women*. That's what all scientists have in common, a curiosity about the world.'

'Excellent, but you'll need a subtitle.'

'The Struggles of Women in Science?'

'That'll do for the moment. And I know you're aware that Catherine wants an outline for the book soon. Now, are you eating? The food's good here. There's a burrata starter that melts in the mouth and I can recommend the sea bream.'

Later, when Stef arrived home, bright-eyed from the evening, all was thankfully quiet. She made some herbal tea and sat cross-legged on the bed in her pyjamas, her laptop open before her. Again, the search for Nancy Foster's name was fruitless. Perhaps she was looking for the wrong surname. But when she tried adding the word 'doctorate', the list of results included the entry 'Dr Nancy Foster, Prince's College, London'.

Quickly she opened the link. It led to a search engine for alumni who had studied at the prestigious institution. Stef entered Nancy's name and read the very brief resumé that came up: 'BSc (Hons) Zoology 1950, PhD 1954.' There was a link to a doctoral thesis, but when she tried to open it a screen came up that read 'Access denied'. She stared at it in surprise, then tried to find it on other websites, using the dates and Prince's College, but without success. There was no mention of Nancy's subsequent career anywhere, either.

Stef's interest was properly piqued. She closed down her laptop and sat thinking, feeling the familiar prickling sensation at the back of her neck that told her she was on to a story. She must meet this woman and find out more.

Downstairs, a door banged shut and a moment later the familiar sound of her neighbour's music started up. She knew it wouldn't go on all night – Gary kept regular hours during the week – and it wasn't at its loudest. She'd learned to ignore it, but it was still a nuisance.

She lowered the window blind slowly so no draught would blow over the birthday cards. Last year, she mused, she'd had five times as many, mostly with some variation of 'Congratulations' on the front. Now they mocked her for getting old.

She sighed. She badly needed a decent advance for a new book. Most of the time she pegged on, trying to be optimistic, but looking at the cards now, for a brief moment she felt unmoored.

Her mother was right, she thought as she climbed into bed. She did need a break. It was too late to ring her, she'd do so tomorrow. If she set off first thing on Saturday morning, she should reach deepest Norfolk by lunchtime. They would go to Nancy Foster's talk and Stef would speak to her afterwards.

The decision made, as if it was a sign, Gary's music ceased. Stef switched off the bedside light and lay listening drowsily to the distant sound of traffic. London was never silent. A peaceful weekend in the country should be the restorative break she so desperately needed.

Three

Norfolk

'Hi, Baxter, old thing.' Stef bent to caress the overweight spaniel who had ambled to the door to greet her, his feathered tail swaying with pleasure. 'Where's Mum, eh?' Mellow red-brick Springfield Cottage lay quiet. Was her mother out or in the garden?

After the four-hour drive, she'd hoped for more of a welcome. Instead, the doorbell was hanging broken behind a curtain of rampant ivy and there was no answer to her knock. Thankfully, when she'd twisted the doorknob and shoved, the door had creaked open.

'Baxter, find Mum!' The dog wheeled round and lumbered off. Stef followed him down a hallway that was bright with her mother's paintings, through a cluttered kitchen and out into a sunny, flower-filled garden.

Her mum had been busy. An ancient claw-footed bath

spilled over with purple petunias, and sky-blue lobelia fronted a newly built artist's studio with a wooden frame and sloped glass roof. Baxter trotted past it on the flagstone path and out through an open gate onto the strip of mown grass that ran behind the row of cottages.

Here Stef stopped, shielding her eyes against the sun, to look at the view. A field of ripening corn gave way to lush pasture dotted with cows and crisscrossed by hedge-rows and green canopies of trees. When she'd helped her mother move in, thick cloud had hung over the landscape. Now, she could appreciate its full summer beauty. A lark sang in ecstasy somewhere above. She scanned the sky, but the bird was too high and the sun too dazzling for her to spot it.

'Stef, darling, I thought you wouldn't be here till later.' Stef turned at her mother's breathy voice and saw her rise from her stool by an easel under a gnarled old oak tree. She looked as slight as always, as though the wind would blow her away, and despite her paint-spattered smock very pretty with her blue eyes and swept-up fair hair. Stef managed to kiss her cheek without getting paint on herself.

'I did say lunchtime, but don't worry. How's it going?' Stef glanced at the broad canvas her mother was working on and felt a mixture of wonder and wistfulness at how clever she was at capturing and transforming the landscape with her vibrant palette. It was not a talent Stef had inherited. Pippa could draw well, but Stef was more like her father, a retired academic historian who was currently writing a book about the Spanish Civil War.

'Oh, you know,' her mother said cryptically. 'I just need time.'

'Is there anything to eat in the house or should I nip to the shop?' Stef was used to her mother forgetting about normal life when she was working.

'Darling!' Cara Lansdown smiled and patted her daughter's arm, her bracelets jangling. 'Don't fuss. I did know you were coming.' She wiped her brush with a cloth. 'Go and put the kettle on while I tidy up here. Oh dear, I haven't made your bed up yet. Would you mind doing it?'

'I take it the sheets are in the airing cupboard.'

'Where else would they be?'

'Could be anywhere with you.' They smiled at one another.

On the way back towards the kitchen, Stef checked her phone and remembered with annoyance that there was no signal around the cottage.

She stopped to look into the studio. It was filled with light and smelled of fresh wood and paint. Stacks of paintings leaned against the walls and a roll of new canvas lay on a table next to a jam jar containing brushes and paint tubes jumbled in a box. A small canvas stood on an easel, shrouded by a dust cloth. Stef stepped closer, lifted the cloth and tucked it aside. The picture underneath was unusual, she thought with surprise, a portrait. Her mother didn't often paint people. She stepped back to see it in focus. It was a man's head and shoulders at a three-quarters angle, the background detail as yet unfinished. The way the light fell on his broad, open face and the intent nature of his twinkling gaze suggested that he was looking out through a window. Who he was she had no idea. She replaced the cloth thoughtfully.

In the kitchen, she was relieved to find the fridge full of food. Some interesting paper packages smelled faintly of fresh fish and thankfully there was milk. She glanced round the cheerful, blue-painted room, finding it strange to see Mum's familiar possessions in their new places. She had to open several wall cupboards before she found the old tea caddy, and then there was another hunt for mugs.

The move from the rambling family home just outside Cambridge had been an upheaval for the whole family. Stef's parents had been divorced for many years, her father moving to a tiny flat in the city near his college. Theoretically, Stef and Pippa could see him often, but in actuality they didn't, for he'd long grown away from the family.

Last year he'd announced his retirement and finally insisted on the sale of the marital home. That was his due. The surprise was that he intended to use his half of the proceeds to pay for his wedding to a Spanish woman he'd recently met who was only a few years older than Stef; and to buy a villa in northern Spain, while keeping on the Cambridge flat.

Stef's mum took the news of the marriage and the loss of the house badly. It was traumatic for her to uproot and sad for her daughters to help empty their childhood home. Stef went to the wedding out of a vague sense of duty, but Pippa refused to point blank.

Initially the idea had been cooked up that their mum would move close to Pippa in Norwich to help with Pippa's four-year-old twins, but once she had seen this pretty eighteenth-century cottage down a back lane in Hickston village, she'd brushed aside her daughters' objections and insisted that she'd live nowhere else. It was near one of the Broads – the network of man-made medieval lakes in North Norfolk – which had been turned into a nature reserve run by a wildlife charity.

'It's such a long way from Norwich,' Pippa had sighed. She'd clearly been hoping Mum would be just round the corner and available at all hours for babysitting.

'Only a dozen miles, dear, and I do have a car.'

'And replacing the broken roof tiles might be expensive.'

'Nevertheless, I like it and I'm the one who'll live in it.'

The sisters had exchanged meaningful looks. They were used to their mother's stubborn moods. There was nothing for it but to shrug and give in. After all, she should have enough money for repairs and to build the studio. Her paintings still had a market, so she'd have an income stream. Pippa had told Stef she thought their mother was settling in well, though she still had her concerns. She'd hinted darkly about some man their mum kept mentioning. His name was Ted.

Stef poured two cups of tea, then, wanting her jumper, for it was cool in the house, went out to fetch her case from the car. As she dragged it up the steep, narrow staircase to her bedroom, she struggled to keep her balance. This was another worry. If the stairs were challenging for her, they could be dangerous for Mum in her sixties. Perhaps someone could come and put up a handrail.

Upstairs had a comfortable feel: rush matting underfoot, more of Mum's paintings on show around the landing, a scent of lavender polish. Stef liked the uneven doorways of the four bedrooms and the single bathroom, though the door to her own room, she remembered as she pushed it wide, would never quite shut. She eyed the bedroom with pleasure, noting the changes since her last visit. The double bed might not be made up, but a colourful painting of the River Cam at Grantchester adorned the wall above it and a pair of flowery blue curtains from the guest bedroom of the old house hung at the mullioned window that looked out onto the lane. She regarded the white stuccoed cottage opposite. An empty pram had been left in its front garden and there were toys strewn over the grass. Of the inhabitants there was no sign, but it must be nice for Mum, who loved children, to have a family nearby.

'Stef, are you there?' her mother called up the stairs. 'The tea's getting cold.'

'Just coming.' She pulled on her jumper and hurried out, glancing into the other bedrooms on her way to the stairs. A set of bunks had been installed in one for Pippa's twins. Her mother had mentioned them on the phone. The mysterious Ted had put them up for her.

'Nice bunks,' she told her mum in the kitchen.

'The kids will love them, though there'll be arguments.'

'About who's on top?'

'Little tykes,' said her mother fondly. 'They'll have to take turns.'

Lunch was dressed crab from one of the fishy parcels. 'We have this marvellous fish man who comes on Saturdays.' Cara heaped green salad on Stef's plate, her fingers still flecked with paint. As usual she hardly ate anything herself, playing with her food as she chattered away about an excellent farm shop she'd found a few miles away, the kindness of the family across the lane who'd invited her to a barbecue the following Saturday if the weather held. She was sure she could wangle an invitation for Stef. 'You are staying for a while, aren't you?' she said, anxiety crossing her face. Stef sighed and said she thought she might only manage a couple of nights.

'I told you. I do have work to do, Mum.'

Her mother looked forlorn. 'Of course, but now you're freelance you can organize your own time, can't you?' She rose, asking, 'Would you like sorbet? There was an offer at the supermarket.' She rummaged about in a freezer drawer and brought out two plastic tubs. 'There's strawberry, but this mango one's delicious.' She peeled off the lid. 'I mean, you can settle yourself at the desk upstairs and get on with things. The internet's a bit slow, but it does work. No one will disturb you. Can you reach me two bowls from that cupboard?'

Stef obliged. 'I can't do all my research online, Mum. I have to speak to people and visit places.' In fact, she was at the writing-up stage for the most urgent feature on her list and she could easily do that here. 'And the phone signal's not great. I can hardly conduct a sensitive conversation in the middle of the village.'

'Use my landline, I don't mind.' Her mum spooned sorbet into the dishes. 'Oh,' she said, pausing, 'Pippa rang earlier. She's popping by with the kids tomorrow morning. I'd told her you were coming. I expect we'll have to feed them. Oh dear, that'll mean another shopping trip.'

'I'll help, don't worry,' Stef said. 'It'll be great to see them.' She hadn't seen Pippa or the twins for ages. She took a spoonful of sorbet. The cold, sweet taste of the mango soothed her annoyance at her mother's assumptions, the way she was being swept up into her life here. 'Rob's not about, then?' she added lightly. Pippa's husband worked as an accountant in London, staying up there during the week, but around for his family at weekends – at least, that had been the original plan.

'I think he'll be playing golf.'

'Golf, eh? Good old Rob.'

'He's under a lot of pressure, Stef. He needs to relax sometimes.'

Stef concentrated on the sorbet but sensed her mother's eyes on her. Rob got away with murder. Quite how she and her younger sister had grown up to be such different people she didn't know. Stef had been biddable and hardworking as a teenager. Pippa, at fifteen, once she'd made herself up to look old enough, had started going to clubs in Cambridge with fake ID and coming home at all hours. She'd managed to scrape a Business HND at a further education college, and afterwards had done a series of administrative jobs locally until she'd met Rob, who regularly visited Cambridge on business. They'd moved to Norwich because property was cheaper. And that had been that. Pippa seemed perfectly happy being a stay-at-home wife, supporting her wage-earner husband – at least on the surface. And the twins, Jack and Jess, were undeniably sweet when they weren't fighting. Stef thought Rob affable but dull, and privately thought he did the minimum when it came to fatherhood. He certainly wasn't her idea of a desirable partner.

'At least he works hard,' her mum said. 'Bringing home the bacon.'

'That is true,' Stef remarked, scooping up the last traces of sorbet. She piled the bowls, rising from the table. 'I'll wash up.'

'Oh, leave it. I'd like another cup of tea.'

'What about the shopping for tomorrow?'

'All in good time.'

Stef took her tea out to the front and walked a few yards up the lane until she reached the sweet spot where her phone began to ping as a couple of text messages landed. One was from Pippa telling her about coming in the morning, the other from her phone company advising her that her bill was ready. When she looked at her emails, one in particular stood out. It was from Sarah, replying to Stef's own message. *'Fascinated to hear what you've found about Nancy's missing thesis. I think you're seriously on to something here.'* Stef smiled to herself. She thought so, too.

Four

Just before six that evening, although the June heat was fading, Stef and her mum set out for Nancy's talk at the nature reserve in bright sunshine, Stef guiding her car carefully between potholes in the narrow lane. At one point, a boat on a trailer turned out of a track signposted 'To the Staithe' and she had to reverse into a layby to let it pass.

The visitors' centre at the reserve, half a mile further on, was a low, modern building that had been designed to blend in with the landscape. Stef could hardly pick it out at first. When they drew close, she saw that its roof was studded with succulents, moss and gently waving grasses. 'Like a Hobbit house,' she commented, laughing.

She turned into a gritted car park area that was already full of cars. The people climbing out of them were mostly of retirement age or families, though there were a couple of youngish hikers laden with rucksacks and binoculars.

'Quite a crowd,' Cara remarked as Stef locked the car. 'Nancy should be pleased.'

Inside, Stef bought tickets at the shop counter from an unsmiling man with 'Josh, Wildlife Officer' printed on his name badge, then they walked through into a large room with picture windows looking out onto the reserve. Chairs had been laid out in rows before a portable white projector screen.

'There she is!' Cara pointed. Stef glanced across eagerly.

At a small table next to the screen, a stylish elderly lady sat close to a young man wearing a navy linen jacket over a pale blue polo shirt. Their heads were bent over an open laptop. Stef only had the opportunity to note Nancy's swept-up silver hair and floaty pink neck scarf before her mother drew her to a pair of empty seats halfway down the rows, next to the aisle, and her view of Nancy was blocked by a large gentleman in a birdwatcher's cloth hat.

Cara proceeded to point out various people in the room. Stef was impressed by how many she'd already got to know since moving to the village. The woman she waved to behind them had two boys with her of nine or ten. 'They go to the primary school near the church,' she whispered, before indicating an older man further along their row with a soldierly bearing who she said delivered the parish magazine, worked with boats at the staithe and kept bees. Stef, in the meantime, was beguiled by a girl of six or seven dressed in trackpants and a T-shirt with a rainbow decoration who was skipping up and down the aisle. She clutched a pack of picture cards and was singing to herself. When Stef smiled at her, she smiled back briefly before resuming her game. She had long, almost black straight hair and striking dark features.

'Who's she?' she asked her mother, who shook her head.

The answer presented itself when the man named Josh, who'd sold them their tickets, arrived at the front and tested the microphone on the lectern. The child darted over to the pair at the laptop and whispered something to the man in the polo shirt before taking a seat in the first row. A strange feeling came over Stef as she watched, but there was no time to identify the cause, for Nancy Foster was walking across to stand beside Josh. Although she looked frail, she held herself upright and her movements were graceful. She conveyed quite a presence, Stef thought.

'We are delighted to welcome Dr Nancy Foster,' Josh began in a confident voice. 'She's here to tell us about the life cycle of the swallowtail butterfly. As you know, this Broad is one of the very few places in the country where this rare insect can be seen. Some of us here had a wonderful time with Nancy this afternoon, didn't we, trying to spot some around the reserve? And it being fantastic weather, they were out and about and we were lucky to see one or two. Nancy, over to you.'

'Thank you, Josh.' Nancy's eyes brightened as she took her place behind the lectern and began to speak. 'Good evening, everybody, and thank you for coming.' She had a low, musical voice and Stef agreed with her mother about the distinctive way she dressed. The soft pinks and greys of her scarf went with her pale skin tones and brought out the grey-blue of her irises, a colour so light her eyes were mesmerizing. Her dress, too, was grey, but below the waist the grey gave way to patches of colourful pastels that ran up from the hem, reds and pale blues, like watercolours running in the rain. For a moment, Stef was too intent on the woman's appearance to listen to what she was saying, but now the first slide clicked up on the screen – a close-up photograph of the rare butterfly – and she began to concentrate on the lecture.

'Butterflies are my favourite insect and British swallowtails are my favourite type of butterfly. I love their unusual shape, with these tiny horns at the base of their wings like a swallow's tail – hence their name – and the intricate patterns on their wings. And their rarity does give them an extra-special glamour. We must take care of our swallowtails. Here on the Broad . . .'

With the help of drawings and photographs which the man on the laptop clicked onto the screen at her behest, Nancy explained how the creature lived and reproduced, and why the Broad was one of the few places providing the exact conditions for it to thrive. In particular, swallowtails laid their eggs on milk parsley, which is what the caterpillars ate when they hatched. Its flower head, like the more common cow parsley that filled the hedgerows in May, was shaped like an umbrella and consisted of a mass of tiny umbrellas, each one made up of minute flowers.

Stef found the talk fascinating. She didn't remember ever going into such detail at school about the complex relationship of insects to their environment and was alarmed by the fragility of it. Take away one of the balance of elements that these tiny, delicate creatures needed to live – something as simple as milk parsley – and the butterfly could not survive. Other types of parsley simply would not do.

Throughout the talk, focused as she was on Nancy and her slides, Stef was also aware of the little girl at the front. The child sat quietly, swinging her legs, but once she dropped several of her playing cards on the floor of the aisle and slipped down from her seat to collect them up.

After the talk, Nancy answered several questions from the audience and then, in her closing words, came the surprise.

'I would like to thank my grandson Aaron for managing the technical side'.

Aaron. Stef straightened then and, with a returning sense of disquiet, rose briefly to look over people's heads at the man operating the laptop. He raised his head and was instantly recognizable. It was Aaron the film-maker whose crew had parked in front of her mother's house on moving day. He was Nancy's grandson? She sank back down, recalling how unfriendly she'd been to him, and blushed with embarrassment.

'Stef, are you all right?' Her mother's nudging elbow startled her. She managed to nod.

Around her the room was erupting into applause. Stef's mind was whirling. Nancy's grandson. If he saw Stef and remembered her, it wouldn't be easy to charm Nancy. She glanced about, wondering what to do.

'We should go and speak to Nancy, don't you think, darling?'

'You go,' Stef mumbled. 'I'll wait for you in the car.'

'I thought you wanted to meet her.'

'Um, I do, but maybe not this minute.' She stood up,

swinging her bag onto her shoulder. 'She's busy, anyway, look.' Over by the screen, people had clustered around Nancy. Others were gathering their possessions, murmuring to one another how much they had enjoyed the talk. Stef started blindly to follow them out, but collided with someone and stopped. The little girl had appeared from nowhere, still clutching her pack of cards.

'I'm sorry,' Stef gasped. 'Are you okay?'

The girl nodded, then turned and darted back to the front where Aaron was busy collapsing the projector screen. She watched the child reach Aaron and point to her calf. He bent to examine it. Guilt washed through her. The girl must be Aaron's daughter. Should she go and apologize? Oh heck, did she have to?

Beside her, her mother grasped her arm. 'Come on, darling, you do need to speak to Nancy. It's the reason you came.' And before she knew it, she was being propelled towards the throng around the lecturer.

But now Aaron's eyes met hers and she saw his surprise as he recognized her. A guarded expression crossed his face. She approached hesitantly and he straightened, his arm still round the child. 'We meet again.' His voice sounded tight.

'I'm visiting my mother.' She addressed the girl. 'I'm so sorry, did I hurt you just now?' The girl hid her face. 'I bumped into her,' she said to Aaron. 'Or she bumped into me. It was an accident.'

'Livy, you shouldn't tear about like that,' Aaron said to the girl, then to Stef, 'She's okay.'

Stef nodded, then rushed on. 'The lecture was amazing. I

came with Mum, that's her in the denim jacket. Mum talks to absolutely everyone. She met Nancy at an art exhibition.'

'I see.' Aaron gave Stef a stiff smile.

She could feel her cheeks flush. 'I should also apologize for the last time we met. Let's say it was … pretty stressful helping my mother move in.'

He gave a short laugh. 'I got that impression.'

'I'm not usually like that,' she said in a low voice. He gave the slightest of smiles.

'Did you enjoy the talk?' she said to the little girl, who glanced up from her playing cards and nodded.

'I need to finish up here,' Aaron murmured.

'Sure.' She turned, feeling miserable, to look for her mother.

The crowd around Nancy Foster had melted away now, leaving only Cara deep in conversation with her. She beckoned and Stef went across with some trepidation, wondering what was being said.

'This is Stephanie, my daughter. I told you she's a journalist. Well, she's dying to talk to you. This book she's writing, it's about women scientists and how badly they're treated by the men. She's dug up some really sensational things, haven't you, Stef?'

'Mum!' Stef stiffened at her mother's direct approach, which must surely be guaranteed to make Nancy close up like a clam.

'How … interesting.' Nancy contemplated Stef, her grey-blue eyes steely in her lined face. She'd applied just a touch of powder and pinkish lipstick, Stef saw.

Stef drew breath and tried a light approach. 'I so enjoyed

your talk, Dr Foster. I wish we'd had a teacher at school like you for Biology. I might have learned much more.'

'You're very kind,' Nancy said crisply as though she distrusted compliments. 'I was a schoolteacher myself for many years, but one had to follow the curriculum and the children didn't always find that interesting.'

'Nancy was a proper scientist before that,' Cara interrupted. 'I mean, in a university. Doing research. What were you researching? Did you discover anything important?'

Mum, stop, you're spoiling things! Stef wanted to shout.

'I don't know about that. I was an entomologist, studying insects. My main research was with locusts.'

Again, Stef met the woman's eyes, definitely flinty now. 'Mum, it's okay,' she said gently.

Thankfully, her mum got the hint. 'Oh, don't mind little me. I'll see you in the shop, shall I? Thank you so much, Nancy.'

Stef watched her drift away, her narrow shoulders hunched, and felt bad. Brushing this off, she turned to Nancy. 'Mum is right,' she said. 'I am a journalist and I am writing a book, but it's not sensationalist, it's a serious exploration.' She mentioned the article she had written about women in science. 'The conference I reported on was concerned with what is still happening, but I want to take the longer view in my book.'

'A great many things have changed for the better,' Nancy remarked. A bitter tone had crept into her voice. 'These women you met at your conference ...' She stopped and, though Stef waited, didn't go on. Instead, she fiddled with her scarf and glanced over at Aaron, who had fitted the rolled-up screen into its case and was putting the laptop away.

'These women . . .' Stef prompted, but Nancy merely smiled and shook her head.

'It was very difficult back in the forties and fifties. There's much more equality now than in the past.' Her tone was mild, but the working of her fingers on the scarf suggested she was mastering strong emotion. Stef felt that sensation again, a prickling of the hairs at the back of her neck.

'I'd love to hear more about your experiences,' she said, trying to keep her tone casual. 'Would you be available sometime for a chat? I'm staying with my mother for a few days.'

Nancy was briefly silent, then said, 'Possibly. Aaron and Livy are here until tomorrow.' The woman's reluctance was obvious. Stef wondered how to pin her down, but feared she had lost her.

'I think it's time we went,' Nancy said with a tight smile. 'We've a table booked for dinner. Livy?' Aaron was ready now. The child skipped across and put her hand in Nancy's. 'So nice to meet you. Stephanie, isn't it?'

'Stef, yes. So I'll come to find you on Monday, perhaps,' she persisted. 'We could have a coffee in the café here? Around eleven, if you're free.'

'Oh, I suppose that should be all right,' the woman said. Stef felt Aaron's gaze on her and it wasn't friendly. She followed the three of them at a distance through to the shop, where they said goodbye to Josh, who was serving customers at the till, then watched them walk out to the car park. Nancy lived in a cottage somewhere on the reserve, Stef remembered her mother saying.

'Over here, darling.' The shop was nearly empty, but her

mother was waving a greetings card from her place in the short queue at the counter. 'I'll just pay for this. It's for Auntie Sandra's birthday.'

Stef nodded, then turned back to stare after Nancy, Aaron and Livy. They had reached Aaron's sleek black saloon car. She saw its lights flash at the press of his key. Aaron stowed the technical equipment in the boot, then they climbed into the car and he drove away with a rattle of gravel.

Stef sighed with sudden despondence. She was still processing the awkwardness of running into the man she'd been so offhand to. If his grandmother knew about it, it would likely ruin her chances to talk to her. It was annoying, too, that Stef's mother had made the book project sound so intrusive and sensationalist. That had obviously set Nancy on edge before Stef had had a chance to explain the facts.

Just then she heard her name mentioned and glanced up to see that her mother was now at the till and chatting away to Josh. Was she telling yet another stranger about her?

Stef barely heard her mother's chatter on the drive home. She was thinking about Nancy. There was something she'd said, bitter hints about her past, that piqued her professional instincts. And she remembered that prickle of excitement she'd felt. There was a story there, she thought. Maybe it wouldn't be much of one, but maybe it would. Nancy Foster had secrets, Stef sensed, and she badly wanted to discover what they were.

Five

Later that evening, Nancy Foster walked alone by the Broad in the fading light. She loved these calm summer twilights when the sweet-scented air was full of birdsong, the chirp of crickets and the soft lapping of water in the reeds. She paused at a viewpoint by the duckboards and rested one hand on the wooden rail as she stared out across the Broad. In the distance, the last rays of the dying sun shimmered on the rippling water. High above, a lone gull sailed across a sky that was streaked with wisps of amber cloud.

Nancy sighed. It was so peaceful here once the visitors had gone and there was no rumble of distant traffic or murmur of human voices. Despite her age, her hearing was still sharp, something she was deeply grateful for, but quietness soothed her. Especially at times like tonight, when the old anxiety surfaced.

She'd enjoyed their supper at a gastropub near Blakeney on the coast. Aaron was always interesting, talking about his busy life. It was funny to think that she'd once loved living in the heart of a city, as her grandson did now.

It was good of Aaron to make time to help her with the talk, and of course she loved any opportunity to see Livy. The child was tucked up in bed asleep now at the cottage and Nancy had left Aaron hunched over his laptop at the old mahogany desk in her sitting room – constructing a pitch for a film project, he'd murmured when she looked in to say where she was going. He hardly seemed to stop working, that boy, even when it was his turn to have his daughter. He was a good father, gentle and attuned to Livy's needs. He lived on his nerves, though, which wasn't good for anybody.

It had been a shame about the break-up, traumatic for Aaron, but he and Crystal, whom he'd met at university in London, had become parents too young and their paths had quickly diverged. How different it was when Nancy had been their age and women were expected to stay at home to raise children. Not always better, but relationships had been given more of a chance. Three years now, he'd been single – at least, she'd been unaware of anyone special. She worried about him greatly – making up for all the years when she hadn't seen much of him because his mother, Nancy's daughter, had left home very young and eventually moved to America. She felt that familiar pang when she thought of Andrea. She'd been such a delightful little girl, but had struggled as a teenager.

It wasn't Aaron or Andrea who were troubling her tonight, though. It was the young woman she'd met after the talk, what was her name, Stephanie something. Lansdown, same as her mother. Nancy liked Cara, she was amusing; a bit scatterbrained, but amusing. She'd found Stephanie more serious, a little earnest, nothing wrong with that, but it was all too obvious that she was a journalist with a nose for a story. Wanting to interview Nancy for a book.

She tensed. Well, she certainly didn't want her past, her secret pain, the injustice done to her, to become fodder for some sensationalist account. She simply wanted to be left alone to enjoy her last years. Aaron had seemed to agree. When Nancy had mentioned Stef, he'd frowned and said he'd met her once before briefly, though he didn't say where or how. Nancy asked what he'd thought of her, but he'd merely shrugged. Livy had piped up then, said Stephanie had bumped into her. 'Only because you were fooling about,' Aaron had told her. Nancy didn't think he'd needed to say it so sharply.

'I'm serious, Gran, you don't have to meet her if it'll upset you. You know what journalists are like – they dig around in your life. It's their job. I'd keep away from her if I were you.'

'I'll manage,' Nancy had told him, a little snappish. 'I'm used to looking after myself.'

A mournful quacking dragged her from her thoughts. She watched as a pair of ducks flew down to the Broad, carving a furrow in the water and sending up golden spray. After the ripples had ceased and peace had returned, she left the viewpoint and walked on. Before long, she entered an area of scrubby woodland and the wooden boards gave way to a loamy path. Darkness was gathering here under the willows and the holm oaks, and moths had started to flutter about. She hardly noticed where she was going until she walked into a spider's silk thread spun across the path, flinched and stopped to brush it from her face.

She considered whether to meet this Stephanie on Monday. The request had caught her on the hop. It would be rude not to, she supposed, and anyway it would be sensible to find out what she'd turned up in her research so far – you never knew what was on the internet. She'd be firm, though, and explain that no, she didn't want to be in this book. Having made this decision and because the midges were biting, she took an early turning back to the main path.

The light was still on in the sitting room and the door firmly shut, so she made herself some tea with a splash of whisky in it and climbed the stairs to bed. As she lay waiting for sleep to overtake her, she remembered something that Stef had said earlier, something she'd forgotten. It was about the talk, how Stef had found it inspiring and how she wished she'd had a teacher like Nancy at school. She'd looked particularly sincere as she'd said this, and Nancy warmed to her thinking of it. She herself had had an inspiring schoolteacher, but her love of the natural world had started way back before that. As she sank into the dreamy state between wakefulness and sleep, it all came back in a series of images, like an old film, that wonderful childhood memory.

She'd been seven or eight. A family outing to Richmond Park. The rough feel of a tartan picnic blanket against her legs. The sweet chill in her mouth of homemade ice cream served from a wide-necked vacuum flask. Deer grazing beneath the oak trees. A dog barking and the sight of the startled herd flowing away across the grass. So beautiful, she'd stood up to watch them, wondering at the lightness and grace of their movements. She was curious. How did they come to be like that?

If anyone ever asked, 'What first inspired you to become a scientist?', that had been the moment.

Six

On Sunday, Stef accompanied her mother to morning church. She'd been reluctant, expecting to stick out among a handful of elderly people, but instead was pleasantly surprised. The vicar, a cheerful, motherly woman named Daphne, led the worship for several dozen people of all ages, including young children who sat at a low table in a patch of sunshine at the back, crayoning template drawings or doing jigsaws, the birdlike sounds of their voices a musical accompaniment to the poetry of the traditional liturgy. Afterwards, there was good coffee and fresh croissants – no doubt a part of the draw.

Nancy was there in front, Stef saw. Livy, next to her in the pew, spent the service dressing and undressing a doll. They didn't stay afterwards, Nancy staring straight ahead as she led Livy up the aisle to the door. Stef wondered if Nancy had spotted her and that was the reason for her quick exit, but there was no way to tell. Instead, she nibbled her croissant, trying not to drop crumbs on the flagstones, and allowed her mother to introduce her to various people she'd got to know in her six weeks in the village, amused that she had no reason, after all, to worry about her mother making friends. The soldierly man with wispy silver hair who kept bees was Geoffrey Stuart. He ran boat trips on the Broad and proved very knowledgeable about the area. He knew Nancy, of course. She'd lived in her cottage on the reserve for two decades, he told her, but last year the new landlord had tried to get her out. He'd failed so far.

'Isn't the cottage owned by the trust who run the wild-life reserve?'

'Oh no, they only have part of the area. The rest is a per-missive access arrangement. It's very complicated.'

'Why does he want her to leave?'

'Accounts vary,' said Geoffrey. 'It's mad of him, really. The place is run-down and damp. I can't imagine he'd find another tenant who'd put up with that.'

'Perhaps he wants to renovate.'

'Possibly, though it would cost him.'

As the numbers thinned out and she waited for her mother, Stef wandered round the building, examining memorials to the long-dead and the biblical scenes in the stained-glass windows. A noticeboard at the back of the church advertised the activities of local societies and businesses. Reading the flyers, she realized that her mother had chosen to move into a thriving village and was reassured once again. She glanced at her watch. Pippa and the twins would arrive soon. She hurried over to remind her mother.

They'd only been home a few minutes when Pippa's

bright blue SUV pulled up outside, blocking the light to the little sitting room where Stef was reading the Sunday paper. Their mother hurried down the front path to greet her younger daughter, but Stef hung back at the door, arms folded, watchful.

'It's good to see you, Pip,' her mum said, opening the driver's door. 'Hello, darlings!' She waved to the kids in the back.

'They've been awful,' Pippa sighed, clambering out and hugging her mother. 'Fighting all the way over a silly computer game.' She looked as lovely as ever, her slim, languorous figure set off by faded jeans, a navy T-shirt and white sandals. Her tanned, heart-shaped face was partly hidden by huge sunglasses and by the brim of a blue and red baseball cap, from which a short, dark ponytail poked out at the back.

Stef banished the usual stab of envy at her sister's effortless attractiveness and stepped forward with an affectionate grin. 'Hi, Pip!'

'Hi.' A half-hearted hug and Stef, sensing Pip looking her up and down, tensed her tummy muscles, aware of the excess half-stone she had always carried. 'You're fat' had been Pippa's favourite insult when they were children and Stef had taken it to heart.

The twins were struggling to escape their child seats.

'Leave your Gameboys in the car!' Pippa cried. 'Or I'll take them away altogether.'

The twins tumbled out, a matching pair of sturdy four-year-olds with smooth, butter-coloured hair, creamy skin and brown eyes like Rob's. Jack was in jeans and a Spiderman T-shirt. Jess wore trackpants, her hair was long and her T-shirt featured a Disney mermaid. They grinned briefly at their aunt, muttered, 'Hi, Gran-gran,' to their grandmother and raced past into the house, shouting for Baxter in high voices. Stef guessed that Baxter, if he had any sense, had retreated to his favourite hiding place behind the heavy Knole sofa. Her mother rolled her eyes and followed them inside, leaving her daughters alone together.

Stef picked up a tiny computer game that one of the twins had dropped on the road, then helped Pippa with the bags of toys and spare clothes she was hauling out of the boot.

'At least they no longer need buggies and high chairs and travel cots,' she said, remembering. 'It used to be like a military campaign.'

Pippa lifted her sunglasses onto her head. 'Thank God that stage is over,' she sighed. 'Never again!'

She was chewing gum like a teenager, Stef noticed, and her oval nails were beautifully painted. Stef glanced down at her own stubby ones.

'How are things going, Stef?' Pippa said casually as she lowered the boot lid. 'Haven't seen you in ages.'

'Not bad. The work's coming in okay. You?'

'All right. Those two are running rings round me.' Pippa locked the car. 'They don't sleep and nor do I.' Between them, they carried the bags inside.

Stef felt on edge. There was always this stiffness between them. It wasn't that affection was lacking, it was simply that the sisters had little in common apart from family ties. They hadn't properly quarrelled since their teens, just gone their own ways. Sometimes Stef wished that they did fight. At least it would be communication of a sort. Instead, they danced round subjects of dissent without actually saying anything that might cause the other deep offence.

Their mother had gone to put the kettle on and, in the sitting room, the children had burrowed behind the sofa – Stef smiled to see the soles of Jack's trainers waving about – and were chatting to Baxter as though he was human. 'How are you today, Baxter? Have you been good? If you have, I'll give you a sweet.' Poor dog. He wouldn't hurt a fly and the twins knew it. It was rather touching, really, how they brought him into their games like an honorary triplet. They weren't unkind. The worst he'd had to endure was hair-ribbons tied round his floppy ears, though he regularly did duty as a pudgy pillow. Then he'd assume a droopy-eyed expression of endurance – even a dog had his dignity.

'Stop torturing the poor animal!' Pippa sighed. She and Stef laid out puzzles and toys on the carpet. Then they followed a smell of frying onions to the kitchen. The kettle had boiled, Stef saw, but their mother had forgotten to make the coffee and instead started on the spaghetti bolognaise – the twins' favourite – for lunch. Pippa binned the chewing gum, made coffee and settled herself with hers at the kitchen table, where she sat in doleful silence. Stef located a tin of tomatoes and fetched a garlic baguette out of the freezer.

'Is Rob really playing golf?' she asked her sister conversationally. She sat down opposite Pippa with the fruit bowl and a knife, intending to make fruit salad for dessert.

'He really is. It's so annoying, but what can I do?' Pippa took a sip of her coffee, examined her pearly nails and looked glum. 'It's a way of letting off steam after a hard week, I get that, but it's hard on the kids – they never see him. And I'd really love some time off myself. Just to flop, you know?' She looked appealingly at her sister.

'Your father was much the same,' their mother told her daughters as she stirred bubbling mince in the pan, 'but it was antique book fairs in his case, not golf. I wasn't able to do any painting when you two were young. You're very fortunate, Pip, that Rob earns such a good salary and you don't need to go out to work.'

Pippa shot her mother a furious look and Stef winced. 'I expect I will work when they're older. It's just nice being with them when they're young.'

'You're lucky to have the choice,' Stef couldn't stop herself saying. 'Most of my friends with kids have to go on working to pay the bills and keep up with their careers.'

'Well, at least I never had a career to keep up,' Pippa said crossly.

Stef nearly said, 'You could have done if you'd tried,' but happily at that moment Baxter barrelled into the kitchen and straight out through the open door into the garden with the twins running after him, shouting, in hot pursuit.

'Stay inside the garden, you two. Don't go out to the field without a grown-up!' Pippa called after them, but there was no indication that they'd heard. 'Honestly, they don't take any notice of me.'

Stef sighed and held out her knife. 'You finish the fruit salad and I'll go and see what they're up to.'

'It's a deal, Auntie Stef.' Pippa took the knife and picked

an apple out of the fruit bowl while Stef washed her hands at the sink.

'After lunch, there's a surprise for them upstairs,' their mother told Pippa.

'You've put up the bunks?' Pippa perked up.

'Ted has.'

'Ah, Ted.' Pippa smirked.

'Who actually *is* Ted?' Stef asked, drying her hands.

'He was one of the men who put up the studio for me and he's been very kind,' their mother said firmly.

'Mum's been painting him.' Pippa's eyes twinkled.

'Oh, really?' Stef stilled in surprise, remembered the mysterious portrait in the studio.

'They're tormenting poor Baxter, Stef. Go and stop them, will you?'

Stef rescued the dog, managed to prevent the twins going into the studio and challenged them instead to do somersaults on the square of lawn. When that became too competitive, she found a football and took them out to the field. After running about on the grass, they grew calmer and sat down with Stef, prepared to engage with her. Jess listed her favourite TV cartoons with occasional interjections from Jack, who was teasing a beetle with a grass stalk.

After lunch, they all went upstairs to view the bunks and the predicted tussle ensued as to who would sleep where when they stayed.

'Me first on top,' Jack cried. 'Can we stay tonight?'

'No,' Pippa said, 'or you won't see Daddy before he goes back to London.'

Stef wasn't sorry that they'd be going home – the twins were adorable, but exhausting. And it was hard to get to know them as individuals because they were so absorbed in one other. As usual, though, as she waved them off, she felt she hadn't had a proper conversation with her sister. She longed for them to be closer, but somehow whenever they met they fell back into their old patterns and it never happened.

Seven

Stef couldn't be certain that Nancy would show up on Monday for their meeting. Or if she did, out of politeness, whether she would agree to be interviewed. Still, soon after ten, she packed her notebook into her bag and set out on foot for the nature reserve. The weather was sunny, the sky a deep blue with cotton-wool puffs of cloud, but neither the beauty of the day nor the healthy exercise could dispel her sense of trepidation.

As she walked the mile to the visitors' centre, Stef passed a newly built house of brick and polished flints, with an arc of horseshoes over the door and a shiny brass knocker in the shape of a squirrel. Then there was the intriguing turning to the staithe with its notice advertising boat trips. By the rotting gate of a crumbly old thatched cottage, a wayside stall displayed plants and honey for sale, with an honesty box for payments. Further on, a ginger cat sitting on a wall twitched its tail in warning when she reached to stroke it. As the line of houses gave out, she ambled beside hedges rampant with wild flowers, breathing in a grassy scent.

At the junction for the reserve, she turned right up the track.

The door to the visitors' centre stood open to the summer air. When she entered, there was no one except a short, round middle-aged woman, who was busy unpacking books from one of an assortment of cardboard boxes and filling the gaps on the shelves. In the café area, the delicious scent of coffee emanated from a machine which was making cheerful sucking and bubbling noises. Several tables with chairs were arranged nearby.

The woman looked up at her entrance, her hands full of books. The name tag hanging from her lanyard read clearly, 'Jackie – Volunteer.' She wore red-framed spectacles, gold dangly earrings and a tunic with a flowery pattern over white trousers. 'Have you come to see the reserve?' She looked harassed. 'I'll be with you in a sec. The boss is late in and there's a school party due, so I'm having to do everything myself.' She set the books on a shelf, then picked up a pair of scissors.

'Don't worry. I'm meeting Nancy Foster. You haven't seen her yet, have you?'

'Ah, you know Nancy.' There was warmth in her voice. 'I haven't seen her, no.' She frowned with effort as she slit the tape at the bottom of the empty box. 'You're a friend of hers?'

'My mother's local and introduced me. I came to the talk Nancy gave on Saturday. Very interesting.'

'I knew it would be. I wish I could have gone,' Jackie wailed as she flattened the box and added it to a pile. 'Saturday was my mother-in-law's birthday and we went out to dinner. Very nice restaurant. The White Hart, do you know it? But if it had been lunch, I said to my husband, we could have gone to the talk, but he refused to change it.' Stef sensed a woman who wouldn't stop talking.

'Nancy's lived on the reserve for many years, I gather?'

'I wouldn't like it myself. Very remote and the cottage is practically falling into the Broad. I'm surprised they let her keep living there, an elderly lady like that.'

'Who's "they"?'

'Oh, I don't know.' The woman frowned. 'The only family I've seen is the grandson and his little girl. Nancy comes in for a chat sometimes, but not all that often. There's another access track to the Broad and she keeps her car in a shelter at the top. She rings us if she's seen a rare bird or spotted a problem on the reserve. Otherwise she keeps herself to herself.'

Stef thought it sounded a lonely life. 'Well, I'm a few minutes early. I'll hang about here if you don't mind.'

'Be my guest, but the schoolchildren are on their way and I have to get on. It must have been a busy weekend here because there's so little left on the shelves.' She lifted a full box onto a table and raised her spectacles to squint at the label. 'Now, this is an important one.' She slit it open eagerly, pulled out a rubber snake and waved it about theatrically, before coiling it into an empty pocket in a Perspex stand of colourful toys. Then she began topping up the other compartments with a lifelike assortment of wildlife, items of bright stationery and branded fridge magnets. 'Some of these kids have a ridiculous amount of pocket money.

Honestly, modern parents. You wouldn't think we'd had a financial crisis.'

'Oh, here's Nancy.' Stef was glad to interrupt this flow. 'Good morning.'

'It is a nice one,' Nancy said and patted her throat. 'Oh dear, my voice. Bricks in a mincing machine today.' She carried a walking stick and looked weary, Stef thought, but at least she had come. She wore practical clothes today, navy slacks and a light blue zip-up fleece, but had taken the trouble to add gold stud earrings, while tortoiseshell combs kept her swept-up hair in place.

'How are you, Jackie dear?' she called.

Jackie complained again about the school party and Josh being late.

'Shall I buy you a coffee,' Stef put in quickly, 'before the hordes arrive?' The jug on the coffee machine was full now, the hotplate gently hissing. It would be awkward sitting here asking Nancy sensitive questions with Jackie listening in and noisy schoolchildren milling about. 'Maybe we could sit outside.'

Nancy must have had similar thoughts. 'Would you like to come to mine?' she said. 'It's not far and, who knows, we might see a swallowtail or two on the way.'

'I'd love to.' Stef was intrigued by the idea of visiting her cottage, and the butterflies would be a bonus.

'Jackie,' Nancy said with a smile, 'we'll get out of your hair. I can see that you're busy.'

'I just wish Josh would turn up. The kids will be here any moment.'

Just then came the crackle of tyres on gravel. 'Talk of the devil,' Nancy murmured as a small red car sped into the car park. It juddered to a halt and the youngish man who'd sold Saturday's tickets jumped out. He took a bulky rucksack from the boot, shouldered it and strode towards them, his face as dark as a thundercloud.

Stef, dismayed, hung back out of the way.

'Bloody roadworks,' he complained to Jackie, then saw Nancy. 'Oh, hello.'

'Morning, Josh,' Nancy said briskly. 'Bad luck about the traffic. This is Stef, by the way. We met at Saturday's effort.'

'Yeah, Stef, I think I remember you.' His tone was polite rather than friendly. 'You must excuse me if I get on.'

Josh crossed the floor, dropped his rucksack behind the counter and began to rummage about in a cupboard underneath, rising occasionally to pile pencils, clipboards and printed forms on the top, all the time calling instructions to Jackie.

Obviously a moody type, Stef gauged. The look he'd given her had not been welcoming. It was as if he suspected her of something.

Meanwhile, Nancy stepped over to the coffee machine and poured coffee and milk into a paper cup. When she gave it to him, his grim, suntanned face crinkled into what passed for a smile. 'Thank you.' His sharp brown eyes almost looked friendly.

'Are we ready?' she said to Stef.

The loudening roar of a bus engine could be heard. The school party had arrived. 'A narrow escape,' Nancy murmured, eyes twinkling, as they crossed the garden. The sound of the engine died; then, as she opened the heavy wooden gate to the reserve, the high voices of children started up from the direction of the car park.

The gate swung closed behind them with a soft thud and the voices were replaced by birdsong. The older woman walked at a steady pace despite her stick and Stef followed her along an earthen path between low hedges where sunshine and shadows flickered on the leaves. Soon, the hedges gave way to a sea of swaying golden reeds. It felt as though they had entered another world.

An incredible sense of tranquillity began to steal over Stef's mind. They paused for a while by a crop of Sweet William flowers to look for butterflies, but without success. 'Mmm, not warm enough yet,' Nancy said. She pointed her stick to indicate a passing dragonfly, then they set off again.

The path gave way to wooden duckboards. It was too narrow for them to walk side by side and there was little urge for conversation, though Nancy, in front, occasionally stopped to catch an unusual twittering from the reeds or to point out some far-off bird that Stef then tried desperately to distinguish in the marshy landscape. They passed a path signposted to the Broad, but Nancy took them onwards until they reached a narrow turning barred by a wood-paling gate. A notice nailed to it read 'Strictly Private'. Nancy opened it and they passed down a footpath overgrown by stunted willows.

'Not far now.' She smiled back at Stef. They rounded a corner and there, nestled in woodland, stood an ancient thatched cottage, wide and low and buttressed by out-buildings. Beyond it, through the trees, Stef could see the shimmering waters of the Broad and a wooden jetty where a rowing boat was tied up, gently rocking. It was calm and peaceful but for the birds and the breeze rustling the leaves.

'Welcome to Dragonfly Lodge.'

'What a lovely name. You'd never guess it was here,' Stef said with delight as Nancy opened a low gate and they entered the front garden, where a line of flagstones led between rampant flowering shrubs to a door sheltered by a porch. Indeed one might pass that 'Strictly Private' sign many times without realizing where its forbidden path led.

'That's precisely its appeal.' Nancy's clipped reply gave Stef a jolt and she sensed as she had done at their first meeting that beneath the elegant charm there was steel. She remembered how her mother's unbridled chattering had put Nancy on her guard. Stef would have to handle her carefully.

'It does sometimes feel very remote,' Nancy said as they paused in the shallow porch. She dug her fingers under a mat and brought out a large iron key, which she fitted into the lock.

'Jackie said that you keep a car.'

'I do. In an old barn at the edge of the reserve. That way.' She gestured vaguely, then turned a handle and the door swung inwards. 'Come in, do.'

Stef found herself in a tiny, musty hallway where a steep flight of stairs ran up to the first floor. Though gloomy, the hall felt cosy with thick rugs on the floor. Prints of birds and flowers studded the cream-painted walls. Nancy thrust her stick into an umbrella stand and laid the key on a console table.

'Do you have a telephone out here?' Stef thought to ask.

'I've never been able to get them to run a cable. Aaron insisted I have a mobile, though, which is marvellous, but the signal is patchy. I was practically marooned during the last cold snap. The paths can be treacherous and I was frightened to drive. Luckily Josh brought supplies and I have a few good friends in the village. Sit yourself down in here' – she pushed open a door to the right – 'and I'll make coffee. Won't be a minute.'

Stef wandered into a cluttered, book-lined sitting room and sat down in one of a pair of fireside chairs. A tabby cat lay asleep in a basket on the hearthrug, only briefly opening its eyes at her entrance. Stef smiled at it, then turned her attention to the room, noticing the evidence of Nancy's many tastes and interests. Daylight fell on the carpet in squares from a mullioned window that gave a view onto the wild front garden. It gleamed on the leaves of a cluster of potted plants occupying one side of the window seat and glinted off the brass fender. The fireplace had been swept clean, and a stack of logs lay ready in a box. On the wooden mantelpiece stood an array of ornaments, invitation cards, a vase of dried grasses, a photograph of the little girl, Livy, in a silver frame and a child's drawing of a house with a rainbow arcing above.

A sofa against the wall opposite was piled with books and papers, and at the back of the room a large table with a reading lamp was being used as a desk. A microscope had been set up to one side, next to a stack of wooden display cases, the size and shape of box files. A small upright piano near the window spoke of musical talents, and framed drawings, prints and a couple of pressed dried flower pictures filled up any wall space not already taken by books. The quiet beauty of the domestic scene, combined with its implication of human activity briefly abandoned, reminded Stef of a painting. A Gwen John, perhaps, with the chair and the umbrella and the open window.

A distant clatter and the scent of coffee drew her from her reverie. She stepped across to look at a shelf of outsized volumes with colourful spines next to the door, books about trees and flowers and animals. The shelf above these was dedicated to travel, containing faded tomes about the Swiss Alps, India and Italy. There was a memoir about the Cairngorms that Stef herself had bought for a walking holiday. Had Nancy visited all these places or merely dreamed of them?

She heard footsteps in the hall and hurried to clear a low table of a pile of birding magazines so that Nancy could set down her tray.

Nancy poured coffee from an old pewter pot into fragile cups decorated with blue dragons. 'My mother's,' she said when Stef admired them. 'They're a very old design, dating from the 1820s, I believe, a wedding present.'

'Were they given this set brand new, though?'

'I believe so. My parents married in 1925. It was usual then to be given dinner services for best. I don't know that young people go in for such things any more.'

Stef thought of the weddings she'd attended recently and felt the usual stab of self-pity. 'Everyday crockery, yes, I've given quite a few dinner plates in my time, but not posh ones, no. Unless I don't know the right class of people!'

'Well, I don't know anyone grand.' They smiled at one another. 'My background was quite ordinary. Though I did have an exotic aunt. Dear Aunt Rhoda. Long dead, of course. My brother and sister are gone, too. I'm the only one left. Now, will you have a biscuit?'

Stef took a piece of shortbread and bit into its buttery sweetness. She wanted to ask about the intriguing Aunt Rhoda, but Nancy got in first.

'I need to be straight with you, Stef, in case you think I've invited you here under false pretences. I'm not inclined to be part of any book you're writing. My grandson Aaron is of a similar mind.'

'Oh.' She wondered what exactly Aaron had said. 'Did he tell you that we'd met before?' It would be best to explain.

'Yes, but not where or how. Was it through work?'

'No, it was actually quite embarrassing,' Stef said and explained what had happened. 'I was rather ashamed of myself.'

'It must have been a stressful morning for you. Anyway, Aaron didn't tell me that, but there was something more important. He looked you up on the internet when he was here and found out about your journalism and about the book you'd written. Which caused quite a stir, I gather. No.' She shook her head. 'I don't want any part in a book like that.'

'I have to say that I was surprised myself by the strength of the reaction to it.'

Stef was dismayed by Nancy's response. First her mother

must have put Nancy off her, and now it was Aaron. She slid the half-eaten biscuit onto the saucer, stared down at it, then said, 'I thought that since you'd invited me here . . .'

'I'm sorry to disappoint you' – Nancy looked embarrassed – 'but I wanted to tell you myself and I didn't have your telephone number. I pride myself on politeness. People can be so unkind these days. Blanking each other and whatnot. So unnecessary.' She paused, then went on. 'And I suppose, too, that I wanted to meet you properly. I like interesting people. Life can be a bit lonely here.'

'Thank you for the compliment. I'd like to have a chance to speak up for myself, to put my case. I feel I've rushed you. My mother . . . dear Mum . . . She must have been offputting, though she'd be horrified to think that she had . . . Then Aaron . . . I mean, of course he cares for you . . .'

'My grandson is very protective.'

'Let me tell you a little about my work. Although I'm a journalist, I only write for serious newspapers and magazines, so I'm not looking for sensation and scandal.'

'I'm glad to hear it.' Nancy frowned. 'However, journalists are on the look-out for stories. They have to make things sound interesting.' She laughed. 'And real life is often dreadfully humdrum. Scientific research, for instance, isn't always exciting. In fact, it can be very dull and painstaking. But the media only talks about the rare thrilling moments of discovery or breakthroughs that make it all worthwhile.' She sighed. 'And journalists . . . I have a little experience there—' She halted and began turning her cup in its saucer. 'My daughter . . . Aaron's mother . . . caused us some trouble.'

When she met Stef's gaze once more, Stef was shocked to see her eyes gleaming with unshed tears. Horrified, she attempted to justify herself. 'I don't deny that I'm looking for stories,' she said. 'They're what sell papers, after all, but it's really the truth behind stories that I'm after. That's what good journalism does. It interrogates the cloud of myth and rumour that blows up around events of public interest and tries to determine what really happened and why.'

'Very admirable,' Nancy remarked. She'd mastered herself again. 'But in my humble opinion, the damage caused by this exposure to the people involved can be considerable.'

'I'm sure we can both think of examples and it's a shame. But it's not always like that. I wrote an article a few months ago about women working in the scientific community. It's online. Perhaps Aaron showed it to you?'

'He did. It was a good piece. Although so much for women has changed for the better, there was a great deal in it that I recognized.'

'The book I propose is an expansion of that article.'

'A splendid project,' Nancy said. 'Simply not one I wish to be involved with.'

Why am I pursuing this? Stef asked herself crossly. *The book will be fine without Nancy Foster. I'm sure there are plenty of others I can interview.* And yet she was intrigued. Why was Nancy quite so determined in her refusal?

'I understand your concern.' There was no point in upsetting her. Keen to take the heat out of the conversation, Stef said, 'It's so fascinating to be here. This cottage, this room. What a life you've made.'

At this, Nancy sat straighter. 'Yes,' she said brightly. 'It's been a real haven for me.'

'A haven,' Stef repeated. That was an interesting word. A haven from what? Nancy didn't explain. 'How long have you lived in the cottage?'

'Twenty years, twenty-two maybe. After I retired from teaching in Norwich, I felt a bit lost. I didn't know what to do with myself. I had no family there. Aaron's mother was living in the States then. I hadn't decided whether to stay in the city or go back to London. I certainly hadn't considered living out in the country by myself, but then a friend who knew Hickston told me about this place and when I saw it I just loved it. I've been very happy here. Such a shame—'

'A shame ...?' Stef looked at her enquiringly, but the cat had woken up and stretched its thin body and it took Nancy's attention.

'Come on, Tabitha.' Nancy bent and scooped her up, settled her on her lap and stroked her. Eventually, she spoke.

'But here I am talking all about myself. What about you, Stef? Did you always want to be a journalist?'

Stef smiled. 'It was one of the few options pushed at me when I was finishing my English degree. Journalism, teaching, publishing. In fact, it turned out that there are hundreds of things I could have done, but I had no idea at the time that they existed. So because I'd written for the university newspaper, I decided to apply for a journalism course. When I got a job on the *Globe*, I thought, *That's it, I'm made.*' She frowned.

'All didn't go well?'

'It's partly the internet, of course. Newspapers are

struggling, advertising is down. The *Globe* cut its staff.' As she spoke, it flooded back, the painful weeks of waiting to find out who was staying and who would go, the impersonal email that arrived delivering her fate. She shuddered. When she glanced up, Nancy was studying her, an expression of pity on her face, and she found herself confessing further.

'I'm making ends meet, just about, and there are advantages to being freelance – I've been able to come and see Mum at short notice, for instance – but it's nerve-wracking not to have a regular salary. And being single, as I am, there's no one to help cover the bills if I'm ill or something.'

'What about your parents?'

'Mum has little spare money. I'm okay at the moment, not struggling or anything.'

'Any other family?'

Nancy seemed genuinely interested, so Stef told her about her father, about Pippa and Rob and the twins. 'Dad would help me out if I asked,' she said, 'but he's always been keen that we stand on our own two feet. Pippa's married to a high-flying accountant, lucky girl, but I'd never ask him. Sorry, that sounds as though I'm envious of her, which I'm not.'

'No,' Nancy said. 'Though we can't pretend that money isn't important. Especially when it's lacking. I remember a time when I—'

Again, she broke off. It was frustrating, Stef thought. Nancy would so nearly supply a reminiscence, then draw back. Now Nancy laid her empty cup and saucer on the tray. 'I oughtn't to keep you,' she said, almost wistful.

'Oh, but you're not ... ' Stef started to say, then deduced

that Nancy was simply being polite and actually wanted Stef to go. 'I'll take the tray to the kitchen.'

'If you wouldn't mind, dear. It's the door on the left, next to the stairs.'

The kitchen was at the back of the house and when she pushed the door open, Stef remembered Geoffrey Stuart, whom she had met at church, describing the cottage as run-down. The room with its old lino-tiled floor must have already been old-fashioned when Nancy had moved in twenty years ago. It was furnished with freestanding cabinets, the worktops scarred by generations of knives and hot saucepans. A chipped ceramic sink sat beside a blackened wooden draining board. The view across the Broad from the wide window above the sink made up for it. She bent closer to look. All was tranquil, with tufts of drifting cloud reflecting on the glassy water. *It's breathtaking*, she thought.

'Can you see the heron?' Nancy had appeared beside her, still cradling the cat. 'To the left, beyond the jetty.'

A few seconds' searching, then Stef saw it. 'It's so still,' she breathed.

'It's waiting for its next meal to come by. Then it'll pounce.'

They watched, but the heron did not oblige and Stef's attention was caught by a more distant movement on the water. 'What are those over there?'

'Teal with the striped heads. And the geese are greylags,' Nancy said. 'Try using those things, if you want.'

Stef reached for the pair of binoculars on the windowsill and raised them to her eyes. The birds sprang into closeness. The teal were pretty ducks, dabbling for food. Two geese with orange beaks floated motionless, like children's bath toys.

When she lowered the binoculars, she saw that the cat was struggling in Nancy's arms. Nancy leaned down, crooning, to release it. It went to a dish on the floor next to a fridge, crouched to eat a few mouthfuls, purring, then sauntered out to the hall.

'Poor thing. Tabitha was old when I was given her a couple of years ago. I only kept her because her hunting days are well over.'

'I was going to say, a bird reserve is not a great place to keep a cat!'

'I'm given all sorts of animals. Come and see.' All talk of Stef leaving appeared to be forgotten.

Nancy shoved open the wooden back door, which was swollen with damp, and Stef followed her careful progress out along a flagged path to one of the stone-built outhouses that adjoined the cottage. Inside, it smelled musty, but the room was dry and lined with cages. Several long, low ones on the floor contained hedgehogs. Small birds fluttered and tweeted in an aviary. A number of smaller cages and tanks, some full of greenery, stood on shelves. Stef, touched to see her tender care, watched as Nancy moved from cage to cage, topping up a hedgehog's water bottle, sprinkling sunflower seeds into a bird feeder attached to the outside of the aviary, occasionally offering Stef useful comments.

'The chiffchaff I found injured on the path. An owl had dropped it maybe. Oh, there's a chrysalis in there. I'm hoping something will emerge, but no sign so far. People from the village are always bringing me hedgehogs. This one had a strimmer injury – very common at this time of year – but it's recovering well.'

They left the outhouse and Stef cried 'Oh!' as she saw the heron spread its great wings and take off awkwardly. It flew over the water towards the far shore.

'We disturbed it, I fear,' Nancy said. Stef saw her smile and watched her walk down to the fence, where she stood to look out over the Broad. She glanced about, thinking how close the cottage was to the water. The ground was raised, but still . . .

'Has there ever been a flood here?'

'Nothing serious. The occasional high spring tide has had its effects on the Broad, but the levels have never given me more than wet feet.' Nancy was more relaxed now than she'd been over coffee, less wary.

Stef glanced at her watch and saw that it was half-past twelve.

'I should go.'

'Of course. Is it lunchtime? I lose track. I ought to get on. Aaron's coming back later. He's staying with friends locally, but he's here for supper.'

'That's nice.' Stef felt a stab of discomfort at the mention of his name. 'What about the little girl?'

'He took her back to her mother last night.' Something about the way this was phrased made Stef wonder if Livy's parents were together, but it would be rude to ask. Instead, she said, 'School today, I suppose. Is she an only child?'

'Yes. Aaron's my only grandchild and Livy's my only great-grandchild.'

'I should think she loves it here.'

'Oh yes, coming here is a great adventure for her.'

Nancy's goodbye was friendly and cheerful. 'I enjoyed our conversation. I stand by what I said about your book, but maybe I'll see you again sometime. You know where I am.'

'Thank you. I'd like that.' They smiled at one another. Nancy might not wish to be interviewed, but Stef felt that they might be friends.

'Do you know the way back?'

'I think so.'

She walked back up to the main path, then followed signs back to the visitors' centre. Nancy intrigued her. It was wonderful how she lived out in the wilds, leading a tranquil life apparently, but what was it that made her retreat from the world? There was something vulnerable and defensive about her, as though, like the wildlife she rescued, she was nursing a deep wound. Something or someone had hurt her.

The visitors' centre was deserted apart from Jackie behind the counter and an elderly couple browsing the bookshelves.

'Did you see the school party on the reserve?' Jackie asked her.

'No.' Stef realized she'd forgotten about them. 'They're out there somewhere, are they?'

'Josh will have taken them off to the bird hides, I expect, but I'm ready for their return. How did you find Nancy?'

'I enjoyed meeting her,' Stef said, taken aback by the direct question.

'Such a pity she'll have to leave.' Jackie's eyes were bright with interest.

'Will she?' Stef's reply was cautious, though she remembered what the soldierly man at church had said about pressure from Nancy's landlord.

'I heard it was on the cards.' Jackie looked flustered. 'But perhaps I'm wrong.'

Nancy had given no indication of it, Stef thought, as she began the walk back to the village. And Jackie was a bit of a gossip. It really had been the most peculiar morning. Ultimately a frustrating one, because she'd been most beguiled by Nancy, but Nancy had made it all too clear that she didn't want to divulge her secrets.

Eight

Nancy, too, felt peculiar. After she'd closed the door on Stef, she hesitated in the hall, her hand on the wall for support. She felt a little dizzy. It wasn't just a physical dizziness but a sense of being overwhelmed.

She'd liked Stef, liked her more than she'd expected after first meeting her on Saturday evening, when she'd found her rather hard-edged, as if cross about something. And Aaron had warned Nancy off her. But Stef hadn't been as inquisitive as she'd feared a journalist would be, nor had she asked manipulative questions. She'd caught the young woman looking at her books while she was out of the room, but that was a natural thing to do, not like nosing around on her desk, which she felt sure she hadn't done. Instead, she'd been respectful, politely interested and genuinely charmed by the cottage and its surroundings.

Having decided not to reveal anything about her past, Nancy had found herself starting to tell Stef certain details.

She'd almost invited her to supper that evening, but had stopped herself in time. Aaron clearly hadn't taken to Stef, and Stef had explained that they'd had some silly spat. Nancy sighed. What was next? Lunch, she supposed, setting off for the kitchen. Bread and cheese and the last portion of bagged salad. Making food for oneself could be so tiresome, she thought, opening the fridge.

Once she'd prepared lunch, she took the plate to the table. She always made herself sit down properly, laying out a placemat and the right cutlery, a glass of water. It didn't do to let oneself go. Her mother would have insisted on a linen napkin in a silver ring, but that was going too far. Her poor mother, long dead. Did they have napkin rings in heaven? Nancy smiled at the thought as she buttered her bread.

Sometimes her mother's voice was as fresh in her head as though it were yesterday and she was still a child. Nancy felt very young and childlike sometimes. She'd spent so much of her childhood trying to avoid what her mother wanted her to do. She'd loved the woman very much, but they had never understood one another.

$\sim$

North London, 1935

'Nancy? Coo-ee! Nancy!' Her mother's high-pitched tones reached her at the bottom of the garden, but Nancy took no notice. It was a hot summer's day and she was lying on her tummy in the long grass near the back gate, watching a ladybird climb a buttercup stem. She liked ladybirds. This one she'd decided to call Ann after the one that hid under the frying pan in the nursery rhyme, though now that she was six she was too old for nursery rhymes. She had a favourite pair of pyjamas with ladybirds all over them, and some picture books with a ladybird on the front.

She'd never examined a real ladybird close up before. It was very pretty, but also interesting and clever, the way it negotiated the fragile stalk, though being so broad in shape by rights it ought to fall off. This ladybird had seven spots on its back, but some of the ones on her pyjamas had only two. As she watched, it flexed its red wing cases. *Ann's going to fly!* She waited, but it changed its mind and refolded them. She stayed as still as she could and wondered if it would try again. Yes. Its wing cases spread to reveal a pair of gauzy brown wings underneath and there, it was off with a buzz, a clumsy aircraft lifting through the air, its wings a whirring haze, the cases like black-spotted red parachutes keeping it buoyant. She watched it land on a daisy as her mother called again, 'Nancy. Don't think I can't see you. Come in right away. Your Aunt Rhoda's here.'

Aunt Rhoda! Marvellous! *Goodbye, Ann*, she breathed as she scrambled to her feet. Her mother was waiting a few yards away, frowning, arms crossed, yet so pretty with her short, light-brown hair newly waved, her cotton frock of a blue like a piece of the sky, its round collar and cuffs as white as the fluffy clouds overhead. Nancy smiled with love for her.

'Oh, look at you, girl, you're filthy. Why can't you be more like your sister?'

Nancy glanced down at herself, seeing with dismay that her beautiful smocked party dress was smeared with green and grass seed clung to her ruched white ankle socks. Her mother bent and picked off the seed, then seized her by the hand. The French doors stood wide and Nancy could see her elegant aunt in the drawing room beyond, speaking to her father, one graceful hand on her hip. Rhoda turned her head, saw Nancy and broke off, smiling. She stepped swiftly to the threshold, her arms wide in greeting.

'Here's the birthday girl. Happy birthday, darling!'

'She's already spoiled her dress, Rhoda.'

Nancy shook off her mother's hand and raced towards her aunt but tripped on a step. Rhoda bent and caught her. 'Dear girl,' she cried and led her inside.

'The child's so clumsy,' she heard her mother sigh behind her, but Nancy didn't care for Aunt Rhoda was here, in a stylish navy suit she hadn't seen before, her clipped dark hair smooth against her neat head, the beauty spot on her upper lip accentuated by the reddest lipstick Nancy had seen. Her mother disapproved of Rhoda's make-up, her high heels and her diamond-studded cigarette holder. Above all, she was sniffy that her husband's sister was single and a career girl. Nancy had overheard her mother tell her friend Mrs Armitage these things when Mrs Armitage had come for tea recently. Nancy had been loitering on account of Mrs Armitage's Jack Russell, which did tricks in return for the biscuits Nancy fed her.

'I didn't know you were coming,' she told Rhoda excitedly. 'I'm having a party this afternoon, with games and a cake.'

'You lucky girl! How marvellous!' Rhoda's brown eyes widened.

'A chocolate cake with jelly sweets on top.' Roger, Nancy's ten-year-old brother, sauntered in, hands in trouser pockets. 'Mummy let me scrape the bowl.'

'Don't spoil the surprise, Roger.' Their peacemaking sister Helen rose from a chair where she'd been quietly listening.

'Five little girls are coming at three,' her mother sighed. 'You can stay if you like, Rhoda, but I would not recommend it.'

Rhoda laughed. 'I'd love to, Marjorie, but unfortunately I'm due at Liberty's to show my new range. I just came by to wish my niece a happy birthday and to give her this.' She delved into a paper carrier bag and handed Nancy a large wrapped box tied with a big red bow.

'Oh my!' Nancy breathed, taking it. She sat down on the floor, undid the ribbon and wrestled with the flowery paper.

'Don't tear it, girl. We can use it again,' her mother said, but too late.

A box was revealed with a picture on it. 'A puzzle, I bet it's a puzzle,' Roger drawled.

Nancy read the words above the coloured drawing: 'A Magic Chemistry Set!' she gasped with delight. She swept the paper aside and lifted the lid off the box. 'Oh!' She ran her fingers over two neat rows of cardboard tubs inside. Glass phials and tubes clinked in their compartments when she touched them.

'Isn't it for boys?' Helen asked, uncertain.

Roger snatched up the lid, studied the picture on it and laughed. 'Of course it is. Look.'

Nancy studied the picture and her lower lip wobbled. It

featured a father and a son sitting together at a table, setting up an experiment. Floating in the background was a roundel containing the disembodied face of a sinister-looking man with a pointed black beard. 'He's a scientist,' Roger said, pointing. 'Only men are scientists.'

'Don't take any notice of the wretched boy,' Rhoda said gravely. 'Though you might need him to help you set up.'

'Say thank you to your aunt,' Nancy's mother said. 'It's very generous of her, I'm sure.'

'Very generous,' her father echoed. 'But not to be used without proper supervision. I don't want you setting fire to the house.'

Nancy stood up, cradling the box, and fixed her aunt with a steady gaze. 'I don't care what Roger thinks and I don't need his help. It's my best present. Thank you, Auntie Rhoda.'

～

A dark shadow flickered across the kitchen table where the elderly Nancy sat over her lunch, pulling her out of her reverie. She glanced up. A bird, perhaps, flying across the window. It had gone. She took another bite of soft bread roll, her mind still caught in the past. That chemistry set. She smiled. She'd taken such care of it. Her mother wouldn't have anything to do with it, even though her father had pointed out to his wife that she was using chemistry every time she cooked something. 'That's different,' her mother had snapped. 'Food is food. And it doesn't have difficult names.'

'Bicarbonate of soda?' Mr Foster had said. 'And what about cleaning fluids – ammonia? Bromide. That's all chemistry.'

'But it wasn't how we were taught at school, Arthur. We didn't have chemistry, it was domestic science. And Nancy would be better off learning how to cook and clean than messing about with these dangerous things. Then she could make herself useful like Helen.'

'Helen is Helen and Nancy is Nancy,' was her father's gnomic response, but Nancy knew what he meant and loved him for it.

Her father had always spoken up for her. Her heart still ached at the memory of him, dead and gone when she was only twenty-nine. Her mother had not understood her, had been bemused by her. It was Rhoda, her father's glamorous elder sister, fabric designer and businesswoman, who had paid for her from the age of eight to attend a reputable girls' day school in North London, near where they lived. A school whose mission was to offer girls a proper academic education. Mr Foster worked for the Home Office. As a child, Nancy hadn't known what he did exactly and wasn't much interested. He left home at eight o'clock sharp every morning in a dark suit and a bowler hat, then reappeared in time for tea at six with the evening paper and a harassed expression.

Nancy smiled at these memories as she carried her plate to the sink. She stood for a while, leaning against it, lost in thought. Those were times of such happiness. She'd felt loved and secure with her family in that comfortable suburban house. There must have been snowy winters, but in her mind it was usually summer and she was in the garden. They'd used the straight lines mown by her father for races. The border beds, colourful with roses and dahlias, had been out of bounds to balls, but the old apple tree with the tree house was theirs, as was the field beyond the garden gate. It had been idyllic, a paradise. But in this Eden there lurked a serpent. Three doors down from Nancy's family lived the Hunters, whose two sons were older than the Foster children. The parents were friendly with Nancy's parents but not close. Mrs Foster played bridge occasionally with Mrs Hunter. Nancy's father and Mr Hunter were both members of the local Conservatives. For two consecutive Christmases before the war, the Fosters invited the Hunter family over for lunchtime drinks. The Foster children had felt too shy to address the boys, Brian and Lawrence, lanky lummoxes who wolfed all the sausage rolls, then hung about whispering together and obviously wanting to go home. Nancy was fascinated by Brian's huge feet that he'd clearly inherited from his father but had not yet learned to manage. He was always treading on people's toes.

By 1941, when Nancy was twelve, much had changed. A stray bomb the previous November had put out everyone's front windows and left a crater in the street, now filled with rubble from the remains of a house further down. An Anderson shelter dominated the Fosters' back lawn and the flower borders had been planted with potatoes and carrots. One of Nancy's jobs was to feed the chickens in their run at the bottom of the garden, where she was overlooked by a silver barrage balloon bobbing above the field like an alien craft. It was out on the field that she liked to escape with a book when it was sunny in the hope that no one would bother her.

Sadly, one day, someone did.

It was the pair of large male feet she saw first, quite close, too close. She was sitting cross-legged in the long grass at the edge of the field, reading *The Thirty-Nine Steps*, which she'd borrowed from the library. She'd been so caught up in the story that she hadn't heard him approach. Her first thought was that it was Brian and she was surprised because the elder Hunter boy, at nineteen, was away somewhere with his unit, fighting the Germans.

'Hello, Nancy.' At the teasing deep voice, her gaze travelled upwards. A pair of pale cotton twill trousers – why was the belt undone? Now he squatted down and she found herself looking into Mr Hunter's smiling face. Despite his affable expression, she felt a deep, incomprehensible sense of unease. 'All alone?' She nodded dumbly and pressed her open book to her stomach, wanting to edge away, but not daring to in case he complained that she was being rude. He was an adult and she'd been brought up to be polite to adults, especially when they were friends of your parents.

'You were reading. Let me see.' He reached out his hand and when it brushed hers she felt her skin crawl with disgust. She loosened her grip on the book and allowed him to take it from her.

'Ah, an old favourite,' he said and sat down to study it. He had surprisingly long lashes for a man, but when he stroked his chin it made a bristly sound. He looked up. 'A funny choice for a girl.'

'It is quite an exciting story,' she managed to say. She hated that his eyes were on her bare legs and instinctively pulled her skirt down. She felt self-conscious these days, aware with dismay of her body changing and having no control of it. It had already happened to her sister Helen, but no one said anything about that in Nancy's hearing, not even their mother. Helen had her own bedroom now and wouldn't let Nancy into it. Though Nancy crept in from time to time when Helen was out and marvelled at its tidiness, a sewing pattern open on the desk next to a half-written letter to her American penfriend the only items out of place, a magazine photograph of Jimmy Stewart pinned to the wall next to her childhood picture of a golden-haired Jesus. In the top drawer of the chest she found a box of Kotex napkins. She'd already suspected that Helen had 'started'.

'I'm glad I found you here,' Mr Hunter said, closing the book and returning it to her. He took off his hat and began to fan himself. 'Rather warm, don't you think? No, don't go, you little minx.' His hand gripped her knee so tightly it hurt and she froze. Then, with his eyes on hers and a cruel smile twisting his lips, he allowed his other hand to slide under her skirt and feel its way upwards. She gasped in shock.

'Does it tickle?' he murmured and edged closer.

'Don't,' she almost sobbed, trying to inch away, but the hand on her knee was clamped too firmly. Then he was pushing her backwards, pinning her shoulders to the ground and fumbling with his trousers.

A movement beside her, then a dog's cold nose brushed her cheek, its breath warm in her ear. Mr Hunter cursed and Nancy felt the weight of him lift. 'Get off!' He pushed the dog away and it growled. She rolled aside and sat up. He flailed at the animal, then stood up, reached for his hat and hurried away down the row of gardens to his own. She watched him go, shaking with dry sobs. The dog, a neighbour's collie she recognized, sank down in the grass a few yards off, panting. Then, at the sound of a distant whistle and a boy's call, it cocked its ears, leapt up and tore away across the field. She clambered to her feet, her knee throbbing where Mr Hunter had hurt it, grabbed the book and stumbled back through the garden gate.

The French doors stood open before her and as she approached the house she could hear high-pitched female tones from within. Mrs Hunter's. She paused and listened. She was saying something about her husband having a day's holiday and that she'd sent him out to dig a vegetable plot in the field.

Nancy could not face her. Instead, she turned and ducked back to the apple tree and managed to climb up to the plywood house. There she lay curled up, crying softly. She only emerged once she was sure her mother's visitor had gone.

She never told anybody about what had happened. After all, she reasoned, nothing had, not really. But for a long time she dared not go out in the field alone. Her perfect place had been ruined.

Nine

'I'm sorry Nancy wasn't helpful,' Cara said as they finished their sandwich lunch. Stef had broken the news that Nancy wouldn't be interviewed for her book. 'Perhaps we could do something fun to cheer you up. How about a trip to the coast?'

'Mum, I must write my article this afternoon.' Stef saw her mother's face fall and hated herself.

'Of course you must, darling. I expect I can find something to do.'

'Perhaps later on,' Stef added hastily. 'If the weather holds.' Her mother brightened again.

Upstairs, Stef made a simple desk for herself by pushing a picnic table under her bedroom window. She opened her laptop and called up a blank document. Then, with her ring-bound notebook beside her, she started to construct a plan for the article, flipping back through the notes and checking information online as she went. The subject interested her, being about the progress of Kew Gardens'

Millennium Seed Bank in Sussex, and she wished she had been allowed more space to write about it. It wouldn't be easy to compress all she'd learned from her recent visit there into the required 1,200 words, but it must be done.

From time to time, she looked up from her work and her eye would rest on the view of the quiet lane and the pretty cottage opposite. A white van drew up below her window. Someone knocked on the door and she heard her mother answer.

Mid-afternoon brought the bright sound of children's voices and Stef smiled to see a small girl and her older brother with their mother, who was pushing a pram, turn up the path opposite. The girl was chattering, while the boy ran ahead to the door, shouting about chocolate biscuits. The scene conveyed a particular idyll of country life – children, a lovely home in a picturesque village. She felt a tender pang of longing.

Her moment of self-pity was swept away by the ping of an email arriving and she returned her attention to her screen. Opening the message, she was rewarded by a rush of pleasure. It was a commission from a prestigious current affairs magazine that paid well. They'd loved her proposal to write about urban rewilding projects and wanted 2,000 words in three weeks' time. She stretched luxuriantly. After writing an enthusiastic reply, she went downstairs, humming to herself. She would celebrate with a cup of tea.

She took two brimming mugs outside to look for Cara in the field, ready to propose an early evening visit to the beach. Her mother had company. Cara was seated at her easel in the sun, laughing and talking. Her companion lay sprawled on the grass, stroking Baxter, who was stretched out asleep beside him. Stef recognized him at once as the man in the portrait she'd seen in her mother's studio.

'Oh, thank you, Stef,' Cara cried on seeing her. 'Stef, this is Ted.'

Ted climbed to his feet, brushing grass stalks from his clothes. 'Hello, Stef, I've heard all about you,' he said in a soft London accent. He was of average height and build, in his late fifties perhaps, with cropped greying sandy hair, a lean, weatherbeaten face and a friendly expression. His checked shirt and faded jeans were spattered with white paint. He regarded her shrewdly with deep-set blue eyes and she couldn't help wondering whether he wasn't a bit of a rogue. Nevertheless she must be polite.

'Pleased to meet you, Ted. Here, have this one. I'll make myself another.' She handed over the mugs of tea.

'Cheers,' he said. 'That's kind. I've just fixed the doorbell. Your ma said you'd complained about it.'

'That's great. Isn't it you who put up Mum's studio shed? You did a super job.'

'With the help of my mate Liam, yeah. We do a lot of work round here. Painted your ma's kitchen, too, didn't we, Cara?' He gave her a lazy grin. 'And put up those bunks.'

Cara's responding smile made her eyes light up and roused in Stef a sense of unease. She hung about and chatted to Ted politely for a few minutes, trying to puzzle him out. Her mother seemed charmed by him, that was clear, making him recount stories about the ridiculous demands of his clients, mainly second-homers from London. He was, however, suitably discreet about their identities. Listening to him speak knowledgeably about the locality and his craft as a carpenter and builder, Stef revised her initial prejudices. Ted was an intelligent man, well-informed and interested in many subjects.

She collected the empty mugs and said, 'It's nice to meet you, Ted. Mum, are you okay to go out about five?'

'That would be lovely.'

As Ted said goodbye, his eyes twinkled with good humour and she couldn't help smiling back. A nice man, she thought, as she returned to her work, but her mother did seem very friendly with him and Stef would do well to keep a daughterly eye.

They were lucky with the weather again that evening. On the beach, they kicked off their shoes to walk by the sea. The evening sun was warm on their faces and they smiled at Baxter's fat little figure waddling ahead over the shingle, swerving occasionally in a comic fashion to avoid the reach of a wave. As a youngster, he would dash in and out of the water and race over the sand, but those days were long gone.

'You are so lucky to have this,' Stef told her mother. 'I'm beginning to understand why you moved here.'

'Ah, you admit it now. No one trusted my judgement at the time.'

'It wasn't that . . .'

'Yes, it was. Silly Mother, doesn't know what's best for her. That's what you both thought.'

'It was winter when you showed us the cottage. It was dark and poky. The garden was a bog. Everything looked grim.'

'But I had a good feeling about it, didn't I? All the possibilities. And it's great for my painting. I love Hickston and the people I'm meeting.'

'Ted?' Stef said, with a smile.

'Yes, Ted. You may well laugh, but friends come from surprising places. In a small community, you have to get on with your neighbours even if you don't have anything much in common with them. You rely on one another. I expect it's different in London, you can be choosy.'

Stef thought her mother was probably right. Her friends were a rarified group, mostly university friends or professional contacts who lived across the city. She hardly knew the other people in her block of flats. The only reason she spoke to Gary downstairs was to ask him to turn down his music.

Her mother had batted her daughter's gentle probing away. Talking about Ted, though, reminded Stef of something.

'Have you thought of asking Ted to fix a handrail onto your staircase? The stairs are so steep.'

Her mother shot her a sharp glance. 'Possibly. I'm not an old lady yet, you know.'

'I didn't say you were. Personally, I find the stairs pretty steep.'

'Ted certainly doesn't think I'm old.'

It was Stef's turn to glance at her mother and she saw mischief in her eyes.

'Mum? I was talking about the stairs.'

'Never mind the stairs. I know what you're trying to say. Ted makes me feel attractive, whereas you and your sister sometimes treat me as though I'm one plate short of a dinner service.'

'We don't!'

'Pip thinks I'm only good for babysitting. Stef, I adore those kids and want to spend time with them, but I've done my share of childcare. I want to enjoy myself now.'

'Of course you do,' Stef murmured, taken aback by the strength of her mother's feeling. 'But ...'

'Don't worry about me, darling. I'm all right.'

'Okay,' Stef said cagily. 'What's Baxter sniffing at there?'

'A dead fish. No, Baxter! Come away! Come!' Stef watched in amusement as her mother broke into an awkward run, splashing ahead through the shallows with the dog limping after her.

It was strange the way relationships changed. Stef, Pippa and Cara had always been tightly bound together by circumstances, but they had constantly struggled with one another. How hard it had been for Stef as a teenager to prove to her mum that she was no longer a child, yet now she found herself questioning her mother's independence. Pippa had gone her own way growing up, kept them both at a distance, but now that she was a mother herself she seemed to need Cara again. Suddenly, Stef felt off-balance.

Cara stopped and waited for Stef to run and catch up. Her face when Stef reached her was glowing with the exertion and her eyes glittered with happiness.

'Let's pick up fish and chips on the way home.'

'Good idea,' Stef said, bemused by her mother's skittishness.

When they set off again in Stef's car, Cara became serious once more. 'I do worry about you, dear.'

'Do you? Why?' The old exasperation.

'Are you managing financially?'

'Just about.'

'Well, you must ask, you know.'

'I'm all right, Mum.'

'And your love life – there's no one special at the moment?'

'No.'

Silence.

'That last young man, Sam. I liked him.'

'So did I, Mum. It just didn't work out.'

'What went wrong? I know you disagreed about the idea of having children, but he'd have come round. Your father said the same thing, you know, and he came round.'

Stef had heard her say this before. 'It's different these days, Mum. Anyway, there were things about Sam . . . he cared too much about money was one. Oh, I don't want to talk about it.'

'I wish you would settle down with someone.'

'So do I, but there's no one on the horizon so that's that. What about your paintings? Have you had any luck with local galleries?'

'I did have one useful conversation with a man in Blakeney. I showed him some of my past work and he said he'd like to see some local scenes.'

'That's hopeful.'

'Yes. I must take you to the exhibition in the village hall

where I met Nancy. I like to support these things, though they're only amateur. There are a few good pieces, you might like to see. In fact, I put one of mine in and it's sold!'

'Who's bought it? Not Ted.'

'No, a couple from London who are doing up the old rectory.'

'Sorry.' Stef reached and touched her mother's hand. 'The fish and chips will be my treat.' It was the least she could do to make amends.

'Thank you. Are you still planning to leave tomorrow? I wish you'd stay longer.'

'Maybe I will.' Stef had thought, guiltily, of returning to London the next morning, but since she'd managed to work well this afternoon perhaps she'd stay on another day or so. Her thoughts ran on. Could she try to see Nancy Foster again? She was more disappointed than she'd realized about Nancy's refusal to be interviewed. There was a story there, she was sure, but it would look pushy to try to see her again so soon. And Aaron was likely to be around, like a grumpy guard dog. No, she'd have to leave it. The book proposal would simply have to proceed without Nancy.

Ten

While Stef and Cara were eating fish and chips in the back garden of Springfield Cottage, Nancy had been checking on the menagerie in her outhouse at Dragonfly Lodge. She'd released one of the hedgehogs earlier and her heart warmed at the memory of it running off into the undergrowth.

Now she bolted the outhouse door against predators and returned to the kitchen, where she changed into her slippers and wandered through to the sitting room. Aaron's headphones and laptop lay on the sofa. He'd been here for supper as promised, had cooked a noodle dish she'd privately found a little too spicy, but now he'd gone out for the evening to meet a mate for a drink.

Nancy felt tired tonight and the morning's dizziness still bothered her. It wasn't bad, just annoying. The cat was asleep on one of the fireside armchairs, so she sat down in the other and wondered what to do with herself. Not much. A warm bath and go to bed early with a library book. Aaron would let himself in. For now, it was pleasant just to sit and recover from a busy day.

Her thoughts roamed back to her conversation with Stef. She'd told Aaron about it, how she'd liked Stef, found her sympathetic, but Aaron had not been impressed. 'You don't want to stir things up again,' he'd warned. But things had already been stirred up – in her mind, at least. Her gaze drifted to the bookcase near the door where she kept her old university textbooks. Out of date now, of course, but the drawings in them were useful if she was identifying some insect or plant. There were some exercise books, too. She hadn't looked at them for years. She stood up and picked one out at random. It was from her last year at school, its paper cover furry with age. She sat and turned the pages, smiling at her own carefully labelled drawings of flowers and leaves. Sixth-form Botany with the eccentric Miss Reeves, that had been a hoot! And the years rolled back.

∼

February 1945

'Nancy Foster. Don't dillydally, girl, come on in.' Miss Everard, her thin figure straight-backed behind the mahogany desk, made a tick on her register, then removed her spectacles to regard the dark-haired fifteen-year-old hovering by the door. 'Take a seat,' she said with a gracious sweep of her hand.

Despite the fire crackling in the grate, the gloomy office felt chilly and was haunted by a dank, Victorian smell. Nancy sat down on the hard chair before the desk and licked her dry lips. Her wary eye met Miss Everard's cool, direct gaze. The headmistress of Northburton School for Girls was past her prime and her faded English beauty and commanding presence inspired admiration rather than love. She'd been a VAD in Belgium in the Great War and a rumour persisted that after the loss of her fiancé, a French doctor, she'd sworn never to marry but to dedicate her life to the service of others. Nobody knew if this was true, but it sounded awfully romantic.

'As you know, Nancy, I like to invite each of the girls in the School Certificate year for a little talk about their future.'

Nancy coughed nervously. 'I understand.' After the public exams, some would choose to stay on into sixth form, but others would be leaving in the summer to make their way in the world. Her sister Helen had been on the brink of leaving, but Aunt Rhoda had stepped in, insisting on paying for her to stay till eighteen, and she was now in the upper sixth with a place at secretarial college planned for September.

'This year's reports confirm that you are one of our brightest, Nancy. Full marks all year across the board. Very commendable.'

Nancy felt herself blush.

'Which makes up for your sometimes ... shall we say ... unladylike behaviour.'

Nancy straightened in indignation.

'You have a tendency, it appears, to be strident.'

'Miss Everard, I—'

'Allow me to continue. Several of the mistresses have complained about you interrupting them in lessons and asking unnecessary questions. It's all very well to be curious, of course. We like to encourage our girls to have enquiring minds, but there is a time and a place. It isn't fair to draw too much attention to yourself or to monopolize your teachers, who have the other girls to think of, too. And contradiction comes across as rudeness. Miss Bodily, for instance, was quite upset by a recent occasion on which I gather you persistently asked why it was necessary to perform a particular scientific experiment.'

'She gave me a detention for it,' Nancy burst out. 'It was so unfair. I simply wanted to understand.' It had been a physics experiment to determine the speed of marbles running down an old curtain track. Miss Bodily had written a mathematical formula on the blackboard beforehand to help them work out the answer but had not explained why the findings were useful. Nancy had thought a whole lesson devoted to timing the descent of marbles utterly boring unless there was a wider point to it. Worst of all, she secretly suspected that Miss Bodily didn't know the purpose of it herself. Or if she did, was not sufficiently interested to try to enthuse her pupils.

'You must learn to be more respectful of your elders and betters. Speech is silver, but silence is golden. Now, enough of that. You have, after all, been punished. I see here ...' She replaced her spectacles and consulted a form at the top of a pile. 'You wish to study Chemistry, Physics, Biology and Mathematics in the sixth form. Admirable ... if a little dry.' She perused Nancy over her spectacles. 'You intend a career in medicine perhaps? An excellent option for a bright young woman such as yourself, though not easy to combine with having a family.'

'Not medicine, no. I've written "scientific research" as my aim.'

'Oh yes, I see. I don't think we've had any girls choose that before.'

'I don't know exactly what I want to do yet, but I like to find out how things work. And why.'

'Splendid, I'm sure,' Miss Everard said vaguely, her eyebrows meeting in puzzlement. 'But perhaps you'd consider balancing your choices by the inclusion of English or History instead of Physics? Or French, what about French? A useful skill and it's good to have wide cultural interests. One needs to be able to sustain a conversation on social occasions and all these sciences might frighten ... people off.' By 'people', it was clear she meant 'men'.

Nancy shook her head. 'I read books all the time and I know heaps of history.'

'Do you now?' Miss Everard frowned. She studied Nancy's list again and chewed her lip.

'And I play the piano,' Nancy went on, 'and go to shows. I do have cultural interests, you see.'

'I understand perfectly. But Physics. I'd counsel against Physics. Miss Bodily ... Her time is taken up with the younger age groups.' She gazed at the window and said to herself, 'I often think we need to recruit another Physics mistress, but good ones are hard to come by and there simply isn't the demand here for sixth form.'

Nancy's heart sank. She should have thought of this herself. The only Physics mistress in the school was Miss Bodily and she was barely up to engaging fifteen- and sixteen-year-olds at School Certificate level.

'Perhaps Botany instead of Physics, dear, then you'd have your sciences and maths and something a bit lighter. Drawing plants is enjoyable and gardening is always a useful skill.'

Nancy nodded, crestfallen, but since it was the living sciences that engaged her most, perhaps the study of plants would suit her.

Miss Everard penned the minor adjustment to Nancy's form, then signed it.

'There we are. Send the next girl in, will you?'

'Thank you, Miss Everard,' Nancy mumbled as she rose with a feeling of relief.

'Good luck,' she whispered as she held the door open for the girl waiting outside. Then she hurried along the hushed, wood-panelled hallway and out into a wide corridor that echoed with the soft footsteps from indoor shoes and snorts of girlish laughter. A comforting savoury smell intensified as she made her way towards the refectory. With luck, there'd be some luncheon left.

She'd loved this school since joining it as a serious nine-year-old in a too-big blazer, eager to learn. Aunt Rhoda had been doubly generous with school fees, insisting that Helen should attend the school, too, though Nancy's mother had argued that her biddable elder daughter was perfectly happy at Mrs Brock's School for Young Ladies. It was a small private school that taught cookery and needlework alongside Maths, the humanities and General Science, preparing its pupils for the School Certificate at sixteen before releasing them into a world where, once the war ended, marriage and children would be their most likely occupation. Nancy's mother thought the curriculum very genteel, and Mrs Brock herself was well-connected. She was cousin to an earl.

'She should have the same academic chances as her little sister,' Nancy heard her father declare with finality one Saturday morning, and her mother had cried, 'Oh, no one cares about my opinion,' and marched off to the kitchen to bottle blackberries. In truth, Mrs Foster was relieved that Rhoda would pay for Helen's schooling. Roger's boarding fees at Rugby, his father's alma mater, were a source of anxiety. *But why couldn't the money be spent on Mrs Brock's?* Mrs Foster moaned to her cousin Ruth on the telephone. Nancy's father often took Rhoda's side over his wife's. 'He hardly listens to me.'

In the refectory, Nancy loaded up her tray. She sat by herself at one of the trestle tables and, while she ate her potato, cheese and sponge pudding, noticed Helen sitting with her friends at the other side of the hall. Helen at eighteen was elegant in her navy tunic and white blouse, her pretty blonde hair curled around her face, her wide brown eyes happy and guileless. She'd hardly acknowledged Nancy's existence at school, but then Nancy didn't expect her to. She herself took no notice of younger girls. Helen had chosen arts subjects for her Higher Certificate. While Nancy's reports said things like 'A brilliant performance, but must learn to be more decorous if she is to succeed in life,' Helen's said 'Works quietly but well' and 'Full marks for effort, Helen.' Her sister was good at netball, had been made a prefect and was expected to scrape through her exams in the summer. It was funny to think that Helen would soon be gone from the school and instead it would be she, Nancy, who would sit up in the gallery at morning assembly with the rest of the sixth form, looking very grown up. These days, she made an effort to dress smartly. Her mother held that a neat appearance 'made up for a lot'. Nancy knew she wasn't pretty like Helen, but she'd once overheard Aunt Rhoda say that with her dark hair and light grey-blue eyes her younger niece was 'very striking'.

She considered her conversation with 'The Ever-Hard' as she spooned up the last bit of sponge and couldn't help feeling disappointment. Physics might be boring, but she sensed the subject was important to her future plans. She'd read in *The Girls' Own Paper* about Marie Curie and knew that she had been a physicist as well as a chemist; her pioneering work on radioactivity had won her Nobel Prizes in both subjects. Well, it couldn't be helped if the school didn't offer it. Nancy wouldn't miss measuring the speed of marbles, and Botany would probably be useful. Perhaps she should ask the advice of another of her teachers, but who? Biology was the subject she enjoyed most, but dear Miss Kingston would never go against the headmistress. It was a pity that so many of the teachers were old. It was the war, she supposed. The young ones had volunteered and left. Miss James, the sweet-faced English mistress who'd become a coder, had been killed in Egypt when the jeep she'd been travelling in had hit a mine. Everything could be blamed on the war – disgusting powdered egg, nights broken by air raids, her brother Roger being called up, even the fact that her father was losing his hair. But Hitler was being beaten, wasn't he, his armies pushed back, and she felt full of hope for the future.

That summer, Nancy took her School Certificate exams. She passed with flying colours and loved the following two years in the Sixth. Botany with Miss Reeves involved a great deal of drawing, gardening and learning Latin names, but little of academic rigour.

Maths and Chemistry made up for that and, crucially for Nancy, Miss Everard managed to persuade a well-qualified young man, invalided out of the forces, to become a Biology master at the school. Nancy caught his enthusiasm for his subject as the class dissected animal organs and marvelled at the delicate threads and fibres of flesh that supported life. Sandy-haired and hawk-nosed, Mr Harris was no Adonis, but as the only male teacher in the school he became the subject of intense female interest. He had an unfortunate habit of blushing uncontrollably and the girls played on this. A lesson about reproduction in rabbits had to be abandoned after sly questions about how bunny babies were conceived. Thank heavens the syllabus didn't cover the facts of life for humans or he'd have died of embarrassment! When it was announced in the final assembly of the year that Mr Harris was getting married during the summer holidays, one of the fifth-formers swooned and had to be carried out. Several others actually wept with disappointment. *Silly things*, Nancy thought.

∼

Sixty years later, in the sitting room of her cottage, Nancy turned a page of the exercise book and smiled at her memories. How innocent they had all been then. She certainly hadn't wept. Mr Harris had been crucial to her for another reason. He'd fired in her a love for his subject.

She looked down at a clumsy drawing of hazel catkins and could almost hear Miss Reeves' tuts of annoyance at Nancy's failure to sharpen her pencil. She closed the frail book and rose to return it to the shelf. She'd done all right in the exams, though.

Time for bed. She shooed Tabitha into the kitchen and poured herself a glass of water. At the foot of the stairs, she felt the dizziness again and paused, her hand on the newel post, until it passed. Then she began to climb, slowly, cursing her stiff knees. Four or five steps up, she took her hand off the bannister to adjust her grip on the heavy glass, but the toe of her slipper caught under a riser and her other foot slid away. Her hand flew to the bannister but missed. For a long moment, she teetered, flailing, and then she fell, the glass spilling water down the wall before landing with a soft thud on the rug beside her.

Eleven

As Stef sat down to work on Tuesday morning, Ted's white Transit van drew up in the lane below her bedroom window and her eyes narrowed as she watched Ted climb out. Funny, Mum hadn't said anything about him coming. The newly mended doorbell rang out, but her mother didn't answer it. When it sounded again, Stef pushed back her chair with a sigh and hurried downstairs.

'Is your ma about?' Ted stood on the doorstep, his eyes shining with good humour.

'I think she must be out in the garden.'

'I'll go through and see, shall I?' He placed a tentative foot inside.

Irritated by this presumption yet too embarrassed to ask him his business, she let him in, but followed him closely through the kitchen and out through the back door. Her mother looked up from weeding and greeted him with a smiling 'Ted, how lovely to see you!', so Stef frowned and left them to it.

After that, her morning was constantly interrupted. First of all, Ted clumped about on the staircase whistling to himself, then he went outside and she heard him fossicking about in his van below her window. She craned her neck in curiosity as he drew out some narrow lengths of wood. Finally, she twigged. Her mother must have asked him to fix a rail to the staircase and he'd come immediately. Stef could hardly complain, having made the suggestion the day before. But her mother would have told her, surely. A thought occurred. Had Ted simply turned up out of the blue and her mother thought up a job for him to do? That idea made her feel uncomfortable.

She sighed. At least the handrail issue was being dealt with. After a while, she became accustomed to the noises of sawing and drilling. By the time she went down for a break, pleased by what she'd written, she felt good-humoured enough to offer Ted a coffee as she passed him on the stairs. He'd screwed the lengths of rail to the wall already without, she noticed admiringly, damaging the wallpaper.

'Nice work,' she commented.

'I should have thought of doing it before,' Ted murmured as he wiped the wood clean of sawdust. There was an expression of concern in his eyes and Stef felt touched by his care for her mum.

'And I should have said something to Mum when she moved in.'

'Ah no, there was lots to do. It's a lovely little place she's got here, but plenty still to sort out. Some of the window frames at the back are rotten, that's another job to do before the winter.'

The sense of presumption set her on full alert. Her eyes narrowed. 'Has she asked you to do those?'

'Not yet,' he said, reaching for a can of wood varnish. 'Getting ahead of myself maybe.' He concentrated on levering off the lid with a screwdriver. 'Will you hand me that brush? That's it, thank you.'

Her nose wrinkling at the stink of the varnish, Stef hurried off to the kitchen, where she put the kettle on.

'I've left your coffee on the kitchen table,' she said in clipped tones on her way upstairs with hers. Ted stood back to let her pass, but shortly after she'd started editing her article she heard his footsteps recede, then a moment later a distant sound of voices from behind the house.

By the time he left, an hour later, his van roaring up the lane, Stef had only a couple of references left to confirm. Once these were done, she closed the document, checked her emails, stretched and sighed, enjoying the feeling that she'd done a good job. Hopefully the ecology magazine's editor would think so, too. She would have another quick look at the piece after lunch before emailing it off. Being careful not to get wet varnish on herself, she went downstairs.

'Ted's done well there,' she said to her mother, who was preparing a green salad in the kitchen.

'You sound surprised. Do you like spring onions? I've forgotten.'

'Sure. I didn't mean to sound surprised. It's just . . . Did you ask him to put the rail up?'

'You and I talked about it!'

'But you didn't explicitly ask him before he arrived, did you?'

'I don't remember, darling. It needed doing and I'm glad he came.'

'So you weren't expecting him this morning.'

'No. It's nice that he popped by, though. He's very thoughtful like that.'

'Mum, are you sure that he's not . . .' Stef paused, trying to choose her words tactfully.

'What, darling? Now, where's the olive oil? I'm sure I bought a new bottle.'

'. . . taking advantage.'

'Don't be ridiculous. Of course he's not.'

'He's charging you for these jobs, is he?'

'I think that's my business, Stef.'

Stef was taken aback by the steel in her mother's voice. 'Sorry. I'm only trying to help.'

'Let's have lunch, shall we, and talk about something else.'

Stef, crestfallen, watched her mother fetch cheese and hummus out of the fridge and decided to say no more. She felt very protective of her mother, but Cara was on the defensive.

Instead, they discussed how long Stef would stay. Stef thought another night. She'd work in the morning and perhaps leave late afternoon. She was surprised to feel sad at the thought.

After lunch, she sent off her article and was suddenly overtaken by a longing for chocolate. Finding none in the house, she called to her mother, who was painting out in the field, that she was going to the village shop.

'Oh, can you get me the local paper?' her mother replied. 'I like Zoe Manners' column on Tuesdays, she's quite funny.'

When Stef opened the front door, the dog trotted up the hall looking interested. 'No, Baxter,' she sighed, then realized that he hadn't had much of a walk. 'Oh, I suppose you can come.' She would tie him up outside the shop, then afterwards they'd explore the field by the church where she'd seen a footpath sign. His lead was hanging by the door. She clipped it onto his collar, closed the door behind them and set off up the lane.

Stef loved Hickston Village Stores. It was everything she thought a village shop should be, with post office facilities, newspapers and a freezer full of locally cooked ready meals. The place was something of a honeypot. Several cars were parked up outside and when she entered, leaving Baxter safely tethered to a ring in the wall, it was to see a short queue at the counter.

She grabbed a copy of the local paper and selected her favourite brand of dark chocolate. After she'd paid, she tucked the rolled newspaper into her shoulder bag, then wandered outside, nibbling a square of chocolate. Baxter lay sphinx-like, watchful, his large eyes mournful, but on seeing her, he stood up, his feathered tail wagging. As she bent to unhook his lead, a shadow flickered over the ground and she automatically looked up. And was surprised to see Aaron passing, heading into the shop.

'Hi,' she mumbled through her mouthful of chocolate and he started, then blinked, nodded curtly and continued inside. *How rude*, she thought, with a bolt of irritation, but then it struck her that he'd looked agitated and, if she was being honest, unkempt. She glanced across the street and recognized his car. She hesitated, wondering if she should wait and find out if everything was all right. She took her phone out and pretended to consult it, but whatever he was doing in the shop took time and after a minute or two she gave up waiting and set off towards the church, Baxter trotting along beside her.

Just as they reached the churchyard, a car slowed beside her and she looked up to see that it was Aaron's. It stopped and he lowered his window. 'Stef, d'you have a moment?' His tone was urgent.

'Sure,' she said.

He killed the engine and stepped out, standing uncertainly, one hand resting on the open door. His shirt was creased and his jaw was dark with stubble. 'Sorry,' he said, 'I didn't recognize you for a second back there. The sun was in my eyes. Then when I came out you'd gone.'

'Is everything okay?' His drawn face worried her.

'Not really. My grandmother had a fall last night. I thought you and your mum would like to know.'

'Oh, I'm so sorry! Is she all right?'

'Basically, yes.' He pushed back his hair and frowned. 'A twisted ankle and she's a bit shaken up. She slipped on the stairs while I was out and couldn't reach her phone. I found her when I got back. Thankfully she hadn't lain there long. I can't imagine what would have happened if I hadn't been staying.'

'Doesn't she have one of those personal alarms?'

'No.' He gave a weak grin. 'Says they're for "old people".
She's still at the hospital. They're running some final tests.'

'That's probably a good thing.'

'Anyway, I'm on my way to Dragonfly Lodge to freshen
up, then I'll go back and fetch her. It occurred to me just
now ... well, I thought I'd catch you and let you know since
you came to see her and I don't know who else to tell round
here. Also, I was wondering, did she complain to you about
feeling unwell? Dizzy, for instance?'

'Nothing like that, no.'

'She didn't mention it to me before, either. I don't know
how seriously to take it.'

'I got the impression that she's not a complaining sort
of person.'

'You're right there.' He smiled grimly. 'That generation.
They're all stoics.' He released his hold on the car door. 'All
right, just thought I'd check. I'd better be off.'

'If there's anything we can do to help,' she said, 'me or
Mum ...'

'Yeah, thanks. I don't know yet how I'm going to manage
things.' His tone was dismissive as he climbed into the car,
as if his thoughts were already elsewhere.

Baxter gave a little woof of impatience. 'Yes, yes, come on,
Baxter, let's go!' *Poor Nancy,* she thought as they resumed their
walk. How would she manage unless Aaron stayed with her?
Even getting her home across the reserve would be tricky.
Perhaps the hospital would lend them a wheelchair.

On the way back to Springfield Cottage, Baxter was
made to wait again while Stef bought a Get Well card with

a painting of sailing boats. Back at the cottage, she and her mother both signed it. Stef added a message offering help and their telephone numbers.

'It's ridiculous that Ted's put up a stair rail for me, but it's Nancy who's fallen,' her mother pointed out.

'One of life's amusing little ironies.'

'Mmm. And yes, by the way, since you were wondering, Ted and I do have an arrangement about the money.' She held herself very upright and Stef read the challenge in her eyes.

'You're right,' she mumbled, embarrassed, 'it isn't really my business.'

Early afternoon, Stef drove down to the reserve with the card.

Josh was in the visitors' centre frowning over his laptop, but offered to pass the card on to Nancy as he was walking down in that direction later. He'd heard about the accident from Aaron, who'd stopped by earlier to tell him, but didn't know whether Aaron had yet returned with Nancy from the hospital.

'They'd probably have gone via the back lane. I'll call in at Dragonfly Lodge and find out. I'm not surprised that this has happened, mind you,' he said. 'That house is becoming a death trap.' His words were so doom-laden, Stef half-expected him to add 'Mark my words' and waggle a finger at her, but instead he returned his attention to his screen.

Stef hadn't long been back at Springfield Cottage when the house phone rang. Since her mother was outside, Stef answered it. There was a shuffling sound at the other end and a quavery voice said, 'Hello, is that Cara Lansdown?'

Stef recognized it at once. 'No, it's her daughter. Is that Nancy Foster?' Concern flowed through her. 'I was so sorry to hear—'

'Is this Stephanie?'

Stef said it was.

'Stef, thank you for your lovely card. I wondered . . . Well, Aaron's gone out, though he'll be back later. Perhaps if you're not busy, you would come over and have a cup of tea?'

'I'm not busy,' she said, surprised, 'and I'd love to. But you've just come out of hospital. Are you sure?'

'I'm very sure.' Nancy's voice was suddenly stronger. 'I need to talk to you.'

Stef straightened, alert. 'Well yes, then, I will.'

'The door's unlocked so come straight in. If you can get past the blasted wheelchair in the hall.'

After the call ended, Stef paused, uncertain. Not only had Nancy just come out of hospital, but she'd invited Stef behind Aaron's back. Perhaps she shouldn't have said she'd go. On the other hand, it was too good an opportunity and she couldn't back out now. She ran upstairs to collect her notebook.

Twelve

'I bumped my head and ricked my ankle. Those stupid slippers! At first, after I came to, I thought I was dying. The pain in my leg was simply dreadful and I couldn't move.'

'You poor thing!' Stef, sitting in a chair across from Nancy on the sofa, viewed her with sympathy. With her strapped-up foot propped on a pouffe and nursing a mug of tea, Nancy looked pale and drawn, though her voice was still bright.

'I couldn't even remember where I'd left my phone,' Nancy continued. 'But I did know that Aaron was coming back. It was a question of when. I had to keep myself alive long enough to be rescued. I did a lot of thinking while I lay there. I amused myself by composing my own obituary in my head.'

'Oh, Nancy, that's awful!'

'Not that anywhere would publish it. I'm hardly famous. What I mean is, I went back over my life. Wondered if I'd achieved much. Had anything I'd done been worth it?' She put up her hand as Stef opened her mouth to object. 'No!

I'm serious. Oh, of course I taught a lot of schoolchildren the difference between xylem and phloem and how the heart pumps blood. I'm sure many went on to be useful citizens. But Stef, I had such ambitions to make big scientific discoveries when I started out as a student. You're still too young, I hope, to understand about failed ambition.'

'You'd be surprised,' Stef murmured.

'But you're doing so well. I'm very admiring of young women these days, they're so brave and purposeful. You can't imagine the struggles we went through in the fifties.'

'My granny,' Stef said, 'that is, my mum's mum, used to tell me how her dad wouldn't let her go to art college, but she was so proud of her daughter – my mum – because she did. Mum went to the Chelsea Art School at the end of the sixties – I think she had an amazing time!'

'All those sit-ins for peace and the Summer of Love! I can imagine!' Nancy's eyes gleamed with good humour. 'Your mother's a landscape painter, isn't she? She showed me something of hers at the exhibition where we met. A view of the sea. Such gorgeous colours.'

'She'd be pleased to hear that you liked it.'

'Anyway, what I was thinking as I lay there, Stef, is that if I gave up and died then there's no full account of my story anywhere. I haven't even told Aaron all of it. And there's something rather sad about that. So I'd like to talk to you. Properly. For your book, I mean.'

Stef felt a rush of pleasure. 'Would you? That's fantastic. But are you certain?' It didn't feel right to take advantage of an injured woman.

'I am. Maybe you won't think what I have to say is interesting enough to include, but I want at least to tell you what it was like for a young woman back then, and it might provide a paragraph or two.'

'Even that would be helpful.' Something, a twinge of excitement, made Stef suspect that it might provide far more.

'My grandson will be furious, of course. That's why I asked you here when I knew he'd be out.'

'I don't really understand,' Stef said quietly, feeling her way along. 'What is he frightened I'll do?'

'His reasons are sound.'

'Oh?' Stef waited.

But Nancy chose that moment to try to place her empty mug on a side table. She missed and the mug fell on her foot. She let out a yelp of pain.

Stef leapt up to restore order. Perhaps it wasn't a good time to pursue this conversation, she thought as she sat down again. She would delay her plans of going back to London.

'I won't stay long now,' she told Nancy firmly. 'I'm sure you need to rest. I can come round another time.'

'No, I'm perfectly comfortable now, I assure you, and I'll just sit here fretting without someone to talk to.'

'Well, if you're sure.'

'I am. Would you go to that cupboard above the desk?'

Stef crossed the room. 'This one?' she asked, pointing to a wall cupboard.

'Yes.'

She opened it and stared at the stack of photograph albums within.

'The one I want is the black one on the far left at the bottom. Careful. Some of the pages are loose.'

Stef eased out the battered album. Nancy was right, the binding was coming apart. She held the book in both hands and presented it to the old lady, who laid it on her lap.

'Sit here next to me,' she commanded, patting the sofa.

Stef obeyed.

Nancy opened the album and together they looked through the photographs inside. Here she was as a sweet, solemn-eyed baby, then as a toddler with some older children playing in a garden. There were pictures of her parents, too – though mostly of her mother, as her father was usually the photographer – then one of Nancy at six, holding up a toy chemistry set and smiling proudly at the camera. Nancy spoke of her childhood in a voice soft with emotion. 'This is my brother Roger and my sister Helen. And this is my Aunt Rhoda.' Nancy's aunt was holding a cocktail glass aloft and laughing. She was tall and willowy and wore a striking black dress. Her hair was cut in a short, blunt style that emphasized her high cheekbones. 'I think I mentioned that I have her to thank for my education.'

'You did start to tell me. And who are these?' Stef pointed to a small photograph of a pair of gawky adolescent boys on the page opposite.

'Neighbours. The Hunters.' Nancy flipped the page without further comment. And now came the school photographs. Nancy at eight or nine in a blazer too big for her and with a cloche straw hat hiding her face. A fifteen-year-old Nancy in the netball team, then older still in a smart shirt-dress, white gloves and a narrow-brimmed boater.

'That was Founders Day, 1947,' Nancy explained. 'My last year at school. I should have won four prizes, but Miss Everard said someone else should have a chance so I only got two. I thought that wasn't fair. It certainly wouldn't have happened at my brother's school.'

Stef smiled. She thought Nancy as a teenager looked charming with her shoulder-length dark hair combed back, her shining eyes and slender figure. She asked questions about her schooling and, returning to her chair by the fire, took the notebook from her bag to write down the subjects that Nancy had studied.

'So why did you decide to read Zoology at university?' she asked.

'Biology was my best subject. And my teacher knew a Zoology professor at Prince's College. They were building up the department after the war.' Nancy looked livelier now and there was colour in her face.

'They were happy to take girls?'

'Oh yes. They couldn't afford to be fussy. I was hurt when someone first told me that, but I came to find it amusing. That we girls were given opportunities only because suddenly they needed us. I can remember it so clearly, though, the early days of my studies. Everything seemed so splendidly new and exciting. And there were young men, Stef. Though we were all very shy together at first. Single-sex schools, you understand.'

For a moment, Nancy's eyes were dreamy as she collected her memories. And then she began to speak. 'I was terrified arriving at the college on the first day. I knew absolutely nobody, you see.'

Thirteen

London
Autumn 1947

The bomb-damaged clock tower of Prince's College in Kensington was still caged by scaffolding, just as Nancy remembered from her interview back in the spring. It dominated the middle of the main quad, where hundreds of students now clustered for the first day of the new academic year, the cacophony of cheerful voices bouncing off the high surrounding buildings. Nancy hesitated under the arched main gateway and breathed in deeply to counter her nerves. She hadn't slept much the night before from excitement.

She reached into her leather briefcase and brought out a much-folded letter, frowning as she read the enrolment instructions again. Then, glancing about to check her surroundings, she made her way across the quad towards a narrow door in the far right-hand corner. It was the entrance to the grim red-brick building that housed the Zoology department.

Room Z.271, where she was to report, was on the second floor. She followed directions on a series of notices, climbing four flights of stone steps around an echoing stairwell before passing along a lino-floored corridor with windows offering views of the quad. Room Z.271 turned out to be a poky office crammed with mismatched furniture and filled with the sound of furious typing. A grim, bespectacled woman sat behind a glass-fronted reception counter at which a short line of new students waited.

Nancy joined the queue behind a handsome, dark-haired young man wearing a long black coat, and a snippet of a girl with ginger hair. The man completed a form with his shiny black fountain pen and swept out past Nancy without a glance, but the girl, who spoke to the secretary in a soft Scottish accent, flashed Nancy a smile as she left. Now it was Nancy's turn. She wrote down her details obediently, then asked the secretary for directions to the venue for the welcome speech mentioned in her enrolment letter.

'It's in the main lecture hall in the Chemistry School at ten,' the woman said briskly, pointing. 'The building opposite. Very simple to find.'

Simple if you know, Nancy thought, thanking her and going on her way.

The Scottish girl was waiting for her out in the corridor. 'Hello. I don't understand where we go now, do you?'

'Apparently it's straightforward. Let's look.' They went to a window and gazed down on the quad. The crowds of students were now swarming like ants up the broad steps to the grand portico of a white-stone building on the far side of the quad. Nancy sighed. 'Chemistry looks a much more splendid building than Zoology, doesn't it?'

'My dad says Chemistry is an older subject and more important,' the girl said solemnly as they moved off, 'but it's harder to get a place and even if I'd wanted to do it, which I didn't, my marks weren't good enough. I'm Peggy Harman, by the way.'

'Nancy Foster.' They grinned at one another.

'I say, it's dreadful being new, isn't it? I don't know a soul.'

'Nor do I.' Nancy warmed to Peggy straight away. Her clear green eyes danced with fun in her small pointed face.

They descended the stairs together, exchanging vital details. Peggy's family were originally from Edinburgh, Nancy learned, but were now settled in Aldershot, where her father was a military doctor. Peggy was an only child and her parents were ambitious for her.

Nancy told Peggy in return that her mother hadn't wanted her to go to university at all, let alone to study science. 'She thinks it's unfeminine.' She rolled her eyes. 'I don't mind about being feminine, do you?'

'My mum says all the marrying stuff will happen when the time is right. And that if you've a good brain, you should use it.'

'She sounds sensible, your mother,' Nancy sighed as they walked across the quad. 'You're not living at home, are you? Aldershot's a good way to come.'

'No, I'm in one of the hostels across the road. Moved in

last night. It's not bad, a bit noisy, but at least I have a room of my own. I've never had to share, you see. I mean, suppose the other girl snored?' She giggled.

'I'm still living at home.' Nancy thought a hostel sounded fun. Aunt Rhoda had been willing to stump up for her niece to live independently, but her mother wouldn't hear of it. There had been quite an argument at home. Nancy's father had been sympathetic, but her mother had tried to make it sound an unfair expense on Rhoda.

Nancy guessed the truth, which was that her mother was keen to keep an eye on her headstrong youngest. Helen, through a contact of Rhoda's, was now working as a secretary to a buyer at Peter Jones in Sloane Square in London, and was being courted by a Bobby Norris, one of the younger managers. She was still living at home and very much under her mother's thumb. Why should Nancy be treated differently? To Nancy, this was infuriating. Helen always did what she was told. Sometimes Nancy wished her sister would do something terribly rebellious and draw attention away from her, but she never did.

She and Peggy climbed the steps to the Chemistry building and followed the chattering crowd across an airy, marble-pillared atrium, along a broad corridor and into a large, high-ceilinged lecture theatre filled with tiered seating. Here they nabbed two seats together.

Nancy, gazing around the noisy hall, was heartened to spot a couple of dozen girls among the hundreds of male freshers. There were also a few dark faces; Africans, Indians and Chinese, she guessed. Of the men in the room, most were no more than boys of her own age, fresh from school, but she was curious to see some who were older. They'd have been in the forces, she imagined. That would also explain their air of having seen the world.

'I wonder how many are Zoology students like us?' she asked Peggy, but before her new friend could answer, a bell clanged urgently and the chatter of voices subsided to a murmur.

Footsteps echoed and heads turned to see a burly man in a black academic gown stride to the front. He took his place at a lectern and stared round at the assembled students, his face like a storm cloud, waiting until silence fell. Then he began to speak in a ponderous voice that reminded Nancy of Mr Churchill. 'My name is Sir Hugh Desmond. I'm the Master here.' He rambled on for twenty minutes about how fortunate they all were to attend Prince's College with its eminent alumni – though the famous names he listed were all male – and commended them to work hard. The star of the show, however, was a persistent wasp, which Sir Hugh stopped from time to time to swipe at, drawing snorts of mirth from the audience.

'I thought I'd die laughing,' Peggy whispered, after he'd finished.

'I was sure it would sting him. They're very cross and sleepy this late in the season.'

As they filed out, Nancy caught the eye of the dark-haired moody young man she'd seen at registration. He raised one eyebrow at her, then moved quickly ahead. As she and Peggy walked back to the Zoology building, where they were to assemble next, she found herself searching for his tall, black-coated figure in the crowd.

The next venue on the day's timetable turned out to be a modest lecture room in the Zoology department, rather gloomy, with a blackboard on the front wall above a table for the lecturer. Its cream-painted side walls were studded with posters of insects and fish. Nancy and Peggy joined a dozen other students idling quietly on the chairs as they waited for the head of department to appear. Some were taking the opportunity to silently eye up the others. Others looked at the floor or the posters. Most were too shy to make small talk.

There were fifteen, all told. Nancy was surprised that seven of them were girls, a high proportion compared to the gathering they'd just left. Two of the men were several years older. She listened with half an ear as they chatted desultorily – something about the difficulties one had getting digs. They wore an air of sophistication, as though they'd seen a bit of life, and Nancy felt a little in awe of them.

Meanwhile, the dark-haired young man sat by himself, staring morosely at a leaflet about the Christian Union that someone had left on a desk. Nancy was just gathering the courage to speak to a girl sitting behind her when she heard jocular male voices and everyone looked round expectantly. A couple of youngish men in tweed suits entered the room. One wore a jovial expression and puffed affectedly on a pipe, the other had thick-lensed spectacles and dramatically receding hair. They nodded at the waiting students. 'I expect the prof will be along in a moment,' the smoker remarked before they returned to their conversation.

'Are they our lecturers?' Peggy whispered with distaste and Nancy said she supposed so.

After a few minutes, the stout, bearded professor whom Nancy remembered from her interview stomped in and walked quickly to the front. The lecturers immediately quietened and at his gesture everyone sat down. Professor Briggs dumped his briefcase on the floor at the front, planted meaty palms on the table and leaned to stare round fiercely at the assembled students, iron-grey hair falling across his forehead.

'Apologies,' he said in a gruff voice. 'Some damn fool drove into the back of my car. Now.' He sat down behind the table and everyone watched as he ferreted in his briefcase and brought out a hardback notebook. As he called out names, Nancy's fellow students began to assume identities.

The older men were both ahead of her in the register, Michael Carlton and Edmund Buckland. Michael answered brightly, but Edmund's cultured 'Here' was oddly hesitant, inspiring Nancy to say a confident 'Yes' when her own turn came. Among the others were two Annes, Anne Durban and Anne Southgate; a Welsh girl, Angharad; a willowy upper-class girl named Diana; and a slender Indian man whose long name the professor stumbled over, but who asked in a friendly manner to be called Raj. Nancy instantly warmed to his good nature. The scowling dark boy was last on the list. He answered 'Over here' in a low but definite tone to his name, which was James West.

'Right.' Professor Briggs screwed the top onto his pen and frowned at them all. His eyes rested on the men near the door. 'Ah. Before I begin, may I introduce Dr Lansdale over there with the noxious pipe, and Dr Mills.' Both men murmured greetings, Dr Lansdale brandishing his pipe in theatrical fashion. 'You'll be meeting the other members of the department in due course. We like to think of ourselves as a friendly team and I'm sure you'll settle in quickly.'

He went on to explain the structure of the degree course. Nancy listened with rapt attention, but was surprised to learn that they'd be studying Geology and Botany during their first year in addition to Zoology. She should have asked more about the course at interview, but she'd felt very shy with the professor, who was a distinguished entomologist, interested in insects of any and every sort. He'd talked to her with passion about his work with bumble bees in New Zealand and fire ants in America, but when he'd asked her why she herself was interested in Zoology, he had hardly listened to her rambling answer about 'loving animals'. He'd simply murmured, 'Splendid! Splendid!' and said that he'd write to her school before sending her on her way.

James West raised his hand and asked the question for her. 'What's the reason we study Geology, sir?' There was a touch of arrogance about the way he spoke, which clearly annoyed the professor.

'I'm surprised that a chap of your education should need to ask that,' he replied, staring down his nose at the young man, who had the grace to look abashed. 'Life on Earth has always been dependent on the nature of the rocks and soil beneath our feet. One cannot study our fauna without understanding that. And should anyone question the need for Botany,' he said to the room, 'well, plants and animals are so clearly interlinked, one cannot appreciate the one without the other. Are there any more concerns? No? Well, Dr Mills here will explain to you about our field trips, then he and Dr Lansdale will squire you around the department and other relevant areas of the campus, which should take us nicely to lunchtime.'

'It's not very big, our department, is it?' Peggy remarked at lunch in the refectory.

The new zoologists had collected their meals on trays from a hatch and congregated at one of the long tables. The boys and the girls sat down on the benches in separate groups, each wary of the other. Edmund Buckland and Michael Carlton, the two older men, had not been unfriendly, but they had stuck together during the tour of what the students were learning to call the 'Zoo' building. There was an understandable division between them and the raw school-leavers, but now they chose to sit down in the space between the two groups, thus uniting them. Peggy was on one side of Edmund, James West on the other. Nancy was opposite Peggy and next to Michael.

'Are you referring to the size of the department building or the numbers of students?' James West asked, clumsily pouring himself water and splashing it on the table.

Peggy flinched at his clipped tone. 'Both, really.'

'They have to build up the department again.' Edmund's voice was gentler. 'It only properly came into being in thirty-six when Professor Briggs arrived and then it practically closed during the war, so there's a great deal of work to do. I took the impression from my interview that he's working hard to increase Zoology's importance within London University.'

'He informed me that he's got the college to invest in a new research institute near St Albans,' Michael chipped in. 'ICP's involved, you know, the big chemicals firm.'

The others stared at the older men, impressed by the extent of their knowledge. None of them had thought to find this out. Nancy had vaguely heard of ICP and wondered aloud what it stood for. 'International Chemical Products,' Michael replied.

'Were you in the forces, sir?' a keen, wide-eyed boy named John Philips asked Edmund.

'You shouldn't call me sir. I'm only a few years older than you.' Edmund smiled, the skin around his eyes crinkling. Nancy liked his grave face and quiet, cultured voice. 'But, yes. Carlton was, too, weren't you? I was drafted in straight after school in forty-two. Eighth Army and the desert for me, but Carlton was the real hero. Spitfires, didn't you say, Carlton?'

'The Battle of Britain?' Philips breathed, his eyes round with hero-worship.

'No, I was still at school in Shrewsbury in 1940.' Michael Carlton grinned as he lit a cigarette, and Nancy noticed how his hands shook slightly. He inhaled deeply before adding, 'Italy in forty-three. We provided air cover for the invasion.'

His audience were silent, over-awed by these war heroes in their presence. Finally, James West said, 'How come you're here now? I thought all the forces men were given priority last year.'

'And the year before, yes,' Edmund said. 'But I couldn't do it for private reasons. What about you, Carlton?'

'Recovering from injury.' His voice wavered.

'What happened to you?' West was relentless. One of the girls, Anne Durban, tutted.

'It's no secret. Had to bail out over Belgium in forty-five, which was bad luck. Landed in a tree – good luck. Impaled on a branch – bad luck. I'll show you the scars when I know you better.'

His black humour finally broke the ice. Everyone laughed and started talking at once.

Later, as they stacked their trays on a trolley, Peggy said to Nancy, 'Must be odd, don't you think, them being here after all that. I expect we must seem rather dull.'

'Perhaps dull is a relief after what they've been through.'

'I suppose. You said you had an older brother, Nancy. Was he called up?'

'Yes, in forty-three, but he spent the following two years not doing very much. His unit never left the country. Now he's refused to study law. Says the moment has passed, he's too old. My father is none too pleased.' Roger had tried several different jobs, but had not been able to settle in any of them. He was currently working as a lowly clerk in their father's department at the Home Office. Nobody was sure if he'd stick it out. Mr Foster grew red-faced with fury if

Roger wasn't up and breakfasted in time to leave with him in the mornings.

'You know, my dad's a military doctor – he's seen a lot of boys like that. Says the war has left them high and dry.'

Nancy and Peggy trailed back with the others across the quad to the Zoology building. Here, the afternoon programme commenced with a talk by the head technician in one of the labs. It was a large, curiously bare room on the first floor at the back, overlooking a main road. The technician, Miss Pick, a brisk older woman in a crisp white overall, listed instructions for the safe use of scalpels and chemicals, reminded them of the need to buy their own dissecting kit and gave the impression that any extra equipment was locked up and would be issued only when absolutely necessary.

Nancy preferred the look of Miss Pick's assistant, a put-upon motherly lady whom Miss Pick addressed as Mrs Hall, who obediently fetched items from a back office for demonstration and took them away afterwards. The students sat on stools at the high worktops, the girls carefully writing down everything Miss Pick said, the boys making the odd note or doodling in their exercise books, though they must have been listening because they were usually the first to put their hands up when it was time for questions.

The rest of the afternoon involved tours of the Geology and Botany departments, which were next to the Chemistry building, then afternoon tea with the Zoology staff, a rather stiff occasion that took place in a small teaching room that was overlooked by a case of stuffed British mammals, whose glassy glares made Nancy feel uncomfortable. After this, there were dissection sets and chunky second-hand textbooks to buy from a stall set up in the library and then the students were free to go. Lectures would begin at ten o'clock sharp the next morning.

Lugging her briefcase, now laden with her purchases, Nancy bid goodbye to Peggy outside the college and watched with envy from the bus stop as her new friend went off in the opposite direction, laughing and chatting with the Annes, who also lived in her hostel.

The front door was ajar when Nancy reached home and she let herself in and started up the stairs to her bedroom as quietly as she could, hoping to avoid a barrage of questions, but her mother had keen ears. 'Is that you, Nancy?' Mrs Foster put her head round the kitchen door. 'I need you to lay the table, please.'

She rolled her eyes. 'In a minute, Mummy. I've got some books to put away.' Instead of questions, there had been no interest at all in how her day had gone. She shut herself in her room, set her briefcase on the desk, then sank onto the bed with a sigh. She looked about her. Today was supposed to have been the first day of a new life. So how could everything look the same?

It had to change. She opened the briefcase, pulled out the textbooks and the dissection set, then swept her colourful collection of school story books off a wall shelf into a cupboard and placed the sombre-looking textbooks in their place. One each for Botany and Geology, both dog-eared, and a newer, formidable-looking two-volume introduction to Zoology.

Finally, she felt in her pocket for her purchase from Boots with the change from the books. A Max Factor lipstick in Rose Red and a powder compact. Helen wore make-up, but Nancy hadn't wanted to before, fearing her mother's beady eye. But thinking of the nice young men she'd met today, suddenly she'd changed her mind.

The new students quickly got into the swing of university life. There were lectures every morning – Zoology every day, with Botany and Geology on two days, each lecture followed by a practical session in a lab.

Zoology, Dr Hillman explained in his opening lecture, was one of the two subdivisions of Biology, the science of all living things. Zoology dealt with animals and covered creatures of one cell all the way up to mammals, humans being at the top of the tree, the most advanced animal of all. The other subdivision of Biology was Botany, the study of plants.

Nancy loved Zoology. They were studying the classification of the animal kingdom, the structure of different animals, their behaviour and habitats, which she mostly found fascinating, though there were too many Latin names to learn. Botany she found tedious, for it mostly involved going over information that she had already learned at school about the structures and life cycles of plants, and there was endless drawing, which she wasn't good at. It was frustrating, but it had to be done. As Peggy said cheerfully, at least Nancy would do well in the exam.

Geology, which was new to her, was an unexpected joy. It gave Nancy a strange feeling to consider the great age of the soil and rocks that they handled and to explore the secrets that they concealed. They drew diagrams of the strata of rocks beneath the South Downs and the Pennines, examined fossils and microscopic evidence of more primitive life. Even the dreariest-looking samples revealed knowledge of long-lost landscapes she'd never dreamed existed. She learned that much of Derbyshire used to be a tropical sea. That the unusual rock formations of Western Scotland were shaped by the restless movements of the Earth. It was exciting, too, to examine charts created to support the latest evidence for Continental Drift, a once contentious theory that was gradually becoming accepted.

'Geological time makes me feel small, that my problems are unimportant. Do you know, I find that soothing?' she told Peggy one lunchtime. They were eating with the Annes in the refectory. Several of the boys were sitting together further down the long polished table, though James, Nancy noted, was not among them.

Peggy had been grumbling to the other girls about having to sketch layers of soil and sediment, which didn't have the same appeal for her as living plants, which she loved and spent hours of her own time drawing. Nancy envied Peggy's skill.

'I can't get my head round the idea of millions of years,' Anne Durban sighed as she picked scraps of fish skin out of her lunch. 'They're just numbers to me. All I know is that the fish in this pie must be prehistoric.'

'Mine, too,' Anne Southgate agreed, wrinkling her nose.

Nancy stared at a bone she'd just picked out of her teeth. 'Perhaps it's left over from yesterday's dissection!'

'What a revolting idea.' Peggy giggled.

'Dogfish is actually very tasty,' Anne Durban said seriously.

'Not after being left out in the lab for hours,' Nancy sighed.

She looked up to see James West approaching. He was carrying two books under his arm and a laden tray and was glancing about for somewhere to sit. Realizing that the group of boys he might have joined had left, Nancy caught his eye. 'Come and join us, if you like,' she called out, thinking it a friendly thing to do.

'Thanks.' He didn't even smile.

Anne Southgate moved her things to make space on the bench beside her. James sprinkled salt on his food and began to eat heartily. The Annes and Peggy began to discuss a piece of homework on photosynthesis they'd been given. Nancy only half-listened. She was liking the way the light from the feeble bulb overhead shone off James' dark hair in the gloom of the refectory and was trying to see the titles of the books on the table beside him.

'You nearly missed lunch,' she said tentatively. Three weeks into the term and, although they'd exchanged comments once or twice out of necessity, this was the first time they'd actually embarked on a conversation.

His dark eyes perused her as he swallowed a mouthful. 'I was in the library and forgot the time.'

'Oh, you must have been absorbed, then. I never met a

man who forgot to eat. My sister and I used to have to race my brother to the table or he'd scoff everything.'

He gave a slow smile. 'I'm an only child, so that didn't happen. But don't worry, I'm not in the habit of missing meals. I was reading this.' He pushed one of the books towards her and she picked it up and examined the spine. *Principles of Physical Geology* by Arthur Holmes. She remembered the lecturer referring to it that morning when talking about the ceaselessly moving continents. It was a key text, she'd gathered, only recently published.

'That's keen of you.' She opened it and turned the pages, frowning, her chin resting in her hand. 'The maths looks complicated. Have you grasped it?'

'His take is that heat from radioactivity moves the earth's crust and that's why land masses move. My Biology master used to bang on about Continental Drift. It was he who suggested I come here.'

'But you chose Zoology, not Geology?'

'Geology never occurred to me. A local naturalist came and gave a talk to our sixth form about insects, so I decided on Zoology and that was that.'

'Where did you go to school?'

'Only one of the London day schools. Nowhere grand.' There was a challenging edge to his voice.

'Same here,' she said humbly. 'I chose Prince's because it's the best place in London for Zoology and a master at our school knows Professor Briggs slightly. Anyway, my parents wouldn't have let me go further away.'

'I must say, I was surprised to find so many girls here. I

suppose Edmund Buckland is right. Briggs is desperate for the money.'

Nancy drew a sharp breath. 'Are you saying that the girls aren't up to it?'

'No, no, of course not.' The other girls were staring at him and it was the first time she'd seen James flustered. 'Just, I thought they were still giving priority to the men coming out of the forces. It's only fair, don't you think?'

'Why? Why's that fair?' Nancy demanded. 'We need educating, too. Anyway, you weren't in the forces.'

'No ... but I'll need to do National Service, which you ladies won't.' He finished his last forkful of pie and started on his semolina.

'Only because we'll be having your children,' Anne Southgate snapped, then giggled. 'Well, I don't mean yours personally.'

'Fair play,' he said, then smiled. 'But you won't be doing science by then.'

There was a silence as they considered this, a silence that Peggy broke. 'Marrying and having kids will be years away,' she said brightly. 'Anyway, you shouldn't assume we'll all want to do that. Or maybe we'll combine a family with working.'

'All right.' James raised his palm in a gesture of surrender. 'Now you're ganging up on me. I apologize.'

'I do think James is on to something, actually.' It was Anne Durban who'd spoken. She was a calm, thoughtful girl with wings of dark hair that framed an oval face with smooth creamy skin. 'Everybody does get married, don't they? I know I want to one day, if some man will have me. Some of the girls from my school are already engaged. Mummy says it's a waste of money me coming here, but I don't think so. I want to learn as much as I can and be useful. Maybe I'll be able to work for several years anyway, so that will be worth it.'

Everybody listened in surprise to this speech, James with an admiring look. Reserved Anne Durban rarely spoke at any length and the girls had never talked about such things before. Nancy certainly hadn't given the matter much thought.

'I came just because it was the next thing to do,' Peggy put in. 'I wanted to study Zoology and my parents encouraged me. I haven't thought about what'll happen afterwards. I'll work as a scientist of some sort, I imagine. But of course I want to get married one day.'

'I suppose it's hard on you girls,' James' tone was measured, as though he, too, was thinking about it for the first time. 'But I'm out to make a name for myself as a scientist. I don't know how yet, but I will.'

Nancy heard this and something stirred in her. It was as though he'd issued a challenge. 'I've got my own plans,' she said crossly, as James piled plates noisily onto his tray.

'Good for you, Nan.' Anne Southgate was glancing at her watch. 'It's nearly two. None of us will get anywhere in life if we're late for the afternoon lecture.'

And with that they all rose and went to stack their trays on the trolley. When they walked out into the autumn sunshine, James strode ahead of them across the quad towards the Zoo building. It struck Nancy with dismay that this clever boy with his good looks, his purposefulness and his arrogance would always be ahead. It was the first time in life that she had been offered such a competitor. She would have to do her utmost to keep up.

Fourteen

2010

In Dragonfly Lodge, Nancy's voice faded and for a while there was silence. The sun had moved round behind the trees, filling the room with restless shadows. A clock ticked on the mantelpiece. Stef lowered her notebook and glanced at the old lady. Her eyes were closed. Her face was drawn, but she held herself upright and Stef didn't think she was asleep or in pain. Lost in thoughts of the past perhaps.

She said softly, 'You described it all so well.'

Nancy opened her eyes and smiled. 'It's years since I've spoken about it, but once I started it's surprising how quickly it all came back to me. The intensity of being young. I still feel it strongly. Hopes, dreams and disappointments.' She laughed. 'And a heavy curtain of ignorance separated us from the future. At eighteen we were very naïve, much more than we'd be today.'

'But you'd lived through a terrible war.'

'Yes, we had, but funnily enough we didn't talk much about that. Even the students who'd been in the forces didn't discuss their experiences.' She paused. 'Not then, anyway. My parents were very bothered about Roger for a while. They felt that he'd completely lost his way. However, his problems took their attention off me and I'm afraid I was grateful for that.'

She blinked several times and Stef saw that she was tired. 'I ought to leave you in peace. Is there anything I can do first?'

'I don't think so, dear. Aaron will be back any minute. I'll have to get used to those wretched instruments of torture, I suppose.' They both looked at a pair of crutches propped against the arm of the sofa. 'They made me practise in the hospital, but I can't get upstairs with them. Aaron is going to move a single mattress down here – the beds themselves are too heavy – but I won't find a mattress easy to get up from.' A vulnerable look crossed her face. 'Old age is a pig.'

'Mum's got a folding guest bed,' Stef remembered suddenly. 'A really sturdy one. Comfortable, too. I've slept on it in the past. I could bring it over if you like.'

Nancy brightened. 'That might be the solution. Would she mind lending it?'

'I'm sure she wouldn't. Though, oh dear, my car's not big enough. Nor is Mum's.' And Ted's van would be full of the tools of his trade.

'Aaron's would be. It looks very sleek, but you could get an elephant into the back once the seats are down.'

They looked up at the clunk of the garden gate. 'Ah, speak of the devil,' Nancy murmured. They watched Aaron's steady trudge across the garden with a bulging carrier bag in each hand, then heard the front door open. 'Hello,' he called out.

'Hello,' Nancy echoed, 'we're in here.'

When he entered the room, his expression darkened to see Stef.

'Oh, hi.' His tone was suspicious. 'I didn't know you were coming.'

'I summoned her here,' Nancy said promptly. 'We've been having a nice chat, haven't we, Stef?'

'Yes, we have.'

'I hope she hasn't been tiring you.'

'Of course she hasn't, Aaron. Did you manage to get everything?'

'Yes, except for more arnica cream, but I'll order some online. I'll go and put it all away, shall I?'

'Please, and then can you banish that dreadful wheelchair? When you're ready, we've another little job for you.'

'No peace for the wicked,' he sighed as he picked up the shopping bags.

Stef watched as Aaron's car drew up outside Springfield Cottage an hour later. He got out and started lowering the back seat, his expression grim. Stef's mother, thrilled that her daughter had made the acquaintance of such a good-looking young man, tried to lure him in with the offer of a glass of wine, but he seemed in a hurry to fetch the bed and leave. She asked anxiously about Nancy's ankle and, while Aaron and Stef eased the folding guest bed and its mattress outside, she flapped about gathering some comforting novels for Nancy to read, chatting all the while. Eventually, they succeeded in packing everything in. Cara slipped a lemon drizzle cake from her larder onto the front seat and tactfully retreated to prepare supper.

'Right,' Aaron said, lowering the boot lid. 'All done.' His eyes glittered, unreadable.

'You'll need help the other end,' Stef said uncertainly. He couldn't possibly carry everything by himself from the car across the reserve to Nancy's cottage.

'Ah, damn it.' He pushed back his hair impatiently. 'Josh might still be about at the visitors' centre.'

'Surely not now, it's getting on for seven.' Aaron was so ungrateful, Stef thought crossly. 'Listen, I don't mean to be bossy, but I can follow you in my car and help.' She was doing this for Nancy, not her unpleasant grandson, she reminded herself. 'You'd need to wait for me to keep up, though, as I don't know where you park that's nearest to the cottage.'

'It's fairly straightforward. Okay, that's good of you.'

She hurried inside to fetch her car keys and explain the plan to her mother, saying, 'I won't be long.' When she re-emerged, Aaron was already sitting in his car, the engine turning and music audible through the open windows. It was a band she liked. She told him so and he suddenly perked up.

'They're great, aren't they? I saw them recently at the O2. Mind-blowing.' For a brief moment they'd connected, and Stef saw a softer side of him.

It didn't take long to drive around the back of the reserve to where Nancy kept her small car in the shelter of an open-sided barn. Wheeling the folded bed and mattress together with a bag of bits and pieces the few hundred metres to Dragonfly Lodge was an awkward business and felt faintly ridiculous, but Stef rather enjoyed proving her competence. Because of her guilt about past rudeness and her intrusion concerning his grandmother's secrets, she was determined to prove to Aaron that she was a decent person and useful in times of trouble. They didn't have the breath to talk much, but she felt very aware of the strength of his lean body, the way his hair tumbled across his forehead. She hoped he wasn't noticing in return how red her face became with exertion and the fold of flab that was exposed when her T-shirt rode up.

Finally, the bed was safely assembled in the sitting room. Stef made it up with linen and a spare duvet she found upstairs.

'It does look comfortable,' Nancy said, smiling with relief. 'Thank you so much. Now, you will come tomorrow, won't you?'

Stef had already abandoned her plans to return to London and promised to return the following morning. She wanted to ask if it was all right to bring a tape recorder, but daren't at that moment because Aaron's expression was thunderous at the idea of her visit. She'd bring it with her anyway, she decided.

After she'd said goodbye, he accompanied her to the gate and she was nervous, but her wariness melted when, instead of grumbling at her, he said, 'I want to thank you. You've been brilliant.'

'It's Mum's bed,' she said with a smile. 'You should thank her.'

'You know what I mean.'

'I do,' she said, meeting his eye and seeing that he was genuinely grateful. 'But I simply wanted to help Nancy.'

'Well, it's very good of you.'

'Are you around for a while, Aaron? As I offered yesterday, if you have to go back to London or something, Mum or I could help do things for her. You must want to see Livy.'

'Her mother will have her.' He looked away and she sensed some sadness there. 'I can stay on here for a short while – I have work I can do from here. What about you? Don't you have to go back?'

Stef shrugged. 'It depends.' This was true, but she also guessed their truce was temporary, that he was withholding himself from her, and she felt compelled to do the same. It was like some silly game.

'What does it depend on?' His eyes narrowed.

She shrugged. 'Oh, various things . . .' She let the matter hang, enjoying his curiosity. 'Why don't you want Nancy to talk to me?' she asked, like a sword thrust.

He flinched, then, after a moment's thought, said soberly, 'Because of all she's suffered. The last thing she needs at this stage of life is exposure.'

'Exposure? Exposure of what or to what? My book is going to be a general one about women's experiences. It's supposed to be supportive of women. What are you worried I'd expose?'

His face closed as though a shutter had come down, but she wasn't letting go easily.

'What is it you're protecting her from, Aaron?'

'Gran has always worried about legal repercussions if

certain things are revealed. I'm not sure she'd be strong enough to endure those.'

'Legal repercussions for what?' Stef's journalist's antennae were on full alert.

He sighed impatiently. 'She worries that someone with a guilty secret will stop at nothing to keep it suppressed. I'm not exactly sure what this is all about, but you've been warned.'

His hectoring tone annoyed her. She said softly, 'Nancy may be old, but she's of sound mind. I think what she tells me is up to her, don't you?'

He made an angry sound in his throat. 'I thought you wanted to help my grandmother,' he spat out, 'but all this nosing about won't help her at all. Quite the reverse, in fact.' He turned and marched back to the cottage, leaving her staring after him. The front door shut so smartly that a flock of starlings flew up from a nearby tree, twittering in alarm. Stephanie stared wanly at the closed door.

Fifteen

On Wednesday morning on her way to visit Nancy, Stef parked by the visitors' centre to buy Nancy a bar of special chocolate she'd noticed in the shop. Josh had just opened up.

'How was Nancy yesterday?' he asked as he put the chocolate through the till. 'I didn't see her, just popped the card through.'

'Well, she hasn't broken any bones, so with luck she'll recover quickly.'

Josh nodded, but didn't send Nancy his best wishes or offer any help as one might expect. Yet he'd readily delivered the card. He was a strange one, Stef thought.

As she walked through Nancy's garden a few minutes later, she saw that the sitting room window was open and Nancy was sitting on the sofa, reading. Thankfully she was on her own. Stef wondered where Aaron was.

'Hello,' she called through the window, 'I'll let myself in, shall I?' But the old lady immediately reached for her crutches and struggled to her feet, and a moment later met her in the hall.

'You're making progress!' Stef cried as she closed the door behind her.

'Yes, I'm much better this morning, after a good night. It's a comfortable bed and, do you know, the hospital sent a carer along to help me dress. Come through, will you, we'll make coffee.' Stef followed Nancy on her slow route to the kitchen, where she handed over the chocolate. 'I thought you'd appreciate the picture on the wrapper.'

'Oh, a dragonfly! Very pretty. And it's fruit and nut, my favourite. Now, perhaps you'd kindly make the coffee, as it'll take me too long with my injury. And you might be relieved to hear that I've sent Aaron back to London. It was his turn to have Livy and I don't like him to miss out.'

'Oh, he said that Livy was with her mother.'

'Did he? Men, as we know, are funny. I don't think he sees enough of his daughter. I know he loves her to bits, but he doesn't make the time.'

'They're not together, he and Livy's mother, I take it?'

'Aaron and Crystal? No, not for several years. They met at university and Livy was, shall we say, an unexpected gift. A child is always a joy and they tried to stay together for her, but one changes so much in one's twenties, doesn't one, and it didn't work out for them.'

Stef listened, but didn't know enough to comment. Still, it was interesting to gain these insights into Aaron. Maybe it was the failure of this relationship that had made him bitter.

'Bring the tray through, will you?' Stef did so. In the sitting room, the bed had been neatly made and the room was tidy. There was no sign of the hated wheelchair.

When they were settled, Nancy on the sofa with the cat beside her and Stef in her fireside chair, Stef drew out her notebook, then hesitated. 'Would you mind if I set a tape recorder running? It's what I usually do.'

To her dismay, Nancy froze. 'You'd record me? I'm not sure I'd like that.'

'I don't have to,' Stef said quickly. 'But it is only me who would use the recording. It helps with accuracy, you see.'

'So you wouldn't let anyone else listen, then.'

'No.' She didn't like to add that she would do as she always did and preserve the recording, as she did with her notes, so that if anyone questioned anything she published she'd have the evidence to defend herself if necessary. That had happened with the previous book – only a small matter, but she'd been able to prove that the witness she'd interviewed had indeed provided the information in question.

'Well, all right. Talking to you yesterday has awoken a lot of memories. It was all such a long time ago, though – are you sure that people would be interested?'

Stef's answer was quick and passionate. 'I am, at least, and I think a lot of people will be. It's a sense of connection to the past. And how it affects the present.'

'That's what Aaron is worried about,' Nancy said with a sigh. 'It's not simply a story from the past, you see.'

Sixteen

July 1948

'It's very long, longer than the one you had for Yorkshire.' Mrs Foster was sitting at the kitchen table frowning at a typed kit list. 'Why all these changes of clothes? Sixteen pairs of socks?'

'It's not my idea, it's just what it says.' Nancy was sitting on the back step in the open doorway pasting dubbin on her walking boots, generously paid for earlier in the year by Aunt Rhoda.

'Can't you take those you already have and wash them? Anyone would think there wasn't still clothes rationing. You'll have to borrow Helen's brown slacks, and I imagine her winter pyjamas will be warmer for camping than your old things.'

'I heard that,' Helen said, coming in from the hall and sitting down at the table. 'And the answer's no.'

Nancy gave her an appealing look. 'Be a sport.'

'I can't see any alternative, Helen,' their mother moaned. 'I simply don't have the coupons.'

'She'll ruin them.'

'I won't. Anyway, you borrowed my windjammer to go sailing on the Broads, remember.'

'I look after things. You don't.'

'I do.'

'Girls, that's enough.'

The first year of college was over and Nancy was packing for the zoologists' field trip, three weeks under canvas in the New Forest. It was a more ambitious affair than the Geology trip to Ingatestone at Easter, which had only been one week and they'd stayed in a hostel.

The group were to meet two of their lecturers at the college on Monday morning and travel down to Hampshire in a small coach. Like the others, she felt a mixture of excitement and trepidation. Excitement because, despite the fact they'd be engaged in full-time nature study, the students couldn't help thinking of it as a merry jaunt after years in which holidays had been curtailed by war.

For several summers running during Nancy's teens the Fosters had gone to Devon to stay for a fortnight with Mrs Foster's cousin Ruth. Ruth was married to a local farmer, who was short of hands at harvest time and welcomed the extra help. Nancy's father usually stayed in London on these occasions and took his meals at his club. Roger, who came for the first two of these trips, was out in the fields all day with the workers, after which he slept like the dead. Helen and Nancy were given less onerous tasks such as collecting eggs and milking cows, which they quite enjoyed. Their mother, however, astonished them. She turned into a different person on these occasions, cheerful and sociable rather than nagging and unhappy. She rolled up her sleeves to help Ruth in the kitchen of the rambling farmhouse, preparing meals for the workers. She smoked and drank cider and laughed at doubtful jokes. It did her good to be away from the anxieties of wartime London, which possibly included her husband.

By the summer of 1947, though, this enthusiasm for farming had run out. The year before, there had been some unpleasantness. A new farm hand had developed a pash for twenty-year-old Helen and tried to corner her in a barn. Then an old carthorse Mrs Foster had been grooming stepped heavily on her foot, causing her agony and nasty bruising that had lasted for weeks.

Now Helen was working as a secretary and couldn't get the time off. Mr Foster rented a cottage in the Cotswolds, but Nancy, who'd just left school, was the only sibling who went. Although she'd loved the beautiful countryside and the pretty villages of golden stone, she found a fortnight under the constant eye of her parents a strain and vowed that it would be the last family holiday.

A year later, the thought of going away with her fellow students filled her with joy.

The trepidation was to do with the newness of the experience. Would it be fun? she thought as she rubbed at her walking shoes. How would they all get on? Especially the girls and the boys. Friendships were gradually forming between the sexes, one or two even teetering on romance. Not for Nancy, though. Something always held her back, something that might have been to do with what had happened all those years ago with their neighbour Mr Hunter. She got on well with most of the boys as friends. They were in awe of her intelligence, the fact that she always put her hand up and answered questions correctly, the hard work that she put into assignments.

'You may have gained a higher mark on this occasion, Foster,' James West said recently, after the results of a test about classification were released, 'but I shan't allow it to happen again.'

She had smiled, delighted with her victory, but also by the fact that he'd acknowledged it with a touch of humour. Some of the boys didn't like to be beaten by a girl. She'd been delighted when he'd then invited her to join him and some of the others in the bar. Only the men were allowed to buy drinks in the men's bar. The women didn't even have a bar in the poky lounge that had been allocated for their use. She hesitated for only a moment, imagining her mother's likely reaction, but her mother wasn't there and Nancy would not tell her.

'Yes, please. I'll have a sherry,' she said boldly, for that's what she was given at home on special occasions, and she went off to sit with half a dozen of their set at a corner booth. Peggy wasn't one of them at this point – her religious parents definitely wouldn't have approved of her drinking – but several of the other girls were, including the darkly attractive Anne Durban and Diana Beauchamp, the pretty, sociable girl from a privileged background, who talked a great deal and was popular with the boys but not very studious.

James brought over the sherry and a beer for himself and sat down next to her. Nancy sipped her drink, feeling the warmth of it slide through her throat, and listened to the conversation about the forthcoming field trip.

'Mummy's insisting on me taking a camp bed. She's worried I'll be cold,' Diana said. 'I don't know how it'll fit into the tent, though, if there are four of us.'

'That's not playing the game. We're supposed to make our own beds out of heather.' John Philips was speaking. 'It should be fun!'

'It's all right for you boys. You've all been scouts or cadets and you're used to it. I've never camped in my life.'

'Honestly, Di, you're like the princess and the pea. We all know about your chilly blue blood.'

Diana shrieked with laughter, which made the others laugh, too. They weren't bothered by her background because she never put on airs.

'I've not camped, either,' Nancy put in. 'Have you, Anne?' Anne Durban was coming out of herself more.

'With my brothers, yes. Daddy used to take us to Scotland and we'd camp in the mountains. Four o'clock in the morning was worst. I'd wake up freezing and everything was soaked with dew, and when it rained hard it was awful because the tent leaked. And the midges ... I was covered in bites.'

'I hope it'll be all right in Hampshire,' Nancy said, thinking that three weeks of that sounded very long.

'At least we've got Dr Hillman and Dr Mills.'

'Yes, they're the nicest of the lecturers.' Everyone agreed.

'It's a pity Dr Bauer isn't coming,' Anne Durban sighed.

Trudi Bauer was the only female lecturer, young, reserved and spoke with a heavy accent. 'I suppose she's going back to see her family in Germany.'

Nancy needn't have worried. The field trip turned out to be magical, one of the most marvellous times of her young life.

The weather was dull at first, but it didn't actually rain and felt pleasantly warm. It wasn't simply beds they had to make from heather gathered from the heath. They had to do everything, from putting up tents and a communal shelter to building a fire with logs round it to sit on. Thankfully, it was the boys who were made to dig latrines and to rig up stalls round them for privacy. Under Dr Hillman's instruction, though, the girls fashioned tripods of sticks to stand tin bowls on for washing up.

'Where do we wash ourselves?' Peggy asked him. His expression was bemused and the girls looked at one another in dismay, realizing that he wasn't used to the needs of the fairer sex.

'Girls do need to wash, Dr Hillman,' Anne Southgate said boldly. He thought for a moment, then quickly issued some more bowls.

There was a mains water tap at the far end of the field and the students made a human chain with buckets to get water for cooking and washing. The slopping of water caused screeches of laughter and by the end of the first day even the shyest among them unbent and started to feel among friends.

The announcement that everyone would take a turn to

cook dinner, though, caused some joshing about girls' roles and boys' kitchen skills, but the first culinary team, which included Nancy, set to with enthusiasm. There was much to learn – how to keep milk cool in a nearby stream, the best way to open meat cans without cutting their fingers, the importance of good hygiene to avoid food poisoning.

When the first dinner was served, the potatoes were still hard and the tinned stew a bit salty, but there was more than enough for everyone, and afterwards they fetched their thick jerseys and sat round the fire to sing. The boys knew all the songs, especially the vulgar ones. And then they went to bed, the girls giggling as they snuggled into their sleeping bags and tried to get comfortable on the springy, sweet-smelling palliasses of heather. The others fell asleep quickly, but Nancy lay awake for a while listening to the soft hoots of an owl and thinking over the day, then she, too, fell asleep. She woke briefly as early sunshine filtered through the canvas of the tent and the world was bursting with birdsong but, still tired, she rolled over and only woke again when a whistle blew a harsh reveille.

The next day, they unpacked their butterfly nets and were sent off in pairs down to the stream to search for dragonflies and damselflies. 'I know we're supposed to have done this in class, but what is the difference again?' Diana whispered to Nancy.

'It helps to think of them as dragons and damsels,' Nancy replied with a smile.

'Oh, dragonflies are thicker and bulkier, like that one,' she pointed, 'and the fragile ones are damselflies.'

'They're both *Odonata*, though.'

'They're what?'

'*Odonata* is the name of the dragonfly Order.'

'Well, whatever, it seems a shame to catch the poor things. They're heavenly!'

And indeed they were. The sunlight dazzled off the water and, there being no wind, the insects hovered above the reeds like bright, gauzy jewels. They each netted a couple and transferred them carefully to jars containing cotton wool soaked in ethyl acetate. Later, when the life had gone out of them, the students were expected to examine them before pinning them to the cork bases of their specimen cases. Nancy squatted to peer through the clear water of the rippling stream, watched tiny speckled fish swim against the flow and watersnails the size of babies' fingernails curled up on the gravel bed.

The days floated by like shimmering bubbles. One morning, she found herself paired with Edmund Buckland, one of the two older students. Although he and Michael Carlton were friendly to the younger freshers and occasionally sat with them at college, on the whole they still kept themselves apart. There was a certain inevitability about this. Michael was married and he generally left promptly at the end of each day. Edmund never spoke about his private life. He'd made some friends in the year above, other men who'd come out of the forces, and he would occasionally be seen with them in the bar, playing billiards or simply chatting. Nancy liked his tall, lean, scholarly appearance, while being shy of his age and experience.

He and Nancy had been assigned to visit one of the various ponds that studded the heath to collect specimens and make notes about their habitat. Peggy was supposed to accompany them, but the poor girl had woken feeling sick. She sat palely aloof while everyone else tucked into breakfast, so Dr Hillman ordered her to stay on base to tidy the site if she felt up to it or to nap in the shade if she didn't.

'I'll share my notes with you, Pegs,' Nancy said as she filled her shoulder bag with lidded jars and selected a pond net. Peggy, her freckles more obvious in her ashen complexion, managed a weak smile of thanks.

The air smelled sweetly of heather and gorse as they trudged the sandy paths in rubber boots, following one of Dr Hillman's duplicated maps, to reach a large pond fringed with grass and shaded by trees. Here, they laid their kitbags on a lichened rock and waded into the water, nets at the ready. There was no breeze and the water was clear and still. Nancy wriggled her toes, enjoying its coolness seeping through the rubber.

'Glad of them now, are you?' Edmund said with a smile in his voice, and she laughed, for she'd questioned the need for the uncomfortable wellingtons in warm weather. 'Right,' he sighed, 'what are we looking for?'

'There!' She pointed at a water boatman darting across the surface, but Edmund's attention had been drawn downwards.

'Look.'

She followed his line of sight. 'Yuck,' she groaned. A strange, formless creature was oozing over his boot.

'A medicinal leech. Lovely.' He planted his net in the silt, took a jar from his windjammer pocket, unscrewed the lid and, bending, urged the invertebrate inside. They peered at it together as it flowed in looping movements over the inside of its new home. Nancy shuddered.

'Sorry, I can't help it. It's the thought of it sucking people's blood. Why on earth did doctors ever think it did patients any good?'

'It's rather beautiful in its own way. I'd always thought they'd be black.' Instead, it was brightly coloured, with greenish-grey and rusty stripes on top, its underneath a greenish yellow.

'I'm not persuaded,' she said with a grimace and Edmund laughed heartily. She hadn't heard him laugh much before. Even in repose, he had rather a sad face, she thought as she watched him pocket the jar, then she lifted her net and concentrated on scooping up a boatman.

They spent a contented hour collecting specimens, though the one Nancy most desired, a bulky male dragonfly with a sky-blue abdomen, appeared to sense her intent, for he continually zigzagged away out of reach. '*Anax imperator*, the Emperor,' she sighed. 'He would have been the star of my collection.'

'You're free to fly another day, Your Imperial Majesty!' Edmund called out across the water and Nancy laughed.

When they'd used up all their jars, they searched for great crested newts but found only frogs. Then, feeling hungry, they wandered back towards the camp for lunch, taking turns to follow birds on the wing through Edmund's field glasses. They'd not really talked about anything personal, only the job in hand, but Nancy realized she felt comfortable with him.

They returned to find that Peggy was a little better. John Philips, a regular clown, unscrewed the pot containing Edmund's leech and threatened to 'cure' her by applying it to her arm. Peggy shrieked in alarm until the others held John down and sat on him. Edmund rescued his specimen while Nancy laughed cruelly until the tears ran down her cheeks.

That night, after it grew dark, a crescent moon crested the trees, bathing the campsite in a pale silvery light, and Dr Hillman declared it a perfect opportunity for a walk. Everyone gathered. Some shone torches, but Hillman said to put them away. 'Use your natural nightsight instead,' he said. 'You'll see more that way.' They followed him across the heath, past ponds, glittering under the moon, and into scrubby woodland, realizing that he was right. Once their eyes became used to the light, they could see everything beautifully.

They found themselves walking alongside a grassy bank that flanked dense woodland. Dr Hillman came to a halt and pointed. Someone gasped. Another said, 'Oh!' and at the same time Nancy saw what they'd seen. 'Glow-worms,' James West said. And now, everywhere she looked, it seemed, were little points of greeny-orange light.

'How beautiful.'

'They're not worms at all,' Dr Mills said. 'They're beetles, but the females don't have wings so they just sit and look pretty to attract a mate. Rather like other parts of the animal kingdom I could name, eh?' There were only a few giggles at Dr Mills' well-worn joke and Nancy sighed audibly.

'The males are equipped with large, far-ranging eyes so they can spot their lady friends easily.' Dr Hillman switched on a torch with a red light, scooped one of the glowing beetles into a jar and invited them to inspect it.

'It's a bit sad to think they're boring old beetles,' Anne Durban whispered as they all set off back to the camp. 'They ought to be fairies or something, carrying lamps.'

'I'm not sure that fairies come into Zoology, Miss Durban.' Dr Hillman had overheard and there was much laughter at her expense. 'What Latin name would we give fairies. Hmm. The word fairy comes from *fatum* – fate, I believe. How about *fata fabulosa*?'

'What's the glow-worm's formal name?' Nancy ventured.

'Anyone?' Dr Hillman asked.

'*Lampyris noctiluca*,' James West said promptly.

'Well done, West.'

'That's a lovely name,' Nancy said to Anne, hoping to soothe her hurt feelings. 'I don't know, it just sounds nice.'

She felt very close to the others, walking through the semi-darkness as though they all belonged together. Edmund and Michael hung together at the back as usual, but when she smiled at Edmund he smiled back, his eyes twinkling at her in the moonlight, and she felt a rush of liking for him. The person she was most aware of, though, was James West.

Two nights later, Nancy shared in another magical experience.

'It's here, look.' James stopped suddenly. 'By the roots of that oak.'

Dr Hillman had pointed out the badger's sett the evening before. The group had passed a number of D-shaped holes burrowed into a bank in a copse of broadleaf trees where they'd gone to look for stag beetles. It wasn't far from the camp, near one of the main paths, so on the presumption that it would be difficult for them to get lost, James, Nancy and Peggy had been allowed to return to try to see the occupants. Dr Hillman had advised them to set out an hour before the light faded and gave them various guidelines to ensure success.

The air was warm and very still, so that they didn't need to worry about the wind carrying the scent of humans to the badgers, but the downside was that it was difficult to be silent.

'No waterproof clothing, it rustles,' Dr Hillman had told Nancy when she'd appeared for inspection in her windjammer after supper. 'And West, you'll need plimsolls, not those clumpy boots, or the badgers will think it's a herd of elephants tramping about. Miss Durban, you look very pretty in pale blue, but I did advise "dark clothing". And I hope neither of you ladies is wearing anything perfumed. Badgers have an excellent sense of smell.'

'I just smell of sausage and onion,' Nancy had grumbled to Anne as they returned to their tent to change.

'Sausage and perspiration, me,' Anne had said with a shameful smile. 'I don't know about you, but I haven't washed for two days so there's no danger of me smelling of soap.'

James was taking charge now, prowling about quietly,

looking for places where they might conceal themselves. There was no sign of life at the sett, just the holes, black and sinister-looking in the fading light, and hillocks of freshly dug earth. Nancy pointed him to another oak tree some twenty yards away with low-spreading branches, and they went to inspect it. It seemed the most obvious observation platform, so James interlinked his fingers as a foothold for Anne, but when it was Nancy's turn she spurned his help and scrambled up by herself. Each found themselves a comfortable perch on their own branch, Nancy with her back against the trunk and her knees drawn up. What a funny lot of roosting birds they were, she thought with a smile. As the light faded and darkness gathered in the hollows, they waited in silence, hidden by the canopy and not daring to move.

For what seemed like a long time, nothing happened. Birds sang their liquid songs around them, a squirrel ran up the tree and froze, startled, to see its strange fruit. A small bug tickled Nancy's hand and she brushed it away. The air grew cooler and she shivered despite her thick jersey. Cramp was setting in and she was just wondering about flexing her legs when she heard James, on the branch above her, give a sharp intake of breath. Slowly, she lowered her gaze to survey the bank with its black holes, her eyes narrowing in the dwindling light.

Something whitish was moving on the ground there. She blinked and a white furry face with a black vertical stripe down each side came into focus. She caught the glint of its eyes as it raised its snout, snuffing the air. The badger was larger than she'd expected, probably a boar. It browsed about in the loam for a minute or two, searching for worms, then returned to the hole. Disappointment seeped through her, but after a moment it reappeared and her spirits rose, for this time it made a low whickering sound and another slightly smaller adult emerged, then several cubs bounded out.

The little family began to bustle about, the cubs tumbling over one another, emitting little growls and yelps. Nancy watched and listened, open-mouthed in wonder. Then she jumped at a movement above; was it James or Anne? A soft curse and something dropped past her, battering the leaves and hitting the ground with a smack. Immediately, the boar badger raised his head on full alert, then opened his maw and issued a loud grunt of alarm. A moment's mayhem followed as the badgers fled back to their hole, and once again the scene was still and silent under the moon.

'Sorry,' James sighed. 'It was the bloomin' case for the field glasses.'

'Never mind,' Anne's voice wailed from above. 'I'm so cold I can't move.'

'Weren't they magical, though?' Nancy cried.

'Magical,' the others agreed as they climbed stiffly down.

As they walked back to camp together in the moonlight, linking arms, with James between the girls, Nancy felt the happiest she'd ever been. Nothing, she thought, could ever match the joy she'd experienced that evening.

Something else happened that really touched her. At the end of the trip, Edmund presented her with a little dragonfly that he'd whittled from a piece of wood. 'Because you like the creatures,' he said with a friendly smile. It was roughly carved, but there was something spirited about it and she accepted it with a cry of pleasure.

Seventeen

'I still have it,' Nancy said and pointed to a bookshelf behind her. 'Can you get it down?'

Stef put aside her notebook and reached up. She examined the small wooden carving, admiring the accuracy of the proportions. 'It's beautiful!' She handed it to the old lady, who cupped it tenderly in her hands before passing it back.

'I've held on to the memory of that field trip all my life. I've often returned to it in times of trouble. It's like a safe haven in my mind. The quiet beauty of the New Forest, the magical experience of seeing those wonderful creatures, the way we all bonded as fellow students. It was perfect.'

'It sounded truly amazing.' Stef turned off the tape recorder.

'I was so fortunate. Do you have anything like that, a golden memory you go back to?'

Stef thought, then said, 'Oh, beach holidays, that sort of thing. Holkham, actually,' she said, naming the vast sandy beach on the North Norfolk coast.

'Of course, I've often been. It's an incredible place.'

'I remember when I was about twelve and my mum and dad were still happy together. It was a really hot summer's day and the sea was shallow and so warm. And I saw horses galloping over the beach. I'd never ridden a horse, but I longed to that day. Sadly, it wasn't something my parents could afford.'

'These experiences are important,' Nancy said. 'You need a stock of them to take out and look at when life is getting you down. The importance of that field trip was that it cemented in me a deep love for my studies. I went home more determined than ever that I would be a scientist. Little did I know how important the memory of it would become to me years later when things turned dark.'

Stef's eyes widened. Should she turn on the tape recorder again? But no, Nancy was now struggling to stand up. 'Would you pass my crutches? I ought to go and check the animals,' she said. 'I sent Aaron in to feed them before he left, but I'd still like to see them for myself. Perhaps you'd come with me. I'm not awfully good at managing.'

'Of course I'll help,' Stef said, jumping up.

She passed a busy half an hour under Nancy's firm instruction, cleaning out a couple of the cages and topping up water bottles. Then, in the kitchen, she laid out the old lady's salad lunch and fetched a warm throw from upstairs. The carer, whose name was Lauren, was returning later to help with dinner and the evening routine. Nancy questioned the need for this. 'I don't object to her particularly, she is very nice. It's the idea of needing anybody.' She sighed. 'I suppose I have to put up with it.'

'Are you sure you'll be okay till she comes?' Stef said as she prepared to leave.

'Of course. So tomorrow, Lauren's coming first thing, then you'll be here at about ten and Aaron will be back in the afternoon.'

'You'll ring in the meantime if you need anything?'

Nancy's answer was to pat the phone lying next to the TV remote on the sofa. Stef had made sure her number, and that of Springfield Cottage, were in the contacts list. While she respected Nancy's desire for independence, she couldn't shake off her unease about the injured woman being on her own overnight.

Eighteen

When Stef returned to Springfield Cottage, it was to find that her mother was out somewhere with Baxter. She made herself a ham sandwich and took it upstairs, where she went through her emails, then wrote one to her agent.

> *Hi Sarah, a quick update. I'm still in Norfolk and have had a good chat with Nancy Foster. She's really interesting so far – I'm still interviewing her – and will possibly do for the book. More anon.*

As she was visiting some websites in preparation for her commission about urban gardens, the reply came in.

> *Hi Stef, good to hear about Nancy Foster. I had breakfast with Catherine this morning and she is very excited about the idea for the new book. How soon can you finish your outline? I'd like to send it to her before I go on holiday at the end of next week.*

Stef was thrilled to hear her editor's response. She thought for a bit, then wrote back, *'Another few days, I think.'* Surely by then she'd have the bones of Nancy's story and could see where to include it. She pressed send and looked up to see that the sky had turned grey. After a moment, rain began to patter against the window.

Just then she heard a vehicle in the lane and shortly after that the sound of her mother's return. 'Stef? Are you there, darling?' her mum called up the stairs. 'We were lucky to miss the rain.'

'Coming!' Stef called back.

In the kitchen, Baxter lay panting on his bed. Cara was making tea.

'Where did you go?' Stef lolled against a worktop, fingertips resting in her jeans back pockets, watching her mother arrange Viennese Whirls on a plate. They had always been her favourite. Stef gave in and took one, its artificial cream and jam sweetness reminding her of her childhood.

'Just for a walk.' Something about her tone made Stef look at her twice.

'Where?' She tried to keep it light.

'The usual. Fields, up to the mill. Here's your tea. Now, I've had a phone call from Pip. She's bringing the kids after school on Friday. You'll still be here, won't you? They're going to stay. The kids have been begging to try the bunks. Pip can sleep in the boxroom.'

'I can't promise. I may have gone back to London by then.'

Her mother's demeanour changed. 'Oh no, please stay. I wanted the two of you together. I hardly see you.'

'All right.' Stef sighed. Fridays were bad for traffic so it was probably better not to drive back then, and it would be good to spend more time trying to be a caring aunt. The boat trips, she remembered. Perhaps she could treat them to a boat trip. *Do you suppose you have to book ahead?* And then a further idea struck her. If Livy came down with Aaron at the weekend, maybe she'd like to come, too? It would be a way of getting Aaron on side, and goodness knew that was needed.

She watched her mother feeding bits of Viennese Whirl to Baxter as the rain came down outside.

'No wonder that dog's so fat,' Stef remarked and her mother threw her a stony look.

Where had her mother been just now? she wondered, then remembered the sound of the vehicle in the lane. 'Was that Ted's van I heard?'

'What is this?' her mother said with a smile. 'The Spanish Inquisition?'

'No. I was only asking.'

'I don't have to tell you everything,' her mother said smugly. 'Like you don't have to tell me about that gorgeous young man yesterday.'

'Aaron?' Stef frowned. 'I shouldn't waste time having hopes of him. He's very bad-tempered.'

'He's the one you were rude to back in March, did you say?'

Stef, having already confessed to this, nodded.

'Well, I thought he was rather nice.'

Stef rolled her eyes. 'How little you know,' she sighed. She hoped she didn't bump into Aaron when she next visited Nancy. Her nerves wouldn't stand it.

Nineteen

April 1949

'For the love of Mike, stand still, Nancy, or I'll never get this hem straight.' Her mother's voice was as sharp as the pins she'd removed from her lips to upbraid her daughter.

'I can't, it's torture, I'm prickling all over!' Nancy wailed. She had been standing on newspaper on the dining room table for what felt like hours but was probably only twenty minutes, encased in a dress with a horrid blue and pink floral pattern that was held together by tacking. She lifted first one foot, then the other and flexed her shoulders, trying to get comfortable.

'Nancy!' She froze and her mother continued to inch the wooden hem marker around the bottom of the dress, folding and pinning the stiff fabric as she went.

Helen was to marry Bobby Norris, the department manager from Peter Jones, in two months' time. It was to be a June wedding in the parish church with Nancy as the only bridesmaid. 'We can't afford to make any more dresses so that's that,' Mrs Foster said firmly, after Helen begged to have her best friend Audrey as well.

With determination and the assistance of Mrs Armitage, their mother had sewed Helen a beautiful full-length, full-skirted white wedding dress with lace overlay and sleeves and matched by a gauze veil. The budget ran out after that and Nancy was to make do with a modest garment cleverly fashioned from a cheap remnant in a pattern that made her feel like a garden ornament.

'It isn't your big day, it's Helen's,' was all Mrs Foster said to her complaints.

Helen had stood quietly for her own fittings, perhaps subdued by Mrs Armitage's presence, and her finished dress now hung from the spare room picture rail, protected by a cover made from an old white sheet. From time to time, she took it out and tried it on, anxious that she was losing weight from wedding nerves.

Nancy's problem was the opposite. The bodice of her dress had to be resewn after her second-year exams because the weeks of revision had involved sitting at her desk and eating too many biscuits. However, by the eve of the wedding, her weight had dropped back to normal so there were further arguments when the dress had to be altered for a second time.

Nancy did not envy Helen's version of 'happy ever after'. She was pleased that her sister seemed elated, but puzzled by the object of her love. Bobby was admittedly a good-looking young man with cropped fair curls and an athletic physique.

His sharp blue eyes fixed upon his pretty fiancée's every movement, but all the Fosters except Helen herself thought him terribly silly.

'What do you make of Mr Atlee's government?' her father asked Bobby one Sunday lunchtime.

Bobby had dismissed the question, saying, 'I don't have time to read the newspapers much,' before renewing his enthusiastic attack on the roast chicken. Aunt Rhoda he spoke to with awe because her fabrics were popular at Peter Jones.

Nancy thought that getting married generated a very anxious type of happiness. Sometimes Helen would trip about the house humming to herself, her expression radiant, but she was also prone to tantrums as sudden and short-lived as summer storms at the tiniest disappointment. Once she burst into tears because Mrs Foster pronounced that the red roses she wanted in the wedding bouquet would 'look vulgar'.

The question of where the couple would live caused the greatest distress. Bobby wanted Helen to give up work after they married, but if she did then they wouldn't be able to afford a place of their own. The different possibilities were discussed endlessly at the supper table and on one occasion Helen sobbed that her dreams were 'in ruins'.

Nancy privately thought that the arrangement eventually agreed – the couple living with Bobby's parents while they saved for a deposit to buy a home – sounded awful. Mr and Mrs Norris themselves were awful. They had come round for a celebratory dinner after the engagement was announced and the Fosters found them to be terrible snobs. At one point between courses, Mrs Norris had turned a side plate over and murmured to her husband, 'Look, it's Wedgwood, Larry, very nice.'

Mr Norris complained about their new neighbour in South London, who was a plumber and was 'letting down the tone of the neighbourhood' by keeping his company van outside the house. The Fosters listened politely, but after the three Norrises had driven away in the Coupé Cabriolet that was Mr Norris' pride and joy, Nancy's mother said, 'I'm glad that's over' in a brittle voice. The girls were helping her clear the table, but Helen threw down a table mat and fled upstairs in tears.

'I don't think she likes them, either,' Nancy observed.

'That's the trouble, you marry your husband's family.' Mr Foster's elderly parents were stiff and old-fashioned but safely far away in a leafy part of Bristol.

'You've been lucky with Aunt Rhoda,' Nancy pointed out.

'Rhoda's been very kind,' her mother conceded.

The wedding itself was spoiled for Nancy by the best man, a cousin of Bobby's, who sat next to her at the top table and regaled her with endless tales of silly horseplay on holidays with the Norrises at Broadstairs. He boasted about his promotion at the advertising company where he worked, and never once asked her anything about herself. All the time, she was wondering whether he meant his leg to be brushing against hers under the table. After she accidentally on purpose knocked her wine into his lap, he kept his distance.

Later, Helen tossed her the wedding bouquet – Mrs Foster's choice of pink roses, cornflowers and Queen Anne's

Lace. Nancy caught it and stared down at it in alarm, before passing it to Helen's schoolfriend Audrey, who'd recently become engaged, saying, 'Here. Your turn, I think.'

Marriage might seem a long way in the misty distance, but Nancy's life was not without romantic interest. After the field trip in the New Forest, any remaining awkwardness between the girls and the boys among the group of students melted away and during their second year they mostly became friends, lunching together, borrowing notes for missed lectures and laughing at practical jokes.

Nancy's special friends remained Peggy and the Annes, but this foursome being a lively and welcoming group they were often joined by others. In particular, there was a good-natured boy with a northern accent and an infectious laugh named Theo and a thin, studious, bespectacled lad named George, who fixed himself like a little dog on Peggy, to her surprise, but was too shy to take things further. And then there was James, who circled the group like a lone wolf and would only sometimes consent to sit among them.

He and Nancy hit sparks off one another, arguing ferociously while the others listened, hardly daring to intervene.

A particularly fierce disagreement was about which animals felt pain. Six of them were sitting in the men's bar at the end of the afternoon before going out to the cinema. James had started it by inexpertly squishing a spider. Nancy accused him of cruelty, James defended himself and the argument broadened.

'Obviously amoebae can't feel anything,' Nancy put in. 'They don't have a nervous system, just sense receptors. But shellfish do. If you nudge simple shellfish like limpets, they respond by clinging tightly to their rock.'

'That's not pain. You'll be saying next that a plant feels pain. That sensitive plant whose leaves curl up when you touch it.'

'Don't be ridiculous.'

'Yes, and then you'll be saying we shouldn't eat vegetables because we're hurting them.'

'You know I'm not saying that. You're just being annoying.'

The argument jumped on to the use of live mice in experiments. Nancy expressed pity for them. Even if they were killed humanely, she thought their use should be restricted. James argued strongly for unfettered use for the betterment of the human race. As ever, it was difficult to discern what his real opinions were. He simply liked being controversial. Then, as often happened, he suddenly lost interest in the argument altogether. Nancy, her face flushed with effort and eyes wide with passion, saw his gaze soften and his wolfish lips curve into a charming smile.

'You are infuriating,' she muttered and sipped her lemonade.

'Do stop arguing, you two,' Anne Durban sighed. 'It's so wearing.'

'If Nancy didn't answer back, we wouldn't argue,' James said, eyes glinting.

'If you weren't such a—' Nancy started, then sat back in her seat with a sigh.

She noticed how he treated Anne Durban differently, with gentle courtesy, but then Anne never got hot under the collar like Nancy. Instead, she merely stated her own opinions and listened to James or whoever express theirs before saying, 'Well, I might not be right, but that's what I think, anyway,' and moving on to talk of something else. Nancy couldn't stand by like that if she disagreed about an issue. She wanted to get to the truth. She knew that this was what made a good scientist, a refusal to let things go. And frankly she enjoyed a spirited argument. It made her feel alive.

James had once told her that she argued 'like a man' and said he intended it as a compliment, but it bothered her. Did Anne Durban argue 'like a woman', then? Would Nancy have to be 'like a man' in order to get on? *I'm just being myself,* she decided in the end, *and so is Anne being herself,* and she stopped worrying.

James irritated and fascinated her in equal measure. She resented how aware she was of him, always subconsciously looking for his tall figure in the eccentric long black coat he wore instead of a jacket, discarding it only on the warmest days. In the classroom, he sat at the back and she could sense his restless movement as he turned the pages of a book, the scratch of his shiny pen in his notebook.

And it became painful for her to notice how he looked at Anne Durban. He wasn't getting anywhere with her, though. Peggy had teased her about James' attentions and she had frowned, with an expression of distaste, though she'd said nothing, but nothing needed to be said. Anne was a popular girl with the boys, but said once that she was 'keeping herself' and that 'she'd know' when she met 'the one'. Clearly that wasn't James.

James never looked at Nancy that way, though he often sought her company and clearly felt comfortable with her. They were good-humoured rivals and often compared marks, for the pair were invariably top of the class. Sometimes the laurel crown went to Nancy, at other times to James.

Nancy had her own admirers. She was friendly with Edmund, though he wasn't around much outside class, which she thought a shame. The good-natured Theo was a more constant presence, and when he asked her at the beginning of second year to go to the theatre with him, she was flattered and spent time choosing the right dress for the occasion, a demure red and black plaid A-line style with a black velvet collar. She basked in Theo's warm friendliness. He made her laugh with his impressions of their lecturers and she enjoyed his insightful comments on the play.

Afterwards, they walked the dark streets to the Underground station and before they parted he took her hand and asked bashfully if he could kiss her, but she felt a flash of fear and hesitated and the moment was lost. She berated herself on the train home for letting the memory of Mr Hunter's unwanted attentions still stand in her way so many years later.

Theo did ask her out again and this time she did politely let him kiss her, but when she felt his tongue probe between her lips, she pulled away. 'I'm sorry,' she gasped, certain it was her fault. She'd overheard girls at school talk about kissing and how to manage noses and teeth, but now it had actually happened to her she found she couldn't relax. In the end, she got quite skilled at it, but her affection for Theo was lukewarm and he, too, seemed relieved when after several weeks she asked if they could go back to being friends. This physicality was almost something one had to get out of the way with men, she thought, after which you could feel comfortable together as pals. She rather envied Diana, who Anne Durban said prudishly was 'getting a reputation', but, seemed to enjoy herself very much while doing so.

Soon after Helen's wedding, Nancy heard that she'd passed her second-year exams with flying colours, beating James by two marks, which gave her great satisfaction. She'd enjoyed the year on the whole and had learned so much, but several things left her uneasy. The lecturers and support staff, bar one, took little notice of the students. The one she thought most warmly of, Mrs Hall, the motherly technician, performed many small acts of kindness for the students. She smuggled into the lab replacements for forgotten scalpels or broken petri dishes. Her boss, Miss Pick, would never have allowed this if she'd known. Mrs Hall also helped Nancy when she had a bad period, taking her to a side room and giving her a bottle of hot water wrapped in a cloth to cuddle against the pain.

Another disappointment was the content of the degree course. Professor Briggs was an entomologist, renowned internationally for his work on bees, and it had been natural for him to recruit other entomologists to the department. So although the undergraduate curriculum adequately covered the basics of Zoology, it would be difficult for graduate students at Prince's College to specialize in anything but insects, for there was no one to knowledgeably supervise them. For the moment, this didn't really bother Nancy. Time seems endless to the young and she had another year to go before decisions about the future needed to be made.

In the meantime, there were the summer holidays – eight weeks stretching out before her. One of these would be spent in the Welsh mountains near Porthmadog. There would be six of them: Anne Durban, Theo, Peggy, George, herself and James. The other Anne had been invited but had chosen to go to Italy with her parents instead. Aunt Rhoda had given Nancy some money for her birthday and, brushing aside her mother's worries that she'd fall down a mountain or find herself in 'a difficult situation' with one of the boys, she declared that she would go.

The cottage lay at the edge of a village in a high valley. Some mornings, once the mist burned off the hills, they could see the tip of Mount Snowdon in the distance, but more often than not it was hidden by dense cloud. George had borrowed a large shooting brake from an uncle, and drove it like a maniac, glowering over the wheel at other road users as he rounded the bends of the narrow mountain roads. The evening they arrived, everyone felt quite weak-kneed with relief as they got out.

It was Anne who proclaimed it 'a darling cottage', which is what they subsequently called it until its real name was forgotten. It was built of grey Welsh stone, its slate roof yellow with lichen. Inside, it was cold and dark and smelled of ashes, but once Theo got a fire going and defenestrated a few of the larger spiders it became cosy. The girls set about cooking sausages and potatoes on the ancient kitchen range, after which everyone was too tired to do much and went to bed, three in each of the two bedrooms, lying top to toe on the huge Welsh bedsteads.

The holiday felt to Nancy like perfect freedom. There were no parents or lecturers to please. They got up when they felt like it, ignoring the early morning habits of a local cockerel, and fell into bed when they were too tired for anything else. Most days, they trekked for miles across hillsides and through dank woodland. One hot afternoon, they ate a picnic tea on the rocky shores of a lake and, since there was no one else around, stripped down to their underwear and one by one plunged squealing into the clear, chilly water. Nancy undulated like an otter as she darted beneath the surface, keeping a professional eye out for water nymphs or fish, though finding little evidence of either. They avoided looking at one another when they emerged shivering, grabbing their clothes and dressing quickly.

The plan was to take turns to cook, but after a couple of disasters the girls ended up doing it all. The payback was in the pub where the boys bought the beer. Here they played cribbage until closing time, then back at the Darling Cottage James brought out a bottle of whisky.

The holiday was memorable for two particular reasons. First, it marked the occasion when, after months of shyness, George and Peggy finally got together after becoming separated from the others on an evening walk. They came back down the hill hand in hand, to the sound of the boys' teasing cheers.

The other was more serious, for it could have ended in tragedy. One morning towards the end of their stay, James rose unusually early and came in for breakfast announcing that Snowdon was clear of cloud and he, for one, was going to climb it. Only Theo and Nancy were eager to join him. George dropped them at a village below the mountain and arranged to come back later.

At first, all went well. The climb was strenuous but not too much so, but there came a point where they were halfway along a narrow ridge with sheer drops on either side and a thick mist suddenly engulfed them. Nancy dropped to her hands and knees and followed James' muffled voice calling instructions from ahead, but though she called behind her many times there was no answer from Theo. She and James reached the safety of a rocky outcrop, where they waited, freezing cold and anxious, but Theo did not appear. Eventually, the mist began to clear. James expressed a wish to go on and claim the summit, but Nancy talked him out of it. They both made their way down, Nancy in dread of what might have happened to their friend, only to find Theo waiting calmly at the bottom reading a book. He'd taken the decision without telling them to turn back rather than go on. Nancy was furious.

One way or another, though, the holiday had brought everybody closer. James was so annoying, Nancy felt, but she couldn't help being drawn to him. He was a spark of light to her, the one most up to her intellectual weight, and she felt alive when she argued with him. And sometimes in bed, as she lay waiting for sleep to overtake her, she tried to imagine what it would be like to feel his arms around her and his lips on hers.

Twenty

Stef saw from the window that the rain had eased. Fingers of pale sunshine illuminated the sitting room of Dragonfly Lodge, playing on Nancy's face, draining it of colour. The old lady seemed particularly tired this morning. Stef had had to ask more questions than she usually did to nudge her memories and establish how she'd felt about past events as they had happened. Everything Nancy described was so long ago, it was inevitable that she'd feel differently nearly sixty years later.

'A couple more questions and then we'll stop,' Stef said and Nancy agreed. 'Were you aware as a student of occasions when you were treated differently to the men? Did you ever experience a sense of injustice, for instance?'

Nancy thought for a moment, frowning, then said, 'We took a great many things for granted then which you'd find unacceptable now. I don't remember minding, for instance, about conventions of dress or not being allowed to buy drinks in the men's bar.' She chuckled. 'That small lounge we girls had to ourselves, I didn't like it. It had once been a laboratory, I think – it still had a horrid antiseptic smell – and we never spent much time there. But then there weren't many girls overall studying science, and since it was a science college, the authorities probably thought that it was all we needed.'

She sighed and went on. 'What I did object to was anything that constrained me intellectually. One of the lecturers used to joke that women were less intelligent than men because their brains were smaller. That made me angry. I put my hand up once and told him he was wrong. He had it in for me after that. He'd call me "the formidable Miss Foster" in a sneery voice. I didn't like that at all.'

'I should think not. Especially since you were often getting the best marks in the class.'

'Yes. It was difficult at home, too. My mother couldn't see the point of me continuing my studies after my undergraduate degree. I think she was proud of me in her own way, but she'd have been happier if I'd studied English Literature or Art History. She did say she was glad she could explain to people that it involved working with animals. Molecules or machines would have sounded far too masculine.' Nancy smiled, then reached out an arm for her crutches. The interview was over.

'The carer left some lunch for me in the fridge,' Nancy said. 'Perhaps you could heat it up – and find something for yourself.'

Stef assured her that she would have her own lunch at her

mother's but would be glad to prepare Nancy's and bring it in for her on a tray.

While she was in the kitchen, waiting for the plate of chicken and vegetables to heat up in the microwave, her eye was drawn to a small pile of post left on the worktop and she couldn't help noticing a letter left unfolded on the top. It was typed in an unusual italic font, which was strange, and because she felt protective towards the old lady she bent to look closer. Her eyes widened at the first line and she picked up the page and read it all with a growing feeling of concern. The letter was making a threat, there was no doubt about it. There was no envelope that she could see anywhere and the type was blotched as if by rain.

The microwave pinged so she laid the letter down. As she transferred the steaming dish to a tray, she considered what to do. Was the letter her business? Should she raise the matter with Nancy? Yes and yes, she decided. Nancy was elderly and injured and would be on her own until Aaron returned. And although she'd found it on top of other post, the sender may have delivered it to the house in person. She shivered.

After she'd settled Nancy with the tray on the sofa, she brought out the letter. 'Nancy, I'm sorry if you think I'm nosy, but when did this arrive?'

Nancy took the missive and glanced at it. She made an impatient noise and tossed it onto the sofa beside her. 'I found it on the mat this morning,' she said in a clipped voice, drawing the tray more securely onto her lap. 'It's nonsense, of course. Like the others.'

'The others?' Stef sat down opposite and regarded Nancy intently. 'What others?'

Slowly Nancy began to eat. She swallowed her first mouthful. 'It's nothing to worry about,' she said. 'There were several last year and Aaron took them to the police. They couldn't find out who'd sent them, but perhaps whoever it was got frightened off, because the letters stopped coming.'

'Nancy, this person wants you to leave your home. They're threatening you.' The threat was unspecified. '*Or you will regret it if you stay*', the letter said in slanted type.

Nancy shrugged and continued eating.

'Do you have any idea who might be responsible?'

'No, but the police didn't think it was my landlord. I don't know why they discounted him because I know he would like it if I left. I've a long lease, made with his predecessor, and this new man inherited the freehold. He lives a long way away so maybe the police believe it's unlikely to be him, since the letters have all been delivered by hand.'

'What are you going to do?'

'I'll show the letter to Aaron. Please don't worry about it, Stef.'

'As I said, I didn't mean to be nosy. I know we've only recently met but, well, I care, I suppose.' It occurred to her that this was true. She was becoming quite fond of Nancy.

'That's very sweet of you.' Nancy smiled and took a sip of water from the glass on the tray. 'But I don't like to bother people. I am used to looking after myself.' Her voice had a touch of steel.

'I didn't mean to imply otherwise.'

'And I do have Aaron. I had thought the matter had gone away, though. I don't like it. I don't like it at all.' It was as if she was talking to herself. 'It takes me back to that time ... No, there wouldn't be any connection ...'

'To ... ?'

Nancy roused herself, took a forkful of chicken, then hesitated. 'I'm being a silly old woman. Don't take any notice.'

Stef left the cottage reluctantly, but she didn't want to outstay her welcome. Aaron would be back later, she told herself. Surely Nancy would be all right until then.

She was therefore surprised when, sitting in her mother's kitchen that afternoon, renewing the batteries in her tape recorder, she received a phone call that proved her wrong. Nancy wasn't all right. She didn't recognize the number and answered tentatively. 'Hello? Who is this, please?'

'Stef, it's Aaron ... Harding.'

'Aaron!' she said, surprised, then concerned.

'My grandmother gave me your number. Listen, I know this is bad of me but I've a favour to ask. Rather a big one, I'm afraid.' He sighed.

'Yes?' she said cautiously, then, 'Is Nancy okay? Are you with her?'

'This is the thing. I can't be there today. My daughter's unwell and her mother's busy with something she can't cancel, so I'm in charge.'

'Oh, that's a shame.' Was Stef imagining the bitter undertone when he said his ex was busy? She picked at a thread on her shirt and her thoughts flew to poor Nancy. 'Can I do anything to help?'

'Ah.' There was relief in his voice. 'I'd be so grateful.'

I wouldn't be doing it for you, she thought. *It would be for Nancy.*

'The carer's coming in for a short while around seven, but Nancy sounded a bit distressed on the phone.'

'Really?' Stef straightened, alert.

'I gather you know about these mad letters.'

'Yes. Aaron, surely it's a matter for the police.'

'I agree, but there's nothing I can do about it today. Nancy wants me to go to the station with her when she's better and talk to them. It's just ... Stef, this is a big ask, but would you pop over and stay the night with her. She said she'd rather have you than some stranger.'

'Yes, of course I will.' She felt a rush of compassion. Obviously Nancy was more worried and vulnerable than she'd conveyed to Stef earlier. 'What time would she like me?' She'd planned to do a little more work this afternoon, but it wouldn't matter if she put it off.

'Well, this is it. As soon as you're able. I'm rather anxious about her. Stef, I'm sorry about this. I wouldn't have asked you, but Nancy says she'd feel comfortable with you.'

'I suppose I'm flattered in that case. Of course I'll go, Aaron. Please don't worry. I hope little Livy recovers quickly and then ...'

'If she's better tomorrow, and I think she might be, I'll bring her down with me. A couple of days off school wouldn't do her any harm. You can either sleep in my room or Nancy's, I expect you can sort that out with her. Plenty of linen in the airing cupboard. And there's a key under the mat.'

'Yes, I know.'

'I told her to lock the door with the duplicate but not to leave it in the lock. That way you should get in easily enough if she can't answer the door.'

'That's fine. Should I pick up some supplies?'

They discussed a short shopping list and then Aaron rang off. For a moment Stef stood frozen, phone in hand, her thoughts running this way and that. Poor Nancy, weaker and more frightened than she'd let on that morning, and seemingly without anyone else local she trusted enough to come. But a welcome change for Aaron to be speaking to Stef in a reasonable manner and relying on her help, rather than treating her as some sort of heartless fiend intent on exposing his grandmother's secrets to the world.

Necessity had changed his view of her, she supposed, as she slung a few essential items into her case and went out to the studio to tell her mother what was happening.

It was nearly five when Stef opened the gate to Nancy's garden. Although it had rained again during the afternoon, the clouds had since parted and the grey sky was patched with blue. The boardwalks were slippery underfoot, the wheels of her case skidding, and she was glad she'd worn her mac as the bushes she brushed against on the narrow path down to Dragonfly Lodge dripped with rain. As she passed the front window, she saw that Nancy was asleep on the sofa, so she trod softly. The heavy iron key was in its hiding place as Aaron had directed and she let herself in as quietly as she could. Not quietly enough, for as she propped her case against the wall she heard Nancy's voice call anxiously, 'Stef, is that you?'

She called back cheerfully, 'Yes, just me.'

'I feel a bit of a charlatan,' Nancy said as Stef entered the room. She was wrapped in a colourful throw and somehow looked small in its folds. 'It was when Aaron rang that I crumbled. I'd been so looking forward to him coming. Of course, he has to put Livy first, but honestly, Crystal can be demanding. I thought of you at once and that maybe you wouldn't mind. I find you so *sympathique*, you see. It's very good of you to come.'

'I was pleased to be asked,' Stef said, feeling rather touched by this speech. 'And I don't think you're a charlatan. You can't walk or do things properly and this morning's letter would have been a shock for anyone. And Nancy, I know what it's like living on your own and being ill. I always feel terribly sorry for myself, as though the world's forgotten me.'

'I didn't realize you lived alone. In fact, I don't know very much about you, Stef. We've spoken about me all the time. My mother would have been horrified at such appalling manners. She brought her daughters up not to talk about themselves. That was how women were then.'

Stef laughed. 'I can assure you, that attitude has gone by the wayside,' she said. 'Girls emote all the time about themselves on social media these days. It's the "me" generation. Can I make you some tea? I did a little shopping under

Aaron's instruction, so we can have some madeira cake courtesy of the Village Stores.'

'How marvellous,' Nancy sighed. 'Madeira cake is one thing that hasn't changed. If you like Earl Grey tea, which I do, the teabags are in the tin with the Taj Mahal picture on it.'

'I'm sure I'll find it.'

When she returned, the room had grown darker and, outside, the rain was coming down once more. It felt rather cold and cheerless all of a sudden, so she switched on a table lamp and under Nancy's direction lit a fire in the grate.

'There's something about fires that makes one want to tell stories,' Nancy sighed as they sat and watched the flames. 'But let's talk about you for a change. Tell me about yourself.'

As they drank their tea, Stef told Nancy about working as a journalist, about the book she'd had published the year before and how unpleasant some of the reactions to it had been. She explained that she'd lost her job on the paper and how renting on her own was a bit of a struggle. 'After I split up with Sam, I couldn't bear to go back to the flatsharing of my twenties. I'm a proper grown-up now,' she said, with a rueful smile. 'Thirty-one and the clock is ticking.' She screwed her face into a look of mock horror. 'Sam's refusal to contemplate ever having children was the main thing that ended our relationship.'

'You still have plenty of time, my dear. Oh, what I'd give to be thirty-one again.' Nancy sighed. 'Of course, I feel sixteen inside, but my body is finally beginning to admit that it's nearly eighty-one.'

'You're very fit,' Stef said softly. 'It's only because of your ankle that you feel your age. Once it's healed, I'm sure you'll be out and about again.' She remembered then what Aaron had intimated, that Nancy was being tested for dizziness, but she chose not to mention it. Instead, she said wistfully, 'Thirty-one feels old to me. I would like to have children one day and it feels as though time is running out.'

'Life is very different today.' Nancy regarded her with sympathy. 'That aspect is hard for young women who have a career.'

Stef was strangely grateful that she hadn't muttered the usual platitude: *You'll find someone soon, there are plenty more fish in the sea,* because there didn't seem to be, or they weren't her kind of fish. There was simply no guarantee that she'd find the right person. And she didn't want to spend her days worrying about something she couldn't do much about.

'Were you married by that age?' she asked.

'Ah, I'll tell you when we get to that part of the story,' Nancy said. She was no longer looking sympathetic or smiling, but rather tragic, and Stef felt a prickle of unease.

Nancy went on. 'Perhaps after supper and when the carer's been, I'll have a little more energy. I don't suppose you've brought your tape recorder?'

'I do happen to have it,' Stef said bashfully. 'A good journalist is always prepared!'

'And I'm sure you're a good journalist, dear.'

Stef gathered up the empty mugs and plates and took them out to the kitchen. The cat came and wrapped itself round her ankles, so she shook some kibble from a sack into its bowl and watched it crouch down stiffly to eat. Poor thing. Like its mistress, it was feeling its age.

The carer arrived. Lauren appeared to be a competent young woman. She claimed to be used to far-flung visits in the countryside and unfazed by the remoteness of Nancy's cottage. While she was helping Nancy wash and change into her nightclothes, Stef investigated the arrangements upstairs. She'd agreed with Nancy that it would be easiest to change the sheets on one of the big old single bedsteads in Aaron's room. She chose the one nearer the window. Judging by the unicorns on the duvet cover, this must be where Livy slept. A seasoned traveller, Aaron had left nothing visible of his or Livy's possessions, but the room had a faint woody scent of soap or aftershave as though he'd been there only a moment ago.

After she'd changed Livy's bed linen for a duvet set with a rose pattern and found a towel, Stef lay down on the bed for a moment to think, alert to the sounds of the house and the cheerful exchange of Nancy and Lauren's voices below.

Outside it was still light, but the rain fell relentlessly and being here, warm and dry in the cottage, far from the world, made her feel safe. Then she remembered why she was here – the threatening letter – and that made her feel less safe. She could understand Nancy not wanting to be out here on the reserve, injured and alone.

She gazed around the bedroom. It was odd being in the room where Aaron and Livy slept, intimate even, yet she couldn't pretend that she knew them. Still, the bed felt soft and unless Nancy needed help during the night, she should sleep well.

Footsteps; then, 'Stef?' Lauren called up the stairs.

'Coming!'

She hurried down to the sitting room to find Nancy in her dressing gown on the sofa with a cup of tea to hand, the fire stoked up and Lauren ready to depart. 'She's comfortable, aren't you, Nancy? Just a little dizziness, that's all.'

'Don't listen to her. I'm perfectly all right,' Nancy said curtly. Lauren merely smiled and said her goodbyes.

'People do fuss,' Nancy complained after the front door closed, 'but I really am all right.'

Stef thought she looked frail, but kept this to herself.

'I have to say that I'm glad you're here, though.' The old lady's eyes twinkled. 'Very glad. Now, did you sort out where you're to sleep?'

Stef assured her that she had.

'Good. Well, if you'd like to prepare yourself something hot to drink, perhaps we could make good use of the evening and I'll tell you the next part of my story.'

'Are you sure?' Stef asked. 'I don't want to tire you.'

'It's odd, but now I've started and it's all in my head, I don't want to stop. Does that make sense?'

Stef nodded enthusiastically.

Twenty-One

January 1950

The third year of her undergraduate degree was a hard one for Nancy. Final exams were approaching at Easter, followed by a term to write a special research thesis that was to contribute to her final mark. Nancy decided that her topic would be badgers, because she'd been so bewitched by them on the field trip at the end of their first year. This would necessitate further visits to the New Forest, but all that would have to wait until after the Easter holidays and there was much to focus on before that.

Their new subjects of study in the autumn term had included the anatomy, habitat and behaviour of mammals. All the students had found it fascinating to study this class of complex and familiar creatures to which they themselves belonged.

At the same time, Nancy despaired when Anne Southgate

claimed mammals to be her 'favourite' aspect of their studies because 'you could have relationships with them'. The girl even used her family Jack Russell's barking habit as an example of territorial behaviour in one of her assignments. The essay attracted a low mark, to Anne's dismay, but when Anne showed her the work in the refectory one Wednesday lunchtime in January, Nancy wasn't surprised, for phrases like 'Joey's annoying behaviour' and 'Mother says he's a naughty boy' were hardly evidence of a scholarly approach. Seeing James enter the refectory and anticipating his joining them at the table where she, the Annes and Peggy were sitting, Nancy pushed the wretched paper back to Anne, urging her to 'put it away, quickly'. She hated seeing the pain in Anne's eyes, but knew that if James got hold of the work he'd ridicule it mercilessly. They'd all learned from humiliating experience that James could spot academic weakness at a glance and skewer it without pity.

'What's up with you girls?' James said as he sat down with his tray, his plate heaped with extra-large portions of meat stew, boiled cabbage and mashed potato, swathed in gravy. 'You're not going to cry, Southgate, are you?'

'Honestly, James, all that food – you must have hollow legs,' Nancy remarked to deflect his attention.

James merely grinned and picked up his knife and fork. Having finished his first course, he attacked the generous slice of jam roly-poly, while the girls chatted. It being Wednesday and Games Afternoon, some of their cohort were off playing for the various college teams. Lectures and practicals continued regardless, however, those who weren't sporty being expected to share their notes with absentees.

That particular afternoon, though, something strange and unpleasant happened that was to darken Nancy's memories of her time at Prince's. At the end of the two o'clock Zoology lecture, Dr Hillman announced that there had been an electrical fire in their usual first-floor lab. Though it had quickly been put out, the room was still being aired and the damage assessed, and thus the afternoon's practical session would take place in a lab on the ground floor that was usually the preserve of postgraduates.

Accordingly, Nancy, Peggy, Raj and James trailed down the main stairs from the lecture room and turned left along the ground floor corridor, past several closed doors, stopping from time to time to check the room numbers.

Raj sniffed. 'It smells nasty down here.' He wrinkled his nose. 'Perhaps something has died.'

'That's a bit obvious in a Zoology department,' James said, his lip curling, 'but you're right, it's vile.' The others agreed.

As they approached the final door, just before the back stairs, the smell grew stronger. 'Oh, it's horrible,' Peggy cried, clamping her hand over her nose.

'I hope it's not coming from in here,' Nancy said as she turned the doorknob.

Their temporary lab, thankfully, smelled only of formaldehyde and rubber. It was a cramped, untidy room, most of the worktops occupied by glass tanks containing insects, machines humming and other paraphernalia. A male technician they hadn't seen before was laying out their afternoon's task on a central table. They were to examine muscle cell samples on slides through microscopes and to sketch and label what they saw. The technician was plump, bespectacled and a bit seedy. He spoke to James and Raj but barely met the women's eyes as they pulled out stools and sat at the worktop. In the face of such unfriendliness, Nancy wasn't even tempted to ask him about the evil smell. Soon, they were caught up in their work, chatting about what they saw through their microscopes and taking turns to borrow Peggy's pencil sharpener. The stink was forgotten.

It hit them once more an hour later when they emerged into the corridor. Nancy glanced to her left to where a flight of stone steps led down to a basement. 'Perhaps it's coming from down there,' she suggested and went to investigate.

'Shall we?' She reached for the handrail. The others were reluctant, but curiosity won out and they followed her down.

At the bottom, a dull black lino floor absorbed the weak flicker from a dying bulb overhead. Several doors ran away into gloom. The stink was overpowering.

'What's that?' Raj whispered. They'd all heard it, a faint wailing sound.

'Definitely animal,' Peggy said, her eyes huge in her pale face.

James tried the handle of the nearest door. It was locked. He bent and applied an eye to the keyhole, then straightened. 'I can't see a thing.'

The wail came again.

Further down the corridor came the sound of a door opening. They looked up to see another white-coated technician emerge, a set of keys clinking in his hand. He flinched when he saw the students. 'What are you doing here?'

'We, ah, wondered what the smell was,' Nancy gabbled. 'And we heard something. What's in this room?

'It's not your business,' the man growled. 'You're not supposed to be down here.' He glided towards them. The students retreated and fled up the stairs.

'He didn't have to be so unpleasant,' Peggy complained as they hurried along the ground floor corridor to the main door.

'We were trespassing, I suppose,' Raj sighed. He was always anxious about obeying the rules.

'How were we to know?' Nancy snapped as they walked out into the darkening quad. 'There weren't any notices.'

The late afternoon air was crisp and cold and they stood together tugging on coats and hats ready for their onward journeys. James and Raj started arguing over a book James had that Raj wanted to read, but Nancy barely heard them. She was thinking about their recent adventure.

'How can we find out what's down there?'

'Leave it, I should,' James sighed. 'The tech chap's right, it's none of our business. Some research project or other, I expect. We'd only stir up trouble. I'm off to the bar. Raj, fancy a jar?' Everyone knew that Raj didn't touch alcohol, but that didn't stop James teasing him.

'You have one for me, West,' Raj called cheerily to his departing figure, then he himself left, calling goodbye over his shoulder as he set off for the gate, one end of his long scarf flying. He cut a lonely figure. No one knew where Raj lived or what his circumstances were. Though everyone liked him, there was a barrier of politeness on both sides. He'd volunteered once that he'd been born in the Punjab and that was all anyone knew.

Nancy, waiting for Peggy to do up her shoelace, couldn't leave the subject of the Great Stink alone. 'I would like to know what happens down there,' she said, 'for peace of mind. Who should we ask?'

Peggy shrugged. 'Mrs Hall?' She picked up her satchel.

Nancy thought she was right. When the opportunity arose, she would ask their motherly technician.

Twenty-Two

It was a Friday lunchtime a week later and the Zoology building was deserted when Nancy crept down the back stairs, breathing through her mouth to avoid the smell. She hesitated at the start of the basement corridor and peered into the gloom, but, seeing no sign that anyone was about, felt in her skirt pocket for the key Mrs Hall had given her the previous day. Its paper label cited only a room number. It had taken Mrs Hall almost a week to get hold of it, and Nancy had had to promise to say if confronted that she herself had 'borrowed' it from the department office. 'Or I might get the sack,' Mrs Hall had warned her. The woman said she did not know what went on in this basement room, but had often wondered and worried about it.

The room was again locked, but the key rotated silently in a well-oiled movement and Nancy turned the doorknob and pushed. A wave of warm, foetid air at once struck her. She clamped a handkerchief to her nose and slid inside.

The room was dark and it took her a few moments to

adjust. The only light came from a point of red shining from a machine that was gently chugging on a worktop, but it was enough to illuminate the room. She found herself in a small laboratory, one side of which was taken up, floor to ceiling, by, she saw, several large wire cages. In each of these, many pairs of eyes gleamed at her through the gloom. The effect was eerie and troubling.

She stepped closer and, although the owners of the eyes shrank from her approach, she saw with a shock that they were cats.

'Someone's experimenting on them. We must do something,' she told the others, out of breath, after she found them in the refectory and described what she'd seen.

'That's the most awful thing I've heard,' Peggy gasped. 'Do you suppose it's allowed? I mean, does Professor Briggs know about it?'

'How should I know? I imagine not, though, surely.'

They stared at one another in horror. There must be rules about this, or if there weren't there should be. Nancy had once asked Mrs Hall about the small animals, rabbits and frogs, that they dissected in practicals and had been assured that they were obtained from reputable sources and killed humanely. None of them liked the idea of any animal suffering, but detailed examination of specimens was the way that Zoology, Biology and Medicine had to be taught. Cats, though, that was horrible on another level. And kept in such dreadful conditions.

'Look,' Nancy said fiercely, 'I'm going to do something.'

*

'You know I've always wanted a cat?' she said to her mother a few days later.

'No, you've never said that.' Her mother was preparing supper in the kitchen. 'A dog, you wanted a dog at one point and the answer's still no.'

Nancy shook her head. 'A dog, a cat, a pet of some sort.'

'We had rabbits and chickens during the war. That was more than enough work for me.'

'They weren't pets. We ate them. Anyway, we've got a cat now.' She opened her satchel and a skinny black cat, little more than a kitten, leapt out onto the table and looked about, dazed.

'Nancy! Get it off!'

'She's called Bonnie and I'll pay for her food.' Nancy picked up Bonnie gently, aware of a sore on the little cat's side.

'Absolutely not!' She'd rarely seen her mother so cross. 'We can't possibly have a cat. Who'll look after it? Especially now when we're getting a houseful again.'

Nancy had to acknowledge that her timing was poor. Her sister Helen had arrived pale-faced the weekend before to ask if she could move back home and bring Bobby with her. 'Bobby's parents are impossible,' she'd sobbed. 'His mother treats me like a servant. She makes me clean the house every day and never lets Bobby lift a finger. And you'll never believe it, she opens my letters from Sadie! She thought my penfriend was an American GI! She's mad!'

Mr and Mrs Foster had looked at one another in dismay.

'And I'm having a babeeee!' Helen burst into fresh tears.

'A baby! Two extra adults to feed and a baby?' Mrs Foster covered her face with her hands.

Bewildered by her mother's reaction to news of her first grandchild, Helen stopped crying and stared at her.

In the end, it was agreed that Helen and Bobby would move in temporarily, but only for as long as it took the couple to find somewhere of their own.

Nancy's cat was the last straw.

'It is not staying.'

'She is.' Mother and daughter locked eyes across the kitchen table. 'I rescued her and she trusts me. She's got nowhere else to go.' She'd told her parents about finding the cats but hadn't thought what would happen to them if they were rescued.

Bonnie snuggled into Nancy's lap and stared appealingly at Mrs Foster with unblinking blue eyes. Though alarmingly thin and with the sore patch, she had fur like black velvet and was very pretty. When the cats had been freed at the behest of Professor Briggs, Nancy knew deep-down she had to have one and Mrs Hall had brought her Bonnie in a cardboard box. She'd told Nancy that a local vet had arrived in a van to take the dozen others. He'd assured Mrs Hall that homes would be found, but from the expression on the assistant technician's face, Nancy feared otherwise. Some might be too poorly to survive. As she'd set off for home with Bonnie, another piece of jigsaw fell into place. Outside the college, she watched the unpleasant man from the basement hefting his possessions into a taxi. The news was that he'd been dismissed.

The foul miasma in the basement of the Zoology building might have lifted and the disgraceful episode be over, but Nancy had not acquitted herself well with the head of the department. Professor Briggs had been outraged when Nancy had presented herself in his office and criticized the running of his fiefdom. She had had to speak quite strictly to persuade him to follow her down to the depths of the building. It was plain that he'd never been there before, but then why would he? There was only a boiler room down there, or maybe store-rooms, he grumbled, not a research laboratory. And the long way down the steep flight of stairs was gruelling for a portly older man like himself. He was puffing like a steam train by the time they reached the bottom.

When he saw the cats, though, Nancy felt justified, for he, too, was horrified. However, rather than apologizing for disbelieving her, he told her sharply, 'I will deal with this, Miss Foster. Please do not mention it to anyone or the department might be brought into disrepute. If the matter gets out, I will know who to blame.'

Though incensed by his rudeness, she realized with relief that he would do something about the cats. Still, he might have thanked her, she thought as she left him.

In the end, Nancy also won the battle to keep Bonnie. Beaten by her daughter's stubbornness, her mother admitted that the dainty cat was 'quite sweet' and she was allowed to stay. Nancy often found them together in the evenings, her mother laughing as Bonnie played with the wool for the matinee jacket she was knitting for Helen's baby, while Helen herself slumped sick and exhausted next to Bobby on the sofa. Bobby's eyes were red and streaming. Such a shame that he was allergic to cats.

Twenty-Three

The spring term was passing at an alarming rate. As well as Nancy being given stacks of new work, revision for finals was pressing. If not attending lectures or practical sessions, she retreated to the library surrounded by books. When she and the others gathered for lunch, the talk was of their studies. At home, she shut herself in her bedroom and tried to ignore the sounds of Bobby and Helen arguing on the other side of the thin wall. Bobby was still adamant that they should save up for a deposit to buy a house, not waste money on rent, but this would take longer to achieve. Nancy knew that he wasn't paying his in-laws enough towards their keep, but that her parents had decided not to complain in the hope that it would help the couple to leave sooner. Helen was urging him to take a job in a firm that paid better, but he liked the one he had. The tension in the house was electric.

After the final exam, in the last week of the Easter term, the students were surprised, but not displeased, to find in their pigeonholes an invitation from Professor and Mrs Briggs to a supper party at their home the following Saturday. This was new. The professor had shown little interest in them up to now. Official social activities in the department had been limited to a drinks party each Christmas in one of the lecture rooms, an informal event to which the entire Zoo student body and all the staff were invited. It was a good-natured occasion with plenty of bread and cheese to soak up the wine, and Christmas crackers containing paper crowns and toy whistles, which led to silliness.

'I didn't even know there was a Mrs Briggs. Do you suppose it's going to be frightfully formal?' Anne Durban asked the others when they met in the bar. 'Only someone spilled red wine on my only good dress last weekend.'

'Oh, I shouldn't worry about what to wear.' Diana eyed her empty wineglass. 'He's hardly likely to throw you off the course now on a point of etiquette.' She reached for the bottle and slopped in some more. 'I'm drinking to forget,' she told the generality. 'That physiology paper was bloody.'

They all murmured agreement.

The conversation turned to the future. Most of the Zoology finalists were leaving in the summer, and although it was only Easter there was already a sense that their time together was ending. They wouldn't see so much of one another after the holiday because there was no more teaching and they would scatter to work on their individual projects.

'I can't believe it's almost over,' Anne Southgate sighed. 'Three years' work packed into my head and poured out on the page. I'll have forgotten it all by next week. Then it'll be great crested newts and nothing else till the summer. And after that? Who knows?'

'July and August off, then I'm looking for a job,' Peggy put in wistfully.

'I will be, too,' George said, sitting beside her. They smiled at one another. 'We've some news actually,' he added, blushing.

'We're engaged,' Peggy said bashfully.

Their corner rang with squeals of congratulations from the girls and hoots of derision from the boys. Sentimental tears sprang to Anne Durban's eyes. James gamely went to the bar to see if they had champagne, but returned disappointed. Nancy, sitting opposite Peggy and seeing her happiness, was glad for her. She liked George and wasn't surprised by the announcement – since that Welsh holiday, the pair had been inseparable – but she bit her lip against a tinge of disappointment, remembering Peggy's delight in her studies. Her ambition would likely now be swallowed up by marriage and children.

Nancy and Anne Durban were keen to stay on to do doctorates. Several of the boys were, too – James, definitely, Raj and, she suspected, Edmund. James would have to wait, though. He and most of the younger men were glumly viewing the prospect of eighteen months' National Service first. Edmund and Michael had already done their stint for their country and Raj, being of Indian nationality, was exempt. The remainder of the year's cohort would go out into the world to be schoolteachers or civil servants or, in wealthy Diana's case, who knew what. She intended, she said mysteriously, to travel and have adventures.

*

On Saturday evening, Nancy was among the last to arrive at the imposing red-brick mansion block in Kensington where the Briggses lived. She pressed the bell for Number One and leaned against a pillar, taking in the quietness of the wide street now bathed in early evening sunlight. When the door opened, she was admitted to an elegant hallway with a black and white chequered floor by a brittle young woman in a maid's white apron whom she recognized as one of the departmental secretaries. 'The Briggs flat is first door on the left,' the girl said sharply, clearly resentful of her role this evening. She ushered Nancy into a high-ceilinged drawing room that was already buzzing with polite conversation. Here she joined a circle of her fellow students. Glancing round, she thought they all appeared unnaturally smart. Except James, who was still wearing his black coat and who looked her up and down, making her feel she looked peculiar. In fact „she'd taken care to look her best this evening, in a calf-length midnight blue dress that she'd sewn herself and a diamanté brooch borrowed from her mother that reflected the sparkle in her eyes. She wanted to make a good impression, particularly on the professor, on whom her future would depend.

'Miss Foster, glad you made it.' The man himself appeared beside her, unusually affable and dressed in an ancient dress suit that smelled slightly of mothballs. He thrust a glass of wine into her hand and introduced her to his wife. Bridget Briggs, a small, quietly spoken woman with a faded prettiness, offered her a sausage roll from a plate with a doily and asked if she'd come far.

'I must have a private word with Miss Foster, my dear,'

the professor murmured and, taking Nancy's elbow, he drew her aside.

'I wanted to talk to you about next year,' he murmured, his breath a warm cloud of whisky, and she glanced up at him in wary surprise. 'You are planning to stay on, aren't you?'

'To study for a doctorate? Yes, I am,' she stuttered, flattered that he'd asked. 'If my results are good enough.'

'Oh, I'm sure they will be.'

Delight filled her. She stood straighter. 'I haven't thought of a precise subject yet. Does that matter?'

'Not necessarily. You must choose something entomological, of course.'

'I wondered if that might be the case.'

'It would suit us best if you did. Easier to find a supervisor in the department. I could advise you. In fact, I might take you on myself if I like your specialism.'

'I'd be very honoured, of course.' In truth, she wasn't sure what she really thought about that. Even though he'd appeared to have forgotten the cat incident, it was difficult to feel at ease with him. And would he have time to take an interest?

'I know mostly what the men's plans are, but what about the rest of you young ladies? Any among you who might be persuaded?'

'To . . . ?'

'Undertake doctorates, of course. What about Miss Durban?'

'Anne? She was talking of it, but you must ask her yourself.'

'Good, good. Any of the others? If you would encourage them, I'd be delighted.'

She met his rheumy gaze with troubled eyes, any feeling of being special dying within her. He picked a sausage roll from an offered plate and ate it in two bites, shedding greasy crumbs down his shirt front.

'I . . . I don't know about the others.' She tried to inch away without him noticing. 'I don't think so, but perhaps if their results are good they might change their minds.'

'Oh, don't worry too much about the results. A reasonable second will be enough.'

'But they'll need to be high enough to apply for grants . . .'

'I can write persuasive references.'

She was puzzled. 'It's encouraging,' she said, 'that you do want us girls. I know someone – I won't say who – well, she applied to a different university and got nowhere.'

'Goodness, I don't mind ladies. If they don't go off in the middle of their course to start families – that's always a danger.' His eyes twinkled. 'Bit of a waste. You're not like that, are you, Miss Foster?'

She stared at him in consternation. 'I . . . I don't think so. It's not my plan at the moment, anyway.'

'Good. Listen, we'll talk about this matter again. I suppose I ought to circulate or Mrs Briggs will be annoyed. It's her idea, this little supper, you know.' And with that he wandered off to speak to Edmund and Michael, who were conversing with Dr Hillman and Dr Lansdale and wolfing down vols-au-vent from a table laden with party food.

Nancy, feeling disgruntled, joined a circle where James was holding forth. She stood quietly, sipping her wine and barely aware of what he was saying; some joke about an elderly scientist who'd muddled his specimen jars. There was, she mused, something wrong with Professor Briggs' approach to recruiting graduate students. Surely it was his duty to engage only the best and brightest of the final year's cohort. If initially she'd been flattered that he'd singled her out, had believed it was because he thought her special, now she thought that he was simply using her to boost finances. She remembered how, at the beginning of the first year, Edmund and Michael had explained that the reason Briggs admitted so many women was in order to build up his department. This approach, then, obviously didn't just apply to undergraduates. Did he actually believe in her abilities as a scientist? Would he support her in her studies? She had no idea. It was very undermining.

The others broke into laughter, bringing her back to awareness, but she'd missed the punchline to James' story.

'You're in a brown study, Foster,' James commented. 'Has something happened?' He leaned and whispered, 'You were very cosy with the prof there.'

'I assure you it wasn't cosy.' She was watching Briggs with the group of men across the room, all laughing at some remark. 'He is odd, isn't he?'

'In what way?'

'Oh, I don't know. He was asking about my plans for next year, then he made me feel I'm just a number.'

'Well, trust me, if you do stay on you should keep in with him.'

She stared at James, wondering what he knew, but he merely smiled and said nothing. James, too, could be infuriating. He liked to give the impression that he was one step ahead of everyone else. And he often was. He had a way of finding out things. It was easier for him, being a man, she thought crossly. It meant he was able to start up conversations with the lecturers, hang out with doctoral students in the bar, which she, as a woman, couldn't even enter by herself.

There were other things. If she was brave enough to join a group of older male students, she was incensed by the way they often shifted the conversation down a level. Instead of continuing to discuss something interesting like department politics or the best way to apply for research grants or the reproductive habits of honey bees, someone would make a flirtatious remark or ask something patronizing such as whether girls felt 'squeamish' about dissection. When that happened, Nancy always steered the conversation firmly back to serious matters and enjoyed seeing the astonished look on the men's faces when she offered an informed opinion. The other women didn't appear to mind these male ways, or were too polite or too nervous to make a stand, but she did mind and was not afraid to assert herself. She imagined that some men thought her blunt, but why shouldn't she be herself?

Twenty-Four

It was after nine and the fire in Nancy's sitting room had died to glowing embers. Dragonfly Lodge lay in shadow. Outside, the rain was coming down heavily. Stef was glad she didn't have to go back to her mother's house that evening.

At Nancy's behest, she rose, drew the curtains across and turned on the lamps so that the room felt cosy. Lauren, she noticed, had folded down the duvet on Nancy's bed and tidied the bedside table.

'Would you mind checking on the menagerie?' Nancy asked. 'Then a tot of brandy would be very nice.'

The sky was thick with cloud, but there was still some light in the sky when Stef found an umbrella by the back door and crept out into the rain. The cat slipped out with her and limped off into some bushes on some business of its own.

Stef stepped over the puddles and unbolted the door of the outhouse. Inside, she went from cage to cage in the gloom.

The hedgehogs in their runs on the ground were awake and rustling about, but all appeared well so she retreated. Outside, she hesitated a moment, noticing the twilit Broad shrouded in mist, listening to the sounds of the rain pattering in the trees and gurgling down the drainpipes. Apart from that, all was reassuringly quiet. Surely there would be nothing tonight to threaten or disturb.

She called, 'Tabitha! Tabitha?', but the cat did not reappear. Either she'd gone back inside already, Stef thought, or would find her own way through the cat flap later.

That night, in Livy's bed, Stef woke in pitch darkness, prickling with nerves. She lay still with eyes open, listening to the steady fall of the rain and wondering what had disturbed her. The room was quiet apart from a clock ticking. And then came a sound, a distant moan. *Nancy*, she thought, and sat up, throwing back the duvet. She listened. There it came again, the moan rising to a cry.

She fumbled for the lamp switch, then, dazzled, reached blindly for her dressing gown. Out on the landing, the lamplight threw shadows on the wall, but all was silent. There came another cry, louder this time, and she padded down the stairs, her eyes adjusting to the dimness. The sitting room door was shut, with no telltale line of light showing. She knocked softly and pushed it ajar.

'No, no, no!'

'Nancy?' Stef whispered. 'Are you okay?'

A muttered answer. Stef could make out the lines of the bed, the pale face of the figure lying in it, restless, fingers plucking at the duvet. Nancy was asleep and dreaming. Then suddenly her eyes fluttered open. 'Yes? Who's that?'

'Just me, Stef. I'm so sorry, I've woken you. I heard you talking and ...'

'Talking? What did I say?' She struggled to sit up.

'Let me ...' Stef stepped forward to assist. 'I didn't hear what you were saying, just worried that you needed something. You were obviously dreaming, I realize that now.'

'I don't remember ... I'd like some water. Bit dizzy.' Nancy seemed confused.

Stef passed her the tumbler from the table, then helped her get comfortable.

On her way back to bed, she thought to get herself a drink and opened the kitchen door carefully in case Tabitha got out. But there was no soft, purring body trying to escape and when she switched on the light, she saw that the kitchen was empty. Still out in the rain, she imagined as she ran water into a glass. She switched off the light and stood in her bare feet peering out of the window as she sipped it. A faint glow from her bedroom lamp threw light across the garden, but beyond the perimeter fence the reserve lay in thick darkness. It felt so remote out here, the night air chilly from the Broad. Stef thought of that stretch of water behind the cottage swelling with rain, lapping against the shore, perhaps creeping up towards the fence. And remembered a teacher telling them at school that the great network of man-made lakes and waterways that constituted the Broads connected up ultimately to the sea and were therefore subject to the tides. Nancy had said that flooding hadn't been much of a problem here, but one never knew. Stef shivered, wriggling her toes to get warm, then checked the cat flap to see that it swung cleanly before going back up to bed.

She must have slept deeply because the next thing she knew was Lauren's arrival at eight. The rain had stopped. By the time she was up and dressed, Nancy was eating break-fast from a tray on the sofa and Lauren was making the bed. Nancy glanced up anxiously as Stef entered and Stef noticed that her hair, though combed, wasn't elegantly tied back, but hung around her shoulders. She returned Stef's good morning, though, then said, 'I'm worried about the cat. She hasn't come in for her food.'

Stef frowned. 'I let her out before I went to bed, but haven't seen her since.' She went outside to look, but though she called repeatedly the only sign of life was the singing of the birds in the trees.

After Lauren left with a promise to return that evening, Stef helped Nancy to visit the outhouse to feed and check on the wildlife, then put the kettle on for coffee. While she was waiting for the water to boil, she heard Nancy's phone ring and Nancy answer it.

'That was Aaron,' Nancy informed Stef when she carried in the coffee. 'Livy is much improved, thank heavens, but not well enough to return to school. I told him to stay in London, but he's insisting on coming. They'll be arriving soon after lunch.' Her eyes shone and she looked much stronger than she had earlier. 'That's marvellous. And it means we'll have some time to chat this morning. If you're happy to stay, that is.'

'If you feel up to it.'

'I certainly do.'

Stef quickly rang her mother to say that she'd be home early in the afternoon, then she and Nancy settled down with the tape recorder running, and Nancy began to talk, picking up where she'd left off.

Twenty-Five

London
July 1950

The summer after she graduated was a time of great happiness for Nancy. At the start of July, a little nephew, Andrew, was born and Nancy accompanied her parents to the hospital for a brief first viewing. The tiny, red wrinkled baby yelled the whole time and Helen looked pale and puffy under her make-up, her fair prettiness quite gone.

Poor Helen went through 'the baby blues'. She stayed in hospital crying for days after the milk came in, until she was sent home, where her doctor gave her 'a good talking to'. After that, she got herself up and dressed to make Bobby's breakfast every morning, 'as was only right'. But Mrs Foster, visiting, reported that 'her eyes looked dead' and she was worried about her. Bobby's mother was 'making things worse' because she kept 'giving unwanted advice' and her high standards were 'impossible' for her daughter-in-law to meet.

After she'd handed in her project, Nancy visited Helen and Bobby's new house in the South London suburbs on several occasions. She learned how to hold little Andrew without dropping him and became quite fond of him. She enjoyed taking him out in the big Silver Cross pram Aunt Rhoda had bought but baulked at changing nappies. Thankfully her mother and Bobby's were often in evidence to do this and various household tasks, glaring at one another territorially over the twin tub when their visits coincided.

Nancy felt sorry for her sister, but her attention was elsewhere. Aunt Rhoda had found her a holiday job working in the stockroom at Liberty's. This occupied her days and enabled her to save some money.

At the end of July, an official-looking letter arrived addressed to her. She opened it with trembling hands and gave a cry of joy. She had been awarded a first-class degree! Shortly after this came another piece of good news – her application for a grant to continue her studies had been successful. Now, at last, she could afford to leave home. Grown-up life would begin.

Towards the end of August, a letter from Professor Briggs caused her momentary disquiet. Although he'd agreed to be her supervisor and she was allocated space in a lab at the college to start work on her doctorate in the autumn, the letter advised her that there would be a point, as yet unknown, when she would be required to move out of London to a research station in Hertfordshire. Brandingfield Park, the place was called.

Nancy had heard about the professor's pet project before, the whole department had, but she hadn't realized that the plans were so advanced. This was the one that would make his name. The gossip was that it was where much of the money – student fees and grants – was being channelled. The professor's letter confirmed that it involved a partnership with the chemical company ICP, who would also be using the building. *Interesting*, she thought, folding the missive away. She wondered what her own role would be there, whether her research might feed into some bigger project. That might be exciting. The upheaval of moving would be a nuisance and she might have to find digs nearby, but it was too soon to worry about that yet. She would begin her doctorate at Prince's College.

One sunny Saturday in mid-September, her brother helped her move into the graduate hostel opposite the college.

'I don't think that policeman likes Daddy's car being left there,' Nancy remarked from the window seat to Roger, who'd arrived out of breath after climbing the stairs with yet another box of her books. She was gazing down at the busy street.

'I'll shift it in a moment,' he said shortly. 'There we are, lazybones.' He dumped the box on the floor.

'I'll start unpacking,' she called after him as he marched out to bring the next load.

Her room in the women's hostel faced the gateway of the college. The four-storeyed, white stuccoed building had once been a grand house for a large family with many servants, but was now a rabbit warren of odd-shaped student bedrooms. Nancy's, up two flights of the elegant staircase, was high-ceilinged with shelved alcoves on either side of a handsome marble mantlepiece, where a modern gas fire had replaced the old grate. The room was simply furnished with a mahogany wardrobe that smelled of camphor, a plywood desk and chair and a chest whose drawers had jammed. A note left above the hand basin by the previous inhabitant explained the idiosyncrasies of the hot water geyser. Despite these glitches, the room was twice the size of her bedroom at home and she already loved it.

She watched Roger below for a moment, arguing with the police constable, then stepped down from her perch and started pulling books out of boxes and piling them on the wooden floor. She'd arrange them properly later, she thought, hearing Roger's heavy tread on the stairs. And beg a bit of candle from the kitchens to rub on the drawer runners to ease them fully open so that she could unpack her clothes.

'This is it,' Roger gasped, dumping two bulging suitcases. 'I'll shift the car to please PC Plod, then let's get some lunch.'

'Thanks, Rog. See you downstairs in a moment. I must just see if Anne's moved in.'

Anne Durban, she'd already discovered from Mrs Cherry, the hostel warden, had, by a happy coincidence, been allocated Room 21, two doors down from Nancy.

'So we're neighbours!' she exclaimed when she found Anne sitting at an identical desk to her own, writing a letter to her aunt.

'Must dash this off, as my uncle will be back in a moment. He gave me ten pounds from her. Awfully generous.'

'I won't stay. Roger's giving me lunch. He's been offered articles with a solicitors' firm in the Strand and wants to treat me.' Nancy glanced round Anne's room, thinking how tidy everything was – the books and clothes already put away, framed photographs arrayed on the mantelpiece. Anne was still scribbling, so Nancy stepped closer to see who they were. Her parents – Nancy had met the genteel vicar and his wife once or twice when they'd come to see Anne – and a snapshot from some college field trip. It was of Anne laughing, a frog sitting on her upheld palm. And close by her, Nancy saw, feeling suddenly wan, was the brooding figure of James.

'Where was that taken?' she said lightly.

'The New Forest – don't you remember?'

'The summer of our first year?'

'Yes. George took it. Don't look at me like that, Nancy.'

'Like what?'

'Accusing. It doesn't mean anything, you know.'

'I don't know what you're talking about.'

Anne rolled her eyes. 'James. You like him. I can tell.'

Nancy stared at the picture and felt her face grow hot. 'I . . . didn't think it showed.'

'Nancy, the pair of you argue like hammer and tongs, but the way you look at him it's impossible not to see it.'

'I don't think he likes me in that way,' she said mournfully. 'It's you, I've always thought.'

'Rubbish.'

'Honestly.'

She met Anne's eye in quiet despair. Anne looked calmly back at her. 'He had a thing about me once, but I put him off. He's not my sort, Nancy. Too ... interesting. I want someone steady and reliable. There's a boy at home, Gerald. We've known each other for years. If he ever asked me ...'

Nancy was surprised to see pain cloud her friend's eyes. All the time she'd known Anne, she'd never suspected this secret longing. On the surface, Anne was serene, rarely ruffled. Nancy had always understood why James should have been drawn to her. She'd seen men – and women, too – turn in the street to stare at the girl's quiet beauty.

'Anyway, I must finish this.'

Nancy returned to her room to fetch her coat, deep in thought. All this time, these three years, she'd kept her feelings about James hidden, had hardly dared acknowledge them even to herself. And now, it appeared that others had noticed – well, Anne had. And perhaps they pitied her. She blushed at the thought as she buttoned her coat.

Anne didn't pity her, she'd been sympathetic. And she had revealed her own hopes and fears. Nancy felt a rush of affection for her. But if Anne didn't love James, it didn't help much because there was no real sign that James was interested in her, Nancy. How did you make men love you? Nancy had no idea. Anne had the sort of beauty that drew men to her. Diana had flirted outrageously. Peggy hadn't, and wasn't pretty exactly, yet George had spotted something in her that answered something in himself.

Nancy had no idea how to flirt, nor the confidence to try. She'd decided she was nice-looking in a dark, intense sort of way, but no beauty. She was argumentative and had brains. Both these things, it seemed, put men off.

Oh well, she thought, as she locked the door to her room, she could forget about romance for the moment. James was square-bashing somewhere. He'd be sent to Germany, maybe, or Korea if he was unlucky. She was free of him for eighteen months, though she'd promised to write. *I'll get on with my studies,* she thought as she ambled downstairs to meet Roger, *and be miles ahead of him when he gets back!* The prospect brought a feeling of guilty pleasure.

Twenty-Six

Stef was washing up after lunch on Friday while Nancy rested and was brooding over the morning's interview. The old lady had spoken very tenderly about her conversation with her friend Anne, and Stef sensed that its revelations had formed a pivotal moment in Nancy's emotional life.

Up to today, Nancy had spoken in a guarded way about her fellow student James West, focusing on her relationship with him as a fellow scientist. Stef had gauged that while she had been attracted to him, she had not been nursing an unrequited love for the young man.

Now she knew otherwise. It must have been hard, extremely hard, for Nancy to have spent so much time with James while knowing that he preferred her friend. Stef knew that she'd have to write about the matter. Although these interviews were an examination of Nancy's professional career, she could hardly ignore matters of the heart when they were pertinent.

Her thoughts were interrupted by the squeak of the garden

gate and she guessed that Aaron and Livy were arriving. She quickly dried her hands and flew to the front door to let them in. Aaron was carrying two laden holdalls, but stood back to let Livy enter first. Livy's eyes were bruised with tiredness. She was wrapped in a fleece throw and clutched a large ragdoll with thick dreadlocks tied up with ribbon. She smiled weakly in response to Stef's greeting and said graciously that she was 'a bit better, thank you.'

'Nancy may be asleep—' Stef started to say, but too late. Livy had pushed open the sitting room door and went at once to snuggle next to her great-grandmother on the sofa. Nancy straightened, dazed and blinking, and hugged the child close.

'How lovely to see you, darlings.'

'How are you feeling, Gran?' Aaron bent to kiss her.

'Surviving,' Nancy said, patting his hand, 'but all the better for seeing the two of you! Though Stef's been marvellous. I don't know what I'd have done without her.'

Aaron switched his attention to Stef, who was watching from the doorway and feeling on the edge of the cosy family scene.

'Yes, Stef, thank you so much.' There was genuine warmth in his smile.

'It's been a pleasure. Your grandma's been very hospitable. I slept in your bed, Livy, I hope you don't mind. It was very comfy.' She'd already changed the linen.

'I don't mind,' Livy sighed, a tiny princess robed in her throw.

'Well,' Stef said brightly. 'I'll leave you all to get on. Goodbye, Nancy.'

Nancy thanked her profusely and made her promise to visit the following day. When Stef went to pick up her case Aaron followed her out to the hall.

'I really am immensely grateful,' he said quietly, his arm reaching past her to open the door. 'I can't think what I'd have done without you, in fact.'

She looked up at him and smiled. 'I've loved it.' They were standing so close in the narrow space, she could see the sun from the fanlight glint on the hairs of his rough-shaven jaw. As she moved past, she became aware of his soapy scent. On the doorstep, she paused. 'Oh, one thing. The cat has gone missing. I let her out last night. I hope it's not my fault.'

'We'll have a look,' he said. 'The poor mog's so old anything could have happened.'

'Yes, I hope she's all right.' They looked at each other and a distressing thought struck her.

'You don't think the letter writer . . .'

'No, surely not,' Aaron murmured. 'But I hope Tabitha hasn't . . .'

'Me, too,' she said swiftly. 'It's the last thing Nancy needs.'

'I'll keep an eye out.'

She turned to go.

'Stef . . .' Aaron said hesitantly. 'May I ring you later? I thought if things were peaceful here, perhaps we might meet for a drink at the Ilex Tree this evening. If you're free, that is?'

Stef stared out at the brooding sky. Did she want to have a drink with Aaron? She bit her lip. Not if he was going to berate her for betraying Nancy's secrets.

'I just thought it would be nice.' His smile was uncertain. 'To say thank you.'

'All right.' She grinned.

'Maybe seven-thirty. I'll text to confirm.'

There was no sign of Aaron inside or out when Stef arrived at the pub that evening. The pub garden felt a bit cool after the recent rain, so she went back inside, smiled at the barman and sat down at a table with comfortable chairs in a sheltered nook to wait, glad of a moment to collect her thoughts.

How different one's mood could make a place. Last time, the old-fashioned oak panelling and the horse brasses decorating the walls had hardly registered. Tonight, the place hummed with conversation and felt friendly and welcoming. She was just wondering whether to order a drink when Aaron arrived. He saw her wave from her corner and with a look of relief came at once to join her.

'Apologies,' he sighed, sitting down. 'Lauren the carer was late and then . . . well, everything took longer than I thought.'

'I can imagine. Don't worry. How's Livy?'

'Upset about the cat.'

'Still missing?' Stef was concerned. 'I can't help thinking it's my fault. Maybe I shouldn't have let her out.'

'She's usually free to go in and out at night, so don't blame yourself, please. I expect she'll turn up. One way or the other.'

'It really couldn't be the letter writer, could it?'

'I very much hope not,' he said feelingly. 'I've reported the letter to the police, by the way. Emailed them a photograph of it. Who knows what they'll do, if anything.' His face was grim, but he made an effort to cheer up. 'Now, what'll you have?'

Aaron stepped over to the bar, where he chatted amiably with the barman. She found herself viewing him as a stranger might, seeing a slim, averagely attractive, youngish man in dark jeans, a navy linen jacket and polished boots and with a scruff of dark hair. But he was more than that, she decided. She liked his quiet laugh, the way he used his hands as he spoke to the barman.

At Nancy's talk in the visitors' centre, she'd seen him tense with concentration and ever since either frowning angrily as he defended Nancy or miserably anxious after his grandmother's accident. Which one was the real Aaron? All of them, probably.

'What are you smiling at?' he said as he returned, bearing two foaming beer glasses and a large packet of crisps.

'Oh, private thoughts. Not very interesting. Salt and vinegar, yum.'

When he smiled back, his brown eyes narrowed, slight crow's feet crinkling. He'd taken the trouble to shave this evening and his deep blue shirt suited his dark hair and tan. She watched him split open the crisp packet and push it between them, took a crisp and sipped her drink, then sat back, wondering warily if this really was just a friendly drink or whether he had an agenda.

The former, it seemed, though he genuinely wanted to know how she thought his grandmother was. 'She's frailer,' he said, in a worried tone. 'This injury has knocked the stuffing out of her. And the dizziness. That's not good.'

'Obviously I didn't know her properly before, Aaron. She's still herself, isn't she?'

'Very much so. Stubborn as a mule!' His eyes shone. 'Lets Lauren do the minimum and is commendably strict with my daughter. Told Livy she can watch television for an hour, then it's upstairs to bed. And Livy's quite happy with that. Funny, she plays up with me like anything!'

'Winds you round her little finger, right?' Stef grinned.

'She tries to.' His expression was soft.

'I can see you're mad about her. She's a lovely girl.'

He sighed. 'She is, but she's had a bum deal with the divorce, being shifted from pillar to post. Crystal ... well, I don't like to say this ... she adores her but treats her like a little adult. You know, lets her stay up and mix with bohemian friends, rarely says no to her. It's one of the things we argued about when we were married. I was too old-school apparently.'

Stef nodded. 'Not having kids, it's difficult for me to comment. My sister's twins are gorgeous but they give her the runaround. They've got each other, you see, so if one is up to mischief the other joins in.'

'They do the twin thing! Do they have their own language?'

'I don't think so, but they seem to know each other's thoughts. They're coming tomorrow, actually. D'you think we should get them together with Livy or are they a bit young for her? They're four years old.'

'We could try. She doesn't know any kids round here so it's a bit lonely for her.'

'Well then, would you like to ask—' She stopped, taken by surprise at how naturally they'd been conversing.

'Is there something wrong?'

She shook her head, then laughed. 'Quite the opposite. You . . .' She hesitated, trying to find the words. 'You're different this evening, if you don't mind me saying. Nicer.'

'Ah!' He sat back in his chair and sighed. 'I've been a bit of a bastard, haven't I? And you've been so kind to Nancy. I don't know where to put myself. Still, you can't blame me for taking care of her. I don't like what you're doing.' His tone was casual, but was there a hint of something harder?

'What I'm doing?' she echoed, trying to gauge his mood.

'You're trying to get her to trust you.'

That glint of steel. She breathed.

'She wants to talk to me, Aaron. And once I hear all she has to say, I'll make a judgement. I won't reveal anything that would mean she gets hurt. Why would I do that?'

'Because it's your job. Journalism, writing exposés. That last book of yours, the trouble it caused. It's my job, too. I'm a documentary film-maker. I know the importance of a good story and getting to the truth behind it.'

She sighed. 'Convince me, Aaron. I don't understand what you're talking about here. What is Nancy's great secret that you're so worried I'll write about?'

'Keep your voice down,' he whispered, glancing around. No one else, however, appeared to be listening. 'Look, I don't know the details, but it's partly to do with an old relationship she had.'

'With whom?' Stef's eyes widened in surprise. She waited, but he only sighed.

'Listen, I'll get us more drinks first.' He waved away her offer to pay, pushing back his chair.

When he returned with fresh drinks, she saw a different Aaron again, one concerned and anxious. He smoothed back his hair, then took a long draught of beer.

'Nancy hasn't said much about her relationships,' she said to encourage him, 'or indeed about her marriage. I know she had a child. Obviously.'

'My mother. Sadly, she and Nancy don't see much of each other.'

'Are they estranged?'

'I don't completely understand the narrative myself, but Mum dropped out of school at fifteen. Became your typical hippy flower child. I never met my father. He was some bloke she hung out with for a while in a London squat, then lost touch with afterwards.' He sighed. 'My grandfather apparently was heartbroken. He died when I was small and I didn't see much of Nancy when I was growing up.'

'That's really sad.'

'Yes, it is. Nancy hasn't told me very much about when she was younger, just that there's this man from her past. He's a very well-known scientist apparently – a giant in his field. I don't know who he is. It's not a world I'm familiar with. The thing is, he's very litigious and he has powerful friends. In fact, I don't fancy the chances for your book if you reveal whatever it was he did.'

'So you don't actually know who he is or what happened?'

'No.'

She stared at him, nursing her glass, her thoughts whirling, then smiled.

'What?' He met her gaze, his eyes troubled.

'Are you jealous?'

He wrinkled his brow. 'Jealous of who?'

'Me. That Nancy is telling me stuff that she hasn't told you?'

'God, no.' His words lacked sincerity.

'You are,' she said, teasing, then frowned at her thought. 'Why d'you think she hasn't opened her heart to you about this?'

'I've literally no idea.'

'Perhaps,' she said carefully, 'it's because you're a man and she thinks you wouldn't understand.'

He blinked and considered this, but said nothing.

Stef couldn't help feeling a pang of victory, but then that faded. She mustn't make an enemy of Aaron. She didn't want to, that was certain, not when they'd started to get on well. A shame, she thought, looking down at her hands, that there was this antagonism between them, as she had to admit that she was beginning to find him very attractive.

They sat in silence for a while, then he asked her if she'd already eaten. She had, she said. She'd had supper with her mother to keep her company. She didn't add that it was partly to keep a clear head so that she wouldn't make a fool of herself.

'I'll have something later. Another drink?'

'Something soft. I'll get them.'

Up at the bar, waiting to be served, a text pinged on her phone and she glanced casually at the screen. It was from Pippa. She frowned and clicked on it, then stiffened. She paid for the drinks without noticing what she was doing and carried them back to the table as if in a dream.

'I can't stay long,' she told Aaron, sinking into her chair. 'My sister's arriving at any moment.'

'I thought she wasn't expected until tomorrow. Is something wrong?' he asked, concerned.

'You could say that.'

She explained that Pippa had left her husband.

Twenty-Seven

It took over an hour for Stef to get Jack and Jess into bed. Pippa had arrived with them at nine-thirty and, attuned to the fact that something was wrong, the twins whinged and fought for their mother's attention. Pippa was a heap of misery and hardly responded, so Stef took the children outside to the field, where for twenty minutes they ran around agreeably enough in the wet grass with Baxter and a tennis ball. By the time she'd given them a bath and hot chocolate, they were getting sleepy, so she herded them into bed, playing Solomon to the impossible judgement of who should occupy the upper bunk. Jack, on top by virtue of promising to lend Jess a particular computer game, fell asleep in the middle of the story Stef read them, leaving Stef to soothe Jess, who'd more immediately picked up that something in her world wasn't right.

'Why's Mummy so cross?' she asked. 'She told Jack to "shut up" and that's rude.'

'She's upset about something, darling. Sometimes when we're upset we say or do things we don't mean.'

'What's she upset about?'

'I don't know exactly, but it's nothing that you or Jack have done.' Stef wondered whether to tell Jess anything further, but decided against it. How did one speak to four-year-olds about parental squabbles? She didn't know. She and Pippa had been older when their parents' marriage deteriorated.

There was so much about parenting she didn't know. She drew the curtains against the darkness, thinking how exhausting it was and perhaps she wasn't cut out to be a mother. She kissed Jess goodnight, plugged in the nightlight and withdrew, careful to leave the door ajar at Jess' insistence.

Downstairs, there was an atmosphere of gloom. Pippa, grey-faced, sat curled up on the sofa with a cup of tea. She looked up briefly at Stef's entrance and enquired after the twins in a distracted fashion while their mother watched her, dismayed. Stef sat down gingerly next to her sister and said mildly, 'So what's all this about?', at which point Pippa dissolved into such a flood of tears it was as though a dam had broken.

Her story poured out. She and Rob rarely saw one another. He lived another life in London during the week, a more exciting one, while she was left in Norwich looking after the kids. She didn't know what he was up to but worried that there might be someone else. And she'd met someone at the gym – not that she'd let it go anywhere, mind you, but it was nice to flirt. Anyway, Rob had arrived home early this evening and found the house in a mess and they'd had a terrible row. He'd said he didn't understand what she did all day while he was earning the money to pay for everything, and she'd said she didn't have a life any more while he had all the fun. What fun was that? he'd asked. She'd shouted something stupid at him, she couldn't remember what, then he'd reached for his coat and walked out of the house. So she'd bundled up the kids and come here.

This utterly predictable tale sounded so individual and distressing the way Pippa told it that Stef was deeply saddened. Pippa was in real agony, lost, heartbroken.

'But Pippa, darling,' their mother put in, bewildered. 'Surely he's right, he is paying for everything. I thought you wanted to stay at home and look after the twins.'

'I did, I did. But I'm so miserable. Why am I so miserable?'

'Poor Pips,' Stef said, touching her sister's arm. 'You can both sort it out, though, can't you?'

But Pippa could not be comforted. Shortly afterwards, she went upstairs and they heard her run a bath. Eventually, her bedroom door closed and there was silence.

Nobody understands a marriage except the two people in it, Stef told herself later, as she sat in bed, failing to take in the words of the novel she was reading. On the other hand, when you were in the middle of a crisis it was hard to see things clearly. She of all people knew that and her heart went out to her sister, who'd often seemed so lost. She remembered Pip and Rob's wedding, only five years ago, how the couple appeared quietly fond of one another and the bride really did look radiant. Everybody had sighed with relief at Pippa's apparent 'happy ever after' following the turbulence of her teens and her directionless early twenties.

Both the sisters had been upset by their parents' separation, but Stef had recovered quickly, glad that the tension in the house was gone. Pippa had been closer to their father, his 'little bird', and adjusted less easily. Then, at fourteen, she'd got in with a bad lot at school and by the time her mother noticed it was too late to detach her. There was a particular boy Pip hung out with who wrecked her confidence by repeatedly picking her up, then dropping her. Jed Burns, he was called.

Stef, at seventeen and a late developer as far as boys were concerned, was both envious and disapproving. Sixteen-year-old Jed was undoubtedly gorgeous, with a raven's wing of glossy dark hair and a bad boy sideways glance that played havoc with Stef's insides if she encountered him in the kitchen at home or on the stairs at school, but as her best friend Gemma said pompously, he had trouble written all over him. After Jed lost interest in tormenting Pippa and dropped her altogether, Pippa stopped going to school for a while and wouldn't eat. There followed weeks of visits to the doctor and counselling sessions until gradually she recovered, but the rest of her teens were by all accounts a rackety affair, which Stef, glad to get away to university, hadn't witnessed at first hand.

Now she wished she didn't feel so helpless, that she'd taken more interest in her sister, been more kind, could understand her better. Surely whatever was wrong in her marriage was fixable, she thought, giving up on the book. She switched off the lamp, but when she rolled over to get to sleep she noticed a line of light shining under the door. Annoying. She blinked at it, frowning. It was stronger than the kids' nightlight. The landing light, then. She sighed and stumbled out of bed. After turning it off, she stood for a moment in the soft glow from the twins' nightlight, puzzling at a strange sound. It was coming from Pippa's room. She padded soundlessly across the landing and listened at the door. There it was again. A sob. Pip was crying. She raised her hand and knocked softly. 'Pip, are you okay?' No answer. Should she go in? 'Pip?' she whispered again, but there was only silence and an abyss that could not be crossed. She returned to bed and tried to sleep, but the thought of her sister crying alone in the darkness was too much to bear. If Pip couldn't sleep, then she shouldn't, either. It was a lonely, senseless vigil, and she was tired. Soon, she slipped into troubled dreams.

Twenty-Eight

Early the next morning, she was rudely awoken by the sound
of the television on high volume and hurried downstairs
to find the twins sprawled on the sofa eating the chocolate
cereal her mother had left out and watching cartoons. She
seized the remote to turn the sound down, greeted them as
cheerfully as she could manage, then went into the kitchen.
There, Stef mopped up spilt milk, swept up scattered chocolate krispies and let an agitated Baxter into the garden. The
clock said eight, but of Pippa and their mother there was no
sign, so she switched on the kettle and, as she waited for it to
boil, yawned repeatedly.

She'd been here in Norfolk a whole week, she reflected, and
so much had happened in that time that she felt a different
person. As for today ... she wondered what horrors it might
bring. Perhaps it would be a good idea to take the twins off
somewhere and give Pippa time to sort herself out.

As she made a cup of tea, she remembered her suggestion

to Aaron about doing something with Livy, if the child was well enough, and felt an uplift of happiness for it meant seeing him again. Curious, she thought, given how annoying he was being about Nancy. And that sent her thoughts scurrying to the interesting problem of how she should use Nancy's story in her book, given what Aaron had said about the mysterious litigious male scientist. She would wait till she'd heard the whole story and then ask Nancy's advice, she decided. Maybe Aaron was overreacting.

Baxter trotted in from the garden and sat pointedly by his food bowl. 'You, too?' she remarked in the same fake-cheery voice she'd used with the twins. 'No peace. Everybody needs Stef today!' *Actually, when you live on your own,* she thought as she reached for a bag of kibble, *it's rather nice to feel needed for a change.*

Both the twins were tired, unsurprisingly. When Pippa finally appeared, in a silky dressing gown, her children fixed on her like limpets, moaning and squabbling over who should sit in her lap on the sofa. Stef placed a cup of tea for her nearby, took another upstairs to her mother and went outside to ring Aaron.

He agreed enthusiastically to her tentative suggestion of a boat trip. She dressed the twins in yesterday's outfits, then, rather than mess about changing over car seats, herded them firmly on the short walk to the staithe. She was surprised and enchanted by the dozens of moored boats of different shapes and sizes bobbing on the water, by the gaily painted boathouses and the bright metallic sounds of the wind in the rigging.

They spotted Aaron and Livy waiting by a wooden jetty. The soldierly man with wispy silver hair whom she'd spoken to at church the previous Sunday emerged from the nearest boathouse. His name was Geoffrey Stuart, she remembered. 'Hello, Mr Stuart.' She waved. 'Could we hire one of your boats?'

'Five of you, are there? I'll be with you in a moment.' He smiled and disappeared inside his boathouse.

The twins and Livy were initially shy with one another, but bonded over a blank refusal to put on the buoyancy aids Mr Stuart brought over.

'I don't need one. I can swim,' Livy told him in an adult voice. She was less tired this morning but a little tetchy.

'Livy . . .' Aaron began warningly.

'I don't want it, too,' Jess whined, rubbing her eyes.

'Look, the grown-ups are having them,' Stef said brightly, taking the life vest that Mr Stuart passed her.

'Nobody's going on the water without one, young 'uns, it's the law,' the older man growled and such was the wildness of his white hair and the fierceness of his gaze, the children obeyed.

'Have you driven one of these things before?' Stef whispered to Aaron as they handed the children down into the little boat. 'I'll have a go, but my experience is limited.'

'My stepfather used to take me out in one,' he replied. While Stef settled the kids on the benches, he slid behind the wheel, clipped the kill cord to his belt, and soon they were puttering out over the Broad, a cool breeze in their faces.

The sky was cloudless and the light beautiful, clear and sharp, as though the world had been washed clean by yesterday's rain, and the boat carved through the water setting off wavelets that rolled outwards and rocked the floating flocks of geese in a comical fashion. The children, awed at first into silence, soon began to point out wildlife and landmarks: the jetty, tiny behind them in the distance, an odd-shaped buoy that they passed, which had a mournful clanking bell. Soon, they were nearing the far side, where the water was fringed with reeds, then Aaron turned the motor right down and the boat glided into a narrow channel.

'This leads eventually to the reserve,' he remarked as the boat nosed quietly between tall bulrushes and stunted trees. After a while, he switched off the engine so that the vessel could drift along.

'Listen,' he said to the children. 'And keep completely still.' And amazingly, they did, with only Jack shuffling his feet, because he never could stay motionless.

After a short period of silence came birdsong. First one bird piped up, then another answered. 'Warblers,' Aaron whispered. 'I don't know which ones, sedge warblers maybe or willow.'

They listened for a minute before he started the motor again. The boat moved slowly along the channel, which gradually opened into a wider patch of water. It sped across this, then slowed again for another narrow stretch before finally emerging onto a second great Broad.

'Look ahead,' Aaron said with a grin and eventually Stef recognized what he was pointing at. Hazy in the distance at the far edge of the lake, sunlight reflected off a tumble of white-painted buildings.

'Nancy's cottage!' Stef gasped, then grabbed Livy, who had stood up to see.

'Better not go any further,' Aaron said, indicating a sign commanding 'No Motor Vessels' that was rooted in the shallows. 'We must go back, but I thought you'd like the view.'

'Who's Nancy?' Jess asked Stef.

'She's my . . .' Livy broke in. 'Who is Gran-gran, Daddy?'

'Your great-grandmother.'

'Aaron's gran,' Stef explained to the twins, who looked curiously at Livy as they tried to work out this relationship. Stef and Pippa's own grandparents had all died before the twins were born, so this was alien to them.

'Is she very old?' Jack ventured.

'She's about to be eighty-one,' Aaron told him. 'Old, but not very, very old.'

They were edging back towards the first Broad now. Stef would have loved to stop again to listen to the birds, but they only had the boat for an hour and they'd used half of that. Also, the wind had picked up and Livy was shivering despite being warmly dressed in jeans and a fleece top under her life vest. Aaron glanced at her with concern. Stef rootled in a locker and produced a blanket, which she wrapped round the little girl.

'A gentle trip up to the far end to see what birds there are, then we'll go back,' Aaron said and turned the boat in a great arc.

By the time they arrived back at the jetty twenty minutes later, the three children were chatting over a pocket guide book about birds that Stef had found next to the blanket. The grown-ups pointed out birds on the water and the children tried to identify them.

'That was fun,' Livy conceded as they climbed out and Stef laughed to see the relief in Aaron's face. He was, she thought, a little too anxious with his daughter.

Other visitors were gathering at the staithe to use the boats and the atmosphere was busy. Stef spotted a tea room next to Geoffrey Stuart's boathouse and suggested warm drinks. Soon, the five of them were seated around a bare wooden table with a view over the Broad, sipping mugs of foaming hot chocolate and sharing cellophane packets of biscuits. Livy fetched a box of colouring materials from the windowsill and the children coloured pictures of birds and chatted together.

'How is Nancy today?' Stef asked Aaron.

'Improving, I'd say. She got herself upstairs to the bathroom with the carer's help this morning. If we make it through the next few days without incident, I reckon we can stand down. I hope so. I can't keep coming and going at this rate.'

'I'll help if I can. It looks as though I'll be here for the rest of the weekend at least.' She glanced at the twins. 'While my sister sorts herself out.' She explained to Aaron in a low voice what Pippa had said about leaving her husband.

'Oh dear, I hope it sorts itself out,' Aaron said, then sighed. 'I have to get Livy back to London tomorrow evening. She has school on Monday.'

'Do you think Nancy would need me overnight again?'

'It's possible. But it's too much to ask of you. And you know what I think . . .' He rolled a biscuit crumb under his finger and cast her an unhappy look.

'Aaron.' She paused, then said in low tones. 'I know what you're trying to say. I won't do anything that causes Nancy trouble, I promise.'

He sighed. 'I want to believe you.'

'What are you talking about, Daddy?' Livy put in.

'Just about Gran-gran. Making sure she's all right, love,' Aaron replied and the girl nodded and returned to her colouring. He lowered his voice to speak to Stef. 'I am starting to worry about her generally, you know. I hate to agree with the poison pen writer, but I don't think she should continue to live out there on her own.'

'She'll take some convincing of that,' Stef remarked.

'I know. I broached it with her this morning. Phew, did I regret it. She said was I in collusion with the letter writer and was I trying to put her in a care home?'

'Fiercely independent is the phrase. She loves that house so much. It would be a terrible wrench for her to leave it.'

'Perhaps there's somewhere in the village. If she was just in a property that was easier for her to look after and where there were people close by. There's no need for her to go far, given she loves the Broad so much. Stef, would you talk to her about it?'

'Me? Aaron, that doesn't seem right. I hardly know her. Why should she take my advice rather than yours? You're family.'

He sighed. 'It was silly of me to think of it. It's just she thinks I mollycoddle her.'

'What's mollycoddle mean?' Livy put in.

'It means overprotect, little Sharp Ears. Nothing gets past you, does it?'

Livy looked at him severely. 'Mummy says you have to ask questions to learn things.'

'Well, Mummy is right, but some things are for grown-ups to know about, not children.'

'I know that, Daddy,' she said, emphasizing each word.

Stef restrained a giggle. Aaron was right about his daughter acting up. Jess and Jack, on the other hand, were deeply involved in their crayoning, apparently unaware of the adults' conversation. Thankfully, the three children seemed perfectly happy in each other's company.

'We ought to be getting back shortly,' she said, wanting to find out how Pippa was.

'If you're around tomorrow, perhaps we could do something with the kids,' Aaron said, his eyes pleading. 'We must leave for London mid-afternoon, so the morning maybe.'

It must be difficult for him to entertain Livy on his own, Stef thought, and readily agreed. 'I'll do a bit of research,' she said, 'and check with my sister.'

Aaron nodded. 'There's something else,' he added reluctantly. 'Nancy wonders if you're free for tea this afternoon. I promised I'd tell you.'

Stef smiled to think of what that cost him. 'I could be. Will you be there, too, or may I bring my tape recorder?'

'I—' Aaron's face creased in a frown.

'We're going shopping this afternoon,' Livy butted in. 'Aren't we, Daddy?'

'Only to the supermarket,' Aaron said sternly. 'I'm not made of money.'

Stef would take her tape recorder. The sooner she heard the rest of Nancy's story, the better.

Twenty-Nine

'Perhaps you know all about locusts.' Nancy was in teaching mode, bright and focused on her subject. She looked much better, too, her hair swept up in its usual elegant style.

'Not really,' Stef said cautiously. 'I mean, I know they're a terrible blight. Otherwise . . . are they similar to crickets?'

'They are related to crickets, yes. Locusts,' Nancy continued, 'are very large grasshoppers in the family *Acrididae*. They are normally solitary, but have a swarming phase when in their millions they devastate crops, causing famine and human misery. Through my research, I came to know locusts very well indeed. Intimately, in fact. Am I lecturing you? I don't mean to.'

'Perhaps a little,' Stef said, smiling. 'But I don't mind. It's interesting.'

'After my conversation with Professor Briggs at his Easter supper party, I sought his advice about a subject for doctoral research. It was he who directed my attention towards locusts. He told me I'd be more likely to pick up grant money if I selected an area of study with practical implications. Locusts, he said, threatened global food supplies. They were a scourge, threatening the lives and livelihoods of rural populations worldwide. There could be little more useful to humanity than investigating how to control them.'

'Wasn't that the time when that awful insecticide DDT was starting to be used?'

'DDT compounds had been in use for some years and were very successful in terms of killing pests. Now, of course, we know how devasting DDT was in other ways, because it killed all sorts of useful insects, too, and affected the birds that ate them, but we didn't understand the extent of that back then. I certainly didn't when I started my research. Anyway, the professor suggested that I might join efforts to test aspects of DDT's efficacy, and so that's what I did. I spent some weeks during that final summer term of my undergraduate studies reading up about them and thought his advice sound. He offered to be my supervisor and, despite my mixed feelings about him, I felt honoured that he'd picked me out. I filled in the forms and was thrilled when that grant came through. At last, I would be a scientist conducting useful research and someone would give me money to do it. The Agricultural Research Council, to be precise.'

'Did you have to propose an exact aspect of the subject for your thesis?' Stef prompted, scribbling a note to look up this grants body. She wanted to be clear about Nancy's studies.

'The aspect I chose was not one that had been extensively tested. It concerned the nature of some of the different dusts that chemical companies mixed in with the DDT to spray crops. You didn't use pure DDT. Was one kind of dust or another more effective on locusts? That was my starting point. Some of the first term of my doctorate the following autumn was spent in libraries around London, reading up on research that had been carried out and talking to other scientists about it.'

'Setting the parameters of your research?'

'Yes. And I spent a great deal of time getting to know locusts. Nasty, bristly, noisy insects, but extremely interesting and highly evolved for what they do. Which is eat things and reproduce.'

'Lovely!' Stef said with distaste.

'Yes, quite. On the professor's instructions, I was given some space in one of the upstairs labs at the college to set up some glass tanks. In these, I kept my locusts. They're used to warm, arid environments and it was a terrible job in chilly, damp old London keeping the temperature of their tanks high enough and the humidity low. It meant using heat lamps. More than once, I arrived on a Monday morning to find that some unhelpful person had turned the lamps off and the insects were all listless, so I had to put up stern notices telling them not to.'

Nancy smiled gently, gazing into the distance, remembering.

'What did you do with your locusts?'

'Do? I fed them on grass and leaves, observing their habits. Sometimes I killed them humanely by leaving a few drops of ethyl acetate on a pad in a tightly closed jar – they wouldn't have felt a thing. Then I dissected them and examined them under the microscope, trying to get to know every aspect. I quickly observed that locusts have a very thick cuticle – exoskeleton – its outer layer, if you like, and this forms a significant barrier against absorbing toxins. Therefore, any dust used to carry the insecticide would have to cling to the creature's side long enough for the poison to seep in and do its job.'

'And you explored different kinds of dust to see which would do this best?'

'That's what I went on to do, yes. There were all sorts of things to consider, but I won't go into those now. It's enough to say that I had to take into account the context for the spraying, the ability of the different types of dust to carry the poison and so forth.' Nancy sighed. 'I shudder now, looking back, knowing that I played a part in promoting the use of these dreadful chemicals, but we simply didn't know then everything that we do now. There wasn't the widespread awareness of the need to take care of the natural environment.'

'I think I understand. Rachel Carson hadn't published *The Silent Spring* by then, had she, about the damage DDT was doing to wildlife in the States?'

'No, that was 1962, ten years later. I was horrified when I read it. And she experienced quite a backlash. Nothing's black and white, though. As well as saving crops, DDT was proving incredibly valuable in the fight against malaria. It killed the Anopheles mosquito that carried the disease and saved thousands of human lives.'

'I didn't know that.' Stef frowned.

'Anyway, by Christmas I was ready to start my experiments, but then everything was briefly up in the air because the great move to the new field station was taking place. But I enjoyed that first term hugely. I was finding out things and being treated seriously. It was quite different from being an undergraduate. Even Miss Pick, the head technician, was moderately less icy. Mind you, she was never as nice to me and Anne as she was to the men. I've wondered since if it was because she was envious of other women. Maybe she had wished to be a proper scientist rather than a technician, but was never given the chance.'

Stef nodded and scribbled 'Explore female technicians in the period' in her notebook. The tape recorder was running, but it was useful to make such notes as she went along.

'Would you excuse me for a moment?' Nancy reached for a crutch and stood up, waving away Stef's offer of help. 'I'll be perfectly all right.'

While she was out of the room, Stef paused the tape recorder and gazed dreamily out of the window. It was sunny this afternoon and her mother had spoken about taking Pippa and the twins to the coast. Stef wouldn't stay long at Nancy's once Aaron and Livy returned from shopping. She'd be glad of an opportunity to catch up with some work in an empty house.

Thirty

London
Autumn 1950

The large, high-ceilinged lab on the second floor of Prince's Zoology building where Nancy kept her locusts was home to half a dozen different research projects. It was cluttered, gloomy and smelled of formaldehyde together with something feral. A large, chugging machine under a worktop near the door sustained an aquarium of whiskery black fish that stared at Nancy with bulging eyes whenever she passed. From time to time, a short, silent student with thick-lensed spectacles arrived to sprinkle flakes of food onto the surface of the water or to check its temperature. He'd make notes on a spiral-bound pad and leave again. None of the other research students knew who he was or what he was doing, and he rarely spoke to anyone.

Nancy's work station occupied a far corner under a tattered

notice on the wall forbidding anyone to smoke. Nearby, Edmund kept a tankful of flies fed on raw meat, which contributed to the feral smell, though no one complained in case their own project attracted criticism.

By one of the narrow sash windows, Anne Durban presided over a green glass terrarium where shy black beetles hid among moss and twigs. Nancy and Edmund used to joke that there was in fact only one beetle, but seen many times. They named it Alexander after the insect in the Christopher Robin poem. Once Anne arrived to find a sign taped to the glass advising her in childish handwriting that 'Nanny let my beetle out, and beetle ran away'. She momentarily panicked that all her beetles had been stolen.

Though Nancy took no part in practical jokes, thinking them infantile, they were common in the labs and woe betide anyone whose sense of humour failed. Since none of the pranks actually damaged anyone's work, which would have been a grave offence, they were largely taken in good part. The only one that fell flat was the occasion when a person or persons unknown placed a large, busty, ceramic figurine in a scanty bathing suit on the sand at the bottom of the aquarium. The silent keeper of the fish did not react or even appear to notice it, and so the statuette remained. By Christmas, its voluptuous curves were modestly clothed in green algae.

Although only Nancy was supervised by Professor Briggs, she, Anne and Edmund had all chosen to work with insects as he'd advised. They understood that this was the best way to get on if they wished to stay at the college.

It was following a discussion with Edmund about this

narrow range of study options that Nancy was granted the opportunity to learn more about him. She was feeling low one Tuesday afternoon in December because some of her locusts had died, and she told him she hated the insects and felt like throwing in the towel. Edmund took her out to a teashop and plied her with tea and cakes to cheer her up.

The place was busy with Christmas shoppers with bulging bags, and it was hard to be heard over the clink of crockery, the tinny music and bright laughter. On each table, a tiny bristly Christmas tree decoration frosted with white had been left next to the cruet, and the cakes, when they arrived, were iced in festive colours.

'I needed a treat,' Nancy declared, selecting a cake decorated with a pink star as Edmund poured the tea. 'And it's lovely and warm in here. I can't believe how cold the lab gets. No wonder my poor locusts die.'

'My blowflies move very slowly when the temperature drops. I can't get them to do anything. We should have a word with the gorgeous Miss Pick, though it's hardly worth making a fuss this side of Christmas. And we'll be moving soon after.'

'I wish they'd give us a date and be done with it.'

A group of them had visited Brandingfield Hall the previous week to inspect the new facilities, and had been impressed by the converted building with its spacious laboratories and state-of-the-art equipment. It was set in parkland, on the site of an old country house partly destroyed by enemy bombs, and was nearly ready for them to move into.

The research students were looking forward to the move

on the whole. The only problem was where they would live. It would take Nancy the best part of an hour to get there by tube and train from the hostel, and travelling there and back every day would become onerous. She supposed she would look for digs in the nearby town.

'What will you do?' she asked Edmund. Despite them being acquainted for so long as fellow students, she was rarely on her own with him, and given the five years between them in age and experience often felt a little shy in his company.

'I haven't decided yet,' he said carefully. 'I have family commitments and it suits me to stay in Kensington at present. In fact, I may not be coming to Brandingfield at all. Briggs and I are at loggerheads over the matter.'

'Oh,' she said, surprised and wondering what he meant about family, for she had thought he was single. 'I assumed ... I mean, is it your parents?'

'My parents? No. They're hale and hearty in Dorset, thank God. I have a child. A little girl named Marianne. She's six. She lives with her mother, but I'm able to take her out.' A fond expression crossed his face, then he looked at Nancy with concern. 'We're divorced, you see. Have I shocked you? You look a little pale.'

'Not shocked, just – I didn't know.' She looked at him with new eyes now, understanding his habitual air of sadness.

'It's not something I broadcast,' he murmured. 'Nobody else's business.'

'No, of course not.' She crumbled her cake and wondered what to say.

He sipped his tea, looking thoughtful, then smiled, reached

in his jacket for his wallet and extracted a scrap of card from it. 'Here she is,' he said, passing it over. It was, Nancy saw, a snap of a merry little girl with her head tilted to one side. Her hair was light-coloured like Edmund's and she had his deep-set eyes. And Edmund's mouth, too, but hers curved in a cheeky grin. 'Marianne was only four when this was taken, but I keep it because she looks so happy.'

'She's very like you,' Nancy said as she passed it back. He glanced at it with a soft expression and tucked it back in his wallet. 'Is your wife—?' She tried again. 'Did you—?'

'Vivienne and I met in London when I was home on leave and married rather hastily. We knew we might be separated for some time and it seemed the best thing to do. Marianne was born when I was in Cairo. It was hard for us not to be together and rotten for Viv. She had no mother to help her out and our flat was up three flights of stairs. It can be a very lonely business raising a young child ...' He let his words hang.

'She must have missed you.' The teashop was packed now. A large woman entered, wearing a thick fur coat. She brushed past Nancy, who felt the cold shock of snow against her cheek. When she looked at Edmund again he was gazing sadly down at his uneaten cake. 'So ...' she managed to say, 'things didn't work out.'

'No,' he said quietly. 'She wrote to me in Italy. Said she'd found someone else. They offered me compassionate leave but I wouldn't take it. Stupid really. Too proud.'

'You wish you had?'

He looked away. 'For Marianne's sake, yes. When I next

set eyes on Viv, I saw a stranger. Couldn't think what I'd seen in her. Does that make me sound cold? Perhaps it does.' He reached in his pocket for his cigarettes and lit one, which gave Nancy time to think of an answer.

'A little,' she said.

His eyes softened as he studied her through the smoke.

'I'm so glad that you are young and came through the war unscathed,' he said. 'You can't imagine what it was like for servicemen like me in the battlefield with only the thought of our loved ones to sustain us through the horror. But it's taken me years to understand what it was like for Viv, struggling alone at home. And to forgive.'

Poor Edmund. Nancy couldn't help but pity him, but she felt humble, for he was right: she couldn't truly imagine what he'd been through.

'It's something I like about you and the others, Nancy,' Edmund went on. 'Your freshness and innocence. I can't tell you what a relief it is to cheer someone up after the loss of a few insects. I've so enjoyed our outing.' His eyes twinkled at her.

She laughed, feeling at ease with him now. 'So have I,' she said. 'And I'm sorry I was petulant. I do like my work and I feel ready to start again tomorrow.'

'Good,' he smiled. 'And don't be afraid to call on me again. We all need bolstering up from time to time.' And he signalled to the waitress to bring the bill.

Thirty-One

At Dragonfly Lodge, the afternoon was waning, but there was no sign of Aaron and Livy. Nancy didn't appear worried, though.

'They've probably gone on somewhere to do something fun – I do hope so.' A fond expression crossed her face.

Remembering Aaron's air of anxiety with Livy that morning, Stef hoped so, too. 'Livy certainly enjoyed the boat trip this morning. It must be nice for you to see so much of her and Aaron.'

'It is lovely,' Nancy said, breaking into a smile. 'I don't know if Aaron has told you, but I didn't see much of him when he was growing up.'

'He sort of hinted at it.'

Nancy sighed at the memory. 'His mother, Andrea, left home when she was fifteen. We had a bit of trouble with her growing up and she got in with the wrong crowd. It was the early seventies, so you'll understand the type I mean – those awful hippies. We didn't hear much from her for a long while after that – and then usually when she was short of money. I'm afraid she didn't wait to get married before having Aaron and we never met his father.'

The way Nancy put it sounded old-fashioned compared to Aaron's account, but the anguish in her voice tore at Stef's heart.

'My husband found it difficult to forgive her for rejecting us. Which was unfair, though I understood why. It's rather complicated … Eventually, Andrea did settle down. She married an American, a musician from New York whom she met on a plane, and seems happy with him, though he's fifteen years older than she is and not in the best of health. They live in Mexico now. I don't often see her, though we do keep in touch.'

Stef waited quietly, but Nancy's attention had moved on.

'Now, there was something I meant to show you.' Nancy shifted herself round and started awkwardly shuffling through some papers on one of the shelves behind her. 'Here it is,' she said suddenly, pulling out a slim volume and passing it to Stef.

Stef examined it wonderingly. It was a privately bound publication. She opened it and read the typed title: *The Effects on Locusts of Different Dusts Carrying DDT.*

'By Nancy E. Foster,' Stef said aloud. 'It's your PhD thesis!' She began turning the pages, frowning at the scientific language.

'That's right.' Nancy beamed. 'Take it away for a few days, if you'd like, though I want it back. It's my only copy. I filed the other with Prince's College, of course—'

'I tried looking it up online,' Stef remembered suddenly.

Nancy looked surprised. 'Can you do that?'

'Yes! Except the website wouldn't let me open it,' A reason suddenly occurred to her. 'They're probably still in the process of digitizing old theses.'

A wary expression crossed Nancy's face. 'D'you think that's why?'

'I don't know,' Stef said simply. An uneasy feeling crept over her.

'I expect you're right. I'm a bit paranoid, that's all.' Nancy glanced at the book. 'You must take care of that. I suppose the college's copy is somewhere in their library, but if it's ... mislaid, then this is the only copy left.'

'Of course I'll take care of it. I won't keep it long.' Stef slipped the thesis in her bag, feeling uncertain. Surely no one would have wanted to suppress this piece of research from more than fifty years ago? The explanation that had just occurred to her was likely to be correct. But the message on the website, 'Access denied', had been unnecessarily aggressive. Perhaps she needed to have been logged in to their system?

The old lady pushed herself to her feet. She went to stand at the window and gazed out sightlessly.

'Are you all right?' Stef asked but Nancy merely nodded. Her thoughts, it seemed, were far away.

As Stef walked back through the reserve to where she'd left the car, she hardly noticed her surroundings, so caught up was she in the events of the afternoon. Everything Nancy had told her to date was fascinating, but she sensed that the story was beginning to turn darker. She was aware of the precious book in her bag. Maybe there would be time this evening to read the thesis.

She was so caught up in her thoughts that she took a wrong path and only realized when she came to a dead end. Here, a dark wooden bird hide hunkered on the edge of the Broad. Apart from the distant sounds of birds, all was quiet. As she turned to retrace her steps, she heard a sound from inside the hut and glanced round to see the door opening towards her. It was Josh, the warden, who stepped out. He was carrying something white in his hand, a piece of folded paper. He pushed this into his cagoule pocket as they stared at each other in surprise.

'Sorry,' he said, speaking first, 'didn't expect to see you!'

'To see me personally, or anyone?' she said with a smile.

'Anyone. We closed half an hour ago, you know.'

His tone was accusatory.

'I've been visiting Nancy,' she said stoutly. 'I'm only down here because I'm lost. So stupid. I'm trying to get back to my car in Fox Lane.'

The suspicion left his face and he nodded. 'Easy to take a wrong turn if you're not concentrating. I was just bolting the hatches here. There's stormy weather forecast. I'll walk back with you and show you the way.'

'Thanks.' She followed his striding figure the short distance back along the duckboards to a junction she'd missed.

'I feel really stupid taking the wrong turn.' She laughed. He'd paused by a fingerpost to wait for her.

'Even I've done it,' he said conversationally, resting one hand on a wooden rail. 'I'll say goodbye here. Have a pleasant walk back. When you get to the old mill, there are lots of swifts this time of day. Worth stopping to look.'

Before she knew it, he was telling her all about the swifts' behaviour. His demeanour was completely different as he talked, not sulky at all; in fact, his face glowed with vitality. He was extremely knowledgeable and spoke interestingly, so she let him run on. Soon, in return, she was describing her own work as a journalist, mentioning a new bird sanctuary that she'd written about, and it was his turn to be interested.

'You're seeing a lot of Nancy,' he said suddenly. 'Is that also to do with your work?' He spoke casually, but something about the restless way his fingers tapped on the rail put Stef on her guard.

'Just to do with a book I want to write,' she said. 'I mustn't reveal any more or my agent will skin me.'

'Oh, okay,' he said, sounding friendly enough, but his fingers tightened on the rail. 'Skinning doesn't sound good.'

Stef remembered something she must ask him. 'You haven't seen Nancy's cat on your rounds, have you? It's been missing for a couple of days now.'

He shook his head. 'Aaron asked me to keep an eye out, but no. Mind you, I've never liked Nancy keeping a cat here, for obvious reasons.'

'It's too old to catch birds, I think.'

'Still, the sight and scent of it is disturbing for them. I've talked to her about it before. I'm sorry, of course, that the mog is missing . . . but I can assure you, I haven't seen it.' His voice was clipped. He was hard work, this man, easy to annoy. Despite being so knowledgeable about the local wildlife, and in many ways probably a good warden.

'I can't think that it will be able to fend for itself for long,' Stef sighed.

'How is Nancy? Aaron seems concerned.'

Again, that casual tone, but there was a lack of warmth.

'She's managing,' Stef said cautiously.

'I don't suppose she'll be able to carry on living here, given her accident.'

'I wouldn't know.' She didn't like the way the conversation was going, but Josh was getting into his stride.

'Has she told you the history of the Lodge?'

Stef shook her head. 'It's Victorian at a guess.'

'Mid-nineteenth century, with later additions. I've been researching it. It was built for an eccentric widow who wanted to escape from the world. She lived out here with only a housekeeper for company. People said she went a bit mad in her old age. Anyway, she disappeared one night and was found drowned in the Broad.'

'Poor woman, how sad.' Stef shivered.

'Her estranged son inherited the house and the land,' Josh went on, getting into the swing of his story. 'He lived abroad, but he rented it out, and then his children and grandchildren inherited it in turn. Sometimes it was used as a holiday home, at other times it was empty. After the Second World War, the reserve was set up and the trustees managed to lease the land around the Lodge – but not the Lodge and its garden. Before Nancy took it on, an elderly couple lived in it. The trouble is that it's been rather neglected, and a few years ago it was sold.'

'And the new owner is keen for Nancy to leave, is that it?' Stef rushed in.

'It would seem so. Before it crumbles into the Broad, I should imagine.'

'And what do the trustees of the reserve think should happen?'

'They don't have any say over the house. It's a little enclave that doesn't belong to them.'

'What do you think, then?'

'I don't have an opinion. It's nothing to do with me.' His face was hard, closed.

You're keeping something back, Stef thought. She'd had plenty of experience interviewing unwilling subjects, could spot evasion or lying a mile off. But what had he to lie about? It was puzzling. Was Josh the letter writer? She remembered the folded paper he'd been holding when he'd emerged from the hide, the way he'd quickly stuffed it in his pocket. *Though, come on, Stef, that could have been anything, a leaflet or a bit of litter.*

She thought more about it as she walked along the path back to the car. It wouldn't have been another poison letter, she concluded. Not so soon after the last.

When she noticed the ruined windmill out on the marsh, she paused, remembering Josh's suggestion that she look for it. She hadn't really studied it before. It was a sad-looking, red-brick edifice, its sails long gone, its roof open to the sky. There were certainly plenty of swifts darting above it, black shapes with distinctive curved wings and forked tails. While she watched them dive and swoop, plucking insects from the air and emitting plaintive, high-pitched cries, she brooded about Josh. He was secretive and mercurial, she concluded, but did that make him the letter writer?

High above, storm clouds were moving in with an air of menace. Soon, she felt the first raindrops on her face and hurried on again towards the car.

As she accelerated along the narrow road that led back to the village, she heard the light toot of a horn behind and glimpsed Aaron's car in her rear-view mirror. It was slowing to turn down the lane to the parking space that she'd just vacated. She waved to them from her open window, then wondered whether she should have stopped and turned round, or if that would have appeared too enthusiastic. She still didn't know how she should act with him.

Thirty-Two

Back at Springfield Cottage, thoughts of a quiet evening to do some work were dispelled. Stef had forgotten that it was Saturday and her mother had been invited to a barbecue at the home of the family opposite. While Stef was out, Cara had popped over the road and rather cheekily had the invitation extended to Stef, Pippa and the twins. Pippa was refusing to go, but wanted the twins to. Cara had begged Stef to accompany her, saying she wouldn't be able to manage Jack and Jess by herself, and Stef had rather grumpily given in. Then she discovered that Ted was coming, too.

'There'll be burgers and sausages, I expect,' Cara said cheerily when Jess expressed a wish to stay with Pippa, 'and there's nothing much to eat in our house at all.' Stef knew this to be true. Her mother's fridge freezer was looking distinctly bare this end of the week and some shopping would need to be done in the morning.

Stef took her bag with the tape recorder and Nancy's

precious thesis safely upstairs to her room, where she hastily applied a little lipstick and dragged a brush through her hair. Downstairs, at her mother's behest, she picked a bunch of flowers from the garden and located a bottle of wine in the larder to give to their hosts.

They left Pippa by herself in the kitchen scrolling through her phone, her face blotched with tears, and herded the children across the road, where a delicious smell of grilled meat was rising in the air.

The barbecue turned out to be an interesting affair attended by a couple of dozen local people, two of whom Stef recognized – Serena Clay, the vicar, and Geoffrey Stuart, the boat owner. Suzannah and Martin Baker, their hosts, turned out to be a friendly couple of incomers who ran a business selling trampolines from a nearby light industrial estate. With their kids at the local school and growing their own vegetables to sell at the shop, they appeared fully invested in village life.

Stef and her mother were seized upon by the chatty Suzannah and introduced to various locals as 'the talented author and journalist' and 'her mum Cara, our wonderful resident artist'. While Cara swelled happily with pride at this attention, Stef wanted to go and hide, but instead sipped her lager and smiled politely.

The twins, on the other hand, were having fun with the Baker children on a giant-sized trampoline, which, with its high safety net, took up much of the back lawn. The food was good, too – Stef enjoyed a hot dog and salad. She also had two notable conversations, one with the Reverend Serena, who expressed concern for Nancy and offered the possibility of lifts to doctor's appointments through a parish good neighbour scheme. The other was with Geoffrey Stuart. He, too, asked after Nancy.

'Everyone seems to know I've been visiting her,' Stef replied, smiling.

'Ay, well, it's a village, news gets round. She's one of our local characters and people don't like to think of her marooned out there on her own on the marsh. That's her grandson you were with yesterday, wasn't it?'

'Yes. We both had children to amuse.'

'The twins are your sister's?'

'Yes, that's right,' she said. Everyone indeed knew everything. She remembered what he'd told her about the ownership of the Lodge at church the previous Sunday, so, referring to her conversation with Josh that afternoon, she asked him if he knew who the landlord was. He didn't appear to know and shortly afterwards their conversation was interrupted. It really was mysterious, Stef thought.

Momentarily on her own, she looked for her mother and saw that Ted had arrived. They were standing near the trampoline together, drinks in hand, keeping an eye on the twins. It was time, Stef thought, to make her excuses and see if Pippa was okay.

She found her sister huddled in a chair under a thick throw in the garden of Springfield Cottage. A bottle of wine, half-empty, stood next to her phone on the table. She was sipping from a glass while staring out at the evening sky.

'Oh, hi,' Pippa murmured on seeing her, her voice dull.

'The kids are having a great time so I left them with Mum.'

'Okay.'

'Ted turned up.'

Pippa merely shrugged. Stef fetched a bottle of lager from the fridge and joined her at the table, wondering where to start.

'Have you heard from Rob at all?' she ventured.

'Endlessly.'

'And?' Stef prompted.

'Haven't answered.'

Stef felt bewildered.

'How do you feel, Pip? Do you ... still love him?'

Pippa turned sad eyes towards her. 'Huh? I don't know. What the hell is love?'

'Pip, what is the matter? The real matter, I mean. What's going on underneath?'

Pippa sighed and a long moment passed. Then she shook her head. 'It's this feeling of, I don't know, is this all there is? Stopping the twins killing each other and keeping the house nice for Rob, who's never there. It's awfully lonely, Stef.'

Stef felt a stab of annoyance. How could her sister be lonely with her husband and children, and her mum nearby? It was she who was lonely, she who wanted what her sister had. She'd never understood Pippa's choices, her apparent lack of effort, and was envious of the amount of attention Pippa had managed to draw from their parents. Pip sounded so low, though, and she pushed down her own feelings to try to help her sister.

'Isn't it funny,' she said wonderingly, 'how when we were

growing up we never used to talk about anything important? I mean, about how we felt about things.'

Pippa's eyes were on her, wary. 'Kids don't, do they?' she said in clipped tones.

'Well, we didn't, anyway.'

'I don't remember.'

'When you went out with whatshisname and it all went wrong, we didn't even talk about that.'

'Jed? That was years ago.' Pippa's eyes glinted.

'What was that all about, Pip?'

'Why are you interested now?'

'I don't know. It's just ... you can tell me stuff, you know. Our lives are very different, but I do care. I sometimes feel guilty. That it was me who did everything ... right, doing well at school, going to university, the career thing.'

'Why would you feel guilty about that?'

Pippa was making no effort to meet her halfway.

'Because ... you didn't do all those things, I suppose.'

'Isn't that a form of judgement, Stef? That you think your life has been more successful than mine, that I've failed in some way?'

'No, no, of course not.'

'Because that's what it feels like. I didn't want to do those things, didn't see the point. But when I met Rob, I thought, *This is what I do want.*'

'That's all right, then,' Stef said helplessly.

'Well, it's not, is it, because it's not working out. I feel miserable, utterly miserable.'

But you have a husband who adores you and two beautiful

children, Stef wanted to say, but didn't. Instead, she said softly, 'You know, I've felt jealous of you.' *Not for having Rob,* she reminded herself, *but for having someone.* Pippa straightened, her gaze now puzzled. 'Being married and having the kids, I mean,' Stef went on. 'I sometimes wonder if it'll ever happen for me. No, please don't say you're sure it will do. It doesn't for some people, you know.'

'I expect it will, though.'

'Yeah, well. And I know it's pathetic, but you have your own house and financial security. Why would you walk away from that if you didn't have to?' She remembered something. 'Pip, you said you were worried that Rob might be seeing someone else. Are you sure? It doesn't seem like him.'

Pippa shrugged. 'He hasn't denied it.'

'Have you any evidence?'

She shook her head. 'He's quite distant. I don't think he even fancies me any more.' Pippa sounded so plaintive.

'Oh, don't say that,' Stef rushed to reassure her. 'I'm sure he does.'

She watched with dismay as tears pooled in her sister's eyes, and reached and put her arms round her. It had been so long since she'd last held her that she'd forgotten what it felt like.

'I don't know what to do,' Pippa said, nestling into her. She was trembling like a little bird and Stef hugged her tighter.

'It'll be all right,' she whispered. 'I'm sure it will. You'll sort it out.' She wished she could be sure.

Thirty-Three

Stef woke abruptly on Sunday to bright daylight and the sound of the doorbell. Squinting at her phone, she saw it was after nine. Baxter began to howl, so she slid out of bed, reached for her dressing gown and hurried downstairs.

'Move, Baxter,' she sighed, trying to get to the door, then spoke a little louder, 'Okay, okay, I'm coming.' She wrenched open the front door and stood blinking in surprise at the sight of Pippa's husband, Rob. His fair hair stuck out at all angles and his cherubic face, usually wreathed in smiles, was blotchy, his good-natured brown eyes sunken wells of despair. The collar of his rugby shirt had what looked like dried egg on it and he held a set of keys with a fluffy pink tag.

'Morning, Stef, sorry,' he said, his usually confident deep voice faded. 'I did text Pip, but ...' He raised his palm in a gesture of exasperation.

Stef gestured for him to enter and his burly figure filled

the little hallway. 'You'd better come through.' He followed her into the kitchen with Baxter shuffling behind.

'Tea?' She took up the kettle.

'Er, filter coffee if you don't mind.' He tucked the keys into the pocket of his chinos and rubbed his eyes. 'No one else up yet?' he said with a sigh.

She shook her head. 'Late night.'

Her mother, Ted and the twins hadn't returned until after nine, then the twins, overtired, had been the devil to get to bed. Ted hadn't left until nearly midnight, Pippa had gone on drinking and somehow it was after one when Stef turned her light out.

She brewed strong coffee and took the tray outside, where the sun was making a feeble appearance. Rob cleared last night's empty bottles from the table and sat down with meaty legs spread and head bowed, the very image of defeat.

'Drink your coffee,' Stef said quietly, filling the mugs and Rob meekly added milk and sugar to his. They sat sipping it in silence for a while, contemplating the view. A line of geese flew across the distant sky, honking faintly, and Stef thought of Nancy out on the reserve. She'd know what kind they were.

When she glanced at Rob, she saw that his thoughts were miles away and she softened. She wondered what to say to him, knowing she must be loyal to her sister above all. Perhaps she shouldn't get involved, but she could see how devastated he was. In the end, she didn't need to say anything because he began to talk and she merely had to listen.

'I genuinely don't know how this happened. I thought she was happy, that this was what she wanted, being at home with the children. I pay the bills and give her money, there's nothing she has to worry about. I'm not one of those bastards who keep their wives under the cosh. I love her, Stef. I wouldn't do that. I like working and knowing I'm providing for her and the little 'uns.'

'I don't think it's me you should be talking to, Rob. It's Pippa.'

'Yes, but I don't know if she'll talk to me. She hasn't answered any of my calls and texts. I guessed she'd come here. It was such a relief to see the car outside. I've never been here before, you know. It's nice.'

'You've never been here?' Stef was shocked. Her mother had lived here for six or seven weeks and Rob and Pippa only lived a dozen miles away now.

'There's never time,' he stammered, shamefaced.

'Okay,' she said. She thought of the games of golf, of Pippa's goodheartedness when it came to visiting Rob's parents regularly, taking the trouble to involve them in the lives of their grandchildren. It seemed a shame that he hadn't made the effort to see his mother-in-law, though she'd never heard her mother complain and indeed hadn't known of his negligence before now. Still, it didn't seem her place to say anything. Instead, she rose and said she'd go and see if Pippa was awake.

Would Pip want to see Rob? she wondered as she mounted the stairs, then paused, uncertain, on the landing. There was no sound from the twins' or her sister's rooms, but her mother's door was open and she must be in the bathroom. Stef knocked on Pippa's door and let herself in. The room was dark and close and smelled strongly of stale wine and Pippa's favourite citrusy scent. She heard Pippa sigh and mumble Stef's name. She sat on the edge of the bed and reached to grasp her sister's hand.

'Pip, I hope you're not cross, but, well, Rob's here. I let him in.' Pippa stiffened and withdrew her hand. 'Did I do wrong? I could hardly leave him on the doorstep.'

'What does he want?'

'To see you, obviously. He seems very contrite. He's come in your little car.'

Pippa sniggered. 'That'll have annoyed him. His head touches the roof and there's no room for his knees!'

Stef smiled, then said softly, 'Will you go and talk to him? The twins aren't up yet, but I'll look after them when they are.'

'I s'pose.' She yawned and stretched, then rolled out of bed. In her short T-shirt nightie, she looked very young and Stef's heart went out to her.

'You must explain everything to him,' she said plainly. 'That's my best big-sisterly advice.'

Pippa stared at her, her eyes glinting in the gloom. 'You've no idea, Stef. You don't know what being married's like.'

'No, I suppose I don't,' Stef sighed, thinking how impossible her sister was. Hearing the bathroom door open, she grabbed the silky dressing gown from a chair and tossed it to her sister. 'Mum's finished. Look, have a shower and come down, please. I'll make you a cuppa.'

Downstairs, Stef discovered her mother and Rob outside in the garden. Cara was showing him the studio and chattering away. Rob was listening and trying to look interested.

Stef smiled to herself and retreated to the kitchen. She'd make breakfast and contrive a way to lure Mum away and leave the estranged couple together.

Thirty-Four

'They are at least talking,' Stef's mother remarked cheerfully half an hour later, peering through the kitchen window as she peeled off her rubber gloves. Stef stacked the last cereal bowl in the dishwasher and came to join her. Rob and Pippa were just visible out in the field, Rob standing with palms raised in despair, Pippa with shoulders hunched and arms tightly crossed. The volley of raised voices was just audible, though not the words themselves.

'What shall we do with the twins?' Stef wondered. Jack and Jess had been excited to see their father, but after breakfast had been easily detached from their parents in order to watch cartoons in the sitting room.

'They can come with me to church,' her mother said, 'or you can take them out somewhere.'

'I vaguely promised Aaron we'd do something with him and Livy,' Stef admitted. Aaron and his daughter would be leaving in the afternoon and the thought induced a tug of panic. She realized how badly she wanted to see him.

She went out along the lane to get a phone signal. Seeing that he'd already tried to ring her, she felt a glow of satisfaction. Quickly she phoned him back. Something local was called for. They would meet at the visitors' centre in half an hour and walk in the reserve. Later, Aaron said, he and Livy planned to take Nancy for a pub lunch.

Once she'd proposed brightly to the twins that they go out to see Livy, they sped upstairs and dressed themselves. They reappeared in grubby clothes from the day before, but there wasn't time for Stef to challenge this. She was hunting for the keys to Pippa's car, eventually finding them under the sofa.

The car seats were, as Stef feared, an awkward fit in her little hatchback, but she managed to strap her charges in safely, while her mother hurried down the garden to let Pippa and Rob know what was happening.

'I won't come, love,' she informed Stef on her return, with a gleam in her eye. 'I don't want to get in your way.'

Jack and Jess hadn't visited the reserve before except by boat, and they were delighted by the merchandise in the visitors' centre. Being a Sunday, it was busy. Josh was there at the till, and Jackie, the talkative middle-aged volunteer, was serving coffees. Stef managed to resist the twins' demands for toys. 'An ice cream maybe later,' she said sternly. 'Look, there's Livy!' She ushered the children through the door that led to the reserve. The twins rushed ahead to join Aaron and Livy, who were waiting beside the entry gate.

'Hello!' Stef sang out and was glad to see Aaron's face light up as he returned her greeting.

The day was cool and cloudy, but the rain was holding off, though she made the twins zip up their cagoules before they set off. The children walked ahead together, the girls chatting and pointing out flowers and birds, while Jack made occasional little dashes off the path, once having to be prevented from climbing a fragile tree. Then he found a fallen branch and charged ahead brandishing it, lost in some mysterious game. Stef called for him to wait.

'They're exhausting, kids, aren't they?' She laughed.

'Boys are exhausting in a physical way,' Aaron agreed. 'Or at least, the kind of boy that Jack is.'

'He's going to be very like his father, I can tell already. Straightforward, not very reflective.'

'Ooh, that sounded strongly felt.'

'Sorry, we've been having a difficult morning.' She explained how Rob had turned up unannounced and how she hoped that he and Pippa were sorting things out.

'Best thing to do, leaving them to it.'

She allowed a beat of silence to pass, wondering if he'd say something about his own experience of marital discord, but he didn't. Perhaps that was a good sign, she mused as she watched him stoop to collect a fallen iris head and give it to his daughter. She'd once dated a man who'd talked incessantly about the circumstances of his divorce and realized reluctantly that he wasn't ready for a new partner.

When Aaron talked about Nancy, Stef was touched by the tenderness of his concern.

'Her ankle is much better. She's able to put weight on it and I don't feel so bad about leaving her again this afternoon. I'd be happier if she slept downstairs for a while yet … if your mother wouldn't mind her keeping the bed a little longer.'

'I'm sure she wouldn't.'

'I don't know when I'll be able to come down again, though,' he said wistfully. 'This week's something of a nightmare. We're filming down in Cornwall on Wednesday.'

She felt a sudden pang. Maybe she wouldn't see him after today. Trying to keep her voice steady, she asked him about the project. It was a biopic about the sculptor Barbara Hepworth and they talked enthusiastically about her work. When she broke off their conversation to tell Jack to stop menacing his sister with his branch, it struck her how easy Aaron was to talk to.

But when he fell back in step with her once more, he brought the conversation round again to their old subject of dissent. 'What about you?' he asked in a suspicious tone. 'Have you finished with my grandmother yet?'

'Finished? What do you mean?'

'Are the interviews over?'

'No, not yet. Hasn't she said?'

'She won't talk to me about the matter. Says it's her business.'

'I suppose it is.' She was sorry, though, if she'd caused him to argue with Nancy again.

His expression stiffened and she sensed with dismay that their warm connection had cooled again.

Their footsteps slowed, for they had come to a break in the

vegetation where a short platform, guarded by a rail, ran out over the water. They waited until another family there moved on, then Stef found a coin in her pocket and lifted Jack up so that he could feed it into a small telescope clamped to the rail. The children took turns to look through it at the distant birdlife.

Aaron, however, waited to one side, aloof, lost in his own thoughts. *Well, let him,* Stef told herself. Her father had been a sulky man and once he'd left the family home it was as though something lifted. But to her relief, Aaron roused himself, his eyes crinkled at her, and he joined the children at the rail, pointing out the dragonflies that were dancing over the water like bright jewels.

I wish this moment would last, Stef mused. She imagined briefly that they were a proper family on a day out, two parents, three young siblings, and liked the feel of it. *Though it's nonsense, of course.* She'd got to know the twins a little more this week. It should be easier as they grew up and became more individual. And Livy, gorgeous with her long, thick hair and striking features, was comical with the adult attitudes she struck.

It began to rain, a desultory shower, but heavy enough for Aaron to help Livy zip up her jacket and for them to move off under the thick canopy of an oak tree. Here, they stood listening to the patter of the raindrops on the leaves and the songs of the birds, who were undaunted by the weather. Jack poked his nose into a bole in the tree and made owl noises. 'Careful, something might nip you,' Stef said, laughing, but this didn't put him off.

'I want a go,' Jess said, butting his face with hers like a baby goat until he shifted. Then Livy had a try, her owl hoots trembling with laughter, before making her daddy squat down to do it, too. By the time the game was over the rain had eased and they were able to move on.

'Shall we try a bird hide?' Aaron suggested when they reached a large wooden shed. As he drew open the door, he raised his finger to his lips. 'Shh. You need to be quiet in here.' The children filed past him inside, their faces solemn and intent.

'You keep quiet, too,' Aaron joked as Stef followed them into warm darkness.

'Cheeky,' she muttered, and was aware of the warmth of his breath on her face as he pulled the door shut behind them. For a second, they all stood huddled close together. When he nudged past her to take Livy's hand, she felt an immediate sense of loss.

It took a moment to adjust her eyes to the gloom, then several horizontal strips of daylight with views of the Broad came into focus. Beneath these ran long benches, partly occupied by several birdwatchers leaning with their elbows on the sills, silently intent behind binoculars or high-tech cameras. Stef, whispering instructions, ushered the twins over to join Livy and Aaron, who had already laid claim to a vacant bench. Somehow she found herself sitting next to Aaron, with Livy to his other side and the twins standing beyond Livy with their arms resting on the sill. Aaron showed a restless Livy where to look and the child shifted onto his lap and leaned forward to peer out. Jack and Jess seemed rapt.

'Wish I'd brought my binoculars,' Aaron whispered in Stef's ear.'

'I don't even have any,' she whispered back, enjoying their closeness, but the peace didn't last for long. The birds were a long distance away and the children were quickly bored. When they began to chatter, a twitcher shushed them. It was time to go. Soon, they were filing back outside, the kids jumping about with relief at their freedom.

'Ice cream, ice cream,' Jess started to chant. 'You promised, Auntie Stef.'

'I did indeed,' Stef smiled and looked at Aaron. 'Shall we? My treat.'

Back at the visitors' centre, the rush had slackened and Josh was sitting at a picnic table outside, going over some paperwork and eating a sandwich. He didn't notice them as they passed, and when Stef went in with the children to buy the ice creams it was to find that Jackie was on duty. When they came out again, Aaron was standing chatting to Josh.

Stef ambled across and passed Aaron his ice cream.

'No chocolate, I'm afraid, so I got strawberry. Hi, Josh.'

'Hello there.'

She glanced down at the papers he'd been examining. They were held together on a clipboard and the top one appeared to be a bill of some sort. Just then a gust of wind blew, the papers fanned upwards and the bill tore off and flew away. Josh dived to retrieve it, leaving the clipboard on the table.

Something about the page now visible caught Stef's eye and she edged forward to inspect it. It was a list typed in an unusual italic font and she frowned. It appeared to concern stock for the shop. At the bottom was a handwritten addition in biro and a sign-off: 'J'.

Josh returned with the torn page and, leaving him to his sandwich, she and Aaron led the children to a far-flung table in a patch of sun. What, she wondered, as she peeled the lid off her ice cream tub, was it about the typed stocklist that was bothering her? Then it came to her.

'D'you know Josh well?' she asked Aaron.

'Not really. He just wanted to know about Tabitha . . .'

'Is he okay?'

'What do you mean by "okay"?'

'I don't know. This is probably a ridiculous thought, but could he be Nancy's letter writer?'

Aaron looked up sharply and his eyes searched hers. 'Why would you think that?'

She recounted her conversation with Josh from the day before and described the likeness of the font on the stocklist to the font on the latest letter. 'What would his motive be?'

Aaron ate a spoonful of ice cream, then licked his lips thoughtfully. 'I can't think of one. He's always been very protective of my grandmother. No, it doesn't wash with me.'

She glanced over at Josh, who was still frowning over his paperwork. It was indeed puzzling.

'I hope giving Livy ice cream hasn't spoiled her lunch,' she said, changing the subject. 'You're going to the Ilex Tree, or somewhere else?'

'The Ilex Tree. Nancy doesn't want to go far.'

'And then you're leaving.'

'Yes.' His smile was thoughtful as his eyes raked her face. 'London for a couple of days, then Cornwall.'

She swallowed. 'I hope Cornwall goes well for you. And . . . everything.'

'Everything . . .' he echoed.

'You have my number if you need it.' She felt her face grow warm. 'I'll definitely be going back to London this week – I've so much to get on with.'

'Those recordings to transcribe.'

'Among other things, yes. It's not just you who's busy!'

She regarded him steadily and he had the grace to smile. The ice creams were finished, so he dealt with the litter as she wiped the twins' faces with paper serviettes.

'Say goodbye nicely,' she urged them and they chanted politely.

'Goodbye, Livy, and goodbye, Aaron.'

Aaron hesitated, then stepped forward and hugged Stef briefly. 'Take care,' he said softly when he'd released her and she nodded.

'You, too, on the motorway.'

She reached for the twins' hands and set off on the way back to the car. As she opened the door to the visitors' centre, she looked back to see Aaron and his daughter disappearing into the reserve and felt a mixture of relief and sadness. Relief because she could get on with interviewing Nancy without his interference. Sadness because she and Aaron had made no arrangement to see one another again.

'I want to see Daddy,' Jack declared as she strapped the twins into the car.

'That would indeed be nice,' she said vaguely, careful not to make pronouncements that might turn out to be untrue.

During the short drive back to Springfield Cottage, her thoughts were fixed firmly on domestic matters. Would Rob still be there? Would Pippa, for that matter? When she turned into the lane, she was relieved to see that all three cars were still parked there. She pulled up behind her mother's to make a fourth.

Immediately the front door of the cottage opened and Rob stood framed in the doorway. His puzzled round face made Stef think uncharitably of a flat-faced dog denied its walk. He smiled sadly at her and sympathy for him surged in. She released the children and they ran to his embrace.

'Hope you've had a good time, kids,' he said, 'it's very kind of your auntie. Ice cream, eh?' Then he looked up at Stef. 'We have to get on the road right away, I'm afraid.'

Stef saw Pippa in the doorway, arms folded, still looking miserable. A tense few minutes followed as children and luggage were stowed into the people carrier, goodbyes briefly said and the two cars moved away in tandem, Pippa driving the twins in the bigger car and Rob in the small one, looking indeed ridiculously large in it.

Stef and her mother stood in the lane, waving them off, then sauntered back inside. As her mother closed the front door, Stef said mildly, 'Well, spill the beans, Mum. What was all that about?'

Cara spread her hands in a gesture of bewilderment, then went into the sitting room. Stef saw over her shoulder that the room was a mess. Together, they gathered up fragments of

Lego from under the furniture, plumped cushions and restored ornaments to their correct places. Her mum talked all the while.

'It's difficult to know what's going on. I left them arguing out in the field and went to church. When I returned, they were packing everything up. All Pip said was that she thought it best to go home, but she looked absolutely tragic. I'm quite worried about her. I don't think that Rob's been unkind – he seems sad and concerned rather than angry.'

'That's what I thought. Should we try to ring her later?' Stef scratched at a blob of dried yoghurt on the arm of the sofa. 'Or wait until tomorrow.'

Her mother paused. 'Tomorrow. She'll be busy with the twins tonight and anyway Rob might be around so she won't be able to say much.'

'You're right.' Stef gave up on the yoghurt and sat back on her heels with a sigh. 'I suppose there's upstairs to deal with, too.'

'Let's do that after lunch,' her mother sighed. 'I could murder a glass of wine.'

Lunch eaten and the beds stripped, Stef took Baxter out for a walk while her mother read the Sunday paper. As Stef closed the front door behind her, a clanking sound made her look up and she saw their host from last night's barbecue, Martin Baker, lugging a crate of empty bottles down his path. She watched him load it in the back of his car, presumably to take to the bottle bank.

'Thanks so much for last night,' she called. 'Did it go on late?'

'Till half-two. I hope we didn't disturb you.'

'No.' She'd been briefly aware in the night of cars leaving, but that had been all.

'Thanks for coming. Not every day we have celebrities to supper.'

'We're not celebrities,' she said, mortified by the idea.

He grinned. 'Geoffrey Stuart seemed to think so. Couldn't stop talking about you and your books. Told me you're writing a new one about that woman at the reserve. Says she's full of secrets. Was she one of those wartime spies or something?'

Stef, horrified, walked across to talk to him quietly so that the whole village wouldn't hear. Who'd been telling Geoffrey Stuart her business? Well, whoever it was had got everything wrong. 'It's not quite like that,' she told him, 'and I'd be obliged if you wouldn't spread it about.'

'Sorry.' He looked abashed as he lowered the car boot and gave her his full attention. 'But I gather it was your ma who told him about a book.'

'Mum?' Stef prickled with annoyance but tried to hide it. 'Dear old Mum. She's got the wrong end of the stick. The book is no more than a twinkle in my eye and it's just about the experiences of women scientists. Nothing to do with secrets at all!'

His brow knitted. 'Whoa! I'm sorry,' he said, raising his hands.

'Will you tell Mr Stuart that?'

'Yes, when I see him.'

They said goodbye and she trudged off, head down, Baxter

trotting along beside. She looked for Aaron's car near the pub. No sign, but it was well after two now. To pass the time, she stopped at the village hall to see her mother's painting in the art exhibition. Since she had Baxter with her, she didn't plan to stay for long. She quickly spotted Cara Lansdown's beautiful picture of distant figures on a sunny beach because its blues and yellows glowed jewel-like in the gloom from across the room. No wonder it had a sold sticker, Stef thought proudly.

She was on her way back to Springfield Cottage when her phone rang. It was Nancy to say that she was home again and that Aaron and Livy had left.

'D'you know, something marvellous has happened.' Her voice quavered with emotion. 'Tabitha's come home.'

Thirty-Five

'She's in remarkably good condition.' Nancy was settled in her usual place on the sofa and was stroking Tabitha, who lay dozing on a throw beside her. The cat raised her head briefly to blink at Stef, then stretched luxuriantly.

Stef put down her bag on a chair and crouched down to examine the cat, reaching to scratch behind Tabitha's ears. Tabitha began to purr. 'She does seem well,' she said. The cat was no thinner than usual and her fur had a glossy sheen. 'Where did you find her?'

'She found me. I was sitting here feeling a little forlorn after saying goodbye to Aaron and Livy, and she sashayed into the room! I hadn't heard the cat flap go, though I don't think she can have been in the house for long because her fur was damp. I went out to the kitchen but she hadn't touched the food I'd left out. She wasn't hungry.'

'It sounds as though someone's been looking after her.'

'It rather seems like it. She's certainly too old to catch mice and birds to eat. But who, and why?'

Stef thought for a moment, then met Nancy's eye. 'This is a bit mad, but you don't suppose it was the letter writer, trying to frighten you?'

Nancy frowned, then shook her head.

Another explanation crossed Stef's mind, and she suppressed a shiver. The cat had reappeared immediately after Aaron and Livy had left. *No!* Aaron would never do something like that. She was horrified at herself for even thinking it.

'Stef?'

'No, it's nothing,' she lied. She straightened, sat down in her usual seat, then hurried on. 'It's possible that she was trapped somewhere where there was food, I suppose, or that someone found her and took her in.'

'Yes,' Nancy said doubtfully, 'though I can't think where. Oh well, she's back. That's the important thing. Thank you so much for popping by. How are things with your family?'

'Pip's not happy,' she said. 'It's odd, isn't it? A stranger would look at her situation and think she had a perfect life.'

'No,' Nancy said feelingly. 'One can never assume that of anyone. I remember people saying that of my own sister and how wrong they were.'

'What happened there?' Stef asked.

'My dear, we were talking about *your* sister. Ours were different times.'

'I'd like to hear, though.'

Nancy looked mischievous. 'You've brought your tape recorder, have you?'

'I might have done!'

'Good.' They smiled at each other. Stef brought the machine out of her bag and set it running, and Nancy began.

Thirty-Six

January 1951

Nancy's early days in Hertfordshire were marked by bad weather. She cycled from her new lodgings in the town through rain or sleet to reach Brandingfield Hall, a hunched mass of buildings in a park on high ground, whose bright lights glowed eerily ahead through the fog.

Once inside, she inhabited a different world. The chilly marble entrance hall with its grand pillars had survived Hitler's bombing, but the back of the house had fared less well, and its classical façade disguised a mishmash of patched-up rooms repurposed as modern laboratories, offices and meeting areas.

Her own equipment, brought up from London, occupied a metal worktop in the corner of an old reception room on the ground floor, where the pattern of the old Chinese wallpaper could still be seen through a new layer of pale green paint.

The room was small and new windows had been installed, which made it easier to keep her locusts warm, though once again she put up notices warning the unwary against turning off the heat lamps.

Anne was still in London and Edmund had been allocated space in a different lab here, and with the building still half-empty, Nancy was disappointed to find herself on her own.

'I fear I'm spending as little time there as possible,' she scribbled in a letter to James West one evening at the desk in her dingy bedroom. James had been deployed to Catterick in Yorkshire for army training, and somewhat to her surprise had started writing her long newsy letters. She always answered them promptly. Like him, she had little else to do with her evenings. Edmund took the train back to London each night and she hadn't yet got to know others at Brandingfield.

She stared up sightlessly at the damp patch in the corner of the bedroom, then wrote:

The hostel forwarded your letter. My billet's now in a very odd household near Brandingfield. My landlady is one Mrs Harrison, who might easily be related to Miss Pick, she's so mean. Here's what her lodgers have to provide for themselves: soap, towels, sheets and pillow cases, lavatory paper, cleaning materials. We must clean our own rooms and not be out beyond ten o'clock without good reason. There was a one-pound deposit for a front door key. I'm not planning to stay here long, but there's so much to become used to at present, I can't get my head round finding somewhere else yet.

She looked forward to returning home at weekends, to the safety of her childhood bedroom and to her parents, who, though irritating, loved her. Yet home was no longer the same. Her brother Roger had recently moved into lodgings with friends.

'Helen has that whey-faced look, don't you think, Arthur?' was Mrs Foster's cryptic remark one Sunday in February as she returned a bowl of hyacinths to the coffee table after the little family's departure.

'She just looked exhausted to me,' Nancy's father replied. 'I'm not surprised, looking after that little rascal.'

Nancy considered this. Certainly Helen had looked unhappy, her skin pale and puffy. And Bob was snappish with her, though he managed the baby skilfully enough. At seven months, little Andrew had learned to roll and Bob was up and down, disentangling the child from the flex of the standard lamp and rescuing the cat from his tight grip on her tail.

'I don't know whether to be worried.'

'About what, Mum?'

'She's not properly recovered from the first one yet, poor girl.'

'Oh.' Nancy twigged. Her mother believed that another baby was on the way. She shuddered. Poor Helen indeed.

'Don't get ahead of yourself, dear,' Nancy's father warned his wife, but another fortnight proved Mrs Foster right. The baby was expected in the autumn.

*

By February, Nancy had started to overcome her early

difficulties at Brandingfield. Her research was going well. The technician was competent, if a bit of a drip. The cleaner learned not to switch off the heat lamp when she plugged in the vacuum cleaner and the locusts thrived in their new home. She bought winter greens to feed them on from a shop she passed in the mornings, leaving enough in their tank to sustain them at weekends. Little by little, she tested humanely killed specimens with different kinds of dust imbued with insecticide and examined them for the effects. It was a slow business, but it was important to be meticulous, to make careful measurements, to note every detail she saw through her microscope and ponder it.

Sometimes the results were puzzling. She felt she was accruing data without knowing how to interpret it, but there was no one to consult. Professor Briggs, her supervisor, was difficult to track down. If he visited Brandingfield, she was rarely told in advance. Only once did he deliberately come to see her, but he merely glanced through her work and asked one or two perceptive questions that left her wanting more before he went on his way. In late February, she wrote to him at Prince's College, asking for specific guidance, but the reply came from a secretary. *'Professor Briggs is in South America on sabbatical and not expected back until early summer. He's out in the field and not easily contactable.'* Her heart sank as she read the letter. She must plod on by herself.

'It's so dispiriting,' she complained to Edmund that same day, making coffee for them both in the galley kitchen off the main common room. She opened the door of a small fridge that hummed in a corner. 'Do you suppose this is all right?'

She passed him a bottle of milk someone had left among the mouldy sandwiches and other items best left unidentified and he sniffed at it.

'Let's risk it,' he said with one of his grave smiles.

It being mid-morning, the comfortable armchairs were all taken so they sat opposite one another on benches at a wobbly wooden table. 'I'm sorry about Briggs,' Edmund said as he mopped a patch of spilled coffee with his handkerchief. 'Dr Hillman isn't much in evidence, either, if it makes you feel any better, but I've found another chap here who knows all about my flies and he's giving me advice.'

'Another student?'

'No. He's a researcher with ICP.'

Nancy nodded. Brandingfield would never have opened if it hadn't been for the generosity of International Chemical Products. She was used to seeing their scientists around the place. They were civil enough, but not particularly interested in the graduate students.

She glanced round the common room. It was different to the Zoo department at Prince's College in that she saw only men. Men sitting in clusters, talking earnestly over paperwork or laughing at each other's stories. Men on their own, smoking and staring into space. She was getting used to this masculine environment and no longer found it remarkable, just sometimes tiresome.

There were other women in the building, but many of them were technicians or administrative staff. They tended to congregate in a smaller, mixed-sex staff common room nearby. Other female scientists used that, too, finding the atmosphere more congenial. Nancy went there often and enjoyed the laughter, though she was careful to avoid one or two characters who liked to rule the roost or spread malicious gossip.

In the scientists' common room, few of the men spoke to her and she felt a need to be watchful, but if Edmund looked her up on his way to have a coffee there or a sandwich, she was happy to accompany him. He didn't care what other men thought of him befriending her and she blessed him for it.

'This chap Rutherfurd,' he went on, 'is on one of ICP's projects. Something to do with pesticides and fruit flies. He keeps it close, as you might imagine.'

'Top secret?' Nancy laughed. *What could be secret about fruit flies?*

'It's commercial research. Of course they want to keep it for themselves.'

'So he gets to know about your research, but you don't find out about his. That doesn't sound fair.'

'The commercial context is very different from the academic, Nancy,' Edmund said mildly. 'We academics are more collegiate in our approach.'

'I do know that.' She blushed at his rebuke of her naïvety. 'There is plenty of competition in our world, though,' she said, to indicate she wasn't completely green.

'Of course,' he sighed. 'We all want credit where credit is due, that's human nature. But as we go on, I expect we'll be working in teams, trusting one another and pooling our knowledge.'

'I'd like that,' she said thoughtfully, then seeing his face, broke off.

'I shouldn't be too generous with your findings, though.' Edmund's eyes twinkled. 'The rivalry for research posts and grants is keen and your reputation will be crucial.'

'We'll just have to prove ourselves, then.'

I've been living in a cocoon, she acknowledged to herself later as she fed her locusts spinach in the safety of her lab. She thought of the groups of men in the common room and glimpsed a vision of how it would be for her as a woman. It had been bad enough as an undergraduate with girls making up half the cohort, but from now on it would be harder. She sighed as she carefully closed the tank. At least she had an ally in Edmund.

Thirty-Seven

Dorothy Winters was a fellow researcher a couple of years older than Nancy. They had met in the staff common room and Nancy was initially drawn to her because she reminded her of Peggy. Dorothy had that same Edinburgh accent and was small and fragile-looking. But her hair was more of a gorgeous auburn shade than Peggy's flaring ginger and instead of freckles she had a clear, creamy complexion. Nancy missed Peggy, though they wrote to one another often. Peggy had become a schoolmistress and Nancy enjoyed her amusing descriptions of her charges in a girls' school in South London. George had taken a training post as a government scientist, which appeared to involve wading through waterlogged fields advising farmers on drainage. They planned to marry at the end of the year.

Dorothy turned out to be a completely different kind of person from Peggy, more intense and serious compared to Peggy's open lightness. She was also the first woman of her own age Nancy had met at Brandingfield who was as ambitious as herself. Her PhD was behind her and she was researching diseases of honey bees with a grant from the Agricultural Research Council. When Nancy asked her advice about analysing data on her own project, Dorothy made a useful suggestion that set her off on a new track. Nancy appreciated her support. In turn, she went out into the frosty air to view Dorothy's beehives outside the portable hut where she operated. Dorothy, too, was supervised by Professor Briggs. 'Notionally, anyway,' she laughed without merriment. 'He's immensely knowledgeable, so it's a shame I see him so rarely.'

It was Dorothy who brightened Nancy's social life at Brandingfield, inviting her to supper at the house in town where she lodged with a senior lecturer and his wife who also both worked at the laboratory. 'The Brauns love meeting new people,' she insisted when Nancy asked if they'd mind another mouth to feed.

She'd enjoyed the evening hugely. Frank and Eleanor Braun, who were about forty, were keen musicians with a large collection of classical gramophone records. After supper, they listened to music and the Brauns talked about art and places they'd visited on their travels. Frank was of Swiss extraction and had relatives in Lucerne. He had worked in Paris for a couple of years after the war and spoke French and German. Nancy, who had never left British shores, was fascinated. It was the first of several such evenings, and then Nancy was thrilled when Eleanor took her aside in the kitchen one night.

'Dorothy mentioned that your current living arrangements are a little spartan.'

'Oh, I can't really complain.' Nancy was flustered at the thought of being talked about behind her back. 'My landlady is a bit of a character, that's all.'

Eleanor laughed. 'I know all about landladies like that. What I wondered, Nancy, was whether you'd like to move in here. It would be a room at the back, not very big, but it gets the sun in the mornings and can be very cosy when the gas fire's lit. Why don't you come over in daylight and take a look?'

'I'd love to,' Nancy gasped. 'Thank you!'

The bedroom was indeed small, but as attractive as Eleanor had described. The sum Eleanor named for board and lodging was slightly more expensive than her present arrangement, but she could use the fire as much as she liked without having to feed it coins and Eleanor's cooking far surpassed anything that Mrs Harrison put on the table. She thought she might also save on train fares home, as here she'd be happier to stay put at weekends, though she was determined to make the effort to see her parents at least once a month.

After she moved in, her life at Brandingfield became instantly more comfortable and less lonely. She'd found good friends in Dorothy, Eleanor and Frank, and through them began to meet others. Once or twice, Edmund came to supper and Frank particularly appreciated his company because of shared cultural interests and wartime experiences. Frank also took an interest in Edmund's research and it wasn't long before Nancy noticed how Edmund's own network of acquaintances was growing. He became drawn into other men's conversations in the scientists' common room in a way that she wasn't. She was pleased for him, but privately it galled her.

Sobering, too, was a conversation she had with Eleanor one afternoon. Nancy had come back early after a frustrating day at Brandingfield, when she'd accidentally dropped and broken a collection of slides containing important samples. She let herself into the house thinking that no one would be home, only to find Eleanor sitting at the dining room table sorting a box of paperwork.

'Oh, I couldn't think who it was,' Eleanor said, looking at Nancy in surprise through lopsided frames. Eleanor famously hated herself in spectacles and was always taking them off and hiding them in silly places where they got damaged.

'Bad day, better tomorrow,' Nancy said briefly. 'How about you?'

'Oh ...' Eleanor waved her hand impatiently over the mess on the table. 'Trying to make order out of chaos as ever. I sometimes think Frank only married me for my organizational skills.'

Nancy squinted at the lists of figures in Frank's familiar scrawl. 'He's writing a paper?'

'I'm writing the paper,' Eleanor said feelingly. 'But both our names will go on it. The Board wouldn't consider it if it were just mine. It's the results of our joint research, I don't dispute that, but I've no status, do you see? I've a doctorate, Nancy, but I was never able to advance any further than a lowly research position. Every paper I wrote got ignored or turned down, and without any publications to my name I couldn't apply for better research posts.'

'But why?'

'It's fairly obvious, isn't it? It's because I'm female. No one actually said, "We don't give grants to women". No, it's more subtle than that. I wasn't part of any network. Some of the men I needed to impress wouldn't speak to me, or mistook me for a technician and asked me to fetch the tea. In the end, I took a position as a technician at Prince's before the war in order to pay the bills. It was only when Frank arrived that things changed.'

'You mean—'

'You know Frank, he'll talk to anyone. We were both interested in water pollution and began to collaborate. Our love bloomed over watchglasses of algae. He proposed to me while we were knee-deep in a stew pond on Epsom Common. But it's me who writes the papers. I was always good at English, you see, and he never enjoyed that aspect of the work. The important thing is that I'm published at all. I love Frank and I love my work, but you can't say it's fair. It simply isn't.'

'No,' Nancy said, wonderingly. She'd never heard the gentle Eleanor speak with such bitterness before. The Brauns had seemed to her a perfect match, both intellectuals, he lively and gregarious, she soothing and supportive.

'Fortunately, I never had strong feelings about becoming a mother,' Eleanor continued sadly. 'Nor did I have the choice. We didn't marry until I was thirty-seven and somehow a baby never came along. Frank would have liked a child,

I think, so it's a shame.' She squared a sheaf of papers by knocking them on the table, then smiled cheerfully. 'Instead, I have lots of paper babies and they give me great pleasure.'

'I didn't know things like that happened,' Nancy said humbly. 'I'm sorry. Perhaps it's getting better now – I hope so.' She thought about the tight groups of men in the scientists' common room, how naturally Edmund had started to move among them, and wondered.

'Maybe it will change, but slowly, I think. My advice, dear Nancy, if you want it, is to be prepared for a struggle. We can count the names of noted women scientists on one hand. In Zoology, being a 'softer' science, it may easier than for our sisters in Chemistry or Physics, but the structures are the same – it's a man's world.'

'Maybe we women should make our own structures,' Nancy said lightly, and she was pleased when Eleanor pursed her lips thoughtfully.

'Perhaps we should!'

There were only the three of them to start with, Eleanor, Dorothy and Nancy, but they sat down together and made a list of possible names. There was a quiet but purposeful-looking researcher in her thirties named Jean Parr, whom Eleanor knew slightly and agreed to approach. 'She's working on a project about fertility in mice.' Jean was pleased to be asked.

Dorothy had befriended Sally Banes, a young technician with a doctorate, who'd married a schoolmaster who was often ill so she had decided not to pursue research because 'life is difficult enough'. Sally was glad to be included in the little network.

Nancy decided to ask Anne Durban. 'She's based at Prince's, but she might be interested to come to a meeting if it's only once a month.' They'd all agreed this to be a realistic frequency.

The six women met for the first time over supper at Frank and Eleanor's. Frank, his expression genial, agreed to absent himself for the evening. 'It's not that we don't love you,' Dorothy insisted the night before, 'but you've got your own networks.'

'I have indeed. I'll be meeting some of my old team from Bristol, Eleanor. I won't be back at all tomorrow night. Bill Jameson's offered to put me up.'

The meeting wasn't one in any formal sense of the word. Eleanor had made a large Lancashire hotpot to warm the chilly March evening. Nancy met Anne at the station and the six women introduced themselves to one another and spoke about their work and experiences, hesitantly at first, but after finding that the others had encountered similar problems, with more confidence.

'I'll be absolutely clear,' Eleanor said, 'this should not be a moaning session. Nor will we have an agenda and minutes and that kind of nonsense. We may be at different stages of our careers, but we're all equal and – I must emphasize this – what we say here stays within these four walls.'

'I agree,' Sally Banes sighed, 'though I can hardly be said to have a career. I work as a technician because we need to pay the bills.'

'You're a scientist and you're a woman. Those are the only qualifications you need to be welcome here.'

'You're all so kind,' Sally said, her eyes shining with unshed tears. 'I feel invisible sometimes at Brandingfield. Some of the men treat me like a Victorian serving maid. Do this, do that, never a please or a thank you. They don't speak like that to the male technicians.'

'I think we should challenge them about that sort of behaviour,' Eleanor said, frowning. 'If we all do it when we come across it, they might take notice.'

'Ask them if they treat their wives like that,' Dorothy said.

'I expect some of them do,' Sally said glumly.

The women were interested to hear of Anne's experiences in her lab at Prince's, where she felt increasingly uncomfortable when the owner of the fish tank was around. 'He stares at me with the unblinking intensity of one of his wretched fish,' she complained, her face pink with embarrassment. 'I hate being on my own with him in case he tries something. I can't report it because nothing nasty has actually happened and I'd sound stupid. Do you understand what I mean?'

Everyone murmured fervent agreement. 'It's monstrous if it stops you getting on with your work,' Jean Parr said.

Eleanor thought for a moment. 'I think it would be worth you having a word in authority's ear,' she said. 'Then they couldn't claim not to have been warned if something unpleasant does happen.'

'Though anything unpleasant should be prevented,' Dorothy said. 'I'd keep something sharp nearby – a pair of scissors – and go for the eyes.'

'I couldn't do that,' Anne gasped amid general laughter.

'What about Mrs Hall?' Nancy said, remembering Miss Pick's helpful assistant technician. 'Maybe she would pop by unexpectedly from time to time and glare at him.'

'I'll think about it,' Anne said weakly. 'Perhaps I'm misjudging the poor man.'

'Misjudging, my foot,' Dorothy muttered. 'He shouldn't be allowed to make you feel uncomfortable in your own lab even if he is otherwise harmless.'

Their meetings continued regularly. They agreed at the end of the first one that they should not become a closed clique, so if other women expressed an interest they would be warmly invited. By the summer, numbers had risen to nearly a dozen and the event was turned into a pot luck supper, with everyone bringing a dish and the atmosphere more like a party than a meeting. It was still enjoyable, the house ringing with lively conversation and laughter, but the group lost something of its early purpose, which was to address serious issues for women at Brandingfield, and, though useful, it became more about friendship and mutual support. Nancy did not mention the supper group when she wrote to James. She was nervous that he might sneer. His replies to her letters were sporadic, but amusing. She giggled at descriptions of his fellow recruits and frowned at the messes he got himself into. *'I'm too slow at everything,'* he complained.

I don't know why, but I never seem to be ready when everyone else is. You can't imagine the hot water I find myself in. I've told you about our sergeant. He calls me the Boffin and says if they'd had to rely on me in the war it would have been all over for us by Christmas. I feel sorry for him sometimes having us lot. Nobody wants to be here and many can't see the point of it. If our platoon were sent on active service, that would be a different matter, but instead it's all square-bashing and cleaning rifles. How I'll stick it out for another nine months without going barking mad, I know not. Now, tell me how old Ed Buckland is. And do you ever hear anything from the lovely Miss Durban?

She read this last sentence with a pang, for it seemed that James still held a candle for Anne. 'Anne is very well,' she wrote back after leaving it a week to appear cooler than she felt, but she kept the matter of Anne's difficulties to herself. Anne would be horrified to think that anyone beyond the original women's supper group knew about Mr Fish Tank. She'd not spoken of the matter again in Nancy's hearing, but Nancy understood that Anne had confided further in Eleanor and that with Mrs Hall keeping a watchful eye things were better.

Thirty-Eight

By mid-July, the inhabitants of Brandingfield began to disappear on holiday. Nancy ran down her supply of locusts because there would be no one to tend them over the summer. She offered the final few to a reptiles expert who presided over a tank containing a large, hungry iguana. Then she filed her papers, tidied her work station and took a last lingering look round the little kingdom where she reigned supreme. Despite all her difficulties, the year had gone well and she'd earned her holiday. She closed the door with a soaring sense of freedom and went to say goodbye to Edmund, who was leaving shortly himself to take his young daughter, Marianne, to stay with his parents in Dorset.

Nancy was to accompany Frank, Eleanor and Dorothy on her first trip abroad, a month driving through France to Switzerland, where they were to stay in a chalet belonging to a cousin of Frank's. Their first stop was Paris, where Frank had worked for a while before the war, and where he still had friends including a married couple who had a young son. It was a bit of a squash in their St Germain apartment, but if anybody minded the forced intimacy they were too polite to say.

Nancy loved Paris. It was extraordinary that, given all that its people had suffered under German occupation, the city itself had been largely undamaged. Coming from tired old London, where children played in weed-infested bombsites and rain made giant puddles of craters in the streets, she felt she'd been set free. She loved the opulent stores in the Champs Elysées, bought beautifully crafted chocolates for her family in a smart little shop full of mirrors and admired the great coloured glass windows glowing out of the echoing gloom of Notre-Dame. She enjoyed sitting outside cafés drinking cups of bitter coffee and watching elegantly dressed Parisians swan by. Eleanor took Nancy and Dorothy to the Louvre, where they wandered endlessly until they were drunk on the richness of Renaissance altar panels, portraits of blowsy nudes and delicately patterned porcelain. Gaps on the walls told a different story, though, as did the haunted eyes of wounded veterans begging on the streets and their hosts' stories of surviving under the Occupation.

All too soon, they said their goodbyes to Paris and headed south-east. The car wound its way through lush farmland, past fields of cows, then sunny vineyards. They stopped for meals in little villages, where they sat outside homely restaurants on squares with pollarded trees for shade, and stayed a night in a lonely wayside hotel. Soon after breakfast the next morning the road began to climb through hill country towards snow-capped mountains wreathed with cloud. The air turned cool.

'Switzerland,' she wrote to her parents, 'is the most delightful place I've ever visited.'

The air is so pure and the animals are beautiful. Frank's cousin Hans has a pair of white-haired goats. The cows wear bells to stop them getting lost, and you can hear these in the distance from the other side of the valley. And the alpine flowers in the high pasture are so pretty and merry. It's just like in Heidi *– do you remember the pictures in my copy? And our wooden chalet is just like in the book. Hans' wife Elsa hangs baskets of flowers from the eaves. There's even a cuckoo clock!*

The weather was clear and sunny, but cool enough for walking, and they were out hiking every day, taking sandwiches with them and flasks of tea. They were there for a fortnight and when it was time to go home Nancy didn't want to leave. '*I feel like I shall be leaving a part of myself in the mountains,*' she wrote on a postcard to Peggy.

She returned home to be told that her sister, now eight months pregnant, was struggling to cope and reluctantly agreed to go and stay with her for the remaining week of her holiday. It was hard trying to amuse a one-year-old who was only interested in gaining his mother's attention, and the twin tub became her personal enemy. She flooded the kitchen twice. The return to Brandingfield and a fresh tank of locusts couldn't come quickly enough in her opinion.

When Nancy entered her lab, expecting all to be as she had left it, she stopped dead in the doorway with surprise. A leather briefcase and a sandwich tin lay on a previously unoccupied worktop, then her gaze was drawn to a black coat slung carelessly over the armed chair under the window. With a prickling feeling, she recognized that coat. It belonged to James.

At the sound of slow footsteps in the corridor, she snapped round to see him enter.

'Hello!' His lopsided smile was as arrogant as ever, as was his air of self-possession, but a walking stick was hooked over one arm and his gait was stiff as he crossed the room, the coffee he carried slopping into the saucer.

'What on earth . . . ?' She stared at him, lost for words. There were other differences. His dark hair was cropped above his ears and his face looked even paler than usual, his eyes larger, with bruises under them. She found her voice. 'Why are you here? Don't tell me they threw you out for bad behaviour.'

He leaned his stick against the worktop, then stirred his coffee, took a sip and nodded with satisfaction. 'Not bad after the stuff in the mess. Honourable discharge is the correct phrase.' He grinned and rubbed his right leg. 'That's the end of my military career. I fouled up my cruciate ligaments on a training exercise. Jolly painful, but it got me a free ticket out.'

Her eyes widened in sympathy, then narrowed with puzzlement. 'You didn't say in your last letter, but that was ages ago. When did you do it?'

'Three weeks back. I've been in hospital for most of that. Doped up after the op.'

'And they just let you go?'

'Nothing else for it. I'm supposed to be convalescing at home, but two days of my mother fussing about and I thought I'd come up here. Briggs is handling my application. Shouldn't be any trouble, he said.'

'Professor Briggs? I thought he was in South America somewhere.'

'Did you? Well, he's back now. He was here last week, in fact, but you were away.'

'Was he? Someone might have let me know and I'd have come in,' she muttered with a rush of annoyance. 'I've been trying to get in touch with him for months.'

'So I'm to join you in here,' he said with a satisfied smile.

His stick fell. Nancy picked it up from the floor, then hung his coat up next to hers behind the door.

'Thanks.'

'What was it like, National Service?' she asked, genuinely curious. 'I loved your letters, but I couldn't tell just how awful it was. Was it awful?'

He shook his head, drank his coffee down quickly and said, 'Boring, mostly. If you'd been to boarding school, you'd feel quite at home.'

'But you didn't go to boarding school.'

'No.' He set down his cup and saucer and his eye wandered to the assortment of equipment at her corner of the room. She saw it through his eyes: the empty tank, soon to be home to the next consignment of insects, the odd-looking bits of kit, the books and ring-binder files stacked on the shelves, flyers and photographs pinned to a cork noticeboard.

'What's that?' He shuffled over to the worktop and reached up for the little carving she kept on a shelf.

'What do you think it is? A dragonfly, silly. Edmund made it for me once!'

'It's not bad,' he said, squinting at it.

She took it from him and set it back in its place, but his curiosity wasn't satisfied.

'May I?' He took down one of the files without waiting for an answer, flicked through its contents briefly and muttered, 'Interesting,' before he put it back.

She was gripped by a sense of helplessness, wondering how she would work with him in the room, given his power both to beguile and annoy her, but if he noticed his effect on her he didn't show it. Instead, he settled himself on the chair under the window. 'Fill me in. What's been going on and what's everyone up to?'

If Nancy had ever complained about being lonely and isolated in her lab, she regretted doing so now. Over the next few weeks, she found it both a pleasure and a pain to accommodate James. He wasn't a constant presence. Being right at the beginning of his studies, he'd not yet assembled all his equipment, but when he did appear she found herself unable to concentrate, for he'd either loiter, engaging her in conversation about his work or hers, or sit sighing over his notebooks and shuffling about. His experience of National Service had changed him, she thought, but she couldn't put her finger on how. He seemed older, definitely. His thin figure had filled out, and he'd lost something of his boyish freshness.

She didn't know whether to be flattered at his interest in her locust project or be alarmed by it, but on the whole she was pleased, for sometimes he offered an astute suggestion or drew her attention to some new article he'd read.

Of his own interests she learned little. Briggs had fixed up for him to study a particular group of grasshoppers. This faintly troubled Nancy, it being close to her own subject, but she tried to assure herself that any overlap would probably be helpful, and anyway, James was a year behind her, so it would be more likely that she could advise him about avenues that were a waste of time, for instance. Yes, a collaborative approach would forward the progress of scientific knowledge and Professor Briggs had always said that this was important to the success of Brandingfield.

But there was something else. Even when James was absent from the room and there was peace and quiet to concentrate on her observations and record her careful measurements, she longed for his presence. *Like a dog waiting for its master to come home,* she berated herself. And James' was a very animal presence. With his restlessness and the way he fixed his intense dark gaze upon her, he seemed to dominate the room. He had her cat Bonnie's way of prowling about, touched things or rolled them between his long, sensitive fingers. She wished she didn't keep imagining those fingers touching her, hated the way that he filled her dreams.

'Could you not do that?' she snapped once. She was poring over some figures that wouldn't make sense.

'Do what?'

'That tapping noise with your pen. It goes right through my head.'

'Sorry.' The noise stopped, but a minute or two later it started again.

'James! I'm trying to think.'

Their eyes met and his twinkled. 'Sorry,' he said again, making a mournful face. 'I genuinely didn't know I was doing it.'

'Yes, well.'

'What are you doing, anyway?' He limped across to her side. He rarely used the stick inside now, though he'd unhook it from the rack for the walk to the station. He was still living at home with his parents, but now he was starting to pore over the local paper, looking for digs.

'These figures are not what I'd expect.' She showed him, explaining her method, and he pointed out a variable she'd forgotten. Suddenly, everything made sense and she thanked him. 'If I'd known how important maths was in this work,' she moaned, 'I'd have tried harder in sixth form.'

'You girls are soft about maths,' he teased, returning to his seat.

She glared at him, then picked up a rubber and threw it so it bounced off the back of his head.

'Ow, that hurt,' he laughed, rescuing it from the floor and tossing it at her, and soon they were throwing it back and forth until it hit Nancy's tank, causing the locusts to thud about in alarm. This stopped the game in its tracks.

Thirty-Nine

One morning, she was setting up some new equipment when there was a commotion in the corridor outside. She raised her head as the door burst open and James entered, his face hidden by a giant cardboard box he was carrying.

'The project begins!' he cried, hefting it onto the worktop. Later, the technician joined him and they spent an hour assembling a complex edifice of equipment. After they'd finished, Nancy examined it, bending to see inside an empty tank that was similar to her own and tracing the muddle of glass tubes and funnels that led from it.

'A veritable Heath Robinson contraption,' she said in admiration. 'What does it do?'

'It's a feeding tract. Saves one opening the lid. I've ordered the inhabitants, but God knows when they'll arrive.'

A box of special grasshoppers arrived a week later and soon the tank was full of the softly rustling, tapping insects. Nancy liked them better than the locusts. 'They seem more friendly,' she explained, which made James roar with laughter.

'Friendly? They're insects, Nance, not pets. You shouldn't get emotional about them.'

'Don't call me Nance,' she said crossly. She was dismayed by his laughter, feeling put down. Dorothy or Anne, she thought, would know exactly what she meant by preferring grasshoppers. Surely she wasn't being unscientific when she expressed such feelings.

More serious than such attacks on her dignity was a rumour that began to circulate. She didn't know where it came from or what she'd done to inspire it. She first suspected something unpleasant was at work when she entered the staff common room and a pair of women broke off their conversation and stared at her like a couple of guilty-looking sheep. A cold feeling seeped through her. They'd been talking about her.

The following day, she encountered one of the secretaries in the entrance hall, hailing her cheerily because they'd always been friendly, but the older woman only gave a nod and hurried past her, averting her eyes. Nancy stopped and stared after her, a tender lump swelling in her throat.

It was Dorothy who explained, an angry Dorothy. 'What is it about some women? They think you're having an affair. Well, actually, two affairs. Apparently you've been seeing Edmund, but now you've dumped him in favour of James. Or you haven't dumped him, you're "riding two horses at once". All rubbish, of course.' She paused, shamefaced. 'It is rubbish, isn't it?'

'Of course it's rubbish!' Nancy stared at her in rage and

disbelief. 'Anyway, what business is it of anyone's? It's not as if either man is married. I mean, Edmund was, but he isn't now.'

Dorothy rolled her eyes. 'Honestly, you're awfully innocent.'

'But I've not done anything. I *am* innocent.'

'Naïve, then. I expect it's to do with the friendly way you have with men,' Dorothy sighed. 'You're always being seen with Edmund, for a start.'

'We're talking about our work. And I'm friendly with him because we're friends.'

'I'm sure that's true, but many other people don't think men and women can "just be friends". And sharing a lab with James, that's asking for trouble. All that time alone with him.'

'Hardly my fault. No one consulted me before they put him in there.'

'They're saying that you and he arranged it between you.'

'Who's saying that? It's nonsense. Why don't they say these things about you, Dorothy? You're prettier than me. Half the men are in love with you. Their eyes fix on you when you pass.'

'Hogswill!' Dorothy said rudely.

There was, however, more than a grain of truth in this. With her auburn hair and flawless skin, she was astonishingly attractive. Nancy had seen men stare after her, but somehow her friend always shrugged off this attention.

'It helps that I've invented Norman,' Dorothy explained with a laugh. Norman, Nancy knew, was Dorothy's non-existent boyfriend. If any man made an advance, 'Norman' would be invoked as the excuse for Dorothy's rejection. 'Their dignity is not threatened if they think you're another man's possession.

Listen, Nancy, I'll do my best to counter the gossip, but perhaps you should do the same. How about a Peter who's in the Foreign Office? Or an Italian? Silvio would sound more exotic.'

'I couldn't!' Nancy said, outraged. 'Anyway,' she mumbled, 'no one would believe me.'

Dorothy sighed. 'You shouldn't put yourself down, Nancy. You're very attractive and dress so nicely. Lots of men fancy brunettes because they look' – her voice turned husky and she narrowed her eyes – 'mysterious and passionate. Like Lauren Bacall.'

'Pish.'

Still, Nancy was flattered. That evening, she consulted the mirror. It was true that her thick dark hair was her crowning glory and her grey-blue eyes were unusual, but her pale skin tended to oiliness and she always seemed to have a spot on her chin. She never usually bothered with make-up during the day, but perhaps a touch of powder wouldn't hurt. Anything more would undoubtedly feed the gossip.

She frowned at her reflection as she cleaned her teeth. Somehow she'd have to ride out this nonsense. The women in the supper club wouldn't countenance it, surely? She couldn't be certain. Dorothy had called her naïve as if she'd brought it on herself. A thought came to her and a blush of shame warmed her cheeks. It was no good feeling self-righteous when it came to James. Nothing had happened yet to vindicate the gossips, but secretly she wished it would.

The weeks passed and Nancy redoubled her attention on her work. She couldn't do much about James, since they had to share the lab space, but she took care only to see Edmund in a group. Doing this bothered her. It felt like giving in to allow the gossip to spoil a good friendship. Had he heard the malicious rumours, she wondered? The thought embarrassed her. Her action was no good, anyway. The mud they'd thrown had stuck. Some of the women remained cool with her, the older secretary and a couple of the technicians, even another female doctoral student, who should have known better. She'd learned a painful lesson. A reputation once lost was not easily regained.

Finally, she decided she didn't care. She would look the gossipmongers in the eye, even if their gaze slid away. She would keep her voice steady when she asked them for information or help with equipment. And when one day Edmund stopped her in the corridor and asked if she'd like to attend a lecture with him at the Royal Society, she abandoned caution. It was about the pondlife of the New Forest, he said. With a rush of pleasure at the memory of the field trip, she said yes, she would go.

The lecture brought back the wonders of that idyllic time at the end of their first year as undergraduates at Prince's College. The lecturer, an earnest, middle-aged professor from Bristol University, was a dragonfly enthusiast.

'That's the one we couldn't catch,' Edmund whispered as a slide of an Emperor dragonfly came onto the screen. 'Perhaps it really is the same one!'

She giggled.

After the lecture had finished, they stayed behind for drinks and spoke to Professor McCall, who was not at all grand or condescending, instead asking kindly after their own studies. He nodded gravely when Nancy described her work with locusts and said, 'Important work. Very important. I know John Briggs, of course. There's a tie-up with ICP, isn't there? These new insecticides, I rather fear we'll come to regret them. I'm not a lone voice in this and there have been examples of human deaths from DDT. No one has got them banned yet, though, they're too useful. Especially in combatting malaria.'

'They're very effective on pests like locusts. Imagine if we could solve the problems of world hunger,' Nancy said, feeling dismayed.

'I very much support that aim,' he said, 'but I suspect that ICP's profits are more important to them than altruism.'

'That sounds a bit grim, though I tend to agree with you,' Edmund put in.

'I see the effects near our weekend cottage in Gloucestershire,' the professor went on. 'This DDT kills all insects, not just pests. We back on to arable fields where they spray and there were fewer bees in my garden this year and no butterflies. You're involved in an important area of research, young lady, but keep your eyes open.'

'Thank you, I will,' Nancy said. Someone else was waiting to speak to the professor and it was with a sense of loss that she watched him turn away to engage with the newcomer.

Later, she and Edmund walked slowly to the tube station where they were to part. They spoke eagerly of the events of the evening, particularly Professor McCall's generous attention.

'If only Briggs were more like him,' Nancy sighed. 'I've still not seen him since his return from South America, you know. It's more than seven months since a supervision. And I know he's visited Brandingfield.'

'It is poor,' Edmund agreed, his brow furrowing. 'Hillman can be elusive but he's not that bad.'

'I should write to the professor again,' Nancy decided. 'If, as Professor McCall says, my research would be so important to the likes of ICP, then surely he should want to know.'

'Perhaps mentioning McCall's comments would ginger him up?' Edmund suggested, and Nancy resolved to follow his advice and write to Professor Briggs.

Forty

'Two bits of news,' James greeted her a couple of weeks later when she arrived late one morning in the lab. 'One is that I've moved into the premises of a certain Mrs Hilda Cartwright off the high street. Top room, shared bathroom, half-board.'

'Congratulations. And the other?'

'Professor Briggs will be here to see us in half an hour.'

Nancy froze in the middle of taking off her coat.

'Really? How do you know?'

'I wrote to him and he's responded.'

A hot flood of jealousy rushed through her. She'd written to Briggs the day after meeting McCall, but had received no answer. James, it seemed, merited a better response.

He pointed to the telephone on the worktop by the door. 'A message came just now. He wants to see both of us around eleven.'

'Oh.' The jealousy drained away to be replaced by panic. 'But I'm not ready ... Oh, Lor.' She snagged her scarf on a hook and, racing over, seized a file from her desk and began sorting papers to the sound of James' laughter.

The professor arrived promptly and spent time with both of them, going through their methods, inspecting their equipment and discussing their findings. When it was her turn, Nancy explained in detail the different dusts that she'd been using to carry the insecticide, and identified which ones had been most effective. 'Naturally, we can't replicate the exact conditions in which they'd be used in real life. There are questions of climate, weather, the equipment used, many things.'

'Of course.' The professor had retreated to the comfortable chair by the window, where he settled himself with hands clasped across his stomach. 'Your research is a starting point. Everybody understands about laboratory conditions. In the field it's a different matter, but that's for others to explore.' After a few minutes, he glanced at his watch and grunted. 'Send me a precis of your findings thus far, will you, Miss Foster? And West, an outline proposal, if you please.' And with that he levered himself out of the chair and took his leave.

'He's so condescending,' Nancy said morosely to James. 'Don't you find him condescending?'

'It's just his manner. No need to get upset.'

'I'm not upset,' she said, struggling to steady her voice. All the strain of the last year was releasing itself. The longed-for feedback had been given, but there had been no time to prepare properly and the meeting with Briggs was over so quickly. Though she was relieved to have his general approbation, she still felt cheated of his attention.

James didn't seem bothered. Briggs had accepted his general approach. He had a tank full of grasshoppers and permission to proceed. Nancy envied his confidence. Was it a male thing? she wondered as she pulled up her chair and stared at the glass plate where her dead locust lay waiting to be investigated. She reached for her instrument box and selected a scalpel. Soon, she was absorbed in her work and forgot Briggs and his condescension.

It must have been an hour later when someone knocked and put their head round the door. 'Hello,' James said in surprise and Nancy, who'd been squinting into her microscope, looked up, blinking, to see Edmund.

'Sorry to interrupt,' Edmund grinned. 'Nancy, may I have a word?'

'Um, yes, though I'd better not be long,' she said, one hand still on the microscope.

Out in the corridor, she glanced round anxiously in case the gossips were about. Edmund said, 'Sorry, I can't use the telephone in my lab without everyone knowing my business. It's just someone's given me two spare tickets for a show tonight. I wondered if you were free.'

'What is it?' she said with genuine interest and when he told her, bit her lip, thinking it sounded fun.

'I'd love to,' she said softly. 'Thank you. What time shall we meet?' She thought again of the gossips. 'Can I meet you at the station?'

'Certainly, if you like.' He looked startled.

They made the arrangement and she returned to her work. Only as she seated herself did she register the look that had crossed Edmund's face and realize to her dismay that her reluctance to be seen with him must have come across as rude.

She sighed and crossed her arms.

'Are you all right? What did he want?' James had come over to lean against the worktop. His eyes searched her face.

'Nothing, really.'

'He must have wanted something.'

'It was private, James.'

'Oh, private? I see.'

'Don't read things into it. If you must know, I'm going to see *Pal Joey* with him this evening.'

'Ah. Very nice.' He was looking oddly at her, as though with new eyes.

'What?'

'I suppose you know he's married.'

'Divorced.'

'Divorced, then.'

'We're just friends, James.'

'All right.' He separated himself from the worktop and shuffled back to his seat. Then stopped and said, 'You never go anywhere with me.'

She froze in surprise, then said, 'You've never asked me.'

'You've never asked *me*.' They glared at one another. 'There I've been at home, staring at the wall every night.'

'I'm sorry, I should have thought,' she said, feeling guilty. 'All right, why don't you come over to supper? You've met Frank and Eleanor, haven't you? You should get to know them, they're fun.'

'I have been introduced and thought them rather splendid,' he said eagerly. 'When can I come?'

'Tomorrow maybe? I'll ask them.'

Pal Joey with Edmund was most enjoyable. She insisted on paying for their drinks in the interval and argued with Edmund over whether the musical's central character, a nightclub manager, was a villain or simply amoral, but Edmund seemed amused by her rather than minding, as James might have done. No, Edmund let her be herself, she reflected on the train home, and she appreciated his straightforward friendship.

When she arrived home afterwards, Eleanor said she'd be delighted for James to come to supper the next day.

This she found a more stressful occasion, even though James was at his most charming. He arrived punctually, with a bottle of wine poking out of his coat pocket for Frank and a bunch of tulips for his hostess, then cackhandedly helped Nancy lay the table, setting the knives and forks at the wrong sides. At supper, he asked Dorothy, Frank and Eleanor in turn about their research, spoke humbly about his own, but so enthusiastically about Nancy's that it made her blush.

'You never say any of this usually,' she mumbled.

'Don't want you getting big-headed,' he laughed and the others smiled.

Afterwards, James helped clear away, then Frank drew him into the garden. As the women washed up, Nancy could smell the smoke from the men's cigars and hear the sound of their voices as they talked in the dusk. While she was glad that they were getting on well, she couldn't help wishing that she was party to their discussion and only half-listened to Eleanor and Dorothy's gossip about the shenanigans in a choir to which they belonged.

Later, Nancy saw James out. It was a mild night, but the skies were clear. 'Oh, look at the stars!' she cried and followed him down the path, away from the light of the porch. They stood on the pavement together for a moment, looking up and pointing out the constellations.

'Do you remember how bright they were in Yorkshire?' James said, remembering a field trip in the Easter of their first year. 'I think that was my favourite trip because of the caves and being so far from civilization.'

'I remember you climbing that dry stone wall and it disintegrating.' Nancy laughed at the memory.

'And you ratted on me to the farmer. That cost me thirty shillings.'

'The sheep would have got out, James. I didn't know they'd fine you.' This was true. Anne Durban had insisted that someone take responsibility and report the problem, so Nancy had volunteered.

'Still, thirty shillings is thirty shillings.'

'You could afford it, West.'

He flashed her a lazy smile and her heart quickened.

'Thank you,' he said. 'It's been a lovely evening. They're very nice, the Brauns.' He gazed sleepily at Nancy for a moment. 'You're like the moon goddess out here, you know, all black and silver.'

He reached and brushed her cheek with his finger, and she flinched in surprise.

'I never heard such nonsense,' she gasped, but he only laughed. Then he turned and set off home. She watched his loping figure until the shadows took it. She slowly returned to the house, closed the front door and leaned against it. Her cheek was burning where he'd touched it, or at least she felt it so.

In the sitting room, the others were waiting for her, Dorothy and Eleanor with knowing smiles. She gazed round at them in surprise.

'What is it?' she asked.

Eleanor said to the others, 'I think our Nancy's in love, don't you?'

'What rubbish.' She threw herself into a chair.

'Come on, Nancy,' Dorothy added, 'you couldn't keep your eyes off him all evening.'

'I don't know about that, but we enjoyed seeing him,' Frank said. 'Ask him again soon, will you, Nancy?'

'All right,' she said simply.

It was to be the first of many such visits.

Nancy entered the lab the next day with a feeling of trepidation to find James already hunched over a delicate piece of work, his back to her. Her spirits sank. Perhaps he regretted what he'd said to her, the way he'd touched her cheek. She was wondering what to say when he glanced round and, seeing her, immediately came over.

'Thanks again for last night,' he said, hands in pockets and looking as uncertain as she felt.

'Not at all, I enjoyed it,' she said, unable to stop herself trembling. 'Frank and Eleanor would love you to come again. If you'd like to, of course.'

'I would. I thought they were charming.'

'And Dorothy?' She smiled, teasing him.

'Dorothy's ...' He looked at her hard, then said slowly, 'Dorothy's pretty enough, but ...' He trailed to a halt.

And with that Nancy had to be content.

It wasn't easy working in the same room as someone you're deeply in love with, Nancy thought, but whom you're not sure loves you. Something about their relationship had changed, she'd be a fool not to recognize it. Whenever James was there, which wasn't all the time, there was a tension in the air. Every time their eyes met, his lingered on hers a moment longer than necessary, a wave of warmth passed through her and she swallowed and shyly turned away. If their fingers touched when she lent him a book from her shelf, or he brushed against her as they crossed the lab, it was as though a charge passed between them.

Even when she was focused on her work, she was constantly aware of him. It was as though she'd developed something very unscientific: a sixth sense. And the situation confused her, for she hardly dared to believe an overwhelming piece of evidence – that for the first time in their acquaintance, he felt the same as she did.

Everything had been turned upside down. Even the things he did that annoyed her she started to forgive. The tapping of the pen on the worktop, the impatient sighs. There was no doubt that this new level of awareness was affecting her ability to work. How could she concentrate when her mind was straying to the other side of the lab? It exasperated her, the way her feelings got in the way. The research had to be done and she wanted to do it. It fascinated her and she passionately wanted to achieve her doctorate and move on. The struggle had to be won.

She changed her routine, determined to regain control of herself. James, who exhibited no sign of being similarly distracted, continued to appear at a random point in the mornings and leave at odd times, often after she'd finished for the day. She took to arriving very early, using a snaffled key to an outside door, and leaving early, but a couple of weeks of this took their toll on her constitution. Her sleep became erratic and she became so tired that she started to make stupid mistakes. Also, the technician didn't clock on until nine, which was a nuisance if she wanted supplies before then, for he kept his cupboard locked. Still, she struggled on because she didn't know what else to do.

Her evenings offered little peace. James often appeared for supper, invited by generous Frank, who enjoyed his company, and Eleanor, who loved matchmaking. Nancy noticed how Eleanor took every opportunity to push her and James together, asking them both to lay the table or wash up or take scraps out for the birds. James cheerfully acceded to all requests and treated Nancy gently, without his usual surliness, apologizing when she chided him for muddling the cutlery or not washing a plate properly. Little by little, she felt she was being worn down.

And yet. Despite her traitorous body yearning for his, something held her back, that deep shyness she'd always felt. To his credit, James seemed to sense her reluctance, for since that night when she'd called his compliment 'nonsense' and he'd touched her cheek, he'd made no further advance, though she was sure that he wanted to. It was different, she mused, than it had been with her fellow student Theo back in first year, a relationship that had felt light and unimportant. Her feelings for James ran deep and were not to be toyed with. A love affair with him would change her utterly and send her down an unknown path to an unknown destination. She thought of her sister Helen, of Eleanor and Frank, Peggy and George, the possibilities of happiness or misery that love and marriage brought. If she had any sense at all, she'd stifle her feelings, ask to be moved to a different laboratory at Brandingfield, ask Frank not to invite James to dinner any more, but she couldn't bring herself to do any of these things.

It was just before Easter that everything changed. A patch of bright weather raised everyone's spirits and the talk in the common rooms was of holidays and field trips. Edmund put his head round the door of the lab, where Nancy was frowning over a petri dish, to ask her to a concert later in the week. James found them chatting about arrangements when he arrived a few minutes later. The two men greeted one another stiffly and Edmund withdrew.

'Edmund doesn't look well,' Nancy remarked as she peered at her locusts, for so she'd thought. His face, usually rosy with health, had been pale and drawn.

James didn't reply. She glanced at him and was surprised to see his cold expression. 'What?' she said.

'Nothing.' He paused. 'Just that he's always hanging about.'

'Don't be silly.'

'You're going to a concert with him.'

'Yes, why not? We like the same music.' She turned away and began unwrapping a newspaper parcel. A fresh smell of greens filled the air. Was he jealous?

'Some people say . . .'

'What do they say, James?' She picked through the leaves, brushing the earth off them, then grasped a handful and, sliding the lid of the tank away, dropped them inside, causing the insects to leap about madly.

'Do you . . . What is the situation with him, Nancy?'

She looked up, surprised. James raked his hair, leaving clawmarks, and his lips drawn back in distress stilled her hand. 'What situation?' There was a rustle and a series of ticking sounds. 'Blast!' she cried as locusts bounded about her. 'Now look what you've done!' She righted the tank lid, then stepped back in alarm, her mouth a shocked O. Four, five, six large insects had escaped and were leaping about the lab, enjoying their sudden freedom. She grabbed at one, but missed.

James, leaning against the worktop, burst out laughing and the tension in the room lifted.

'Don't just stand there!' she cried, lunging at another. 'Oh, there's one by your elbow. Look, look!'

He covered it with swift cupped hands, then stepped over and returned it to its prison.

'There's another!'

He pounced, but missed, he was laughing so much.

'It's not funny!' But now she was laughing, too. Soon,

the pair of them were dodging each other round the lab as their prey bounced about, Nancy giving excited squeals, James laughing helplessly. One by one, using James' coat as a net, they hunted them down. Nancy scooped up the last one from its refuge on the windowsill, but as she turned in triumph she collided with James, who was right behind her, and cried out in despair as the locust sprang through the cage of her fingers.

'Oh!' She gazed up into his face, her fists clenched. 'I nearly—'

'Never mind that.' And suddenly his arms were round her, pulling her into a clumsy kiss.

She found herself kissing him back, withdrew briefly for breath, then their mouths met again in a long, searching kiss. She pressed herself into him, her senses filled with his salty scent. His mouth tasted of peppermint and coffee, and his body was lean and hard against hers. She was melting against him, could hardly stand without toppling, but he held her.

Finally, they fell apart, panting like swimmers bursting to the surface of a lake, and stared at one another with wild eyes. 'Crikey,' he said softly, pulling her to him gently. She nestled against his shoulder. His grip tightened and soon they were kissing again.

After a moment, he drew back slightly. 'Don't move,' he whispered, 'but the wretched thing's in my hair. If you're careful, perhaps . . .'

She tried, but it was too quick. They were laughing so much, they didn't hear a knock on the door before it opened. The technician who found them together, Nancy sprawling on the floor giggling, James standing over her, took no time to spread the story. After that, the common rooms of Brandingfield were buzzing with the information that the rumours about Nancy Foster were true.

Forty-One

Stef glanced at her watch, then quietly switched off the tape recorder. Nancy, prompted by Stef's occasional question, had been talking for over an hour. Now she was silent and it was as though a spell lay across the room. When she spoke again, it was clear that she was still lost in the past.

'That moment,' she said. 'What happened that day. After that, there was only one way to go forward and that was with James. Somehow I would have to pursue my ambitions with him beside me. He'd broken down all my resistance. I loved him, Stef. Passionately and completely.' She gave a short laugh. 'And I thought he felt like that about me.' She paused, then said softly, 'I believe he did then. Oh well.' She plucked absentmindedly at the embroidery on a cushion beside her.

Stef wondered what this hesitation meant, but said nothing. Instead, she pushed the 'record' button on her machine and waited.

'It was difficult to concentrate with James being in the

same room, but we sorted it out in the end. I had to be quite strict. The lab was for work, I told him, and he wasn't to disturb that.' She smiled. 'Finally, he understood. He'd shoot me smouldering looks, then act hurt when I frowned at him, but in a funny way this fed our relationship. Outside Brandingfield, we could do as we liked, of course.' She gave Stef a wicked grin. 'As long as his landlady didn't find out.'

Stef smiled back, then had a thought. 'What about Edmund?'

'Oh, I had to give up seeing Edmund. It was cruel, he was awfully hurt, but I'd surmised correctly. James was jealous. It was no good me arguing that there was nothing to be jealous of, that Edmund and I were just friends. There was the gossip. People had seen me with Edmund before, and Dorothy said they believed that because one part of the rumour had been proved, the other one must also be true. Honestly, you'd think people at Brandingfield, intelligent, educated folk, had better things to do than gossip. All it took was one or two, I suppose, and there was no one in charge stamping that sort of thing out. There wasn't a personnel department I could go to.'

'What about Professor Briggs?'

'Oh, he would have taken no interest in that sort of thing. Office politics was beneath him. He was a brilliant academic and a wonderful fixer, canny and single-minded, but all he really cared about was research. Empire-building for the cause of knowledge.'

'A lot of the women scientists I've come across complain about heads of department who are like that. And they're usually men.'

'There you are. But poor old Edmund. It transpired, I found

out later, that he was going through a difficult time. His ex-wife had married again, and she and her new husband had moved with Marianne to Edinburgh. Obviously he wasn't going to be able to see his daughter often. I still met him occasionally in the scientists' common room. James could hardly complain about us having coffee together there and the gossips could make of it what they liked.'

Stef smiled. 'So you finished your doctorate?'

'I did. My grant ran out in the summer of 1953, but it took until November to submit my thesis. Fortunately I was offered a proper research post before then. It was a twelve-month contract funded by ICP and meant I could stay at Brandingfield with James, who had another year to go on his PhD. They were extremely interested in my work on insecticides, you see, and wanted me to continue. It appeared to be a perfect match. At last, I was on my way. It was awfully exciting.'

Forty-Two

Nancy found the autumn of 1953 exhausting. She'd spent most of the summer working on her thesis, while trying to manage on very little money, not liking to keep asking her family for support. Her first payment from ICP came through at the end of September, which was a huge relief, but the sum involved was not much more than she'd received as a student on a grant. What was more, it was contingent on her submitting her thesis and obtaining her doctorate within a short time frame. So the pressure on her was tremendous for a couple of months. During the day, she was starting work on a fresh line of research, and her evenings were devoted to writing up her PhD. For the time being, owing to some necessary building work, she would remain in her current surroundings, but eventually she'd move to join her ICP colleagues in their lab.

'You're not bored by locusts?' James joked after she broke the news of her new job. He tapped the tank, making the creatures jump about.

'Don't, you wretch. And no, they're fascinating,' she replied. 'I'm sure I'll want a change sometime, but for the moment I'm happy. It's science being useful, you see.'

'Feeding the world by destroying pests?'

'Exactly.'

'I wish I could say the same of my research,' he said, staring moodily at his grasshoppers, hands in pockets.

'You know what the professor says. "Even when your research doesn't appear to lead anywhere ..."'

'"All knowledge is useful." Yes, I know that, but it's very frustrating. I want the blasted thing finished so I can move on.'

Nancy was used to James' moodiness now and no longer believed it was connected to her. It was simply built into his character. She saw that he was suited to the meticulous work involved in scientific study and he usually got on with it happily enough. Every now and then, however, something would go wrong and he'd lose sight of what he was doing and fall into a pit of despair. It became Nancy's job to talk him out of it. He hadn't shown this uncertainty in his undergraduate years because, she supposed, everything had been laid out for them. They'd merely carried out instructions and absorbed information. The lab work they did now, testing the reliability of any promising result, was slow and repetitive. It could be lonely. Sometimes a line of research led to a dead end, but one's observations still had to be written up, depressing though this might be. Even negative results were useful to science.

James' moodiness, though, extended to other parts of his life and Nancy fathomed that his cool arrogance disguised insecurities. For a cheerful, self-confident person such as herself, this was a struggle to endure. Usually he was charming and warm towards her, but if he was unhappy he might give her the sharp edge of his tongue. That wasn't fair, she thought. Weren't men supposed to be the strong and reliable ones, like her father? It was a puzzle. Sometimes she soothed him in return, but at other times she'd lose patience and answer him back. Then he'd look hurt, as though she'd struck him, which made her feel guilty.

After she met his parents properly on a couple of visits to their comfortable home in Hampstead, she began to understand him a little better. His father, a professor of Chemistry at Duke's, another London college, was a dour, bespectacled man of nearly sixty with a spare, stooping figure and thinning grey hair. He would cross-question James about his research, then dismiss his son's answers, instead coming up with some thesis of his own that Nancy knew was rubbish. The effect on James was undermining and he would stutter and twitch with nerves.

James' mother's behaviour was damaging in a different way. She was the complete opposite of her husband, overwhelming her precious only child with gushing affection. James looked embarrassed when she referred to him as her 'darling boy' and her refusal to countenance that her son could ever be wrong was as pointless as her husband picking holes in anything James said or did.

Nancy sensed that both parents disapproved of their son's choice of girlfriend. Mrs West thought her work sounded 'unfeminine' and often hinted how important it was that men had proper support from their wives.

It was a relief that her own parents liked James and she often brought him to Sunday lunch at home. He engaged respectfully with her father's observations about politics and complimented her mother on her cooking. As she'd observed with the Brauns, he could certainly charm people when he wanted.

Early in November, Nancy sent her thesis to be professionally typed, then submitted two copies of it in person to the office in Prince's College later in the month. Feeling light with relief, she hurried away to meet Anne, who had also recently completed hers.

They went to the same teashop where Edmund had taken Nancy several years before. There were no Christmas decorations this time, no snow outside, either, just a foggy mizzle. As they hung their coats on a stand, Nancy glanced over to see that a pair of elderly ladies were sitting at the table where Edmund had first told her about his unhappy marriage and shown her a photograph of his daughter. Then she forgot about Edmund altogether when they were seated by the window with tea and cakes and Anne told her some exciting news.

'I'm engaged, Nancy. Gerald asked me.'

'Oh golly, Anne. Congratulations!' Gerald, she recalled, was the boy from home whom Anne had once told her about, yet had since hardly mentioned. 'Honestly, you are a dark horse!'

Anne's eyes sparkled.

Nancy glanced at Anne's left hand. 'Where's the ring, then?'

'It's being altered. The whole thing's quite recent, which is why I hadn't told you anything before. Then because we'd known one another all our lives, he thought there was no point hanging about.' Anne chattered on happily. 'He asked me last weekend. The ring was Gerald's grandmother's. It's very pretty, a sapphire between two diamonds, but it's miles too big. We're thinking about April for the wedding.'

'That's what, only five months away?'

'I know! There's a cottage in the grounds of Alton Manor, his family's house, and we'll be living there once we're married. He works for his father in the estate office, so it's awfully convenient. So I'm moving back to Gloucestershire now my thesis is in. There's a lot to do.'

Nancy watched her take a large bite of sponge cake and felt a pang of melancholy. She was glad for her friend, but also puzzled. 'What will you do in Gloucestershire?' she asked.

'Do?'

'Yes, I mean, you've just finished a doctorate, Anne.'

'Oh, it's work you're talking about. I don't know. I want a break after all that study, frankly. Gerald's awfully keen that I do something that uses my brain, but his family have a position to keep up socially. He thinks it would look odd for me to go out to work. I expect there'll be something I can do locally. There's no hurry.'

'Oh, Anne,' Nancy exclaimed. 'You're not giving up, are you? After all your hard work. You're good, Anne. '

'Giving up? No, heavens, I'm proud of my achievements. But come off it, Nancy. It's hard, isn't it? How would I combine a life as a scientist with a husband and children? I might as well admit that now and put any thoughts of a career behind me. Gerald's right, there are other ways I can use my brain.

And managing an estate, as he has to, my knowledge can be put to good use. He wants to restore the old stew ponds, for instance, and stock them with fish. I'm sure I can help.'

Nancy looked down at her plate with its half-eaten fruit cake and sighed. One by one, the cohort of women from her undergraduate days were bowing out, dispersing. Peggy was married and expecting her first child, now it would be Anne. The other Anne was teaching Biology in a girls' school in Sussex. Of the remaining three, one had married and moved to South Africa, another was working as a wildlife officer for the Ministry of Agriculture and nobody quite knew what had happened to the glamorous Diana.

So now there was just herself soldiering on in research. Thank heavens for the other women at Brandingfield, for Dorothy and Eleanor, loyal friends and serious-minded colleagues.

'How is James?' Anne enquired, licking cream from her lip. 'I'm so glad that you got together. Is he "the one", d'you think? You're well-matched in my opinion.'

Nancy studied Anne's eager face, realizing that her friend had altered, was happier, more sure of herself, more open. She wasn't bothered by Anne asking such a personal question, but didn't honestly know the answer. 'It's too early to say,' she said finally and changed the subject.

Later, on the train back to Brandingfield, she considered the matter. James had not talked about marriage and she was relieved. It meant she could push the issue into the future. Life as it was had many advantages. She was doing work she loved and was with a man she loved. That was enough for the time being. Once she'd established herself in her career, that would be the time to think about marriage and children. At present, she didn't think she wanted a family. Certainly, what she'd seen of her sister Helen's life rather put her off.

Helen's second little boy, Terence, had been born earlier in the autumn and Nancy had visited her at home. She'd looked exhausted and depressed, was snappish with their mother who went every day to help out. Bobby, Helen said, was no use in the house. In fact, he over-excited two-year-old Andrew every evening so that the child wouldn't settle at night. What she wanted, she moaned to Nancy, was some time on her own. Five minutes' peace to have a bath and wash her hair without someone coming in and wanting something.

Remembering this conversation, Nancy groaned aloud. She'd never cope with all that.

'Are you all right, dear?' a motherly fellow passenger asked, dragging her out of her reverie.

'Yes, yes,' she mumbled, peering anxiously through the dirty window. The train was slowing and soon her station slid into view. 'Thank you.' She smiled at the woman. 'I was daydreaming and would have missed my stop.'

As she walked through the lamplit streets to Frank and Eleanor's, from time to time she glimpsed the distant, frowning facade of Brandingfield Hall peeping between the houses. The sight made her shiver. Some of its lights were on and, wreathed in fog, the hall and the tumble of buildings around it emitted an unearthly glow the colour of old bone.

In daylight the following morning, Brandingfield, while still shrouded in mist, appeared less threatening, and Nancy's footsteps were light as she entered its grand hallway. Having submitted her thesis, she felt as though a great burden had fallen away. There would be the dreaded viva interview to endure after Christmas, when she would have to defend her findings, but fingers crossed all would be well and she would be awarded her doctorate. Now she could work normal hours, focusing properly on her new job and the discoveries she hoped to make. Life was opening out and it was exciting!

Forty-Three

One morning a week later, Nancy paused at her pigeonhole outside the main office and gathered up several thin envelopes, holding them between her teeth as she unlocked the door to the lab. Inside, as the light flickered on, the locusts startled into noisy life. She tossed the letters and her keys on the worktop, hung up her coat and went across to the tank, checking that all was well before reaching into her bag for a package of fresh green leaves.

Her brief from ICP was related to her thesis. The company manufactured insecticides containing organochlorines, in particular DDT.

Now she was to move on and work with the effect of other organochlorines on locusts, and she had started to consider what equipment she'd need in order to conduct her experiments.

She dropped some fresh leaves into the tank and watched the insects feed, fascinated as ever by the speed and efficiency with which they shredded the greenery until there was nothing left but a few dry stalks.

After adding another handful and securing the tank lid, she remembered the envelopes and drew them towards her. The first she opened was a routine memo about keeping the kitchens tidy. She read it, then tossed it into a basket of scrap paper. The contents of the second envelope piqued her interest. It contained a couple of pages torn out of a scientific publication. There was a note pinned to it in Edmund's neat handwriting. *'Have you seen this?'* he'd written. *'Not my area, but it might be of interest to you.'* He'd signed it impersonally, *'E'* . She glanced at the title of the article and stilled; *'Unwanted effects of DDT'*. The first line read, *'DDT is considered a panacea for farmers' ills worldwide, but there are wider issues to consider.'* She frowned at the author's name – it meant nothing to her. An American from some college she hadn't heard of, either, nor had she come across the magazine in which the article had appeared. It wasn't an academic periodical, just something the Iowa college produced to inform members about different areas of research. She wondered how Edmund had got hold of it.

She sat down to read the article. It was general in nature, its observations based on interviews with wildlife wardens, farmers and members of the public rather than on rigorous research. The thrust of its argument was not unknown to her, but she'd not seen it expressed so passionately before. Chemical agents containing DDT were not simply killing insects that were considered pests, but useful insects including bees, butterflies and moths. And what of the birds and animals that fed on insects? Were they affected? *'Further research is needed,'* the article ended rather lamely.

Nancy folded the article back into its envelope, her mind working. She remembered what Professor McCall had said about DDT after his lecture on the New Forest. Further research was undoubtedly needed – but who would fund it? Not agricultural bodies or chemical companies, she thought, although perhaps in the future they might profitably develop compounds that killed only certain insects. She couldn't see presently how that might be achieved, but if there was a will, there could be a way. She glanced at her locusts. No one wanted them eating their crops, certainly, and it was clearly her job to get on with her particular line of research. Leave it to others to worry about the wider effects of toxic compounds designed to save crops and feed poor communities. She remembered what Professor Briggs had once said to her. That science wasn't about ethics or morals, it was about establishing facts. He'd said it in a general, throwaway fashion and she'd appreciated his point. But after reading the article, the idea made her uneasy. She must talk to Edmund about it. The thought of his measured, kindly attitude was reassuring.

She dropped the article into her wire 'pending' basket. She was about to open the final envelope when the door flew open and James entered in a draught of cold air. 'Good Lord, overslept,' he muttered, coming to press an icy cheek against hers, then threw his coat over a hook, missed, picked it up and tried again. 'How d'you get on at Prince's yesterday?' he asked, then cutting short her answer said, 'That chap Staunton from ICP came looking for you. We had quite a chat, actually.'

'My supervisor?' she echoed. She looked down at the envelope she held and turned it over. 'ICP' was printed in black letters on the front. She opened it to find a handwritten note from Dr Staunton inviting her to see him at her earliest convenience to discuss the progress of her research. The idea didn't fill her with joy – Staunton was a dry, depressing individual who was a stickler for budgets and rotas, but did not go out of his way to be encouraging.

'Well, what did the man want?' James asked later. His eyes were bright with interest.

'There's a change of plan.' Nancy sighed. 'I must adjust my experiments to include a different pesticide. One of the organophosphates they've started to use. It's called Zalathion. They're finding it more effective out in the field, but want to find out exactly how it works.'

'It sounds more purposeful than anything I'm doing,' James grumbled.

'You're building a body of knowledge about your grass-hoppers,' she said absently. 'And doing it awfully well. Only another year and you'll be on to something fresh.' Her mind was already on any changes she might need to make to her methods.

'Oh, there's something else.' She feared his reaction to this piece of news. 'The building work's finished and I have to move labs. They want me to join their other researchers.'

His face fell. 'That's a shame. A terrible shame.' He paused. 'I don't know what I'll do without you here. It'll be dread-fully lonely.'

'I know, but what can I do? And perhaps it's a good thing, James. It'll give us both a chance to concentrate fully on our work.'

Actually, the idea of joining her colleagues rather cheered her. It wasn't healthy being with James all the time. It could be quite stressful and claustrophobic, in fact. She still loved him as passionately as ever, but it would be a good idea, she concluded, to separate work and pleasure. If only he didn't appear to be so disappointed.

Forty-Four

'How is Helen?' Nancy asked her mother, the Sunday before Christmas. She hadn't seen her sister for weeks.

Mrs Foster was making mince pies and her hands were sticky with pastry. 'Pass me the flour, will you?'

Nancy, who was stirring cake mixture, nudged the open tin across. 'What's wrong?'

'With Helen?' Her mother sighed. 'She's talking a lot of nonsense.'

'What kind of nonsense?'

'Oh, about Bobby.' Mrs Foster flattened the ball of pastry on the board and reached for the rolling pin. 'That he's not interested in her any more. I'm sure if she made a bit of effort, kept the house better and did her hair nicely ... But she bites my head off if I say anything.'

'Poor old Helen,' Nancy said softly.

'I'm thinking you should talk to her when they come on Christmas Day.'

'Me? What do I know about marriage and babies?'

'It was just a thought,' her mother sighed and began to roll the pastry. 'You're more her age. She might listen to you.'

As it turned out, Christmas Day at the Fosters offered little opportunity for private conversation. As well as Bobby, Helen and their infants, Roger came, proudly bringing his fiancée, Sally, a shy girl who came out of herself as the day went on, helping little Andrew build brick castles and playing charades with little skill but much bubbly laughter. Aunt Rhoda didn't stay long after lunch, but showered the family with lavish and beautifully wrapped presents. Nancy's was a soft grey-blue angora scarf that went with her eyes.

James telephoned after lunch to wish Nancy a happy Christmas. 'Deathly,' he said when she asked him how the day was going. 'Great-Aunt Fanny's snoring on the sofa and Mother is making me play cribbage.'

'Poor you,' Nancy laughed. 'It's not much more exciting here.'

Helen, Nancy thought, looked dull and miserable. She'd lost all the weight she'd put on during her pregnancy and more – her clothes hung off her. Baby Terence cried every time he was laid down, so she and Bobby had passed him between them and taken turns to eat.

The sisters found themselves alone together briefly during tea when Nancy was fetching cake from the kitchen. Helen wandered in with an empty teapot, put the kettle on and slumped down at the table, waiting for it to boil.

'Here.' Nancy placed a slice of cake in front of her.

Helen picked at the icing, then pushed the plate away.

'Aren't you supposed to eat properly when you're feeding?'

'Honestly, Nancy, I couldn't. The pills make me feel sick all the time.'

'Pills?'

'For my nerves. Listen, I know Mother's been telling you things.'

'Not about pills. Is there anything I can do to help?'

Helen smiled sadly, but shook her head. 'No, I've just got to get through it, I suppose.'

If that was what having children did to you, Nancy decided she would put it off as long as possible. Forever, perhaps. She wondered if James wanted children. They'd never talked about it, but then they hadn't talked much about the future. She was beginning to half-wish they would. Many of her friends were getting married now, not just Anne and Peggy but girls from school. What would it be like, being married to James? There'd never be a dull moment, that much was certain, but could she depend on him in the way you were supposed to? She didn't know. Helen had to depend on Bobby for everything, for he held the purse strings, and look where that had got her. Nancy definitely didn't want to end up like Helen. No, the more Nancy thought about it, she wanted a marriage of equals. James would support her work and she would support his. How they would manage having children she didn't know. Were nannies expensive? Perhaps they'd have one child. Or two at most. And if she and James were both working, they could pay someone to look after them. Couldn't they?

Forty-Five

1954

The year turned and Nancy's experiments with Zalathion were underway. Demand for it was growing, apparently, she was told by Dr Staunton, to whom she reported, but they wanted to make improvements. The sooner she could give them results, the better.

There were five researchers including herself in the ICP lab, the other four all men working on a variety of projects, with only one, Philip Saunders, doing something similar to herself. Her tank of locusts and her microscope were soon joined by a wooden box containing electrical equipment to provide a charge, also a pump to deliver Zalathion in a saline solution. Though under time pressure, it was important to be as meticulous as ever. No one should be given reason to question her results. Her brief period of regular hours was over and she worked as hard as she could.

At the end of January, after a gruelling interview at Prince's College to defend her thesis, she was informed that she had passed.

'Dr Nancy Foster!' James shouted, punching the air after she'd rushed into their old lab to show him the letter formalizing her achievement. The irascible man who now occupied Nancy's space glared at them, but they ignored him and he stomped out, muttering something about 'hysterical women'.

She laughed it off and assured James, 'You'll do it, too, you'll get there.'

He put his arms round her. 'I'm proud of you, Nancy, I really am.' When he released her, his face was grave. 'We'll make a fine pair of scientists, you and I. We'll do great things.'

She blushed with pleasure at his enthusiasm, but still felt a frisson of unease. How many senior scientists had she come across who were women? None. She was ahead of James at present, but for how long? She thought of Eleanor, recognized for her achievements because she worked with her husband. Frank tried always to put her name before his on their publications, but editors would frequently change them round. And why wouldn't they? An article by a man carried more authority.

What about Dorothy? Her work on honey bees was important, but she'd found it a struggle to be taken seriously. Only now were her results beginning to be published.

It was after a conversation with Frank, Eleanor and Dorothy over supper one night that Nancy realized something else important. They'd been discussing Nancy's research and the structure of the department where she worked at Brandingfield. Nancy had been complaining about it being like a male club.

'They go out to lunch together on Fridays and never invite me,' she complained. 'Not that I can afford it, but it would be nice to be asked.'

'Have you ever asked yourself why you can't afford it but they can?' Dorothy said sharply. 'How many of them are on your level?'

'Two, I think, are junior researchers like me.'

'And how long have they been in their jobs?'

'One of them a year, the other only a month longer than me.'

'Find out how much they earn.'

'How do I do that? Nobody discusses that sort of thing.'

'Yes, yes. Bad form to talk about, I know all that. I could never persuade the supper club to see how unfairly we're treated. It doesn't matter that we're women, we're doing the same jobs as the men. Find a way to ask.'

So Nancy picked Philip Saunders, who'd been least stand-offish, took him for coffee and asked him direct what he earned. He was taken aback, but when she begged him, explaining her suspicions and resulting sense of injustice, he told her. She was staggered. His salary was a third higher than hers. 'You have to remember, though,' he said, 'that I'm married and my wife's having a baby soon.'

'But I do the same work as you!' she cried.

Philip's eyes slid away in embarrassment. 'Just don't tell them it was me who took the lid off.'

'I won't,' she replied, but she was furious.

'Go carefully,' Dorothy warned when Nancy told her, but to no avail.

Everything was thin about Dr Staunton. His physique, his hair and his voice were all thin and so were his excuses. When she marched into his office the following day and demanded to talk about her salary, he looked outraged.

'You're very full of yourself, young lady. And you're new. Perhaps when you've been here a full year, we'll look at making an adjustment. In the meantime, I'd rather you didn't discuss such private matters with your colleagues. It causes an unpleasant atmosphere, I find.'

He was adamant in his refusal to discuss the matter and she sensed that there was little more she could do without endangering her employment. She'd just have to argue hard when her salary review came round. But she felt so angry and overlooked that she could hardly concentrate on her work for the rest of the day.

In many ways, she'd been right that it was good for her and James to be working apart. She hadn't realized before how much they'd come to rely on one another in their professional sphere. But there were downsides. Among new colleagues, she had to stand up for herself and face insults and indignities she'd never had to deal with before. Philip Saunders was pleasant to her, but two of the other three were definitely not.

Burly Jim Davies played prop forward for a local rugby team and had locker room manners. He also had a threatening way of looming over her when he was making a point, which he did after she had to ask him for a second time not to let his equipment encroach on her part of the worktop. 'Crikey, it's like working with one's nanny,' he sneered. 'Tidy up, do this, do that.'

'Don't be ridiculous,' she said, though she took a cautious step back.

After that, he started calling her 'Nanny' instead of Nancy, which brought smiles from the others. When she asked him to stop, he accused her of 'not being able to take a joke'.

She confided in James, but he advised her not to speak to anyone higher up about it. 'You'll be seen as a troublemaker,' he said, and she knew in her heart that he was right.

If the nickname had been the only jibe, she might have frowned and borne it, but Jim enjoyed needling her. She went about her business one morning unconscious of a notice pinned to the back of her overall that read 'Kiss me quick' in Jim's distinctive scrawl. Fortunately no one tried to take up the invitation, but she couldn't understand the giggles until a female technician took her aside and detached it.

'Jim Davies only treats women nicely if he finds them attractive,' the woman told her, then realized the unintended insult and bit her lip.

'Don't worry, I'm rather glad he doesn't,' Nancy said in a heartfelt tone. 'I just wish he wasn't so horrid.'

'You can either play along with him,' Dorothy said later when Nancy told her, 'and make him laugh, or you can try ignoring him.'

'I'd rather die than play along with him,' Nancy spat. So

ignore him she did and she tried her best to concentrate on her work. But he persisted in calling her Nanny.

Worse, though, were the attentions of an older technician, a fatherly man who was initially friendly and helpful to Nancy when she needed anything. There came a time when, if he found her alone in the lab, he would stand a little too close and she'd have to edge away. Then one day, she felt his clammy hand on her back, warm, stroking her, then moving downwards to her bottom. Utterly disgusted, she pushed him away and fled to the ladies' room, where she waited, staring at herself in the mirror, until her heart stopped pounding. She dared not say anything to anyone about it, it felt too shameful, but she avoided being alone with him again. He'd got the message, anyway, she thought, for his manner towards her became more guarded and he would not meet her eye.

James, too, she gauged, got on much better without her constant presence supporting and reassuring him. Having lost his emotional prop, he 'manned up' and gained confidence in his own abilities. He talked of the future, of seeking an academic research post under Professor Briggs or perhaps a post abroad. Hong Kong, maybe, or South Africa. 'There are more opportunities and the money's good. Just for a few years.'

The prospect made her prickle with alarm. 'What would I do?' she asked, her voice plaintive.

'You could come, too. Though we would have to get married, of course,' he said, smiling as he drew her to him.

'Oh, James.' It was the first time he'd mentioned marriage and she felt a rush of love for him. But the time wasn't right. 'I do want to marry you some day.' She kissed him to show she meant it. 'Just not yet. You know what would happen to my work. No one would take me seriously if I were "Mrs James West". Look at Frank and Eleanor. She wouldn't be anywhere without Frank's name on her work, and they treat her as his assistant in the department. No, I couldn't put up with that.' She gently withdrew from his embrace. 'It's too early to think about marriage. We're all right as we are for the moment. Time's on our side.'

'For the moment, yes, Nancy,' James said softly, looking into her eyes. 'But I'll be applying for positions in the summer and I don't know where I'll end up.'

A lump formed in her throat and she had to look away. The truth was suddenly clear. If they wanted to stay together, she would have to follow him. His career came first. It was a blow, but then she was stupid to be surprised. She'd always known he was ambitious. Her heart was full, remembering the support she'd given him. Now it came down to it, he would not support her work as a scientist if it hindered his. If he took a post abroad, she would have to go with him and hope for the best. A little job in his lab, perhaps? Or perhaps not. They were likely to be even more traditional out in the Empire than in London. She'd be expected to stay at home and have children, most likely. No, she certainly wasn't ready for that.

Forty-Six

One sunny Friday in June, Nancy's colleagues lingered in the pub at lunchtime and she was alone in the lab. She was carefully preparing a dead locust for an experiment. It was a delicate job that involved her finest instruments. After taking some general measurements, she connected the creature to a network of equipment that enabled her to detect the effect of an injection of Zalathion on its nervous system.

A disturbing thought suddenly occurred to her and she stilled. She left the microscope and, going over to a shelf of reference books, withdrew a heavy, well-thumbed volume. She flipped to the end, consulted the index and turned to the page she wanted. After she'd read the entry carefully, she paused to think, then pulled her notebook towards her. As she wrote, her sense of unease grew and remained with her for the rest of the day.

'James, I need to ask your advice.' She found him later in

his lab, fortunately alone. He was reading a letter, but when he saw her, he quickly put it aside.

'Ask away,' he said. His eyes were on the notebook in her hand, but his tone was guarded.

'Is something wrong?'

He shook his head, so she forged on. 'I don't know why I didn't see this earlier. I mean, I've been studying these wretched insects for so long. Perhaps I didn't want to see it.'

'To see what, Nancy?'

'I'm not certain. I'd have to do further tests, but it seems to me that the way this organophosphate works on the locust's nervous system is very similar to how it would work on a human's. It's the same part of the brain . . . No, I'm not explaining it properly. Look.' She showed him her workings and the diagram she'd sketched earlier. He studied it with interest and asked her to explain it again.

'The thing is,' she said, rubbing her forehead as though it hurt, 'you'd think that all this would have been checked before they started using the compound. I mean, there are basic standards and rules about safety. Surely.'

'You would have thought so, but then we know the way the world works.'

'Do we?' Nancy regarded him doubtfully.

'ICP are a commercial organization.'

'I do know that.'

'And we are aware of the problems with DDT. You showed me that paper Buckland gave you. Yet they go on using it because it works.'

'But if what I've noticed is true and these new chemicals could harm people, surely they're no good, either.'

There was a silence. James began to pace about the room, his hands in his pockets, his expression saturnine. She leaned against his worktop with arms folded, watching him, wondering what he really thought. 'Do you think I ought to report it?' she asked finally. 'I mean, yes, of course I ought to, but I'd feel silly if I'd made a mistake.'

'Do you think you have?' he asked, looking hopeful.

'I should do further tests, I suppose.' She tucked away a stray lock of hair and frowned.

'Yes, I would if I were you. The best idea, I think. You wouldn't want to make a fool of yourself.' His words trailed away and his eye fell on the discarded letter. 'There's something I need to speak to you about,' he said, reaching for it. 'One of the posts I've applied for. Well, the professor must have put in a word for me, because they want to meet me. It means flying to Boston next week. They've offered to pay for my flight.'

She stared at him in dismay. 'Boston,' she whispered and swallowed against the lump rising in her throat. 'You've applied for a job in Boston?'

'Yes.' He handed her the letter. 'I'm surprised they're interested in me, to tell you the truth, given that I've only just submitted my doctoral thesis, but Briggs knows the head of department there. It's initially only for a year.'

'I see,' she said. She scanned the letter quickly. '"And with the option for renewal",' she read aloud.

'If it works out, I suppose. You could come with me to America, Nancy. If I get the job.'

'If you get the job,' she echoed miserably. 'But you will, I expect. You're good, they'd be lucky to have you.'

'Thank you. They want someone with exactly my research interests.' His smile was sheepish. 'Briggs must have pushed quite hard on my behalf.'

Lucky James, Nancy thought. The professor had never offered her that kind of support.

She decided that she must share her concerns about Zalathion with Dr Staunton. A few days later, she worked up the courage to knock on the door of his office.

He glanced up at her entrance and his thin lips turned down in a frown.

'May I have a word?'

'I am rather busy, Miss Foster, so it had better be quick.'

Dr Foster, Nancy thought as she sat down, but it wasn't worth correcting him.

He steepled his spidery fingers and peered enquiringly at her. 'I'm all ears,' he said in a clipped voice.

'There's something that's worrying me. About my research.' She paused, was reassured by his murmur of encouragement and hurried on. She summarized briefly what she had found, that the Zalathion she was using in her experiments attacked the nervous systems of the locust in the same way that it would in humans. In short, the substance was dangerous to people. 'Small doses could cause muscle weakness or developmental problems. Larger doses could kill.'

When she'd finished, Staunton said nothing for a moment, but stared at the wall somewhere above her head. Then he absently rubbed a glass paperweight on his desk, cleared his throat and said, 'Yes, that's all very interesting. However, to the best of my knowledge the organophosphates that ICP has developed for commercial use have been tested extensively and are ruled safe to use.' His tone implied, what did she, a junior researcher, think she was doing challenging this conclusion?

'I understand that they would have been extensively tested, but I have conducted various experiments,' she went on bravely, 'and so far the results underpin my hypothesis. What I'd like to do, with your permission, is to test more extensively, but of course that will take up time, time I should be spending on other aspects of my work.'

Again, he regarded her over his clasped hands. Finally, he said, 'I am most grateful to you, Miss Foster, for bringing this matter to my attention. I will report your findings to my superior, but for the moment I should like you to continue to focus on what you are paid to do. We are under a certain pressure of time to produce results. Time is money, Miss Foster. Time is money.' He paused for a moment, then appeared to come to a decision. 'Which reminds me, the salaries board meets soon and I will put in a word on your behalf. No promises, though. So good of you to come and see me.' And with that she found herself dismissed and outside in the corridor.

'He made me feel small,' she complained to James later. She'd caught him just before he left Brandingfield for the airport to fly to Boston. 'I feel so angry.'

'I did warn you,' James murmured, checking his coat

pocket for his passport. 'It's good news that your salary might be reviewed, though.'

'Whose side are you on?' Her eyes blazed.

'Oh, yours, undoubtedly yours,' he said. He leaned in and kissed her, then stood back, regarding her thoughtfully. 'But the man's right, confound it, what else did you expect? You are only a junior researcher and unfortunately your word doesn't count for much. They've already invested heavily in producing this stuff and using it in the field. Your job is simply to help them to develop the damned product more effectively.'

'But what if I'm right and people die? Won't ICP be taken to court?'

'By poor farmers out in the colonies? I doubt it.'

'James, that's a monstrous way to look at it.'

'I'm just putting myself in ICP's shoes. They're interested in turning a profit, Nancy, not in the good of mankind. Look, I must go.'

'I do hope things go well,' she said, giving him a hug.

'I'll be back in a few days. Just stop worrying, Nancy. Everything will work out, you'll see.'

She followed him out to the hall. One last wave and he was off into the sunshine, suitcase in hand, his long coat flapping. Maybe, she thought wistfully, he'd always be walking away. Far into the distance and she'd be left behind. She wanted to run after him, to tell him to stop, but that would be ridiculous. Instead, tears filled her eyes, blurring a last sight of him. She brushed them fiercely away, turned and plodded slowly back to her lab.

*

'Nancy? Hello, can you hear me?'

It was eleven o'clock at night when the Brauns' phone rang out. Nancy scampered down to the hall to answer it. James' voice was distant, but unmistakable.

'It's awfully late here,' she said. 'Hang on. I don't want to disturb the others.' The flex of the phone just reached into the sitting room. She pushed the door to and leaned against it. 'I'm here again. How are you?'

'Fine. I had to tell you right away. They've offered me the job!'

'Oh!' She paused, then said brightly, 'Congratulations, that's marvellous.'

'Nancy, I'm going to accept it. It's ...' The voice crackled and faded, then returned: '... miss.'

'What?' She slid down the door and crouched in a miserable heap.

'It's too good an opportunity. Look, this call is costing me an arm and a leg. We'll talk when I get back ...' Something inaudible, then, 'Goodbye.'

'James?' But the line had gone dead. She stared at the receiver for a moment, then slowly replaced it in its cradle.

They met to celebrate on Saturday evening in an Italian restaurant off Piccadilly. 'I start in September,' James said after the waitress had taken their order. His eyes sparkled like his champagne, despite being red-rimmed with jetlag.

He raised his glass and she hastily did the same. 'Congratulations again, dear,' she said cheerfully, while not feeling she meant it. 'It's a brilliant achievement.'

And it was. The news had travelled like wildfire. Brandingfield was buzzing with it like a hive of Dorothy's bees. That someone so young and newly qualified had landed such a prestigious research post was astonishing, unheard of. When Nancy had coffee with Edmund, the other men in the common room had looked curiously at her and quietened when she walked in. 'I'm afraid they're envious,' Edmund murmured. 'They put the job offer down to Briggs putting a word in. I'm sorry if that sounds mean-spirited, but that's the way it is. We chaps are so competitive, we have to find a solution that makes us feel better about ourselves.' She understood, thinking that it wasn't just men who were like that.

Their minestrone arrived. Sipping it, she found it glutinous, but pretended to eat it while listening to James talk. The Americans had opened a new faculty in Boston. The labs were new, everything was new and James' research interests exactly fitted what they needed. He'd be a member of a team under the renowned Professor Weiss. As for accommodation, he'd find digs initially, but they could look for an apartment together.

'Together,' she echoed dully, crumbling a piece of bread.

'Yes, together,' he said, his eyes fixing on hers. 'You'll come, won't you? Perhaps not immediately, there's a great deal to arrange, but we can get married whenever we like. It doesn't have to be a big affair, neither of us is bothered by that sort of thing, are we?'

She looked hard at him, then smiled. 'I don't know what my parents would think about that. My mother likes things done properly.' She knew exactly how her mother would react to a hole-in-the-corner wedding. She'd be furious, worry that the neighbours would imagine that they'd *had* to get married. She bit her lip. 'But I don't know yet. What would I do out there, James? We've talked about this before.'

'You'd find something, of course you would.' He frowned. 'I'll ask Professor Weiss, if you like.'

He did ask, but the answer wasn't encouraging. 'They don't need researchers with your experience at present,' he said, failing to meet her eye. 'But there are some technician posts you could apply for.'

'A technician?' she said, her eyes blazing. 'After all I've worked for?'

'It would only be a starting point, Nancy, I'm sure.'

'No, James. I couldn't. I have my pride.'

'Think about it. Please.'

Over the next few weeks, the problem lay heavily on Nancy. She went through her daily tasks as meticulously as ever – indeed work, despite its difficulties, seemed her only salvation. The thought of James going away was awful, but what could she do? She didn't want to go to America, to leave her family behind and to face an uncertain future. She'd worked so hard to get where she was now, and if the job wasn't perfect she'd at least have more of a chance here of a position of the status she wanted. She discussed the matter with Eleanor, Frank and Dorothy and appreciated the wisdom of their advice. America, Eleanor told her, was even more traditional in its attitude to women scientists than

England, and it would be tougher still to find a job of the status she deserved if she was married. 'They'll assume you'll leave to have children,' she warned.

'I probably will,' Nancy said, biting her lip as the thought of her poor sister flashed in her mind. 'But not for years.'

'Don't leave it too late like me,' Eleanor said lightly and Nancy's heart went out to her.

As the weeks passed, Nancy's relationship with James grew strained, as every discussion ended in stalemate. She knew that he was trying to wear her down and she couldn't see how it could end well for her. Either she would cave in and prepare to go to America as his wife or she would risk losing him altogether. James didn't seem to think that he had to make the same choice. He was taking up this job and it was her duty to go with him. It simply wasn't fair.

Forty-Seven

Alone in the lab late one July afternoon, Nancy drew a reference book from her shelves. As she did so, a blue exercise book slipped down onto the worktop. She felt a stab of guilt as she picked it up and opened it, knowing what it contained. It was the one in which she'd noted her suspicions about the probable toxicity of Zalathion to humans.

Since her meeting with Dr Staunton, she'd obeyed his orders and put the matter to one side. Her dilemma about James' posting to Boston had filled her mind instead.

She flicked through the pages. Staunton was likely to have been right. The insecticide had surely been thoroughly tested by others at ICP. She was far too junior to challenge any official findings. As she glanced through the lists of figures and the diagrams she'd drawn, though, she felt uneasy once more. Something James had said came into her mind, that ICP were ultimately primarily interested in profits. The idea that people's health, their lives even, might be secondary to making money was anathema to her. Surely, if Zalathion was dangerous to humans, the firm's reputation would be at stake. Wouldn't the management be grateful if she alerted them?

Nancy sighed. Dr Staunton wouldn't be pleased if she addressed him on the matter again. Her salary rise, it had already occurred to her, could be interpreted as buying her compliance.

A freshly dissected locust lay under the microscope. She checked a diagram in the exercise book, then adjusted the eye piece until the insect's head came into sharp focus. The damage to its nervous system wasn't visible, but the range of tests she'd carried out showed that it was there. She was certain. Zalathion and other organophosphate compounds inhibited the action of an important enzyme, disrupting the transmission of nerve signals. This enzyme worked in the same way in other parts of the animal kingdom, including humans.

Now she had verified this, she couldn't just forget about it. What should she do? She'd think about it a while longer, she decided, and returned the exercise book to the shelf. A couple of days later, Dr Staunton called her into his office, but she was relieved to find out that it was nothing to do with organophosphates. He looked harassed, his scanty hair sticking out in all directions. 'I simply wanted to let you know that your salary is definitely being increased.' He named a sum that was almost, but not quite, commensurate with her colleague Philip Saunders. 'This rise will take effect immediately.' He gave no reason for the decision.

Her first reaction was relief. 'Thank you,' she said. Part

of her wondered whether she was indeed being bought off. Staunton was looking at her curiously. 'Is there anything the matter?' she asked. She wondered if he had spoken to his superior.

'No. Only I'm assuming that you are continuing to concentrate solely on the research you're employed to do.'

'Yes, of course I am.' So she was right.

'Good.' His expression lightened.

She left his office with a sense of deep disquiet. It was hard to interpret his enquiry as anything but a warning. But why, she wondered, was he so reluctant to engage with her findings about Zalathion? Did he fear for his position if he asked difficult questions? She'd come across his type before, ticket collectors at train stations who told her, 'It's more than my job's worth,' if she asked to be let off a supplementary fare, while others would give her a wink and pass on with a 'We'll say no more about it.' Staunton was a faceless sort of man. He knew his science – she had no doubt about that – but he gave away nothing of himself. She didn't know if he was married or where he lived. Only that he grew rhubarb – he'd once brought in a bag of it, saying that it had 'gone mad this year'. She'd taken some home but found it as sour as he was.

After brooding on the matter for a further few days, she came to a decision. She'd write up a formal report of her covert investigations after hours rather than in ICP's time. Surely Staunton couldn't object. This did mean having to explain to James why she'd be too busy to see him for a few days.

'I must do it,' she said when he raised his fears that

she'd endanger her job. 'It's my duty. I can't keep this to myself, James.'

James said he understood, but he didn't look happy.

The following evening, after most of her colleagues had left for the day, Nancy fetched a fresh exercise book from the stationery cupboard and sat down to handwrite a report. She glanced round to see who was left. Just Philip, talking to their technician about a piece of faulty equipment. 'Still here, Nancy?' he asked as he passed her with a new rubber tube in his hand.

'Some results aren't making sense,' she said quickly, but moved her hand instinctively to cover her work. After he left, she was aware of the technician tidying up in the background before he too departed.

'Switch the lights off when you go, will you?' he bid her, dragging her from thought.

'Of course,' she muttered absently. 'Bye.' After he'd gone, she began to write in earnest.

A few nights later, she had finished. She read her work through, made a few corrections, then at lunchtime the following day took the exercise book to the typist in town that she'd used for her doctoral thesis. No one would be able to accuse her of taking up a Brandingfield secretary's time. The typist, a Miss Bateman, was booked up, but quoted a price and said she'd produce two copies of the report as soon as possible – in two weeks, she thought. Yes, she still had the Brauns' telephone number from last time.

Nancy walked back slowly to Brandingfield, aware for the first time for weeks of the warmth of the sun on her face and the colour and scent of roses in the gardens she passed. Her research was done and she was certain that she'd proven her hypothesis. This organophosphate was extremely dangerous to the populations whose crops it might save and ICP's chief scientist should be informed. How to do that was the hardest part and she wasn't sure how to proceed. Going over Dr Staunton's head would lead to bad feeling, perhaps even dismissal. Should she send the report upwards anonymously? But there were problems inherent in doing that. It might not be taken seriously. All her worries came flooding back.

James was of little help.

'I'll read the thing if you like, but you're damned if you do anything with it,' he remarked. 'Honestly, Nancy, I admire your spirit, but you'll just be bringing trouble down on yourself.'

'I suppose you'd be happy if I lost my job,' she said bitterly, dismayed by his lack of support. 'You think I'd then come to the States with you.' She slumped in her chair and examined her nails, which she'd bitten right down.

'That would be the only good thing to come out of it,' he joked feebly, but she didn't smile.

At Frank and Eleanor's, she hung about miserably. Frank, Eleanor and Dorothy were preparing to go off on a month's holiday to the Continent and piles of freshly ironed clothes, butterfly nets and specimen cases lay around ready to go into suitcases and boxes. She and James had elected to go away together in August to the Cairngorms, where a Scottish cousin of James kept a shooting lodge. They didn't intend to shoot anything, but they'd have the place to themselves in a beautiful wilderness.

The typist was as good as her word, except that she rang the wrong telephone number. On Friday, a fortnight later, Nancy was elsewhere in the building all day at a first aid training session, but feeling wretched from her period, she returned briefly to the lab at lunchtime in search of aspirin. Here, she found a message on her worktop. It was initialled by one of the secretaries. *'Miss Bateman telephoned. Your report is typed and ready for collection.'* She was annoyed, having asked the typist to ring her at home, but perhaps she had called the number and found no one in.

She glanced about, but the lab was deserted. All at the pub, she imagined. *How silly you are,* she thought crossly. *Why would any of them be interested?* She dropped the screw of paper into a bin, took two aspirin with water and set off in search of a restorative cup of tea.

As she passed the closed door of Dr Staunton's office, she heard voices from within. She paused for a moment. Funny, one sounded like James. She couldn't resist moving nearer to listen, but couldn't hear what was said. James' voice sounded close suddenly and the door handle turned, so she stepped back. 'I'll do that,' she heard him say, and something about the serious tone alarmed her. The next-door office stood open and empty so she dodged into its shadowy gloom. From her hiding place, she witnessed his purposeful figure striding by, but stilled again as Dr Staunton followed. When silence fell, she went on her way, puzzled and disturbed. Why had James gone to see Staunton? She knew the two men were barely acquainted. She glanced at her watch. Bother, she didn't have time to go in search of James now.

She stepped into the corridor and just at that moment the door of her lab opened and someone came out. It was James. He didn't see her, but strode off in the opposite direction. She called his name and started to hurry after him, but he couldn't have heard, for he vanished through a fire door. Her belly twisted with pain and she grimaced.

As she poured herself tea in the common room, she wondered what she would have said to him. She could hardly admit to eavesdropping, could she? She'd have to think of some way of asking him about the incident the following day – he was due, she remembered, to meet an old schoolfriend this evening.

The afternoon's training was interesting to Nancy as it dealt with chemical burns and other accidents in the laboratory. It finished at half-past four and she hurried back to her lab, thinking she'd settle her locusts for the weekend, then see if Dorothy was free to walk home with her in the sunshine.

The door of her lab stood ajar and she heard laughter and conversation from within as she entered. They were all there, her colleagues, looking up at her, then falling silent one by one.

'Hello, Nanny,' Jim said finally.

She ignored him, instead smiling round at the group. 'Your first aid officer is fully trained,' she said with studied lightness, going over to her work station. 'Burns, cuts, anaphalactic shock. I can deal with them all.'

She then saw why they were quiet. Her work station was not as she'd left it. The wire filing tray no longer rested on the shelf, its contents neatly stacked, but askew on the worktop, the papers in it awry. Books that the tray had previously propped up lay tumbled on the shelf like fallen dominoes.

'Who's done this?' she asked, spinning round, her voice cracking with anger, but her colleagues shrugged and mumbled their ignorance or contemplated the floor.

As she righted the books, fighting a tender lump in her throat, a thought sprang into her mind and she began to search, increasingly frantic. The notebook containing her rough workings – where was it? There was no sign. She rummaged in the filing tray, checked the drawers under the worktop and the floor. It had gone. What else had?

As far as she could see, all her equipment was intact. The specimen cases containing neat ranks of glass microscope slides stood in their usual place, the box of paraffin blocks she used to administer chemicals and the smoked drum that recorded results looked untouched. The thief had been careful not to disturb her routine work, that was something.

She leaned on the worktop, her palms pressed onto its surface, and thought hard. *Who could have done this? Who knew about her clandestine research?* In the lab, Dr Staunton, that was all, and she was fairly certain that she'd allayed his suspicions. The only others she'd told were Frank, Eleanor and Dorothy, and James.

She straightened and glanced round. Her colleagues had returned to their places and were doing their best to appear absorbed in their individual research. *They know something,* she thought, *but are fearful, which suggests . . .* She didn't know what it suggested.

She glanced down at the bin, somewhere she hadn't searched, and the screw of yellow paper there reminded her. The report itself, of course, she had to fetch it from the typist. She glanced at her watch – it was too late now, the office would be closed. She'd go first thing tomorrow. They were open on Saturday mornings.

'It's already been collected,' Miss Bateman said the following morning, the high arch of her pencilled eyebrows disappearing under a wing of blonde hair as she gazed at Nancy in surprise over her typewriter. 'A gentleman came by yesterday after lunch. He said you'd be nipping in to pay the bill.'

Nancy stared at her in shock. 'A gentleman? Who?'

'I'm sure I don't know. He didn't give his name.'

'I didn't ask anyone else to fetch it.' She sank into a chair opposite, rubbed her forehead, then glanced up. 'What did he look like? Was he old, young? Dark, fair?'

'Young, dark hair and good-looking, if you know what I mean.'

'I don't, exactly.' She couldn't think of anyone like that. Except James. She felt a worm of unease.

'I'll want paying all the same.' Miss Bateman folded her arms and looked grim. 'A day's work, that was. Twelve shillings and sixpence.'

Nancy opened her purse with a sigh.

Outside, she loitered by the window of a second-hand bookshop, not seeing the dusty volumes within. Perhaps, she thought, it *had* been James. She'd seen him come out of the lab the previous lunchtime. He could have seen the note in the bin, and, knowing that she wouldn't have time to fetch the report, had gone on her behalf and not told her. Her heart lightened and she hurried off in the direction of his digs, hoping that he'd be there. He was. His landlady eyed her suspiciously, but called him down to the dingy hall.

'I don't know what you're talking about.' James stared at her with a bewildered expression when she asked him for the report.

'It's just that you match the typist's description. Who could it be, then?'

'Not Staunton, obviously.'

'No,' she said, picturing Dr Staunton's thin, ageing figure. None of her colleagues answered to Miss Bateman's recollection, either.

'So tell me again, more slowly. The woman gave the report to this unknown cove.'

'A gentleman, Miss Bateman said.'

'That means anything these days. And your rough notes have gone, too.'

'Stolen from my shelf.' Her voice quavered as the scale of her loss dawned on her. 'Oh, James, all that work.'

'Someone must have seen the note about the report being ready.'

'Before I saw it, then. I put it in the bin. James,' she said suddenly, 'I'm not accusing you, but what were you seeing Dr Staunton about at lunchtime?' She watched with dismay as his eyes narrowed and glinted like steel.

'How do you know that?' he murmured lightly.

'Because I was passing his office and heard your voice.' She felt herself flush, remembering how she'd hidden in the next office and seen where he went next.

'It sounds as though you were spying on me.'

'I wouldn't do that.' Her face grew hotter. 'It was coincidence, I assure you.'

'I wanted some advice. Someone told me Staunton knows Professor Weiss in Boston. I needed to know what he'd be like to work with.'

'And?'

And my informant was wrong. We had a bit of a chat, then I apologized for bothering him and I left. There, do I pass muster?'

'Of course.' She bit her lip. 'I'm sorry. I'm all over the place. I don't know what to do now. And with the Brauns and Dorothy away, I'm on my own at home.'

James sighed and she thought he might embrace her, but his landlady was hovering nearby, dusting the houseplants in a very obvious manner, so instead he said, 'Wait for me to fetch my jacket and I'll take you to lunch. It might cheer you up.'

Later, he offered to stay the night, but she knew he'd promised to accompany his parents to a family party in Gloucestershire.

'I'm sure I'll be all right,' she assured him. 'I expect I'm just being stupid.'

Forty-Eight

Monday morning, and Nancy's feet dragged on her walk to work. She'd passed an anxious weekend and was now certain that she'd be called into Dr Staunton's office, that something admonishing would be said, that she'd lose her job. No one higher up in ICP would ever see her research, consequently people would die and she would have failed.

By the time she arrived, she was a bag of nerves. It wasn't quite nine and she was the first in the lab. While she was buttoning her lab coat, she heard Dr Staunton unlocking his office and stilled, waiting, but nothing happened. She checked her locusts and fed them, then scooped two out for her next experiment and set to work.

One by one, her colleagues arrived. She smiled at Philip, but his mouth only twitched slightly before he turned away. When Jim, too, hardly acknowledged her, she found she could hardly concentrate and felt the pressure of tears. Whatever was going on, she felt that they knew something. Whether they were afraid for themselves or contemptuous of her, she couldn't guess. Well, she wouldn't let them win. She would carry on. And carry on she did, but all morning she was wondering what had happened to the evidence of her undercover research, and what would happen to her as a result of it being found.

There came to her, oddly, a story in a Ladybird book of Greek myths that she'd read as a child. It was called 'The Sword of Damocles'. There had been a picture in it of King Damocles, terrified by the vision of a sword hanging by a single horse hair above his throne. If the hair broke when he was sitting there, the sword would fall and he would be killed. She felt like Damocles.

Finally, she took her courage in her hands. She knocked on Dr Staunton's door and at his thin 'Come' entered. He finished pencilling a note on a closely typed letter, then looked up and, seeing her, frowned.

'Miss Foster. How can I help you? Sit down, do. You seem anxious. What's the matter?'

She sat. 'I—' Her voice was a croak. She tried again. 'My work station has been searched, some of my research stolen.'

His eyebrows shot up. 'That's a serious accusation. Who would have done such a thing?'

'That's what I'm wondering.'

'You've spoken to your colleagues, have you? And the technicians? There must be a simple explanation.'

She closed her eyes against a wave of panic. 'I've tried.'

'What exactly is missing?'

'A notebook. And possibly some loose papers. I . . . haven't been through everything properly yet.'

'Then I suggest that you do, before I make any enquiries. This is to do with your legitimate research for us, is it?'

She swallowed. 'It's related.'

'I see.' He stared at her coldly.

She wondered whether to mention the loss of her typed report, then thought better of it. Either he knew already or he'd quickly realize the full extent of her secret project and she'd get herself into deeper trouble. Whatever game was being played, she was being outmanoeuvred.

All she could do was appeal to his better nature. 'Surely this is a question of principle. Whatever work we're doing here, we have to be able to trust our colleagues.'

'Quite,' he said crisply and she caught his meaning clearly enough. He couldn't trust her. 'I suggest that you go through your papers again. It may simply be that a cleaner has moved something. I once came back from leave to find my books out of order. Apparently, the shelves had slipped and been repaired in my absence. It took some anxious enquiries to find this out. Most disturbing.'

He returned to his letter and she saw she was dismissed.

Nancy had reached home that evening and was fumbling her key in the front door lock when she heard the telephone starting to ring in the hall. Flinging open the door, she rushed to answer. There was an echo initially and it took her a moment to identify the typist, Miss Bateman. 'Did you find out who it was, Dr Foster? Who collected your report?'

'No. The copies are still missing.'

'Oh. Well there's some good news, at least. The gentleman

only took the typed reports, not your handwritten original. My colleague found it under her desk. It must have fallen out of the envelope. I have a quiet patch tomorrow. I can type it again if you like, though you'll have to pay another twelve and six.'

Nancy closed her eyes in relief. 'Yes, please,' she sighed. 'But it must be me who collects it this time. Nobody else, do you hear?'

'I understand, Dr Foster. I wonder who that gentleman was. It's quite the mystery, isn't it?'

'Quite.' Nancy gave a nervous laugh. After she replaced the receiver, she sank down on the hall chair feeling dizzy with relief. But she'd have her report back. Then she'd have to think what to do with it. She couldn't wait to tell James.

When she found him alone in his lab the following morning and told him, his expression darkened.

'I'm glad, of course, but Nancy, haven't you learned anything? It's very clear that Staunton isn't interested in this research. Either that or he doesn't want it getting out. Aren't you worried about your job?'

'Of course I am. Terribly worried, but how can I go on with my work when it's clear that the substance I'm investigating is dangerous and shouldn't be used in its current form? And what if they don't know, further up, and it's just Dr Staunton who's blocking it. I can't square it with my conscience, James.'

'I do see that, yes.' He paused to think. 'Why don't you let the matter lie for a while? Things change,' he said, flapping his hand vaguely. 'The way might become clearer.'

'Perhaps I ought to confront Dr Staunton again and have the whole thing out.'

'Do you really think that would help?'

She remembered the previous interview. The man's coldness, the way he dodged her questions. 'I don't know,' she said.

The day passed slowly, and the atmosphere in her lab was charged. The others hardly spoke to Nancy and everyone worked quietly. She was glad. A break from Jim's banter was welcome and she could lose herself in routine tasks. At lunchtime, the lab emptied and she used the moment's privacy to go through her books and papers again, knowing it was hopeless, but she felt better doing something. At least by the evening she'd have the typed-up report from Miss Bateman. She'd ring ahead to check that it was ready, then leave early to collect it.

Knowing that James had left for a few days in London and Edmund was away, she took her homemade sandwich to the staff common room, but found it, too, was empty. Many were on holiday and, it being a glorious day, those remaining were sunning themselves outside. She made herself a cup of tea and sat down, feeling suddenly terribly fearful and alone.

Forty-Nine

It was after six when Nancy reached home with the precious typed report and its handwritten original safely sealed in an envelope. She closed the door and stood in the hall a moment listening to the ticking clock. The sense of a vacuum was horrid. She left the envelope on the kitchen table and set about grilling the chop she'd bought for her solitary supper. After she'd eaten, she sat in the garden for a while listening to the birds and the rhythmic purr of the neighbour's lawn mower, then, when it became chilly, went inside to telephone her mother, promising to go home to see them the following weekend. After the call ended, she wandered back to the kitchen, her mind full of the family news. Roger and Sally's wedding was fast approaching, Helen was struggling with her little Terry's sleeplessness. At moments like this, she missed them all.

She glanced at the envelope on the kitchen table, then sat down and with trepidation opened it and drew out its contents. Flicking through, she saw with relief that the report was accurately typed and all was in order, though annoyingly there was no carbon copy. The question was what to do with it now. She couldn't decide.

The telephone rang, startling her from her reverie. She rose and went to answer it. '5173? Hello?' She was rewarded by a click, then a crackling sound like bacon frying in a pan. 'Hello?' she said again, but the crackling continued. Finally, she replaced the receiver. It might have been Frank or Eleanor ringing from the Continent, she supposed, and hoped there was nothing wrong. She stared at the telephone but it didn't ring again, so she returned to the kitchen.

This time when she sat in a reverie, a shadow darkened the window. She glanced up with a sense of disquiet, but saw only a cloud crossing the purpling sky. There was little point, she thought, her attention returning to the envelope, in keeping the report and the handwritten notebook together. The house was secure, she was sure it was, but just suppose . . . oh, that was silly, she should pull herself together. Still, best to be on the safe side. She took the notebook and hid it under the mattress in her bedroom, then drew the curtains in the sitting room and stowed the envelope with the typed report under the carpet by the bureau. Feeling more confident, she tried ringing James at his parents' house but there was no answer, so she settled down for an early night.

It was dark when she was awakened by the telephone. Three o'clock. She scampered down in bare feet to answer it. Again, there was a click, then the fizzing noise. 'Hello?' she said, 'Frank? Eleanor?' The fizzing stopped and the line went dead.

She went back to bed, but lay there, sleepless, waiting for the telephone to ring again. It didn't, but other more routine sounds bothered her. A scraping noise above the window must be a bird – they had martins nesting under the eaves. The dripping of a bathroom tap, the normal creaks and groans of the old house settling. But what was that? The rattle of the letterbox. Was someone trying the front door? Footsteps along the side of the house, the creak of the side gate, or was it her imagination? She threw back the blankets, went to the window and lifted the curtain. The small back garden lay silent, bathed in moonlight. The window squeaked as she opened it. She looked down and drew a sharp breath. She was sure she'd seen a movement. Had that been a figure retreating down the side of the house? She hurried into Frank and Eleanor's bedroom, where the curtains stood open, but could see no one from the window. Whoever the figure might have been, he had either concealed himself or had gone – or had she imagined him?

Unable to stand it any more, she stumbled downstairs, picked up the receiver and when the operator answered requested to speak to the police.

'I don't think they believed me,' she said to James when she finally tracked him down at his parents' home the following evening. 'They imagined I was being hysterical. Oh, James, where have you been, darling? I rang your mother earlier, but she didn't know.'

'I stayed with Malcolm Gifford last night. Old schoolfriend. I told you about him. We had a bit of a late night.' He sounded defensive. 'What did they say, the police?'

'They waved their torches about, waking all the neighbours, told me to buy a padlock for the side gate and that was it.'

'Would you like me to come over now? It's late, but I suppose there might be a train.'

She heard him sigh and her pride got in the way. She wasn't the helpless type. 'No, that's ridiculous. All this stupid business, it's given me the jitters.'

'If you'll just let it go, Nancy, things will settle down.'

It was her turn to sigh. 'I can't, you know that.'

'We'll talk about it on Friday. I'll be back at Brandingfield first thing.'

After he rang off, she replaced the receiver and sat with her face in her hands. Things were not right between her and James. The warmth had gone. He should be supporting her, but instead she felt increasingly abandoned by him. Her mind roved over the events of the past week and now she saw with clarity how the clues stacked up. The many ways that he had discouraged her from following her conscience. His conversation with Dr Staunton, which he'd brushed away with a weak excuse when she'd challenged him. Miss Bateman's description of the 'gentleman' who'd collected the copies of the typed report, who sounded astonishingly like James. Individually all these things could be argued away, but putting them together now the evidence against him was strong. Suddenly, she felt sick. She roused herself, went to the kitchen for a glass of water and stood slowly sipping it until she felt better. She must be wrong about him, she thought. What, after all, could his motive be? He had no obvious connection with ICP, had nothing to gain by placating them. And if he loved her, why would he plot against her and make her suffer in this way? These truths briefly sustained her. Of course he loved her and had nothing to do with this.

That night, as the light failed, she prowled the house, locking the doors and tightening the window catches. She'd bought a padlock for the side gate, but it didn't fit. In Frank and Eleanor's room, she paused to look out. She could just see the ghostly glow of Brandingfield in the distance above the rooftops. She shivered. Even here she couldn't escape its threat.

She left the landing light on when she went to bed, but the sound of the wind kept her awake and, when she slept finally, dark ghoulish shapes haunted her dreams.

The following day, she was so exhausted that she had to drag herself through the hours in the lab. She hardly cared whether the eyes of her colleagues were upon her. All she knew was that she couldn't go on like this. It was driving her mad. She had to make a decision. ICP's headquarters were at Watford nearby, but she could hardly just turn up there.

She could send the Chief Scientific Officer the report in the post. Then at least she'd have done her duty. But if she made that choice, what would happen next? Either she'd be thanked and applauded or, at worst, lose her job. Be disgraced. And if that happened, who would want to employ her?

As Nancy walked home that evening, a light rain began to fall on the dusty pavements, so she quickened her pace. Later, she watched it grow heavy as she sat in the kitchen eating poached eggs on toast. Far away, thunder growled and flashes of lightning made strange silhouettes of the trees. Normally she loved a good storm, but tonight it made her feel cut off from the world and lonelier than ever. After her supper, she went round the house locking up, listened to the wireless and finished sewing a summer dress for her holiday, then, in a bid for much-needed sleep, she had a hot bath and made a comforting mug of cocoa. All to no avail.

For hours she lay sleepless as rain battered the window and rattled down the pipes, while the wind howled through the trees and the house rang like a glass. This weather, she thought grimly, was like a stage set for the nightmare her life had become.

Eventually, she must have dozed, for a noise snatched her to sudden wakefulness. She lay quiet, her skin clammy, the room alive with shadows. The rain had dwindled to a gentle patter, but this had been a different sound, something strange and wrong. There it was again, a clink of metal, somewhere outside, but close enough to worry her, very close. Then came a scraping noise, as of a spade across stone, followed by a silence. Someone was in the garden, she was sure of it. She dared not move but knew she had to. To reach the telephone. She threw back the covers, then paused. What was the point of summoning the police? She remembered two nights before, the weariness in the sergeant's voice as he'd tried to reassure her: 'There's nobody here, Miss.' She wouldn't trouble them again, not until she'd investigated for herself.

She flinched at a tapping noise downstairs. 'A twig,' she

muttered aloud, 'it's only a twig blowing against the sitting room window. Get up. Go and see for yourself.' She swung her feet down to the warmth of the rug, but fear sapped her strength. *Get up!* She stood.

She froze. Something hard had pattered against her window. What could that be? Heart pounding, she took a step towards the window, and another. Grasped the curtain, took a breath and snatched it aside. Stared out in wonder at the sky. The storm was passing. Clouds like black cobwebs veiled the moon. She blinked at its brightness, then gathering her courage, looked down. Her eyes widened in relief. 'Oh,' she breathed, seeing a bent figure searching the ground below. 'It's *you.*'

She opened the window. 'Dorothy!' she called down. 'What are you doing?'

Dorothy straightened, dropping the pebbles she'd collected. 'Oh, thank heavens. I haven't got a key. I knocked and knocked, didn't you hear?'

'Actually, I thought you were a twig!' Nancy almost choked with laughter and relief. She went down to let her friend in.

They sat together in the kitchen for an hour, talking and drinking whisky. Dorothy had fallen ill in Paris, and though she was on the mend she had decided to return home early. She had tried to phone. Nancy explained everything that had happened while Dorothy had been away and cried as she confessed how she felt that James had let her down. Oh, what a blessed relief it was to pour out her problems to a friend who understood the pros and cons of each course of action. They agreed that she should make no decision about the report until she'd slept on the matter, but when she woke up on Friday morning she knew what she wanted to do.

She and Dorothy wrote a covering letter addressed to ICP's Chief Scientific Officer. After Nancy had taken the package to the post office, she hurried into work and went at once to tell James. It was after ten and she was lucky to find him alone in his lab. He was examining some glass slides. He looked up from his microscope at her entrance and, when he saw her expression, the smile died on his face.

'What's happened?'

'I've sent my report, James.'

She wasn't expecting the force of his reaction, how he spat out the words. 'I guessed you would in the end, knowing you, but it's stupid, Nancy, self-destructive!'

She reeled as though struck. 'James?' she said faintly, but he turned from her. She touched his arm. He flinched and she stepped back.

Finally, he faced her and sighed. 'I tried my best to help you. Maybe you'll be all right, I don't know. But Staunton, he won't forgive you. You'll have made him look stupid.'

'How have you tried to help me, James?' she said in a low voice. 'You don't know what it's been like, how frightening it all is. When your work is stolen, but no one believes you. When your colleagues freeze you out, and even you . . .' She swallowed. 'Even you . . . I needed your support, James.'

'And you had it,' he said, but there was no strength in his words.

'I didn't. You took yourself off and . . . some of your behaviour has been suspicious to say the least.'

'That's an appalling thing to suggest.'

'Was it you? Who stole my report from the typist?'

'Of course it wasn't me!' He sounded so adamant that she believed him. She wanted to believe him.

She closed her eyes and her shoulders sagged and suddenly he was there, she felt his arms round her, his lips on her forehead, and she leaned into his warmth and remembered how much she loved him, had yearned for him. And yet there was something, that old sixth sense, that told her something was different. It was to do with trust. He'd let her down. She didn't trust him any more. Her eyes flew open.

He must have felt her stiffen, for he straightened and held her from him. She tucked a stray lock of hair behind her ear and said, 'We have to talk. You're going away soon?'

'The end of August,' he said gravely, then he smiled. 'And I'd like you to come with me. You will now, surely? It'll be too difficult for you here at Brandingfield now.'

She stared at him as something fell into place. 'So you no longer deny it? That is what this has been about?'

'What d'you mean?'

'No.' It still didn't make sense. 'Forget that I said that.' He had, after all, discouraged her from doing anything with her report precisely because it would endanger her job.

James wasn't letting the implication go. 'I have always tried to support you professionally, Nancy. But now you're accusing me . . .'

'I said forget it!' she wailed. Both hands flew to her face. 'I don't know what is what any more. Nothing makes sense. All I know is . . .' She gazed at him with sudden pity. 'I can't come with you to America, James. And I can't marry you. I'm sorry. I wanted to, but not after all this. I simply can't. Not now.'

He paled, reached for her blindly, but she stepped back. 'I can't,' she repeated with a sob. 'I still love you, but something's gone. Don't you see, James? You don't have my back. I simply don't trust you any more.'

And with that she turned and left him.

Fifty

Heavy rain pounded down on Dragonfly Lodge and runnels of water streamed down the window. Nancy leaned across wearily and switched on a table lamp. Its gleam was feeble against the darkness of the storm. Stef waited, wondering if the old lady was too tired to go on, but Nancy straightened and continued.

'After that,' she said softly, 'I went home. Home to my family. I took sick leave, whatever they called it then. I suppose I had a kind of nervous breakdown. I couldn't sleep and I cried all the time. My mother called the doctor and he prescribed some dreadful knock-out pills. I refused to take them after a bit because of the side effects, but a fortnight or so later I began to feel better. Strangely, what helped was going to visit my sister. Andrew and Terry were sweet little boys and it took my mind off things looking after them. And Helen was grateful, I could see that. We became closer.'

She smiled to herself, lost for a moment in the past, then said, 'Where was I?'

Stef ventured, 'You said you'd gone home. What happened about your job and . . . everything? The report?'

'Oh, the report.' Nancy laughed softly. 'Absolutely nothing. I went back to work for a couple of months, but nobody said anything, not a thing. I waited and waited for the blow to fall, it was terribly stressful. I hardly saw James. We both avoided one another and then, of course, he left for the States. That was a relief. I simply finished the research that I'd been paid to do, wrote it up and turned it in. It was a matter of pride. I hope that they were pleased with it. I never heard that they weren't.'

'But then?'

'ICP declined to renew my contract. No reason was given.' She spread her hands. 'So that was it. My glorious career as a research scientist.'

'That's awful.' Stef was shocked. 'But wait, surely you could have found another research post, couldn't you?'

Nancy considered this. 'I probably could have, yes, but I'd lost the appetite for it. It sounds a dreadful thing to say, not very brave at all, but I felt a door had been closed. All my ambitions, everything I'd worked for . . . Gone.'

'How did people react?' Stef wanted to know.

'My family were extremely sympathetic. They'd been so concerned about me, you see. As for my friends, Eleanor understood, but I think Dorothy felt let down when I told her I was going to become a schoolmistress. Our little supper club was important to her and I'd been a founding member.

We kept up for a while, but our paths eventually diverged. She did very well, got a job in the Natural History Museum and married someone she met there. No children, though.'

She sighed as she gazed out at the rain, then said, 'It took me a long while to get over James. I felt that he'd let me down and it was devastating.'

Fifty-One

1954

At home in early August, recuperating after her ordeal, Nancy was touched one morning to receive a letter from Edmund.

My dear Nancy,

I returned from Edinburgh on Sunday. A pleasant stay with my Aunt Phoebe, and the weather being fine my former wife allowed me to take our daughter out on Saturday. There was a big funfair with rides at one of the parks, which she seemed to enjoy, but it's hard work, Nancy. Marianne sees me so rarely and she seems on her guard when she's with me. Still, she's a dear little girl and I soldier on.

Enough of my ramblings. I was concerned to hear on the grapevine that you were ill, and this letter is really to wish you well again soon. I miss seeing you at Brandingfield. I bumped into James and asked after you, but he didn't appear

to know much. Is everything all right there? Nobody's
saying anything here if that comforts you. I know you
hate gossip.
   With good wishes,
   Edmund

She smiled to read this. Dear Edmund, always hitting the right note. Concerned but not overly so. It was comforting to learn that the end of her relationship with James was not a topic of conversation at Brandingfield, though perhaps this wasn't surprising. James would keep such matters close, and the only other person who knew about them breaking up was Dorothy, who was a loyal friend. Edmund didn't mention Nancy's work problems, but perhaps he was being tactful. Dr Staunton might be discreet – it was not in his interest to be otherwise – but her colleagues in the lab loved to gossip.

She kept herself to herself when she returned to work for that short period. Frank, Eleanor and Dorothy were marvellous, making sure that she was never alone in the evenings. Dorothy sometimes visited Nancy's lab during the day. She was a popular figure there and, being beautiful and outgoing and brooking no nonsense, did not suffer the banter or patronizing attitudes that Nancy had to put up with. Dorothy was like a bright sword protecting her friend. The men feared her ire, so largely left Nancy alone.

Once or twice, she ran into James in a corridor or a common room. The first time he avoided her eye, but she spoke to him and saw his relief that at least they could be civil. When she asked after the progress of his doctorate, his face lit up. 'I've passed my viva,' he told her, 'without corrections.'

'Congratulations, Dr West,' she said, meaning it.

'I know I have to thank you for your help when it was difficult,' he mumbled.

She nodded, surprised but grateful for this acknowledgement.

Soon afterwards, he left for Boston. She found a note from him in her pigeonhole and read it when she was alone.

Dear N,

By the time you read this I'll be in the air over the Atlantic. A new life ahead! I wanted to tell you that I bear you no ill will for what happened. I see now that you would never have settled for being number two to anyone, especially me, and we can't change who we are. Be assured, though, that the motive behind my actions in this unfortunate matter was simply to help you, to help us. I will always hold you close in my heart and hope that one day we will meet again. In the meantime, good luck and take good care!

Yours truly,

JW

A fierce anger leapt in her. So much for her trying to be civil to him. He'd bear her 'no ill will'. She would 'never have settled' for being his number two. The condescension, the obfuscation, the refusal to acknowledge any guilt. James had clearly reviewed the whole episode that led to their break-up and come up with his own interpretation. Well, good rid-dance to him. *No, James, I hope we never have to meet again.* She screwed up the cheap writing paper and was about to throw it into the bin, when, through the flames of anger, a small voice of calm stayed her hand. If she was ever accused of anything by ICP, she would need to marshal every piece of evidence she could and, vague as it was, the letter was an indication of James' interference. She smoothed out the paper and folded it away in her briefcase.

At night, Nancy didn't sleep well. Her dreams were full of noise, of being chased through swirling darkness. During the day, after James' departure and with Dorothy's loving kindness, most of the time she found peace in her work. However, sometimes a sharp word from the technician or a shirty response from a secretary caused tears to threaten.

It was from one of those occasions that Edmund rescued her. She'd dictated a short update on her work that needed to be properly laid out and typed and gave the tape to the office with a deadline, but a week later the work hadn't been done. When she asked why not, she was told in no uncertain terms that her colleague Jim's work took precedence.

'Why?' she asked the woman. 'I happen to know that he submitted it after mine.'

The woman pressed her lips into a straight line and said Jim had told her to do his urgently.

'Mine's urgent, too,' Nancy protested.

'Perhaps he asks nicely,' the woman snapped and Nancy was left without words.

'Dr Foster asked very nicely, I'm sure,' a mild voice said behind her and Nancy looked round to see Edmund. 'Those letters I gave you on Thursday, Miss Weeks,' he said to the secretary, 'with a deadline of today. They're routine. Do Nancy's instead. Please?'

Nancy had noticed before how people liked Edmund. He never patronized anyone, nor did he try to charm. He just treated everyone pleasantly and as though they mattered.

The secretary nodded, muttering, 'It'll be ready late afternoon,' to Nancy. Then she turned her back on her.

'Coffee?' Edmund suggested.

'Mmm.' They walked to the common room together. 'That was kind of you,' she said in a low voice, 'but you don't need to fight my battles.'

'It was an easy victory for both of us. My letters will generate some tedious work that I don't actually want to do.'

'Oh dear.' She smiled. 'And I do need to submit that report. So thank you, Edmund.'

It was late for morning coffee and the scientists' common room was almost empty. They settled themselves in two comfortable seats by the window looking out onto the park, now bathed in amber September sunshine.

'How is it going?' he asked her, spooning sugar into his coffee. 'I try not to listen to rumour, but as I said in my letter, I've heard enough to realize life has not been easy for you.'

She understood that he knew very little of everything that had happened to her and so she started to tell him, awkwardly at first, but then the words tumbled out in a rush. She explained about the findings concerning Zalathion that had alarmed her and how Dr Staunton had blocked her attempts to communicate them to ICP. All the things that had happened sounded ridiculous to her now, but she ploughed on nevertheless. She couldn't, however, bring herself to tell him the scale of James' involvement. It was still too raw and personal, and since she couldn't get it to make sense to herself it was difficult to explain to him. Dorothy had understood, but she was a woman and knew about men like James. So all she said was that she hadn't felt she could move to America and that she and James had decided mutually to end the relationship.

Edmund expressed his condolences, but asked no questions, which she was relieved about. Instead, they drank their coffee and she asked him about Edinburgh and how his daughter was, and he told her with a sad light in his eyes that he didn't know how long he'd be able to keep up the contact.

'I see her so rarely that she finds it difficult. She's puzzled by me, I think. You know, she calls her stepfather 'Daddy' now. Her mother encourages her to. And says it might be better if I didn't visit.'

'Don't give up,' Nancy said, filled with compassion for him.

'It might be kindest. After all, it's unlikely to become easier. Marianne's getting older and hardly remembers London. Her life is in Edinburgh. You know, she speaks with a lovely Scots lilt now.' He chuckled. 'I must seem strange to her. With my English vowels.'

'I'm sure you know what's best for her, Edmund, but it seems sad that you should be made to feel this way.'

'You think I should keep trying?' His face was troubled.

'I think so.'

'Thank you. I like your sort of advice.'

They smiled sadly at one another.

'I suppose we must get back to work again,' he sighed. He paused, contemplating her with an uncertain gaze, then added, 'I'll understand if you say no, but might you be free for dinner on Friday?'

It was the first of many such arrangements, and Edmund's steady friendship helped Nancy through her last days at Brandingfield. He listened to her complaints about Dr Staunton with sympathy and mopped up her tears when she heard in late September that her contract was not being renewed. And he took a day off to accompany her to a school in nearby leafy Radlett one beautiful October morning, where she had been invited for interview.

He waited in a tea room in the high street with a novel to read and she hurried to join him there. The sight through the window of his lean, grave face frowning as he turned a page gave her an astonishing little frisson of pleasure.

He glanced up as she pushed open the door, admitting a gust of dead leaves. Seeing her delighted expression, he broke into a smile and closed his book. 'Yes?' he asked, as she plumped herself into the chair opposite.

'Yes!' She unwound her scarf and sat back in relief. 'They need me right away. The usual teacher's gone off sick halfway through the term. Goodness, those cakes look delicious.' She reached for one and Edmund ordered another pot of tea. 'The thing is, they don't know when she'll be back, poor thing, so it might only be for a few weeks, but it's a start.'

'Well, let's hope she recovers soon but needs a long conva-
lescence. Did you like the school?'

'I did. The headmistress was very warm-hearted and I
could see that the girls thought so, too. The ones I encountered looked bright and cheerful. I'd be teaching the younger
children to start with, but once I've caught up with the syllabuses – is it syllabuses or syllabi? Never mind – they'll let me
loose on the exam classes.'

'That doesn't sound like a short-term job to me.'

'No, it doesn't, does it? Oh, Edmund, I think I'm going to
enjoy myself. It'll be such a lovely change from Staunton and
his blasted disciples.'

'Forget Staunton. You deserve some happiness, Nancy.'

His hand touched hers where it lay on the table and very
slowly they laced fingers. She raised her eyes to his and they
sat together in quiet wonder for a while. Then she said in a
low voice, 'I never thought I'd be happy again, but a month
away from Brandingfield and I feel a different person. I'll
miss research, I can't pretend otherwise, but I couldn't continue to work in those circumstances, Edmund. I see that now.
It's so hard for women. Our work is as good as the men's,
but they seem to resent us. They don't see that things need
to change. They won't give up their old networks, their old
habits. Not without a fight, and I've run out of fight.'

'You fought well,' Edmund said, his face full of concern,
and his hand tightened on hers. 'And you haven't closed the
door on research.'

'I may well have done,' she said thoughtfully. 'At least for
the time being. And I'm sure there will be other scientists

questioning the use of DDT and organophosphates. There must be. I say, I'm still dreadfully hungry. It must be the relief. Is it too early for lunch?'

Over ham and eggs, they talked about practicalities. Nancy could stay at Frank and Eleanor's for the time being and take a bus the few miles to the school. The money was better than her research grant had been, so the extra cost wasn't a problem. 'And if the job doesn't last . . .' She gave a mournful sigh.

'Then something else will work out,' Edmund said, wiping his mouth. 'Take life a bit at a time.'

'Yes, that's the best idea.'

He checked his watch. 'We've an hour before the bus. Shall we explore the town?' He laid out some coins and they called their thanks to the waitress as they left.

They ambled in bright sunshine along the high street, looking into the bow windows of quaint old shops. Edmund stepped into a tiny florist's and came out bearing a posy of late roses. 'To say well done,' he said, giving them to Nancy and brushing away her thanks.

Eventually, they came to a small park with smart wrought-iron gates. 'Shall we?' he said.

Inside, there was nobody about except an old gardener slowly sweeping leaves. They wandered the gravel paths beside beds of neatly pruned shrubs, sniffing smoke on the air from some distant bonfire. Edmund pointed out an unusual crop of fungus growing in an old stump. Swings and a slide occupied a corner beside autumn trees where rooks were gathering noisily among untidy nests. Then, at the far end, they almost missed a break in a long laurel hedge where a narrow loam footpath led them out of the park into a patch of ancient woodland. In the coolness, fingers of sunlight reached between the branches and made Edmund's fine hair shine like gold.

Here in their secret bower, they stood close together for a long moment with locked gaze, then Edmund, brushing a strand of hair from her face, bent and kissed her. And now she was in his arms, kissing him back, pressed against him, feeling the beat of his heart against hers, smelling the warm, woollen scent of him and knowing that somehow, this time, she was safe.

'I love you,' he whispered in her ear. 'I've loved you for years, Nancy. I always thought you were special, ever since we spotted dragonflies together in the New Forest back in first year.'

'You must have thought me very young and silly then.'

'Young, yes, but never silly. I loved your bright spirit, your enthusiasm. But I was too preoccupied by my own difficulties then. And you must have found me very grim.'

'I was in awe of you, Edmund. I sensed that you'd suffered so much. But I appreciated your kindness. And I still love that dragonfly you gave me.'

His face lit up in a smile.

'It's funny how everything has turned out, isn't it? A few months ago, the future seemed so different. And now ...' She reached up and kissed him again. 'To save any doubt, I love you, too!'

Fifty-Two

'We were married the following summer,' Nancy told Stef. 'It was a quiet town hall wedding because of Edmund being divorced, but once my parents got over being upset about that they were content enough. They saw how good Edmund was for me. The only sadness was that he wanted Marianne to be a bridesmaid but his ex-wife refused to allow it. I personally thought she couldn't be bothered to bring Marianne down to London, but Edmund, who's kinder than me, said that wasn't it. That it was more to do with the look of the thing. People thought divorce very shameful then and appearances were everything. Rather than white, I wore a pretty suit in the palest of blues and the sun shone for us that day.'

'It sounds a wonderful ending after all your troubles.'

Nancy inclined her head. 'It wasn't an ending, of course. Real life is not like that.'

'No, I suppose not.' Stef waited.

'But we were married for twenty years and were very

happy together. Edmund left Brandingfield as soon as he could. We thought it for the best and he loved it at the museum in Cambridge. But we experienced much sadness to do with our children. He'd been right, it was very difficult for him to keep up with Marianne, and he became quite bitter about it. I sometimes wonder if that bitterness infected his relationship with our daughter, Aaron's mother; whether she thought she was second-best in her father's life.'

'Where did you say Andrea is now?'

'Mexico. A rather bohemian existence, but she sounds happy enough. Aaron has been to see her and we write to each other sometimes.' Nancy cleared her throat. 'Anyway, Edmund was forty-nine when he became ill. It was an aggressive form of cancer and there wasn't anything the doctors could do ... It was very quick.' Her voice trailed off, her thoughts far away.

Eventually, Stef said, 'That must have been awful. Still so young.'

'Yes, it was awful. I wasn't working at that point, but I knew I had to. I answered an advertisement for a post at the school in Norwich. A fresh start seemed right. So there we are, you know the rest. I've brought you up to date!'

'What about your sister Helen?'

'Ah, Helen. You're too young to have known a BBC children's television show called *Storytime* with Helen Royle.'

Stef frowned. The name didn't mean anything.

'When Andrew and Terry were safely at senior school, she decided she was going out to work. There was a bit of a row. Bobby wasn't at all happy. An old schoolfriend of Helen's got her an interview at the BBC for a job as a part-time typist. And when they were casting around for a female presenter for a new children's show, one thing led to another.'

'That's wonderful! Did Bobby come round to the idea?'

'He learned to put up with it, let's say. Helen died ten years ago and I miss her still,' Nancy said with a sigh. 'We became quite close after my parents died. Roger and his wife Sally settled in Oxford, but we lost him, too. They never visited me here, which is rather sad, but I've never minded my own company, Stef. Getting to know Aaron and Livy has been marvellous, though.'

They smiled at one another. Nancy looked tired and Stef, glancing at her watch, was shocked to realize that she'd been talking for several hours. She knew she had learned everything that she was likely to, and it was time to leave. But before she did, there was an important thing to clarify.

'I need to check with you, Nancy. Would you really and truly be happy for me to include your story in my book? Not the very personal stuff, obviously, but the experiences of being a scientist. I'd run everything past you and you'd have the final word.'

Nancy's eyes were steady on hers. 'Yes,' she said very firmly. 'I think it's time. I wouldn't like to think all this wallowing in the past has been for nothing. I often wonder, you know, what happened about my report. Whether it did any good. Oh well, it's all a long time ago now.'

They sat for a moment, watching the rain coming down. Stef rose and went to the window. 'There's no sign of it easing,' she sighed, 'but I ought to get back.'

'You can borrow my golfing umbrella if you like. It was Edmund's once. I've never played golf.'

'Thank you.' But when Stef opened the front door, she was shocked to see a stream of water flowing across the path. 'Nancy,' she said, turning to the old lady in dismay, 'I don't like the look of this.'

Nancy came close and peered past her. 'It's just surface run-off,' she said, but her tone was doubtful, then she straightened. 'Let's have a look at the Broad from the kitchen.'

She retreated up the hall, one hand on the wall for support, and Stef followed. In the kitchen, the cat was nosing at the cat flap, the tip of her tail twitching. Nancy bent and pushed the flap. 'There you are!' But the sound of rushing rain loudened and the cat backed away.

'Oh, Nancy!' Stef gazed out of the window in dismay. 'This isn't good.' The heavy raindrops pounded the surface of the Broad so that it simmered. Tongues of water lapped at the shore, exploring the slope. The jetty was still clearly visible, but lower in the water than usual, and she couldn't see the boat.

Nancy joined her, rubbing condensation from the glass. After a moment, she said, 'It'll be all right. There's never been a flood while I've been here. The last time I believe was 1953.'

'That's nearly sixty years ago,' Stef calculated.

'Goodness, though, I suppose we'd better move the animals. Oh, Stef, do you think you could? It's best to be on the safe side.'

It took a while for Stef to bring Nancy's menagerie inside. Everything had to come, even the cages up on the shelves.

After all, the outhouse was very near the Broad and, even if the building itself didn't flood, it could become difficult for Nancy to reach it to tend her little zoo. Soon, every downstairs surface in the house had its cage or crate. Stef took care to leave nothing on the floor – just in case.

'What about you?' she asked, coming in soaked, carrying a last sack of seed. 'Will you be all right?'

'Of course I will,' Nancy said brightly, passing her a towel. 'I tell you, this house hasn't flooded for years. It's just a bit of rain, that's all.'

Stef, drying herself, felt uneasy, but there was little she could do. 'Keep your phone by you, will you?' she pleaded.

'Of course.'

When she left, the old lady was sitting happily on the sofa with a cup of tea amid her cages and tanks and the scuttlings, scufflings and pungent smells of their inhabitants.

Fifty-Three

Despite the umbrella and the towel, Stef's clothes were quickly sodden and she was shivering by the time she reached Springfield Cottage. Her mother sent her straight up to run a bath.

She sank into the hot water with a blissful sigh and closed her eyes. For a moment, she thought of nothing but enjoying her own animal comfort. Soon, though, memories of the afternoon began to intrude. The story that Nancy had told her was extraordinary. Her doomed love for James, her thwarted ambition, the traumatic bullying she'd suffered and, finally, the nature of the secret that she'd concealed all these years. She knew all about ICP – they were now a huge multinational company. They would easily brush off a sepia-tinted scandal from fifty-odd years before – they'd undoubtedly dealt with much worse in their time – but, like Nancy, Stef was curious to know what had happened to Nancy's research into Zalathion. Had the chief scientist she'd sent it to even read the report? Was it gathering dust in their archives somewhere? Was it possible to find out? It would be fascinating and, more importantly, it might reassure Nancy.

Her thoughts ran on. There was a great deal that she needed to explore. She guessed from what Aaron's account what had happened to James, that he'd made his life in America. He'd have retired by now, of course, but it might be possible to speak to him.

The cast-iron bath was elderly and the water was quickly losing heat. Stef reached for the hot tap and ran more water. Poor Nancy. She hoped that she was all right out there in the rain. She'd ring her later. And go back to see her tomorrow. There were things she still wanted to clarify. Her mind roamed over some of the characters in Nancy's story. Anne Durban and Peggy. Colourful Aunt Rhoda. And Nancy's sister Helen. Helen had obviously finally rebelled against the constrictions of her life. She'd taken work outside the home against her husband's wishes and become something of a star in her time.

By the time Stef had dried herself and dressed, a delicious spicy smell was wafting up the stairs. She padded down to the kitchen and was surprised to find Ted there in a plastic apron, stirring a pan of curry on the stove. A saucepan of rice bubbled on the back burner. He grinned at her, showing a chipped tooth. 'Coming up in fifteen minutes,' he said and gave her a teaspoon of the curry to taste.

'Very good,' she said sincerely and poured herself some red wine from the open bottle on the table.

'Your ma's gone up for a rest. She was over at your sister's earlier. The twins were a handful. They always know when something's up, kids.'

'Oh yes?' Stef said, interested. 'How was Pippa?'

'I expect Cara will tell you herself,' he said. Their eyes met and she nodded. It was tactful of him. 'Listen,' he went on. 'I know you don't . . . I mean, it must be odd to you . . . me and your mum.'

'I'm getting used to it,' she sighed.

'But I do care about her. Really. She lights up a room, doesn't she? My wife was like that. God, I missed her when she passed. There's been nobody else for years. Nobody to match her. Until I met Cara.'

Stef straightened. 'I didn't know you'd lost your wife. I'm sorry. But it's just that it's strange, you and Mum.'

'You mean I'm not the right sort?' His eyes twinkled. 'Your dad being a lecturer and me a builder?'

'No!' she gasped in embarrassment, then admitted, 'Yes, a little bit, but whoever it was would be odd, do you see?'

'Yeah, I understand. Now, would you like to call your ma down? We're just about ready.'

At supper, Stef's mother explained that Pippa was slightly less miserable than she had been. She and Rob were going to go to couples counselling, a big step for both of them, but astonishingly it had been Rob who'd suggested it. He'd apparently been dismayed by Pippa's fears that he'd been having an affair and was desperate to reassure her. 'Do you think all this is because of your dad and me?' Cara asked Stef, her eyes full of guilt. 'We haven't been a good example, have we?'

'I don't think it's that at all,' Stef said earnestly. 'Their situation is completely individual to them.'

'I suppose you're right. Pippa's also talking about looking for work. She loves going to the gym and mentioned the idea of becoming a personal trainer. I suppose there are courses for that sort of thing.'

'I'm sure there are,' Stef said warmly. 'It's a good idea. She could work that around the children.'

'Your sister has plenty of hidden talents, I'm sure,' Cara said. 'Now, you haven't told me how you got on with Nancy this afternoon. Is she comfortable?'

Stef told them she was worried about the old lady. 'Marooned with all those cages like something out of *Doctor Dolittle.*'

'Give her a call,' her mother said firmly. 'Tell her we'll go up and fetch her if she likes. Though how we'd get her to the car, Lord only knows.'

'I reckon I could manage it,' Ted said with a gleam in his eye. 'I'm a volunteer fireman.'

'Are you? How wonderful! With luck, though, it won't come to that.' Stef took up the golf umbrella and stepped outside. The rain was still pouring down from a sky the colour of iron, and it was hard to avoid the puddles on the potholed lane. When she tapped Nancy's name on her phone Nancy took a long time to answer. Then, after some clattering about at the other end of the line, she was rewarded by the old lady's voice. 'Hello?'

'It's Stef here, Nancy, just ringing to find out how you are.'

'We're managing very well, aren't we, Tabby? I'm having

to watch her near the mice. She's far too interested in them, aren't you, pussy cat?'

'What about the water levels?'

'I haven't been outside, but we're all dry in here.'

'Perhaps you should sleep upstairs?'

'I think I will,' she laughed. 'It'll be too noisy down here with this nocturnal brood.'

'Be careful,' Stef said vaguely, feeling a bit helpless. 'We don't want you falling again.'

'I assure you, I have no intention of doing that.'

'And take your phone with you.'

'Stef,' Nancy said calmly. 'Stop treating me like an old lady. I have all my marbles.'

'Sorry,' Stef sighed and managed not to say, *But you are an old lady!*

After she rang off, she paused, still worried. A vision of Aaron entered her mind. Swiftly she found his name. Phone or text? What might he be doing now? Text first, she decided and sent one quickly asking him to ring her. She waited for a couple of minutes, her feet getting wetter, but there was no reply. She gave up and returned to the cottage.

She opened the door to hear the sound of singing. Her mother's high voice and Ted's out-of-tune bass belting out a lively Beatles number. She went to the kitchen doorway and stood there, amazed, watching them dance about, Ted brandishing a tea towel and her mother a handful of cutlery. Baxter sat watching by the back door. When Ted and Cara saw Stef, they fell about giggling like a couple of schoolchildren.

Stef rolled her eyes and her mother collected herself enough to ask, 'How's Nancy?'

'Fine, I think,' Stef said. 'You carry on. I'm going upstairs to do some work.'

There was no doubt that Ted was making her mother happy, she thought. As she settled down with her laptop, she herself felt lonelier than ever. She shrugged off the feeling and opened a file named *A Curious Nature*. It was the proposal for her book. She went to the Contents page and after a moment's hesitation typed a new entry just before the Conclusion. 'Chapter 20: Nancy Foster, Zoologist.' It needed a title. 'A Life Suppressed'? No, that didn't sound fair to Nancy, who'd achieved much. She'd have to give the matter more thought. She scrolled to the end of the document and began to type:

'Nancy Foster (1929–) dreamed of a brilliant future as a zoologist. Following her doctorate, she began work as a researcher for International Chemical Products in 1953, the only woman in her department. Within a year, she found herself edged out and her most important work quietly ignored . . .'

Stef typed two paragraphs quickly, read them through, then sat biting her lip. Nothing there that Nancy was likely to object to and she did have her approval to include her in the book. But was this the right slot for her in the proposal? It packed a punch as a final chapter and Nancy was, after, all still alive, but the rest of the book was arranged chronologically and the experiences to be covered had taken place in the 1940s and '50s. She should move it to earlier in the proposal. It only took a moment. She reordered the Contents and read the whole document through again, making tweaks here and there.

Perfect, she thought. She wrote a brief covering email to Sarah, then pressed 'Send', sitting back and stretching as she watched it go with a feeling of lightness. Tomorrow, Sarah might read it. By the end of the day, the proposal might be with her editor and then it would be a matter of waiting. Would Catherine like it? She sighed and closed her laptop. No point in counting her chickens yet.

Her phone lay on the desk. She picked it up and glanced at the screen, but there was no mobile signal. Ten past nine. Over an hour since she'd texted Aaron. Perhaps he'd replied by now. She padded downstairs. Her mother and Ted must be in the sitting room, for the television was squawking through the closed door.

She shuffled on her wet trainers with a grimace. Outside, the rain still poured down, so she grabbed the umbrella and squelched up the lane. At the sweet spot, she stared at the phone, but nothing came in. Aaron hadn't rung or returned her text. *Perhaps he's busy,* she told herself, *or doesn't have his phone with him,* but this didn't stop dejection washing over her. Quickly she sent him another text, this time giving him her mother's landline number.

It proved difficult to get to sleep that night. There was so much to think about. She was worried about Nancy out there on the marsh in the storm. There was Nancy's story running through her head. But there was also something else, something eluding her. She was finally drifting towards unconsciousness when she remembered what it was.

It was the stocklist on Josh's clipboard that she'd seen earlier that day, typed in that unusual font and signed with a handwritten 'J'. She remembered going into the visitors' centre and buying the ice creams from Jackie, who as usual was wearing her volunteer's name badge. And suddenly her eyes flew open. Perhaps the 'J' hadn't been for Josh after all. Perhaps it had been for Jackie. *No*, she thought again. She couldn't think of a motive. *Why would Jackie, a kindly middle-aged woman, want to frighten an elderly lady like that?* It made no sense. Eventually, Stef dismissed the matter, turned over and closed her eyes once more.

Fifty-Four

Stef was awakened at first light by the sound of the house phone ringing downstairs. She heard the stairs creak, then her mother answer it, and lay listening, on full alert.

'Stef,' her mother called up softly.

'Coming.' Stef rolled out of bed and hurried down, fumbling with the belt on her dressing gown. 'Who is it?'

Her mother held out the handset with a look of concern. 'It's Aaron.'

She took it. 'Aaron. I'm so sorry, I didn't need you to ring me so early.'

'Your texts are not the reason.' His voice sounded distant, echoey.

'Where are you? Not Cornwall?'

'At home still. Has Nancy rung you yet?'

'No, what's wrong?' Her heart sank. She'd already guessed.

'The house has flooded, Stef.'

'I feared it might,' she groaned.

'She's marooned upstairs. Says she's okay, but she's worried about her bloody animals. The water's knee-deep in the hall apparently and getting worse. Stef, I'm just getting dressed, then I'll come. I told her to ring the fire brigade, but she won't have it. What if she tries to rescue the blasted things herself and falls over?'

'I think we should ring them. Shall I do it from here? It might be simpler. Being local.'

'If you wouldn't mind.'

'And I'll drive over there. I mean, if I can get through.'

Her mother was hovering at her elbow. 'Ted will take you,' she hissed. 'He's fire brigade.'

'Oh yes!' Stef said. 'Thanks. Aaron, Mum's friend Ted will take me over.'

'Amazing. Thank him for me. And thank you to you, too. I'll start out soon.'

'What about your daughter?'

'Livy's with her mum. Oh, Stef, this really is the last straw. Nancy will have to move now.'

'You'd have thought so,' Stef said crisply. 'Don't worry, Aaron. Drive safely. I'll try to let you know what's happening.'

Stef rang the emergency services, then raced upstairs to get dressed, while Ted went out in the grey dawn and got the van going. She'd left her trainers stuffed with newspaper in the airing cupboard overnight, and found them warm but still wet. Never mind. Coat. Umbrella.

Outside, Stef's mother was piling blankets into the back of the van and arguing with Ted, who told her firmly, no, she couldn't come as well or there would be no room for Nancy on the return trip.

What state would they find Nancy in? Stef's fears began to spiral, but she pushed them away as she climbed into the van beside Ted. As Ted backed up, a bright light snapped on in the hall of the cottage opposite and she watched her mother scurry over the lane to speak to the neighbours.

'The whole village will know by the time we get back,' Ted remarked with a smile as the van moved off with a roar of the engine. Stef clutched the seat as he swung it into the road to the Broad.

They barely spoke as he manoeuvred the van between puddles. Luckily, the roads were not flooded and they reached the narrow lane and the barn where Nancy's car was parked without incident. No sign yet of any emergency vehicle, but Ted took care to leave the van off the road and they continued on foot, splashing through muddy water.

Thankfully, the rain had finally begun to ease and the clouds to thin. Ahead in the eastern distance a patch of clear sky shone a beautiful peach and gold. Soon, it would be sunrise.

When they reached the wooden boardwalk, Stef was shocked to see how the landscape had changed. The marsh was flooded on each side, the ruined windmill marooned in a lake, and streams gushed across the path. There were short stretches where they had to wade, Ted clasped Stef's arm to steady her, but they made progress easily enough. Stef began to look for landmarks and soon the black mass of a bird hide loomed to their left. It wasn't long after that when they reached the gate to the secret path that led down to Dragonfly Lodge and Stef was filled with alarm.

The path was inundated, the water pouring through the gate, and when Ted pushed it wouldn't open against the weight of it. He immediately began to rip off the palings until he'd created a wide enough gap for them to duck under a cross-bar and squeeze through. They waded on grimly, Stef shuddering with cold.

Soon, they came to the cottage and Stef stilled in shock, for it was completely surrounded by water, the garden an extension of the lake. The water swirled around weird mounds of shrubs and the trunks of stunted trees. The sharp points of the surrounding paling fence peeped above the water like a row of jagged teeth. Beyond, the jetty lay submerged, but just visible. There was still no sign of the boat. Perhaps it had slipped free and floated off.

'The tide's ebbing, I think,' Ted remarked, though it didn't look that way to Stef.

She was more worried about Nancy and stared in dismay at the porch, where water lapped against the front door. 'What do we do now?'

Before Ted could answer, a window upstairs creaked open and they looked up to see Nancy's pale face peering down. 'I'm so glad you've come,' the old lady said in a calm voice. 'It's very good of you. The animals are all safe, you'll be glad to know.'

'Oh, Nancy!' Stef said, then laughed with relief.

Beside her, Ted gazed at Nancy, grinning, hands on hips,

his hair plastered across his forehead. 'I'll have to carry you to the car, I reckon, but first we have to get in.'

Just then, they became aware of a loudening mechanical buzz and saw a distant blob of orange bouncing across the Broad towards them, the waves it made sending ducks flying up, quacking in alarm. As it neared, Stef saw that it was a rubber inflatable dinghy with three figures in waterproofs sitting inside. It slowed, but its swell still surged against her thighs and she clung to Ted to keep upright. No matter. They were going to be rescued.

Fifty-Five

Later that day, Nancy sat safely on the sofa in Springfield Cottage with an old Lansdown family photo album open on her lap and a mug of steaming tea at her elbow. Stef, sitting next to her, was explaining who everyone was in the photographs.

Bright despite her ordeal, Nancy had expressed interest in everything since her arrival. Stef's mother had already given her a tour of the cottage. Nancy had admired Cara's paintings and exclaimed over the smallest bedroom, where she was to sleep. Cara had insisted that the old lady must stay for the near future and Nancy agreed, though she had petted Baxter a little sadly. Aaron had recently left to take Tabitha to a nearby cattery. 'Just for a few days until things are sorted out,' he'd assured his grandmother, though in truth no one knew when that might be.

Stef turned to the final page of photographs. 'And this is Pip and Rob's wedding,' she said. 'It's the church by Norwich Market.'

'Your sister looks so happy,' Nancy sighed. 'And St Peter Mancroft's lovely, the school used to have its Christmas carol service there.'

She seemed tired suddenly, Stef thought as she closed the album, which was hardly surprising given the exertions of the day. She would never forget the poignant sight of Nancy sitting brave and upright in the rescue boat, a blanket round her shoulders and the cat basket beside her on the bench, as the crew cast off from the waterlogged jetty at Dragonfly Lodge. She and Ted had stood watching as the boat reversed, then set off slowly into the sunrise. She was relieved that the old lady was safe, but also strangely melancholy. It felt like the end of something.

'D'you think Nancy will ever be able to come back here?' she'd asked Ted wistfully as they turned away.

'She knows her own mind, that one.'

'She certainly does,' she'd laughed.

And so it proved. Nancy had rejected a plan to take her to hospital once the boat reached the staithe. Instead, her rescuers had reluctantly agreed to drive her to Springfield Cottage. There, Cara received her while Stef and Ted made their way back by road.

Ted, Stef thought as she returned the photograph album to its place on the shelf, had been brilliant today. Once Nancy had gone, not only had he waded into the house to check that her menagerie were indeed clear of the water, but he managed to phone the emergency number for the visitors' centre to warn Josh about the flood and to arrange for the creatures to be collected and looked after. Josh, sounding unusually concerned, had promised to start out at once.

Ted had brought Stef back to the cottage, then gone off to sort out pumping equipment. Now, following reports that the water levels had fallen, he and his business partner Liam were at Dragonfly Lodge seeing what they could do to rectify the damage. Cara was in the kitchen, making a huge lasagne for supper. Aaron, who'd arrived at breakfast time, had been running errands ever since. He'd accepted an invitation to stay overnight, and no, he didn't mind sleeping in one of the bunks.

'I wonder when I'll be able to go home,' Nancy said dreamily.

'I don't know,' Stef replied. The old lady had not taken on board the momentousness of what had happened and the likely state of her house. It was the shock, she supposed. Aaron would have to have a serious talk with her.

'I can guess what you're all thinking.' Nancy was sharper than she'd let on. 'That I should move.'

'We'll know more about the extent of the damage when Ted gets back.'

Nancy gave her a long, mournful look. 'I think it must be bad. All the furniture downstairs will be wet. And some of the books.'

Stef bit her lip. 'I expect a lot can be dried out.'

'That might take time.' Nancy spoke quietly, as though to herself. 'We'll see.'

Before Stef could question her further, her mother came in to ask if Nancy wanted more tea.

Nancy smiled. 'No, thanks. I've had enough to float a bat-
tleship. And we don't need any more boats launched today!'

'I quite agree,' Stef said fervently while her mother
laughed, then they looked up at the sound of a car outside.
'It's Aaron,' Stef said. 'I'll go.'

When she opened the front door, he was right there close
and their eyes locked. She felt her cheeks grow hot and had to
look away. 'How was it?' she murmured as she admitted him.

'The cattery's lovely,' he replied. 'Not cheap, though.' He
went in to greet his grandmother, who sat up, concerned.
'Tabitha looked perfectly happy,' he assured her. 'It's really a
cat hotel if you ask me!'

'That is marvellous.' Nancy relaxed.

As she spoke, the mass of Ted's van darkened the window.
It was Cara's turn to answer the door and all eyes turned to
Ted as he entered the room.

'There's good news and bad news,' he said, his face solemn.
'The good news is the water's gone down. There's no more
rain forecast and the tides won't be as high. But.' He sighed.
'Less good is the damage. It's not just your furniture and your
books. The walls are old plaster and it's sodden. You'll want
to let your landlord know. He'll need to sort it out.'

'I've already phoned his office,' Aaron said quietly.

There was silence for a moment as Nancy digested all this.
'I see,' she said finally. 'Thank you very much, Ted, you've
been ever so kind.'

After supper, at which she sat toying with her food with
sadness in her eyes, Nancy excused herself and said she'd

like to go to bed. Cara went up with her to make sure that she had everything she needed. Ted and Aaron helped Stef with the washing-up, then Stef asked Aaron if he'd like to walk Baxter with her.

'Of course,' he said, reaching for his jacket.

It was a beautiful evening, the world still fresh from the rain. Fleeing shreds of grey cloud streaked a sky of purple and gold. Baxter, energized by the evening scents, pulled on his lead, then stopped suddenly to sniff at something, causing Stef to bump into Aaron. She laughed as she apologized, but Aaron merely smiled. He was distracted this evening, not fully present, and they walked on in silence.

'What are you thinking?' she asked eventually.

'Oh, you know, what to do about my grandmother.'

'Mum's really happy to look after her for the moment.'

'I know. She's being immensely kind. You all are. But what will happen next? What if I can't persuade her that it's time to move?'

'It's only just happened, Aaron. It's too soon for her.'

'But I can't keep coming up and down the motorway. It isn't sustainable.' She felt his frustration.

'No.'

'I'm sorry.' He sighed. 'This isn't your problem.'

'Aaron, I know it isn't. She's your grandma and I'm practically a stranger, but I care, I do.'

'Thank you. I know.' His smile was warm, but she still felt that despite everything he kept her at a distance and that hurt.

He walked ahead now, lost in his thoughts, and all she

could do was follow. He wasn't an easy man, she pondered, but something about him drew her to him. He was good, she thought, and tried to do the right thing for the people he loved, his daughter, his grandmother, but it was clear that you had to work to earn his trust.

They came to a stile, and he helped her get Baxter through the gap underneath before standing back for her to climb over.

She waited till he was safely over it himself and returned his tentative smile. 'Sorry,' he mumbled. 'I don't mean to appear rude. It's odd,' he went on, falling into step beside her. 'I was suspicious of you when you first turned up two weeks ago.'

'I did notice that.'

'Yes, well.'

'But I understood. Especially after I'd been so offhand. So embarrassing.'

He laughed loudly.

'But Nancy's told me her whole story now and says I can write about it.'

'Does she now?' His face clouded.

'You're not to worry, Aaron. I won't bring her trouble. It will help her, in fact. I want to celebrate her achievements. I don't have to name names. But there is something that I need you to know about. I want to find this man James West and clear up his side of the story. If Nancy allows me to, that is. That's my plan, but I won't say anything to her yet. There's plenty of time.'

'We'll ask her together if you like. When we think she's ready.'

'Thank you.' He did trust her, after all. 'That would be marvellous, Aaron.'

Then she remembered something. 'Aaron, you may think this odd, but those poison pen letters. It's a bit mad, but I've had an idea about who might have sent them.'

When she told him, he looked at her in amazement.

'The font on the stocklist was definitely the same as on the latest letter.'

'Yes, I understand that, but Stef, why Jackie?'

She shrugged. 'I don't know,' she said simply. She understood that the matter wasn't of the great importance at that exact moment, but was relieved when he muttered that he'd mention it to the police.

They'd gone a fair way and the evening was growing chilly by the time they turned back. Aaron was mostly silent as they walked back to Springfield Cottage, not morose, just overwhelmed, Stef thought and didn't mind. After all, she had plenty to think about, too. Not least that work was calling. Soon, very soon, she must return to her lonely flat in London. She glanced at Aaron beside her, deep in thought, and wondered if he'd mind if she suggested they meet up there sometime. Just as friends, of course.

Fifty-Six

Massachusetts, USA
September 2010

Three months later, Stef mounted the steps of an old brownstone in Boston, pressed the bell and waited. It was a beautiful autumn day and the leaves were turning to shades of crimson and gold. She'd arrived in the city only two days before, with a short list of academics she'd arranged to interview. This was the first and the most important and she would need all her professional skills to succeed in her task.

After a moment or two, the door was opened by a young woman, who regarded her suspiciously with shrewd dark eyes.

'I'm Stephanie Lansdown. I have an appointment with—'

The woman's wide grin was transforming. 'I know who you are, lady. He's been antsy all morning 'bout you coming.' She ushered Stef into a deep shadowy hallway and hung her coat up. 'Wait in here, will you?' She pushed open a door to her right and stood aside to let Stef enter a lovely bright drawing room.

'I'll tell him you're here,' the woman said and withdrew.

Stef looked round with interest. The room reminded her very much of Nancy's sitting room at Dragonfly Lodge. It wasn't the room itself, which was much larger than Nancy's, with high ceilings and long windows looking out onto the street, but the contents of it. The walls of books were similar, as was the desk with a microscope on it next to boxes of glass slides and haphazard piles of papers. A fire had been lit in the grate against the chill of the morning, and next to the mirror above the mantelpiece hung the shell of a giant horseshoe crab. One of the pair of fireside chairs had recently been occupied, for a folded *New York Times* had been left on the table next to it and a pair of spectacles lay on top.

She turned at the sound of the door opening. The elderly man framed by the doorway was tweedy in dress, with ruined good looks. His tall, lean figure was a little stooped, but Professor James West possessed the air of someone effortlessly important. 'Miss Lansdown,' he pronounced in clipped English tones, 'you're early.'

She wasn't, but decided not to argue the point. 'I thought I'd have more trouble than I did finding the house. It's kind of you to see me, Professor.'

'Not at all. I like to have visitors. Don't get many these days.' He came forward to greet her, his dark, hooded eyes glaring at her intensely out of his lined, cleanshaven face as he shook her hand. His iron-grey hair was neatly trimmed and combed back and he smelled pleasantly of something citrusy.

'Cynthia's bringing us coffee,' he said. 'She's marvellous. Does everything for me. Let's sit down, shall we?'

So this was Nancy's James West, Stef mused as she watched him settle himself. She'd Googled him thoroughly in preparation for this interview, but even the photographs hadn't prepared her for the discovery that he had been a very attractive man – was still attractive, if she was honest. He seemed engagingly unaware of the effect he had on people. No wonder Nancy had fallen for him.

They were chatting about Stef's journey by the time Cynthia arrived with a tinkling tray and set about pouring coffee from a silver pot into fragile porcelain cups. There were tea plates, too, with napkins, and a dish of homemade cookies. Professor West had done very well for himself, but then Stef had expected this. You didn't get to be the Head of Entomology at a prestigious Ivy League university and win so many prizes without becoming quite well-to-do. He'd married and had a family, she'd discovered from the internet, but his French wife, Sylvie, had died ten years ago and his two boys were grown and gone. It must be lonely rattling about in this big house, and he would be glad of the cheerful Cynthia's company.

Stef sipped her coffee, nibbled at a cookie and waited until Cynthia had left before she reached into her tote bag for her tape recorder. Once the door had closed, she switched it on with his grudging permission and started confidently taking charge of the interview.

'Professor, as I explained in my letter, I have questions only you can answer about Nancy Foster.'

'Dear Nancy,' he murmured, then shot her a genial look. 'I think of her sometimes. How is she?'

'She's very well,' Stef replied cautiously, suspicious of his charm. 'Well, actually, she went through a bit of an ordeal recently.' She described the flood and its aftermath, and West looked suitably concerned. 'But she's now living in the village not far from the Broad.'

Dragonfly Lodge had swiftly been declared uninhabitable by the landlord and those of Nancy's belongings that survived the flood, including most of her books, had been dried out professionally and placed in storage. Then Stef's mother learned that a small bungalow was coming up for rent on a leafy lane leading out of the village. Aaron had acted quickly and Nancy had moved in a couple of weeks afterwards. Stef had gone down to help. It was an attractive little house, with rooms that received plenty of daylight. There was a stubby front garden full of flowers and a sunny terrace at the back.

There was something less pleasant that she didn't tell James. Soon after the flood, Aaron had reported Stef's suspicions about Jackie, and a policewoman had gone to interview her in the back room at the visitors' centre. Jackie was flustered and broke down in tears. She was indeed responsible for the threatening letters and had a pitiable story to tell. Her husband, it appeared, was Nancy's landlord's brother, who, having a financial share in the property, had taken it upon himself, without the landlord's knowledge, to try to remove Nancy. He was either hoping that his brother would do the place up and let it more profitably to holidaymakers, or that he would agree to sell it. He was, it appeared, an overbearing sort of man and Jackie had reluctantly agreed to type up the letters and deliver them.

She had also, at his suggestion, stolen Tabitha, but had felt wretched about it and returned her. The police reported all this to Nancy and Aaron, but Nancy had felt so sorry for Jackie that she asked them not to prosecute. Aaron felt less sympathetic, but didn't try to argue with his grandmother, who would find any conflict stressful. Jackie resigned as a volunteer and Jackie's husband was incurring some of the expense of renovating Dragonfly Lodge, so a sort of justice was working itself out. Nancy was simply glad that the problem had gone away. She missed Dragonfly Lodge, but loved her new bungalow.

'I'm glad to hear that she's living somewhere more comfortable.' James cleared his throat and changed tack. 'As you know, it was a bit of a surprise to receive your letter and I admit that my initial response may not have been gracious.'

'I think I can agree with that.' It had, in fact, bordered on the rude.

'But then I read the typed article you sent me.'

'It wasn't an article. It was the chapter about Nancy for my book on women scientists.'

'Yes, of course. Women scientists indeed!' he said as though such a thing was exotic. 'And I saw that perhaps I needed to speak to you, after all, to put you straight on one or two matters.'

Stef had been, as she'd promised Nancy and Aaron, very circumspect in her writing about James' involvement in the events that ended Nancy's research career. She hadn't actually accused James of colluding with Dr Staunton in the suppression of Nancy's research, or of lying to Nancy about what he'd done – after all, there was no definitive proof. But she had stated that James had put Nancy under considerable pressure to prioritize his career at the expense of hers, and to accompany him to the States in the role of supportive wife – and had spelled out various ways in which he had acted nefariously. In doing so, she had deliberately taken a risk. No doubt her publisher would insist on cutting out some of these implications for fear of being sued for libel, but the draft had enabled her to achieve her aim with West. He'd finally granted her this interview.

And she'd come fully armed.

The last three months had been some of the busiest of her career. The week after her return to London, Sarah, her agent, had telephoned in high excitement to report that Catherine had offered a large advance to publish Stef's book. Shortly afterwards, her American publisher had done likewise. Once the contracts were signed and the first tranches of the advances paid, Stef's financial problems were over for the time being. For a whole week, when she woke up in her London flat she reminded herself of this fact and felt a rush of relief. This would be followed by a moment of panic, though, and she'd jump out of bed, ready to do a hard day's work. The research stage was the thing she loved best, conducting interviews and transcribing them afterwards, visiting libraries and archives and surfing the internet for new lines of enquiry.

Stef had collected the stories of a range of women scientists from the previous hundred years. There were famous names from the past, such as Marie Curie, Rosalind Franklin and biochemist Chi Che Wang. Contemporary examples included the neuroscientist Susan Greenfield. But it was critical to her vision of the book to include half a dozen women that no one had heard of, some because their men had taken the credit or their careers had been held back. Nancy Foster was a prime example of one of these.

The chapter about her was the first that Stef drafted, even though it was to be placed halfway through the book. It was the one she felt most personally committed to and she wanted to do her best for Nancy. Catherine, her editor, had also made clear that while all Stef's subjects would offer important revelations, Nancy's was possibly the most poignant. The actual suppression of a woman's scientific research was an invidious injustice only trumped, in Catherine's view, by the experience of Rosalind Franklin in the early 1950s. Franklin's X-ray photographs of DNA, the result of long hours of skilled and careful work, had been borrowed without her permission and employed without sufficient acknowledgement by a trio of men who, after her early death, went on to win the Nobel Prize for determining the structure of DNA. Not only had their findings depended on her work, but one of the men, James Watson, subsequently published a bestselling book that boasted of his success and disparaged Franklin and her work.

One by one, Stef went through her questions, testing West's memories of every aspect of the traumatic episode that, ended Nancy's career as a researcher. His weakness, she quickly discovered, was that he responded well to being buttered up.

She asked about his own meticulous work with grasshoppers, the impressive doctoral thesis that had underpinned his subsequent move to Boston.

'Nancy remembers the brilliance of your work,' she said, 'how privileged she felt when you explained it to her. It must have been amazing, the two of you working in the same lab at that time on your individual projects.' She could see him puffing up his chest at the compliments. 'And I believe Nancy was very helpful to you.'

'She was indeed a marvellous sounding board for my ideas and made one or two very pertinent suggestions.' While he was too cunning to admit the full extent of Nancy's support and advice, he was generous enough in his replies. After all, given the great heights he'd reached in his career, what had he to lose?

He corroborated Nancy's memories of being bullied in the ICP lab, had himself heard her colleagues' derogatory comments about her in the chauvinist atmosphere of the scientists' common room: that she was 'stuck up', 'too brisk and mannish'.

'And what did you do when you heard these insults?' Stef murmured and watched his gaze slide away.

'These men were confounded cads and naturally I ... I asked them to pipe down.'

'To speak more quietly, you mean?'

'Yes. No. To keep their opinions to themselves, anyway.'

'And what did they say to that?'

'They had the grace to look embarrassed. And after that, I didn't hear more of it.'

'Do you think they were embarrassed because they knew of your relationship or because they saw the error of their ways?'

'I don't know. I suppose the former. That was how men were then. I couldn't have changed anything.'

Stef squared her shoulders and moved on through the questions. What conversations had he and Nancy had about her discoveries concerning the toxicity of the organophosphate, Zalathion, she was working with? How had he supported and encouraged her? What did he think she should have done about revealing her findings? All these he handled with suave ease and she could see him relax.

When she was sure that he was off his guard, she pounced.

'What were you doing that day in Staunton's office, knowing that Staunton was Nancy's supervisor?'

'Ah.' He flinched. 'Um. I was picking his brains. I believed that he knew the chap who headed up the department here in Boston. I, um, thought Staunton could put in a word.'

'About what?'

'Oh, you know.'

'No, I don't. So you didn't discuss Nancy's position at all?'

'Why would I do that?'

'Nancy heard you both talking and later observed you leaving her laboratory.'

'Yes, I went in to look for her. She wasn't there, but I had a word with one of the chaps in there.'

'But when she went in later, after you left, her work station was in a mess and some of her notes were missing.'

'I don't know about that.' He crumbled the cookie on his

plate. 'Anyway, what was she doing stalking me? It didn't show much trust.'

'Perhaps you had lost her trust by then.'

'Mmm.'

Stef had hoped the next question would be the killer. 'Miss Bateman at the secretarial agency claimed that a man answering to your description collected the typed reports of Nancy's research without Nancy's permission. Was that man actually you, Professor?'

'Absolute rubbish!' His hand quivered as he placed his empty tea plate on the side table. 'Turn off that confounded machine, will you?'

Reluctantly, she did so, but picked up her notebook and pen, determined to keep a record. 'What would your motive have been for endangering Nancy's job?'

'Why would I have wanted to do that?'

'Was it because if she lost her job, it would be more likely that she'd go to America with you?'

'Of course not. That decision was Nancy's and Nancy's alone. I simply advised her not to continue the line of research in question. That was to ensure that she kept her job. I could have kept silent and let her get herself into hot water if my motive had been as you suggest.'

Stef paused her notetaking and considered this. It was indeed true. Yet Nancy had been very clear in her belief that he'd aided Staunton in the suppression of her report, and Stef was inclined to accept her account. The puzzle was establishing West's motive.

Then an idea came to her.

'Were you jealous of Nancy?' she asked. 'Did you resent the fact that she had made this discovery that everyone else had apparently missed?'

He stared at her, his lips working. 'Pah!' he said finally. 'My concern was purely for Nancy. And I was right to be concerned. She lost her job, didn't she? And that was the end of her career as a research scientist.'

Stef sat back in her chair, stunned by the baldness of this statement. It had a ring of truth about it. 'Professor West!' She was outraged. 'Even if you were concerned for her, going over her head like that is inexcusable.'

'I thought someone should take responsibility for her.'

'Was she not capable of taking responsibility for herself?'

Professor West refused to look at her and she knew he was being as slippery as ever.

But now came the most important moment of all. She had one more card to play. 'You know,' she said conversationally, 'I've spent some time recently in the archives of ICP.' Finally, he met her eye and she continued. 'The staff were very helpful once I explained what I was looking for. I think because it was so long ago and so much water has passed under the bridge. Everyone knows about the damage that organophosphates do to the environment, even the ones that are still in use.' She paused. He cleared his throat but said nothing. 'They're in the process of digitizing their archive, but hadn't got back as far as the fifties. The file I was looking for was in an old cardboard document box. Nancy's report was in there among a sheaf of related correspondence.'

She closed her eyes briefly and smiled, remembering

Nancy's face when she'd told her the news last week. At first, her expression had been shocked, then disbelieving and then, finally, joyful.

'ICP withdrew Zalathion from the market at the start of 1955. That was several months after Nancy's report reached them. The correspondence explains it all. The Chief Scientific Officer read Nancy's report, then passed it to a colleague for assessment. That colleague, one Eric Frank, was away on holiday and by the time he replied to his boss, Nancy had left ICP's employment. There was then lots of to-ing and fro-ing between people higher up and the outcome was that though other organophosphates continued to be used, Zalathion was declared too powerful, too much of a risk. Nancy had, in fact, succeeded!'

Professor West stared at Stef. He gripped the arms of his chair and pushed himself up straighter. His lips moved, but no sound came out, so that Stef was concerned that he was having some kind of seizure. But then he recovered himself.

'I'm ...' he said weakly, 'so glad. That's wonderful.'

'Isn't it?' Stef said triumphantly. 'She was overwhelmed.' She thought tenderly of how happy the old lady had been. Her work all those years ago had been noticed, corroborated and acted upon. If only ICP had let her know.

'And what's more, ICP have just given permission for the evidence to be included in my book.' The important email had arrived just before she'd left for America. 'Nancy's discovery will be publicly acknowledged. Of course, as her supervisor Staunton won't come out well, but he died thirty years ago, leaving no heirs. I'll try to deal with him fairly, but—'

'He was a mean-spirited sort of chap,' West muttered. 'A stickler for hierarchy.'

'Well then.'

'I'm glad to hear this news, though.' He sounded sincere. 'Nancy was treated roughly, I always thought. I won't say my own part in the affair was blameless, but I'm not as bad a fellow as you and she seem to think.'

It was Stef's turn to be surprised. Where was the fierce, litigious ogre Professor West had been painted to be? He did seem genuinely pleased at Nancy's belated success.

'I was extremely fond of Nancy and would have married her, but I was young, we were both very young, and my career was important to me. I simply couldn't pass up the opportunity to come here. I regretted her loss, but it was she who broke off the relationship and I resent any suggestion that I'd betrayed her. At the time, I thought I'd acted in both our best interests. Now I can see that I was possibly wrong to go over her head like that.'

'You mean you admit—?'

He held up his palms. 'I admit nothing. You must remember that old adage that "all is fair in love and in war". We were in love, but we were also at war with one another, and neither of us would back down.'

You wily old prevaricator, Stef thought. She had seen the letter James had written Nancy after their break-up. He was, even now, after all these years, impossible to pin down. Would she and Nancy ever know the complete truth? Probably not.

'So,' he said, sitting back, his gnarled hands gripping the arms of the chair, 'I think we must come to an arrangement.

You may write about this matter, but there must be no implication that I acted, er, unprofessionally in it. I've made some notes on your draft chapter.' He stood up stiffly and went to collect the document from his desk. 'Perhaps we could discuss them,' he said, passing it to her, 'and arrive at some agreement.'

An hour later, Stef stepped down into the street with the strange sense that she'd faced some hugely important adversary and emerged with life and limb intact. They'd argued over every line in which his name was mentioned, but she'd gradually whittled down his opposition and had a signed agreement to let her publish. He would not allow any implication that he'd stolen Nancy's notes from her laboratory, nor that he'd collected the typed reports from Miss Bateman. But his enigmatic meeting with Staunton and the fact that he'd entered the laboratory 'to look for Nancy' could remain. Stef was to quote his insistence that he'd supported and encouraged Nancy and that the rift in their relationship was 'inevitable given their youth and respective ambitions'. Any intelligent reader, Stef thought, might still work out from Nancy's evidence what had really happened.

There was one thing he'd requested of her that she wasn't sure of being able to grant, and she considered the matter as she walked back to her hotel through the autumnal streets.

He had asked to meet Nancy again.

Fifty-Seven

Easter 2011

'Do I look all right, Stef?'

'Of course you do.'

Nancy had been nervy all morning, her face unusually pale. She was sitting in her favourite chair by the fireplace in the bungalow, adjusting the knot of the gossamer scarf at her throat. Stef, perching on the chair opposite, thought the old lady looked beautiful in her sky-blue woollen dress and neat navy shoes. Nancy had made herself up carefully and combed her silver hair into flattering waves, beneath which a pair of diamond earrings glinted. The living room had been swept and polished, and a vase of fresh spring flowers stood on the mantelpiece. Tabitha the cat was curled up on the sofa, deeply asleep.

A sleek shadow fell over the room. 'I think this is him now,' Aaron murmured from his post by the window. 'Yes,' he confirmed, as the black saloon car pulled up outside. He went to open the front door. Stef and Nancy watched as the driver assisted an elderly gentleman in a cream linen suit and a Panama hat. He straightened and glanced at the window, and Stef heard Nancy draw a sharp breath. 'It's him,' she whispered, her face pale under the powder. 'James. It's really him!' Outside, Aaron was shaking the elderly professor's hand, then showing him into the house. Stef whisked out to the kitchen to tell her mother that the visitor had arrived.

It had taken months to arrange this meeting and everything had been carefully planned. Nancy had initially not wanted to meet James again, but then, at Christmas, when Stef and Aaron were visiting, she'd suddenly said she would. 'If he'll come here, of course,' she said regally. And James, who still sometimes travelled to attend conferences around the world, had readily agreed.

Stef's mother had laid out a simple salad lunch for two on a prettily decorated table in the conservatory and every-one had agreed that the thing to do was to leave the couple together to renew their acquaintance. Cara would stay in the kitchen and Stef and Aaron would absent themselves for a few hours. Aaron had suggested that they go to the coast. Stef went to greet their visitor in the hall, then showed him into the living room. She smiled as Nancy rose stiffly from her chair. Tears sprang to her eyes when she witnessed the joy in the old lady's face.

'Come on,' Aaron whispered in Stef's ear. 'I suppose we're taking Baxter?' At the sound of his name, the dog, whom Nancy only allowed here because he was too slow and stiff to bother her beloved Tabitha, waddled from the kitchen, his ears pricked hopefully.

'Coming, old boy?' The plumed tail waved in response, so Stef clipped the lead onto his collar and they followed Aaron up the road to where he'd parked.

They were quiet as Aaron's car purred along, negotiating the confusing network of narrow country lanes that he'd come to know like the back of his hand. Stef was tenderly aware of his long, strong fingers moving from wheel to gearstick as he slowed to take the bends in the road. From time, to time he glanced across at her and smiled, and once he reached out and briefly stroked her thigh, causing her to feel a hot wave of desire.

After Stef had mustered the courage to ask Aaron to meet her for a drink in London, their closeness had grown in fits and starts since the previous summer. Eventually it had turned to passion and Stef had been surprised and over-whelmed by the gentle power of his lovemaking, which left her gasping with happiness. And how she in her turn could move him to tears. There had been harder times at first, though, times when he'd withdraw into himself and not answer her phone calls, but gradually she came to understand that these were not about her, but about his fear of revealing his deepest self to another person. He'd been too badly hurt in his life, by poor parenting and by the breakdown of his marriage, and she had to earn his trust.

A particular delight had been getting to know his daughter. Stef and Livy had taken to one another quickly. Livy's artless chatter amused and touched Stef, but she learned that the little girl had a more vulnerable side. Stef had met her mother Crystal several times, and though she liked her stylish looks and bubbly personality, she saw what bothered Aaron. Crystal was always giving Livy things to placate her if she was upset, rather than letting her be a child who needed her mother's help to navigate life's difficulties and grow. Stef's friendship with Livy was joyful and uncomplicated, but it was also a bit like walking a tightrope, for she didn't wish to be considered interfering or critical by the girl's parents. Fortunately, so far she'd avoided these dangers and gained the child's friendship in the process.

They passed through a quiet village which had an old pub with a blackboard outside advertising food. 'Shall we stop here for lunch?' Aaron said, signalling and slowing the car. 'It says dogs are welcome.'

'Looks good to me. What about you, Baxter?'

They found a picnic bench in the orchard behind the pub, where Stef settled Baxter under the table while Aaron fetched pints of lager and a menu. The sun climbed overhead in a sky of depthless blue. A thin young man with a white cloth tied as an apron took their order, then brought them each a cheese ploughman's, as well as a special dog sausage, and they laughed when Baxter sniffed at it suspiciously before gulping it down. They themselves ate lazily, without speaking much, enjoying companionship, the clink of cutlery the only sound apart from birdsong and the buzz of passing insects.

'I wonder how the happy couple are getting on,' Stef said as she forked up coleslaw.

'I can't imagine.' Aaron smiled. 'They've so much to talk about. D'you think they'll quarrel?'

'Perhaps they should and get the past out of their systems.'

'An odd situation, isn't it? I mean, they both married other people and had meaningful lives. They're not the same as they were fifty-odd years ago.'

'I think the outcome will depend on whether James gets on his high horse. Nancy will be gracious, but steely, too. She's not going to let him off the hook easily.'

'Do you know that?'

'No, not really, but honestly, Aaron, you'd have thought she was twenty-five again the way she was this morning.'

'I thought that, too,' Aaron laughed.

Stef grinned at him. 'We're older already than they were when they last met.'

'Christ, that's true. Makes me feel ancient at thirty-three!'

'And I'll be thirty-two this year. What have I achieved?'

'A flourishing freelance career? One successful book behind you and another in the works? Oh, Stef.' He covered her hand with his on the table and looked grave. 'You're amazing.'

'There are other things I want, Aaron.' She gazed at him steadily.

'Children. I know.' He said this softly and sighed.

They'd discussed the matter recently. It had been Stef who'd asked him, in a playful kind of way as though she was asking whether he'd ever let Livy have the pet dog she hankered after: 'Do you think you'd ever have a brother or sister for Livy?'

Aaron had first of all been adamant that he didn't want any

more children, but seeing how unhappy this answer made her, he'd sighed then, too, and said he supposed he didn't know, but anyway, not for a long, long time. Having babies was so much trouble.

She'd swallowed the lump in her throat and nodded sadly. It was a deal-breaker for her. Much as she adored him, she couldn't stay with him if he didn't want a child with her. She'd always known she wanted them. The longing came from deep within her. It had been worse lately. She could imagine having Aaron's children. They'd look a little like Livy, but not as dark; a little like the twins, but not as fair. The twins were nearly six now, happy at school. Rob and Pippa were much happier as well. Pippa had started training for a career in fitness and Rob was applying for accountancy jobs in Norwich. Stef and Pippa's relationship had deepened, too. The sisters were more at ease with one another nowadays.

Now Stef stared out across the pub's country garden, where late daffodils waved under fruit trees that were beginning to green. They'd only just started discussing the future, she and Aaron, tentatively, both getting used to the idea that they might be in it for the long haul. She stayed over at his more than the other way round. After all, she had her neighbour Gary with his obnoxious music. Aaron's flat in North London had two bedrooms, the smaller one painted in the style of a forest glade with trees and stencilled woodland animals, rabbits, foxes, a fawn or two. Livy loved it. He hadn't asked Stef to move in yet, but she guessed that he was thinking about it. He needed faith and courage, she thought, to make the leap. It wouldn't do to force it.

Aaron was feeling in his back pocket for his wallet. 'Shall we go? There won't be time for the beach if we hang around.'

She nodded, climbed out of her seat and unwound Baxter's lead from the table leg. 'Let me get this.'

'Certainly not. My treat,' he said.

It was a further twenty minutes to Holkham. They followed the coast road, then turned off down a long, narrow drive with cars parked on either side. Aaron pulled up alongside a horsebox, from which a shaggy grey pony watched with interest as they put on jackets and changed into wellington boots. Then they set off with Baxter on a lead along a sandy boardwalk with pinewoods on either side until they reached the dunes, where a wooden ramp led down to the beach.

At the top they paused, Stef's hair tossed by a gusty wind. The beach lay spread out before them. Below, a patch of marshy sand crisscrossed by shallow channels, then an expanse of beautiful yellow sand that rolled on towards more dunes, and beyond, in the distance, the sea. Stef gave a whoop of joy at the glory of it, making Aaron laugh. But Baxter was funniest, waddling down the ramp ahead of them, then bounding off across the beach as though he were a pup and not an ungainly twelve-year-old with the figure of a badger.

'He'll have a heart attack,' Aaron groaned as they followed more carefully.

'No, he won't,' Stef replied. 'Or if he does, he'll die happy.' They caught up with him when he ran out of energy and lay down panting in a muddy puddle to wait for them. 'Daft animal,' she told him fondly. And laughed as he padded about again, sniffing at smells, his ears blowing comically in the breeze.

They waded across channels of rippling water, then strode hand in hand across the firm sand towards the sea. It was freeing, Stef thought, to feel so tiny in this vast landscape, the wind blowing away her anxieties. When they reached the high tideline, they paused, Stef's hand on Baxter's collar, to wait for a pair of riders to pass. Their horses galloped through the shallows, kicking up spray and tossing their heads in delight. Stef remembered her conversation with Nancy back in June, how she'd told the old lady wistfully that Holkham Beach was her haven and that she'd always wanted to ride.

'Can you ride, Aaron?' But he shook his head. Suddenly, anything seemed possible. 'If I lived here, that's what I'd do.'

'If you lived here. Is that what you'd like?'

'Not now, it wouldn't work, but maybe in the future. What about you?'

He considered this. 'Perhaps. Anyway, we'll be down this way a lot seeing our folks, won't we?' She liked the way he said 'we' and turned fully to face him, pushing back her windblown hair.

'A lot, yes. Maybe I should learn to ride.'

'Why not? And I'd learn to sail. Maybe that bloke Geoffrey Stuart would teach me.' He squeezed her hand and smiled, then kissed her and rested his forehead against hers. She reached up and touched his cheek.

'You know . . .' he said, then sighed and tried once more. 'I didn't think I wanted anything serious again after Crystal.

Opening yourself up, trusting someone, it seemed too hard. And life was busy enough, what with work and Livy and my grandmother.'

'I understand,' she said softly. 'You know that I felt that after Sam.' She had told him about the sadness of her previous relationship.

'But I want to try again, Stef. And get it right this time.' She met his gaze and read the appeal there.

'Aaron?' she whispered.

'And I was also thinking,' he said, with a wicked grin, 'that here would be a brilliant place to bring our children.'

'Our *children*? Oh, Aaron!' Such joy rushed through her.

'So I'm asking you to marry me, Stef. Do you think that you would?'

'Do I? Yes, yes, Aaron!' She wound her arms round his neck and their mouths met in a long, lingering kiss. When they sprang apart, she found she was crying and the wind was blowing her tears away. 'Oh, I'm so happy, Aaron. I didn't think I could feel so happy.'

He laughed. 'And so am I!' And she saw that he was. All the tension had left his face and his eyes were alight. Then he put his arms round her and she laid her face against his shoulder and closed her eyes, and they stood together for a long, tender moment.

Baxter gave a sudden whine. Stef glanced down to see him sitting sphinx-like watching them, his brow furrowed. A stick he'd found lay on the sand before him.

'Sorry, old boy, but we're busy,' Aaron said, laughing. Baxter gave an impatient bark, so Stef collected the stick and tossed it into the shallows. Somewhat regally, he stood waiting until the waves returned it.

Hand in hand, Stef and Aaron walked slowly together along the beach with gentle waves lapping their feet, the dog at their heels and their faces bathed in a golden light.

Epilogue

June 2013

'Are you sure this is Prince's College?' Nancy asked the driver, puzzled. The black cab had drawn up in front of a modern building, where a set of shallow marble steps led up to a vast glass frontage with revolving doors.

'This is the main entrance, ma'am.' The driver smiled as Cara paid him a large tip. Ted wrestled open the vehicle door.

Nancy stepped out first and stood gazing around, bewildered, searching for familiar landmarks. The white Georgian terrace opposite the college was not the same as the student hostel she'd known, and the traffic signs, the spacious paved areas and the cycle lanes confused her utterly. And as for the college itself, where on earth was the Victorian gatehouse? Then, to the left, she spotted a road name and everything clicked into place. The old entrance must be round the corner.

Cara offered her an arm as they climbed the steps, and Nancy gladly took it for she felt a little strange. It wasn't one of those old dizzy turns – which the doctors said had been caused by a virus, now long vanquished – but a sense of being unmoored. The last time she'd visited Prince's College had been in 1958, when Edmund had been presented with an award. It had been odd being there as Mrs Edmund Buckland rather than as Dr Nancy Foster, and she hadn't enjoyed being patronized by the new head of department, though she'd certainly been proud of her husband that day.

Inside the atrium, Cara approached a young woman with blue-streaked hair sitting behind a huge semi-circular reception desk. 'We're a bit early, but we've come for the party for my daughter's book.'

The woman smiled and pointed wordlessly to a freestanding notice next to a rope barrier. It read, 'Launch of *A Curious Nature* by Stephanie Lansdown, The Old Library', and an arrow pointed towards another set of glass doors that led out into dazzling early evening sunshine.

'I've no idea where we are!' Nancy gasped as they crossed a spacious plaza towards another, identical, notice at the far side. Modern edifices rose all around. Several cafés with gay canopies bordered the busy square. Students of all types occupied the tables and chairs that were scattered about, their conversation and laughter echoing upwards to form a kind of background music.

They entered a gloomy passageway beyond, the end of which opened into another sunlit space, and Nancy gasped, for here was the old quad she remembered, with the Victorian gatehouse to one side and the clock tower in the centre.

'This is the Prince's I knew,' she cried. 'We've just come in via the Zoo building, that grand portal is Chemistry and over there's the library – the Old Library, I suppose.' Stef had told her they had a huge modern one on the campus now. Nancy was delighted to hear that Stef had found a copy of Nancy's doctoral thesis safely filed there.

'It's like going back in time,' Nancy whispered, her voice quavery with emotion. And it was. She'd been preparing herself mentally for this moment for weeks, ever since Stef had announced the date and venue of the book launch. Stef had asked her publisher specifically for it to take place at Prince's. Not only had it been Nancy's college, but a Prince's Chemistry professor she'd interviewed had suggested the Old Library for the event.

Now that she was actually here in the old part of the college, Nancy felt surprisingly calm and reassured. Talking about her experiences for the book had helped her come to terms with the past. She'd been happy here at Prince's, she realized. She thought of all the people she'd known here. Occasionally she still heard from Peggy in Hampshire. Anne Durban was still going and sent a Christmas card from the Manor House every year. Somewhere Nancy had read that Raj had done well in what they now called Mumbai, but which in her day had been Bombay.

'Come on,' Cara said. 'I want to catch Stef before it all starts.' She started walking briskly in the direction of the library and Ted and Nancy followed. Nancy liked Ted immensely and felt that he was good for Cara. He was a steadying influence but fun, too. At Aaron and Stef's wedding in Hickston a year ago, he'd driven them to the church in a horse and carriage that Cara had decorated with flowers. Such a beautiful wedding it had been, with a reception at a local converted barn. Stef had become her granddaughter-in-law – she grinned at the cumbersome title. It meant, crucially, that she was family and Nancy was very pleased indeed about that. The only sadness was that Andrea, Aaron's mother, had not felt able to leave her ailing husband, but Aaron and Stef had plans to fly out to Mexico and see her, and had invited Nancy to go with them. Nancy was considering this. It would be a big trip for her, but she longed to see her daughter.

There was a lift up to the Old Library that hadn't been there in her day and Nancy was happy to take it. When the door opened at the first floor, she recognized the wood-lined lobby at once and the rubber-edged doors into the library swung open just as silently as ever.

She blinked in astonishment to see the broad open space where once had been rows of bookcases. At one end was a raised area and a lectern with a microphone. People had begun to gather near a table with a white cloth on it glittering with wine glasses.

'I'll get drinks,' Ted offered and set off.

'There's Stef!' Cara cried and began to march towards the lectern. Nancy had spotted her, too, looking radiant in an amber-coloured trouser suit, but hung back. Stef was sipping orange juice and talking to a striking, willowy woman with cropped auburn hair: Sarah, Stef's agent. Nancy had met her at the wedding and found her friendly, but fierce. All of a sudden, she felt a little lost. She wasn't used to crowds these days. She gazed about. The room was filling up rapidly with strangers. Then suddenly, Stef appeared at her side.

'Nancy!' She returned Stef's kiss.

'You look lovely, Stef dear. Glowing, if I might say!' Stef and Aaron had come to see her a week ago to break the happy news.

'We're so excited. Livy can't wait for a little brother or sister!'

'A wonderful Christmas present for us all,' Nancy had breathed.

Ted returned with a glass of wine for Nancy. And here was Aaron looking happier than she'd ever seen him. And, oh, darling Livy, giving her a hug. Was that Stef's sister and her husband coming to say hello? No sign of the twins. Surrounded by people she loved, she felt strong again.

The party passed in a haze of noise and activity. Various women came over to speak to her. They'd read her story in Stef's book, they said, and had been shocked and angered by it. Two had featured in the book themselves. She shook their hands, listened to words of admiration and support, repeated their names, trying to impress them on her memory. Ted twinkled a smile as he refilled her glass.

Then came the speeches. Stef's editor Catherine, a short, round woman with a powerful presence, was most eloquent; now came Stef with a long list of thanks. And then Nancy heard her own name called and started in surprise.

'Go on,' Aaron said in her ear, so she made her way to Stef's side, felt Stef's reassuring hand on her arm.

'*A Curious Nature* would not be the book it is without Dr Nancy Foster's input,' Stef said into the microphone. 'Many women in the book have shown great bravery in sharing their experiences, but Nancy has arguably been the bravest of them all. Many of you know that Nancy is an alumna of this college, one of their brightest and best. Women like Nancy were pioneers who paved the way for later generations. We have much to thank her for.'

A swell of applause filled the room and Nancy looked round at everyone in amazement and gratitude.

'And many of you know I have something else to thank her for. Through her, I met her grandson Aaron, now my husband, and darling Livy, her great-granddaughter.' The applause grew louder and some people cheered.

Nancy felt tears threaten, but blinked them back as she took the microphone from Stef.

'Thank you, everyone,' she croaked, then cleared her throat and went on. 'It's a great pleasure to be here, to visit my old college again and to celebrate Stef's book about the challenges faced by women scientists. I'd like to be able to say that I achieved something as a scientist in the early fifties – that I made great discoveries or added to the betterment of humanity – but I cannot make that claim. Still, I went on to teach generations of schoolchildren, and that's a noble cause.' There were murmurs of agreement at this. 'It gives me great pleasure to have met many women here tonight who are achieving more than I was ever able to, and I'd like us to celebrate them by raising our glasses. A toast! To *A Curious Nature* and women scientists everywhere!'

As the room vibrated with the enthusiastic response, Nancy stepped aside with a sigh of relief. The speeches were over and everyone was returning to their conversations.

'That was a nice touch, your toast, Nancy,' someone said in her ear. She looked up to see Stef's agent, the fierce Sarah, smiling at her. 'Tell me,' Sarah went on, her eyes glinting, 'did you think of asking Professor West to come tonight?'

'James?' Nancy replied cautiously. 'Boston's a long way to come from for a party. Anyway . . .' She paused.

'Skeleton at the feast?'

'Something like that.' She smiled. 'I couldn't allow him that importance. Or indeed blame. He was, after all, just one man among many.'

'In a system that gave men the upper hand,' Sarah nodded. 'I get that. But that doesn't let him off the hook. Doesn't let any of them off the hook.' She scowled and Nancy saw that Sarah would be a formidable opponent to any man who challenged her position in the world.

'I think you're right,' Nancy said softly, 'but it was many years ago and we're both old now. I've forgiven him. We're friends again, good friends.'

And now Stef was hurrying to join them. She took Nancy's hand and squeezed it. 'Nancy, your speech was wonderful. Everybody is saying so. Thank you so much.' Stef looked so happy, Nancy thought with a rush of affection as she squeezed back.

'I'll leave you two to it,' Sarah murmured. 'I want a quick word with your editor about the next book. See you again in a moment.'

'The next book?' Nancy enquired. 'You've only just published this one.'

'I know. And I'm going to have a baby. Somehow I'll have to fit it all in. They're giving me plenty of time. It's the biography of a 1960s woman artist whose archive has just been released. Should be very interesting!'

'Stef.' Nancy shook her head. 'You're amazing!'

'Not really. I'm actually quite nervous. I've never been a mum before!'

Nancy smiled. 'I know you'll be a good one, Stef. Better than I was, though I did my best.' She sighed, thinking of her estranged daughter. 'I'm thoroughly enjoying being a grandmother and great-grandmother, though! I can't wait to meet your little one!'

'I'll tell you a secret,' Stef whispered. 'We've discovered it's a girl. We're still discussing her first name, but we've already decided that her middle name will be Nancy!'

Acknowledgements

The Secrets of Dragonfly Lodge was inspired by the experiences of my mother and my aunt, Phyllis and Anne Harlow, identical twins who studied Zoology at Imperial College London in the late 1940s and went on to complete PhDs and work as scientists before turning to secondary school teaching. Each later married and had three children. They very generously shared with me a great deal about their lives as women scientists, and although my characters and their stories in *The Secrets of Dragonfly Lodge* are fictional, much of what they told me has informed Nancy Foster's narrative. This includes my aunt's exploration of the effects of pesticides on locusts for an international chemical company. Otherwise, my research has relied on science textbooks from the 1940s, biographies and other accounts of lived experience. Particularly useful were *The Exceptions* by Kate Zernike, *Women Scientists: the Road to Liberation*, ed. Derek Richter and *Rosalind Franklin* by Brenda Maddox.

I am lucky enough to live near the Norfolk Broads and often visit the Norfolk Wildlife Trust nature reserves at Hickling and Ranworth. Hickston Broad is fictional, but typical of these beautiful wild places where rare birds and insects can thrive in the face of many threats to their delicate ecosystems. The reserves are staffed by wonderful, knowledgeable and dedicated people, and some of what I've learned from their talks and tours has made its way into the novel.

I wish to thank the following for their support in the writing and publishing of this book. Sheila Crowley, my amazing agent at Curtis Brown, and Suzanne Baboneau, my wonderful editor at Simon & Schuster, have between them steered my whole publishing career thus far. They are supported by excellent teams, including at Curtis Brown: Rachel Goldblatt, Helena Maybery, Tanja Goossens. And at Simon & Schuster: Louise Davies, Sara-Jade Virtue, Sian Wilson, Sam Combes, Laurie McShea, Amy Fulwood, Mathew Watterson, Olivia Allen, Madeline Allan, Dominic Brendon, Richard Hawton. Many thanks are also due to my copyeditor, Sally Partington, and proofreader Dan Lockwood.

My husband, David, continues to be an unfailing source of love and support. This time, he was happy to trail round Broads villages with me when I didn't know what I was looking for but I'd know when I saw it, to supply examples of 1950s slang and to reassure me, when my courage failed.